Sue Moorcroft

Under the Mistletoe

avon.

Published by AVON
A division of HarperCollins*Publishers* Ltd
1 London Bridge Street
London SE1 9GF

www.harpercollins.co.uk

HarperCollins*Publishers*
1st Floor, Watermarque Building, Ringsend Road
Dublin 4, Ireland

A Paperback Original 2021

1

Fist published in Great Britain by HarperCollins*Publishers* in 2021

A catalogue copy of this book is
available from the British Library.

ISBN: 978-0-00-839305-2

Typeset in Sabon LT Std by
Palimpsest Book Production Limited, Falkirk, Stirlingshire

Printed and Bound in the UK using 100% Renewable Electricity
at CPI Group (UK) Ltd

MIX
Paper from
responsible sources
FSC
www.fsc.org   FSC C007454

This book is produced from independently certified FSC™ paper
to ensure responsible forest management.

For more information visit: www.harpercollins.co.uk/green

UNDER THE MISTLETOE

Sue Moorcroft writes contemporary fiction of life and love. *A Summer to Remember* won the Goldsboro Books Contemporay Romantic Novel award, *The Little Village Christmas* and *A Christmas Gift* were *Sunday Times* bestsellers and *The Christmas Promise* went to #1 in the Kindle chart. She also writes short stories, serials, articles, columns, courses and writing 'how to'.

An army child, Sue was born in Germany then lived in Cyprus, Malta and the UK and still loves to travel. Her other loves include writing (the best job in the world), reading, watching Formula 1 on TV and hanging out with friends, dancing, yoga, wine and chocolate.

If you're interested in being part of #TeamSueMoorcroft you can find more information at www.suemoorcroft.com/street-team. If you prefer to sign up to receive news of Sue and her books, go to www.suemoorcroft.com and click on 'Newsletter'. You can follow @SueMoorcroft on Twitter, @SueMoorcroftAuthor on Instagram, or Facebook.com/sue.moorcroft.3 and Facebook.com/SueMoorcroftAuthor.

By the same author:

The Christmas Promise
Just For the Holidays
The Little Village Christmas
One Summer in Italy
A Christmas Gift
A Summer to Remember
Let it Snow
Summer on a Sunny Island
Christmas Wishes
Under the Italian Sun
A Home in the Sun

Acknowledgements

A host of people have helped me bring you *Under the Mistletoe* and I'm grateful and thankful for them.

Sue McDonagh, writer and artist, was my first port of call when creating Laurel's life as an artist. Laurel's work is inspired by the paintings of artist Ismael Costa and also Sue McDonagh's own gorgeous portraits of children. See her work at www.suemcdonagh.co.uk. Also, if you like my books, you might well enjoy hers. I do.

For (sometimes long) conversations about education, truancy, teaching and the processes of a school, huge thanks to Siobhan Hutchinson, Lynne Hallet, Beryl Hales, Paul Matthews and Hollie Matthews. Further thanks to Beryl for letting me 'borrow' an art month for Middledip, along with the Google map idea.

Mark Lacey, retired detective superintendent and independent member of the parole board, very kindly provided me with the likely view the police might take on teenage pranks that cross the line.

Social media friends contributed an unusual amount to this book. Thanks to those on Twitter who joined the fascinating discussion about being disappointed in a sibling. You made me think hard about how Grady would deal with learning the truth about Mac. My Facebook friends also helped me on the subjects of horses and Christmas gifts.

My writing life's enriched by the members of Team Sue Moorcroft. Thanks to them for constant support and for providing names and occupations when my inspiration runs dry. (If *you'd* like to join the street team then visit www.suemoorcroft.com and click the sign-up link at the top of the page.)

My brother, Trevor Moorcroft, does my early research and this time he searched out information on bullying, infertility, agoraphobia, auto art, decorated gourds and more for me to study. He also kindly maintains several spreadsheets, including the Middledip Bible that allows me to keep track of characters and what they do in the village.

Fellow author Mark West has been my beta reader for most of my writing life and provides me with a fresh perspective, a keen eye for detail and an entertaining commentary. I frequently discuss my plots with him as they evolve. If I couldn't chat about writing I think I'd go bonkers, and another thing that's kept me grounded during tricky times is my Sunday evening video call with Pia Fenton and Myra Kersner – better known to their many readers as Christina Courtenay and Maggie Sullivan.

I couldn't get my books to readers around the world without some very special professionals. Love and thanks to Juliet Pickering and the Blake Friedmann Literary Agency team and Helen Huthwaite and all at Avon HarperCollins. Working with you is a joy and a privilege.

Most of all, thank you for being one of my readers.

You make it possible for me to spend my days conjuring stories for you to enjoy. Thank you for reading *Under the Mistletoe* and my other books, connecting with me on social media and sending me lovely messages and – of course! – writing good reviews. You make me happy.

For my family
Here or gone
Near or far
In my heart
Is where you are

Chapter One

'So, while I battled round Tesco for the food shopping you went to the craft shop and bought baubles and bits of wire . . . and a *Santa suit?*' Laurel demanded of her fourteen-year-old niece Daisy as they drove the winding road home to Middledip. Her windscreen wipers swished away tiny flakes of snow in the fast darkening afternoon.

Daisy giggled. 'I know it's mid-November but I have to start making Christmas wreaths. I can't make the compostable ones yet or they'll fall apart by Christmas Day, but I can make the ones that are all baubles and plastic holly. The Santa suit's for the Year Seven Christmas party I'm helping with at school. It's only five weeks till the end of term.'

'I suppose school Christmas events will be starting,' Laurel acknowledged. 'Whoa, holy crap!' She stamped on the brakes as a man loomed out of the snowy dusk and jumped in front of her car, signalling wildly.

'Where'd he come from?' Daisy gasped as the SUV fish-tailed and shopping bags slithered noisily off the back seat.

1

'There's a car on the verge. Maybe he's broken down. Don't open your window,' Laurel added hastily.

'There's another man with the car.' Daisy peered through the glass, squinting from beneath her dark, curly fringe. She giggled. 'That's weird. He's holding the car door handle and wearing a coat around his bum. He's got bare legs and socks without shoes.'

'That is weird.' Laurel chewed her lip as she took in the bizarre scene. Should she drive off? They were still three miles from Middledip, on a quiet road with the only illumination coming from her headlights. Visions of car-jackings flashed through her mind. She had a teenage girl in her car.

Then the man who'd leaped out in front of them ran up and knocked on her window. Laurel jumped, as she recognised him.

Grady Cassidy.

Though she was aware Grady still lived in Middledip – because Daisy was buddies with him and his nephew Niall – he'd once occupied a special place in her teenage heart and his sudden appearance was a shock.

At the same moment, Daisy, still staring at the man beside the other car, snorted a laugh. 'That's Niall's dad, Mac Cassidy, our head of year. He's been pantsed!'

Laurel's head shot round and she stared at Grady's brother Mac, frozen – in more ways than one, probably – beside his car, short hair rippling in the gusty wind. It *was* Mac Cassidy, minus trousers. What the hell?

Slowly, she turned back to regard Grady. No longer the conservative, doe-eyed teen she remembered, his straight hair fell to his shoulders and was tucked behind his ears, his brows thick and black. Though still recognisably the same person, his shoulders were broader, his

2

jaw stubbled, his forehead wider and set in iron furrows as he tried to peer into her car.

Until she'd left the village at sixteen, she and Grady had been a bit of a thing. To him, she'd confided her dreams of becoming an artist, and the hollow, sinking grief around the loss of her mum two years earlier. In turn, he'd unburdened himself about family-shaking clashes between brash Mac and their domineering dad. Then Mac and his horrible mates had done what they did that night . . .

'Can you help us?' Grady called through the glass. 'Someone tricked us into stopping and took our phones. My brother's frozen.' Grady looked cold, too, hugging his hoodie around him. It was probably his coat around Mac's bottom.

Heart rate uncomfortably rapid, Laurel buzzed her window open half an inch and Grady edged closer. There was no recognition in his gaze but it had been nineteen years and she knew she'd changed. 'Some young lads overtook us, then pretended to break down. When we stopped to help, they jumped out – five of them. Some held on to me while the rest set on Mac and took his jeans and boots then attached him to the car door with cable ties. Hilarious, to them,' he added bitterly.

Laurel glanced back at Mac, his back to them perforce but his head half-turned as if trying to catch the discussion, squinting against the snow blowing into his face. 'They took your phones?' she repeated, to give herself time to envisage driving off and leaving Mac Cassidy to his indignity and discomfort. The revenge would be so sweet that her fingers actually flexed on the gear stick. Then, knowing she ought to have grown out of petty payback, however much she owed the elder Cassidy brother for his past sins, she pulled on the handbrake and switched on her hazard lights. 'I've got something in the boot that will free him. Then you can drive home.'

'Little bastards took Mac's car keys too,' Grady snapped, retreating so that she could open her door. 'They left me my keys but they're not much good when my vehicle's three miles away.' Then, as if Laurel's silence was a question, he added grumpily, 'I know I could have run to the village but I needed to stop any cars careering round the corner and hitting my brother.'

Laurel had to acknowledge that as a real danger, the car being positioned just after a curve. Then she saw Daisy had her phone out and was discreetly training her camera on the hapless Mac. 'Cut that out,' she said sharply. 'I mean it, Daisy. I don't care if he's your head of year and he gives you detention. It's never right to pass images like that around, ever.'

'I was only going to send it to Niall.' Daisy grinned as she lowered the hand that was holding the phone.

'Stay in the car, please,' Laurel began.

But she wasn't fast enough to prevent Daisy springing out of the vehicle with a cheerful, 'Hello, Grady! Evening, Mr Cassidy.'

'Shit,' Laurel muttered, scrambling out and yanking up her hood against the freezing air. She didn't catch any reply Mac might have made to Daisy as she hurried to open her boot and search out her Leatherman multi-tool, kept for when she was out painting and needed to hack her way into gummed up paint tubes. Nor did she enquire why Mac had been pantsed and not Grady. It was probably the same as it had always been: Grady made friends and Mac made enemies. Keeping her distance from Mac, she opened the device to the spring-loaded scissors and offered it to Grady.

4

Relief flashed over his face as he took the tool. 'Thanks.' His mouth relaxed into a sudden smile. 'You're a life saver.'

Laurel nodded and Grady reached around Mac to free him with a couple of well-placed snips. 'Thanks.' Mac nodded in Laurel's direction but focused on simultaneously rubbing his wrists and keeping a grip on the coat clutched around his waist. Neither man showed any sign of recognising her.

Daisy opened the back door of Laurel's car and stuck her top half inside, emerging seconds later with an air of triumph. 'Here you are, Mr Cassidy. I bought these for when I help at the Year Seven party but you can have them.' She beamed angelically at Mac as she proffered the scarlet trousers of the Santa suit, complete with copious white fluff around the ankles.

'Oh. Erm, thanks, Daisy,' Mac muttered gruffly.

He took the folded red felt with such a ludicrous expression of dismay that an insane urge to giggle ballooned inside Laurel. Voice quivering, she said, 'Daisy, let's get back in the car and give Mr Cassidy a moment.'

Mac mumbled a sheepish 'thanks,' but Grady cut across him, peering into the depths of Laurel's hood as if trying to read her expression. 'Erm . . . I don't want to sound ungrateful, but you're not going to drive off and leave us, are you?'

Daisy was already back in the front passenger seat and Laurel hesitated, just for the instant it took for her to envisage doing exactly that. In her head she heard her best friend Fliss's soft California tones. *I accept the gravity of what happened to you, but hanging on to your negative feelings will only hurt you and prevent you from moving on. You're not that hurt teenager, now, Laurel. You're a strong woman. You've empowered yourself by learning self-defence and safety techniques.* Fliss had delivered those sessions and Laurel had been a star student. But . . . she was also human and she drew out the moment as she pretended to deliberate.

In-her-head-Fliss added gently: *Sometimes life doesn't go the way you expected. You have to let go of what you once pictured and take joy in what you have.*

Mac had struggled into the too-small Santa trousers behind the car and was now staring at her, the red felt hanging ludicrously at half-mast above his wet socks. Around them, the fine snow was dusting the hedge tops, outlining each bare twig.

Grady smiled at her, clearly not really thinking they were going to drive off. And he had once been her friend . . . She gestured towards her car. 'Hop in the back. You'll have to share the space with my shopping. The boot's full.' She'd only moved back to Middledip yesterday – Friday. She'd unloaded her personal things into her old room in The Nookery, where dormer window overlooked ploughed fields and lines of poplar trees, and her pictures had been crated and sent ahead, but her paints, brushes and easels still waited in the SUV's capacious boot. There was no reason to share these details with the Cassidys though. Or how adrift she'd felt to leave Alex and their little blue house in West London after ten years – nine together, and one spent apart but living amicably under the same roof. Then Alex had acquired a girlfriend called Vonnie at the same time as he'd gone for trendier glasses and a hipster style to his brush-like brown hair; Laurel's much-loved sister Rea, Daisy's mum, had suffered an acceleration to her agoraphobia and then Daisy had begun uncharacteristic attempts at truanting. Laurel had known it was time to return to the village . . . like it or not. Hopefully, her absence would allow Alex to move on, maybe achieving with Vonnie what Laurel had been unable to provide. She remembered her last words to him. *You're a good guy, Alex Lasienko*. Laurel's infertility ending the love they'd known had not been his fault.

'Thank you.' The voices of the Cassidy brothers broke into her thoughts as she climbed into the car. Laurel brushed snow off herself and jumped back into the driver's seat.

With a quelling look at Daisy, who was grinning all over her round, teenaged face, Laurel started the engine and resumed their interrupted journey to Middledip, wondering if even Fliss could counsel her to look forward when such an uncomfortable part of her past was currently sitting in her car.

The first couple of miles passed in silence apart from the hiss of tyres on wet asphalt and the swish of the windscreen wipers dislodging the snow. Then Grady, as if belatedly recovering his manners said, 'How are you doing, Daisy?'

Daisy turned in her seat and beamed. 'Good. Are you going to run the village art show thing?'

'Seems like it. Hope you'll get involved.' Grady's voice was light and warm.

Daisy nodded. 'Cool, I will if Mum's OK with it.' Then she added brightly, turning her gaze Laurel's way just as Laurel pushed back her hood. 'Maybe you'll join in now you're here, Auntie Laurel.'

'*Laurel*?' Both the Cassidys spoke at once, Grady sounding astounded and Mac taken aback.

'Hi,' she said laconically. Her right foot got heavier on the accelerator and she shot into the village. She forced

7

herself to touch the brakes and take a breath. 'Can you tell me where you need dropping? Our frozen shopping will be thawing.'

Grady said, 'We'll go to Mac's, please. It's 148 Port Road.'

Good. At least that wasn't too near Great End, where Laurel's family home, The Nookery, stood. She turned sharp right out of Main Road into Ladies Lane. 'Number 148? Do I turn right at the end? Or left?'

'Right, please,' Grady said, when Mac made no reply. Then, cautiously, Grady added, 'Nice to see you, Laurel. Sorry for not recognising you—'

'It's dark and I'm nearly twenty years older,' she cut in swiftly. 'It must be about here, right?'

'Just under this lamp,' Grady agreed quietly. 'Thanks again. I think Mac would have got hypothermia if you hadn't helped.'

Laurel answered more genially. 'Someone else would have stopped, I expect.' She halted the car, watching the snow make tiny starbursts on the windshield as the men fumbled with their seat belts.

Daisy and Grady said their goodbyes. Mac, who'd been completely silent since Laurel's identity had been revealed, gave a hoarse, 'Thank you very much,' before he hurried from the car and the brothers left their footprints in the veil of snow up the garden path, Santa trousers brushing Mac's calves. Laurel hoped his silence had come from consternation at her turning up again rather than mere embarrassment. He deserved every anxious moment.

Daisy laughed. 'Poor Mr Cassidy in his boxers, stuck at the side of the road.' She whipped out her phone while Laurel turned the car around.

'Daisy,' Laurel murmured. 'Just hang on before you

start messaging anyone about this.' She felt rather than saw Daisy's surprised glance, but she had the satisfaction of seeing the phone screen gradually going dark in her peripheral vision. Three minutes later they drew to a halt outside The Nookery, its back to the farm fields that surrounded the village. Oddly spaced windows punctuated uneven walls and a mad thatched roof undulated over the large, sprawling cottage, a thatch partridge silhouetted at one end. The Nookery sat back from the rest of Great End like an awkward child at a party. Both it and the studio in its garden had belonged to Isla, Laurel and Rea's mum, so they now belonged to Laurel and Rea. As Rea had little interest in the studio, Laurel was about to make it her new workspace.

She killed the engine, flicked on the internal light and met her niece's dark, dancing eyes. 'I can't stop you messaging your friends or posting what happened on social media, but I want you to think carefully before you cause Mr Cassidy stress and humiliation. Humiliating someone is bullying, and bullying is something we should all find unacceptable.' Even if Mac Cassidy was the victim and damned lucky Laurel was doing him this favour. 'And he's your friend's dad.'

Daisy dropped her gaze and sighed disconsolately. 'The *faaaaaark*.' Laurel already knew that 'the faaaaaark' was Daisy's thinly veiled attempt to get away with saying 'what the fuck'. Rea discouraged it but Laurel felt that as Daisy had a mum who panicked at the idea of leaving home, and an aunt who'd left Middledip for good reason and hadn't wanted to come back, a little pseudo swearing wasn't worth worrying about. Daisy muttered, 'Niall would know it's a joke.'

'When it's his dad?' Laurel probed gently.

Daisy shoved her phone away. 'But Mr Cassidy's my head of year and he was *pantsed* and *cable-tied*. And I got him to wear my *Santa trousers*.'

Laurel grinned at Daisy's air of injury, leaning over the centre console to reward her niece with a hug. 'It's really hard not to take revenge on people. I'm not a fan of Mac Cassidy either but you've told me you're friendly with Grady and I remember him as a good guy. Let's do it for him if not for Mac, all right?'

'Oh, all right.' Daisy opened the car door. 'Grady's great. He does cool stuff.'

Laurel didn't ask what kind of stuff, pretty sure she wouldn't be crossing his path much. It was nineteen years since they'd been more than friends and the reason the relationship ended wasn't a subject she liked to dwell on.

'So you're friends with Mac's son when Mac's a teacher at your school? How does that work for you?' She got out to join her niece in the frigid November evening, careful of her footing.

Daisy shrugged. 'He's my head of year, which is weird, but he's Niall's head of year, too, which is weirder. Kids who have teachers for parents have to put up with weirdness.' She glanced at her aunt. 'Why don't you like Mac? Don't you like Grady either?'

They began to gather the shopping from the rear seat. Laurel hooked three bags on one hand. 'I was friends with Grady but I didn't get on with Mac.' She'd stopped being friends with Grady to protect him as much as herself.

She changed the subject. 'Your mum will be pleased we've got all the ingredients she wanted for her Christmas baking.'

Daisy grappled with her share of the shopping bags as she tried to skid on the snow. 'Do you think getting all the stuff for the mince pies and sausage rolls so early is part of her agoraphobia? It's six weeks until Christmas, bet she won't make them till Christmas week.'

Laurel didn't know. Maybe Rea was trying to exert extra control over some parts of her life because she'd lost control in others? If so, Laurel had made the wrong choice when she persuaded Rea not to order the ingredients online and had piled Daisy into the car for a real-life shopping expedition. But she knew how it felt to be fourteen and facing horrible life events so she gave Daisy the best hug she could manage around all the shopping bags and made her voice reassuring. 'I think she just wants us to have a really lovely Christmas so she's getting in the spirit early.'

Laurel wouldn't mind a good Christmas. Last year, she'd been unexpectedly miserable at the finality of her decree nisi, and so had Alex. Earlier Christmases had been blighted, too. Once, she'd miscarried a week before Christmas. Another year she'd been sure she'd been pregnant but the test had proved negative. The worst had been the year she'd been pregnant but not daring to hope she'd go full term – and losing the baby the day after Boxing Day. Bad things always seemed worse at Christmas. This year, it was time to put the past behind her and look forward.

If she could.

Grady followed his brother up the long front garden of the tall red-brick Victorian house Mac shared with his wife Tonya and their son Niall. The warmth of their home hit him as they kicked snow from their boots and stepped inside, and it was incredibly welcoming after a quarter-of-an-hour shivering at the roadside. His bones felt turned to ice. Mac must feel worse but he was all grim silence and downcast gaze.

Grady had a couple of things to say but could wait till Mac was warm and dry.

Across the hall the sound of the TV blared from the sitting room along with the raucous laughter of Niall, Mac's fourteen-year-old son, whose voice had deepened in the last months. Mac swung round and hissed at Grady, 'I don't want Niall to see me like this,' then raced upstairs in his wet socks, two-sizes-too-small Santa pants looking uncomfortably strained in tender places.

Grady caught Tonya's voice, high and worried, and Mac's answering rumble, soothing yet frustrated. Grady winced. He loved his mercurial sister-in-law but explaining where your car was and why you were wearing Santa trousers? One thing Grady hadn't missed since his relationship with Pippa ended last February was awkward questions.

About to stroll into the sitting room and hang out with his nephew to share an episode of *The Mandalorian*, Grady paused when he heard Mac hiss his name. Seeing his brother beckoning over the upstairs banister, he cast a longing look into the sitting room and the fire he could see blazing in the hearth, then altered course to trudge up the carpeted stairs. Rounding the top, he found Tonya, hands on hips. Her eyes were huge in her pointed face and she reminded Grady of a pretty (if confused) elf, pink hair spiked up from the sides to meet in the middle.

Mac, still huddled up in his coat and Santa pants, glanced at Grady and indicated his wife with a nod. 'Tell her what happened. She thinks I'm making it up.'

Tonya jumped in before Grady could get the first word out. 'I'm not accusing him of lying, Grady, I just don't understand. He was late. I rang you both and no one answered. Then suddenly your phones and Mac's car keys were lying on the doormat in the hall. I opened the front door and Mac's jeans and boots were piled on the step. It was like a scary movie. I was about to ring the police.'

'Our phones and the keys were put through the door?' Grady repeated incredulously. He glanced at Mac. 'That's a relief. I presume we are going to ring the police, though, aren't we? When you've got warm clothes.' Then, realising he hadn't reassured Tonya, he said, 'We were coming home from watching Peterborough play and stopped to help some guys. They'd overtaken us a minute earlier and it looked as if their car had broken down.'

Tonya's fair brows flew up towards her upswept hair. 'You stopped in the middle of nowhere?'

'They were teenagers,' Mac put in. 'It was precisely because it was the middle of nowhere that I stopped. It was snowing.'

Grady jammed his chilly fingers in his pockets. 'You're right; it was like a thriller where innocent people are targeted for no reason. We got out of the car and three of them went for Mac and two for me.'

'Must have been a bloody squash with five of them in their old Fiesta,' Mac commented dourly, shivering.

Grady went on. 'It was easy for them to squash me against the side of the car. I could barely move, let alone fight back.' It had been a horrible experience, being made helpless even if only for a couple of minutes. 'They searched my pockets and took my phone. I thought we were being robbed but they ignored my wallet . . . and now you say the phone's been left here?'

'Yes, sorry. I'm not thinking straight.' Hastily, Tonya pulled his phone from her pocket and handed it over.

13

With a word of thanks he brought the screen to life. The handset seemed undamaged but he'd change the passcode later. 'I was shouting to Mac and he was yelling and swearing and the blokes were laughing. Then they gave me a shove and sent me into the hedge.' He rubbed a scratch on his neck. 'By the time I'd picked myself out of the hawthorn their car was disappearing up the road, and Mac was tied to his car door handle, minus trousers and boots.'

A frown appeared above Tonya's amber-coloured eyes and she tweaked Mac's red felt pants. 'You make a cute Santa but why on earth would they take your trousers?'

Mac sighed. 'I think they were former students because they called me "Mr Cassidy". I guess it was a practical joke. I'll have to decide whether to report it.' He sent Grady a frown. 'I'll get changed. Will you take me back to the car in your truck?'

'Sure.' To give Mac time to warm up, and Tonya a chance to get over her anxiety about their little adventure, he ran downstairs to grab two minutes by the fire. 'Hey, Niall,' he said, dropping comfortably onto the end of the sofa nearest the crackling grate.

'What's up?' asked Niall, barely taking his eyes off *The Mandalorian*. His hair wasn't the Cassidy black but fair, like Tonya's when she hadn't dyed it one of the colours of the rainbow.

As Grady and Niall's relationship included lots of teasing and play-fighting, rather than answer Grady grabbed the remote and switched off the TV.

'Hey!' complained Niall, laughing, twisting round to pit his gangly strength against Grady's more solid bulk. 'Don't be a knob.'

From upstairs, Grady could still hear Tonya questioning

14

and Mac responding. Mac loved Tonya too much to get impatient with her. 'Don't say "knob", you knob,' he teased, shoving the remote behind his back. 'Just seen Daisy in her aunt's car.' He omitted the circumstances.

'Yeah. Daisy said her auntie was coming to stay at theirs.' Niall burrowed behind Grady, snatched the remote and switched the TV back on.

The sound of feet running down the stairs was followed by Mac giving a low whistle, no doubt a discreet attempt to get Grady's attention.

Niall barely looked up anyway. 'Is that Dad home?' He looked more interested in the Christmas ad for Xbox that had flicked onto the screen than the comings and goings of a mere parent.

Grady gave Niall's hair a parting ruffle. 'Yep. And now we're going out again. See you.'

Mac waited in the hallway, one hand on the front door handle. He held two woollen beanie hats and tossed one to Grady before they stepped back out into the freezing cold, pulling up their collars. 'Brr,' said Grady, the warmth gained from his brief sojourn by the fire instantly dispelled. It was snowing harder now, making the nearby cottages look as if they were slowly being coated in icing sugar. They hunched their shoulders and strode down Port Road, where red and green Christmas lights decorated the lamp-posts. It was a two-minute walk to Grady's house, Mistletoe Cottage on the corner of Ladies Lane. On the drive stood his double-cab pick-up, the words "Grady Auto Art" airbrushed on the bonnet in swirling black, blue and purple that popped from the scarlet paintwork even through the powdering of snow. Grady dragged out his keys and soon they were rumbling out of the village, all the heaters on, including those in the seats.

15

Grady brought up what neither of them had so far said. 'So, Laurel Hill's back in the village?'

Mac grunted, gazing out through the passenger window, though there was little to see but the snow settling on the village they'd both grown up in, lights shining cosily from behind drawn curtains.

Grady swung the truck out of Ladies Lane and left into Main Road, heading towards Bettsbrough past hawthorn hedges and dank ditches, snow flurrying in the headlights. He thought back to teenage Laurel: dark red hair streaming down her back, her laugh, her weird home life of being looked after by a sister not much older than herself.

Most of the village kids had gone to Bettsbrough Comp but the Cassidys had always had to travel into Peterborough to the Catholic school. They'd hung out in the village out of school hours, of course, and he'd had a bit of a thing going with Laurel. They'd gone 'over the fields', the village term for anywhere outside the village proper, and Laurel had stolen rides on a pony on the Carlysle Estate. Some kids had been jealous of Laurel's 'luck' not having 'proper' grown-ups to answer to, but Grady had known the reality. Her dad died before Laurel was two, trying some motorbike stunt. In Laurel's mid-teens, her mum, who had diabetes-related kidney problems, had died, too, meaning Rea taking a job instead of going to uni. If that was 'luck' then it wasn't the good kind. Even if Grady's dad had been strict and rarely challenged by Grady's mum, the Cassidy parents had provided a comfortable home. Grady had never had to do half the cooking and half the housework on top of schoolwork, like Laurel.

'She might just be visiting her family,' Mac said suddenly.

'Yeah.' Grady slowed as his headlights illuminated the

bulky shape of Mac's car, relaxing on the verge like a drunk who couldn't find his way home. 'I got on her shit-list years ago.' He didn't know why she'd stopped talking to him, unless it was because he'd said he'd meet her at a village hall party and then not turned up because he'd broken his ankle. He'd had a Christmas gift wrapped and ready to give her but once he'd been up and about on crutches, she'd blanked him. Mac had said she'd probably turned funny because she didn't want to have to buy a Christmas present for him; told him girls were weird, hormonal things.

Grady had written a new tag for the gift and given it to his mum. If Mum had been bemused to receive a Sugababes T-shirt, she hadn't said so.

He smiled faintly to remember the young him feeling so bewildered and hurt at the change in Laurel. Judging by her wary, unsmiling attitude at the roadside this evening, she hadn't changed back. He addressed Mac again. 'Do you really think the guys who stopped us were your students, muffled up with hoods?' He turned the truck around in the lane and switched on the hazard lights.

Mac rested his hand on the door handle but didn't get out, the reflection of the flashing lights going on and off in his eyes. 'I think they were former students who probably saw my personalised number plate. I recognised the voice of one of the more challenging kids who left the school last year.'

Grady 'accidentally' used his elbow to activate the door locks so Mac couldn't get out until Grady had finished asking questions. 'So you're going to take it to the police, right?'

Mac sighed. 'I suppose I'll have to, but he has an apprenticeship now and a chance to make something of

17

himself. I'm reluctant to get him in trouble, despite what he did. They returned what they took so it was pretty much a prank.'

'You softy.' When his brother got all understanding over the antics of tricky teenagers it was as if someone had reached into Grady's chest and squeezed his heart – maybe because Mac had been a tricky teenager himself.

Mac grunted. 'Teachers do try to make things better for kids, even if kids don't realise or accept it. I'm going to put it to the police as a prank.'

'OK.' Shrugging, Grady was about to unlock the vehicle, but paused. 'Daisy Grove's at your school. This story's going to be everywhere.' Young Daisy was great but he'd seen her glee as she'd taken in Mac's discomfiture.

Mac tugged his beanie lower, over his eyes. 'It won't need Daisy for that to happen. The perpetrators took photos and videos because kids these days just don't seem to be able to help themselves. Now, can you unlock the door so I can go home and get warm?'

Grady released the button and they both jumped out. Mac beeped open his car and got in to start the engine, letting the wipers clear the whitening windshield.

Grady shivered as he watched Mac try and coax the car off the soggy grass. Twigs snapped and the wheels spun but that was about it. When Mac turned to look at him through the car window, Grady nodded and returned to his truck to get his tow rope. Sometimes he and Mac didn't need words. Mac needed towing back onto the road, so Grady would do it.

Chapter Two

A slow start to a Sunday over croissants and coffee was a pleasure, but Laurel felt odd because this Sunday began in The Nookery with her sister and her niece instead of the blue terraced house in Park Royal with Alex.

She must have sighed because Rea asked, 'How are you doing? Is it strange being here?' peering over an issue of *Homes & Gardens,* the cover tastefully illustrated with swags of festive greenery. The magazine's title neatly summarised where Rea felt comfortable – so long as it was *her* home and *her* garden. Laurel had tactfully established that Rea hadn't set foot past the bottom of The Nookery's drive since early summer and had spent a couple of hours last night reading how to help a loved one with agoraphobia. She was determined to encourage Rea all she could.

Laurel wrinkled her nose. 'It's a bit disorientating. It'll be better when I get the studio set up.'

'We could help you,' Rea offered. She closed her magazine. 'If I wasn't being so stupid you wouldn't have to be here.' Rea was five years older than Laurel but, even at forty, there was something waif-like about her.

Laurel dusted croissant crumbs off her hand to pat Rea's arm. 'You're not being stupid, you're suffering from agoraphobia.' With Rea living like a recluse, Daisy had been skipping lessons at school. When the electronic register was called, Daisy would not be present and might later be found loitering in an empty classroom. Or, after the register was taken, she'd complain of period pains or nausea and spend the lesson in the loo. Sometimes she told teachers she was late for school because she'd been collecting prescriptions or shopping for her mum. When the pastoral team contacted Rea, Rea admitted she had those things delivered.

The truancy worried Rea, which made her anxiety worse and discouraged her still more from leaving the safety of home. Her inability to face the world had risen sharply in the early summer, which was why Laurel had volunteered to return.

Daisy looked up from her phone. 'There are so many women living here now we should change the name of the house from The Nookery to The Knickery.' She considered her mum and aunt thoughtfully. 'Nobody would think we're even related. Mum's got fair hair and hazel eyes and is thin, Auntie Laurel's auburn with blue eyes, my hair and eyes are both dark, and we're both curvy.'

Like Laurel, Daisy had developed those 'curves' early. Laurel remembered feeling conspicuous to have thirty-six double-Ds in her mid-teens and wondered if that was why Daisy so often wore oversized hoodies. Some girls might have relished the eye-catching boobs but Laurel had found the ogling and lewd remarks unwanted and unnerving, particularly as she'd struggled with the nightmarish aftermath of her mum's death.

Daisy went on, putting down her phone. 'And Laurel

and me have names that sound like addresses. Daisy Grove and Laurel Hill.'

Laurel smiled. 'I was already known as Laurel Hill in the art world when I married Alex so I didn't take Lasienko. You'll have to blame your father for Grove.'

Daisy snorted. 'If I ever saw him, maybe I would.' Rea had shared The Nookery with Ewan Grove during their brief marriage. Daisy was the only good thing Ewan had given Rea and he was no longer in his daughter's life. Daisy frowned. 'Aunt Terri's not a Hill, is she?'

'No, she's Terri Chapman,' Laurel explained. 'She was the sister of our mum – Isla – but didn't marry. When I lived with her while I went to art college in Peterborough, instead of sixth form, she went out with a few men but never seemed to get serious.' Wanting to attend college in Peterborough wasn't the reason she'd gone to live with Terri – it was just the reason she'd always given.

Laurel tapped a glossy image in Rea's magazine depicting exposed beams and a brick-built fireplace just like The Nookery. 'Your mum's got this place looking like a magazine feature now, but our mum bought it as a wreck. Plaster dust and the smell of paint was a theme in our childhood. One Christmas we twined tinsel round the legs of the wallpaper table rather than fold it up and put it away.'

Rea nodded. 'Dad made buying The Nookery possible – unfortunately. When he was killed, there was life insurance, but also compensation from his employer. He was a sports journalist and the accident happened when he was out on a job for his paper. He was messing about on a trials bike, which shouldn't have been allowed. A lot of that money went towards buying and doing up this place, which meant we could stay here when Mum died.'

Laurel looked at Rea. 'You're underplaying. We couldn't have stayed here if not for you working hard at a job you hated because it paid well.'

Daisy's eyes were like saucers. 'What? Like lap-dancing?'

Laurel grinned. 'Well, no, not that.'

'Telesales for an industrial flooring company, selling epoxy resin floors,' Rea said repressively. 'Bigger the floor, bigger the bonus. It was in a call-centre. And,' she added, 'I wouldn't say I hated it.'

Raising her eyebrows, Laurel told Daisy firmly, 'She hated it.' The urge to grin deserted her. 'Aunt Terri offered us a home with her but Rea getting that job convinced the authorities she could look after me, which she did until I, in a total about-face, went to live with Aunt Terri two years later, leaving her stuck here.'

The laugh Rea gave sounded forced. 'Being "stuck here" is perfect for an agoraphobic.' She leaned over to embrace Laurel. 'You went to art school. It was fine.'

Laurel returned the hug but they both knew 'art school' had actually been a school in Peterborough with 'Community Arts College' in its title. Laurel could have travelled to the school from The Nookery daily and her conscience had known Rea had felt abandoned rather than relieved of the responsibility of a teenage sister.

Worse, over the following years of uni, an arts barn in Cornwall and then life with Alex, Laurel had been so wrapped in her own dramas that she'd hardly noticed Rea's mental health issues increasing, and that avoidance of city driving and multi-storey car parks had been joined by avoidance of crowds and public transport. None of those aversions had seemed to Laurel to deserve the label of 'phobia'. They'd just been situations that made Rea flustered.

Then dislikes grew into anxieties and triggers multiplied.

This spring, Rea had begun experiencing panic attacks when out of the home. She'd changed jobs so she could work remotely and it had been like the final lock turning to shut her into The Nookery. Though Rea owed Laurel nothing, Laurel owed Rea a lot, so she'd come back. Here. Where she didn't want to be. During the past five years, selling through galleries, online and via the busy events calendar of the studios in Chiswick where she'd rented space, she'd earned repute in the art world and could have worked anywhere. The reason she hadn't moved out of Alex's house immediately post-divorce had been because she'd been looking into once again finding a studio in the mellow light of Cornwall. Later, she'd planned, she might try Wales and then France or Italy. Such a travelling life was now on the back burner while she helped Rea and Daisy through their respective issues, but at least a period in Middledip would give Laurel time to put her divorce behind her and move on.

Daisy's gaze flitted uneasily between her mother and her aunt and her voice climbed several notes. 'Maybe keeping up Nan's work on the house is why you don't go out, Mum?'

'Maybe,' Rea agreed, though her smile wavered.

Laurel's heart faltered. It seemed as if something she'd said had worried an already worried youngster. Now she and Rea were both gazing anxiously at Daisy. Perhaps the three of them were trapped in a cycle of worrying about each other and they'd never break free.

She tried not to believe it.

Surely a time would come when Rea felt able to live more normally? Daisy would get over her truanting and in a year, or even in a few months, there would be no need for Laurel to remain in this house, which she half-owned but had not considered her home for a long time. She could pick up those travel plans again.

Shoving these fruitless thoughts away, she tried to lighten the atmosphere. 'Are you inviting Aunt Terri for Christmas, Rea?' Terri was busier as a retired person that she had been when she managed a bookshop. Now she travelled, joined community projects, read voraciously and lunched a lot. 'Or maybe she's been invited to spend Christmas with Opal,' she added. Opal had been Terri's best friend even when Laurel had landed herself on Terri, all those years ago.

Rea looked relieved at the change of subject. 'I've already invited her. She didn't seem sure if she'd be going to Opal's for part of Christmas because, apparently, Opal's husband doesn't always like guests.'

'I'll visit her when I'm more settled and see if I can persuade her to come to us for all of it,' Laurel answered. She had lots of affection for her energetic aunt and it would be nice to share Christmas with her. 'I don't think they do their own Christmas baking at Opal's and Aunt Terri loves the traditional stuff, like homemade mince pies.'

The bell pealed at the front door.

Rea put aside her magazine, now turned to a feature on decorating your garden for Christmas, picked up her phone and opened the doorbell app. Laurel had bought a doorbell camera for Rea for her birthday, because while Rea was OK with visitors she already knew, she wasn't super-keen on answering to strangers. 'Oh, it's the Cassidy brothers,' Rea said. 'I suppose it's about last night. You'd better answer, Laurel.' Laurel and Daisy had, of course, told Rea all about the roadside rescue they'd performed on the way home from Bettsbrough.

An unpleasant knot formed in Laurel's stomach. 'I suppose so.' Reluctantly, she left the cosy kitchen. Behind her, she heard Rea chatting to Daisy and the clink and scrape of crockery being cleared.

The front door was the kind with a sidelight so Laurel moved the curtain to peep at Grady and Mac. Even though she knew exactly who would be standing in the porch beside the bare, thorny rose bushes, yesterday's snow still clinging to the ground around them, Mac's presence prompted her to make it obvious she was checking before answering.

The pair looked back at her, their breath forming twin clouds that told her she was keeping them waiting in the cold. Both had hair so black and glossy they could give Claudia Winkleman a run for her money.

Laurel dropped the curtain and opened the door. 'Hello.'

They returned her greeting. Politely, Mac said, 'I wonder if I could have a word with you and Daisy about last night. Is Rea here?'

Laurel supposed it was second nature to a teacher to check an appropriate adult was around when he wanted to speak to one of his students out of hours. 'We're all here,' she confirmed. 'Come in.'

They both ducked under the low beam over the front door. Grady gave her a quick, courteous smile and a pang shot through her. She hid it and showed them into the cosy kitchen, which was cheerful – much cheerier than Laurel felt – even on a winter's day thanks to the sunny yellow Rea had painted the walls.

Being this close to Mac Cassidy brought Laurel out in a sweat.

The past was refusing to stay where she'd put it. Panic jumped up into her throat and her breathing refused to behave, causing her ears to buzz. For several seconds she was back in that dark night on the playing fields with the 'teasing' that had got out of hand. She remembered the smell of cider. Mac and his poisonous girlfriend Amie. Two of Mac's friends, Ruben and Jonny. The shrieks of laughter. Amie's high, excited little voice squealing, 'Hold her!' Laurel shuddered as she remembered the malicious hands that had carried out the assault.

The next day, when Laurel had still been dazed and shocked, on the school bus Amie had snarled at her, 'You watch yourself in future, right, or Mac's going to tell all the other boys you're a slut.' She acted as if Laurel had invited what had happened. *Had she? She'd been the one to walk alone at night across the playing fields.* To reinforce her message, Amie had followed Laurel off the bus and got physical.

Laurel had stopped going out and about in the village after that.

She'd pretended she wasn't at home when Grady called. Rea had thought they'd had a falling out and that Laurel was heartbroken. It had been convenient to let her think it. Rea had been fighting her own battles – against tough sales targets and back-stabbing colleagues who regularly reduced her to tears. No way would Laurel pile a single extra care on her valiant-but-fragile older sister's shoulders.

So Laurel had told no one. The shame, and the fear of retribution or that she'd deserved punishment had been too much. Who would have believed her when there were no impartial witnesses? She knew now from Fliss that women frequently didn't report assaults . . . and fear of not being believed was the number one cause.

Laurel had attended school only until she'd finished her

GCSEs and then left Middledip as the ink on the final exam paper dried.

Swallowing the lump in her throat, she said, 'Mac and Grady want to speak to us.'

Rea turned with a smile. She'd cleared the table while Laurel had been at the door and switched on the kettle. In her own home or garden, with people she knew, she was fine. It was Laurel who was feeling as if she might have a panic attack.

While Grady and Mac pulled out chairs and joined Rea and Daisy at the kitchen table, Laurel yanked her head out of the past and busied herself making hot chocolate and coffee. Then she found the seat left available for her was between Daisy and Grady, who were discussing Art December, the village art month, as they pored over a Google map, though Laurel wasn't sure how the two things were connected.

Mac cleared his throat and addressed Laurel and Daisy, his expression remote and tone neutral. 'Thanks again for rescuing us last night. I've come to mention that I have to report what happened. There's a chance the police will contact you.'

'The police?' Daisy muttered, dropping into teen mode with a whiff of sullen scorn. 'For a pantsing?'

Laurel couldn't let this go. '"Pantsing" is a fun name for a horrible thing – a sexual assault,' she put in quietly. 'I think Mr Cassidy's right to report it.' She caught Mac's expression of shocked alarm and suddenly felt more powerful. *Yeah, mate, the truth is sometimes uncomfortable to hear.*

Grady rubbed his jaw. 'I hadn't thought of it like that.'

Mac's Adam's apple bobbed before he went on quietly. 'Some students like to get back at teachers they hold

27

something against. That's what I think happened. Those lads knew me, my car and where I live. By the time we got home, the phones and car keys had been dropped through my letterbox.' He forged on. 'I'll be presenting the incident to the police as an outrageous prank. We weren't permanently deprived of our property and the car wasn't damaged. Also, I think I recognised one of the lads and most of the time he's making an effort with his life.'

Daisy's expression shifted slightly, as if his viewpoint was becoming more acceptable.

Rea joined in. 'They should be grateful you're taking that attitude, Mac.'

He shrugged and smiled. 'Some kids deserve a break now and then. I'm hoping—' he paused and turned the smile on Daisy '—that Daisy might be equally considerate towards me.'

Daisy's soft eyebrows curled in confusion as she gazed at him.

He smiled. 'I expect it was a great temptation to tell your friends—'

'Oh!' Enlightenment dawned on Daisy's soft, young features. She grinned. 'Auntie Laurel asked me not to spread what happened, so I didn't.'

Surprise flitted over Mac's face and he was left with little choice but to meet Laurel's gaze. 'Thank you very much.'

Though she heard Grady say, 'That was good of you, Laurel,' her gaze remained locked with Mac's as she formulated a reply that would let him know she'd neither forgotten nor forgiven. 'I have a real problem with people who inflict humiliation by displaying someone's body without their permission.' A silence followed her words but she couldn't find it in herself to soften them with a smile. Just looking at Mac Cassidy was like rubbing a freshly burst blister.

Her comment acted as a full stop to the discussion and the Cassidy brothers finished their coffee and rose to leave.

As Laurel showed them across the small, square hall, which Rea had made bright with pale green emulsion and would probably decorate much like the scene on the cover of her magazine, Mac turned back. 'Laurel, do you think we could have a word in private?'

Laurel kept her voice and face expressionless. 'I'm afraid I don't allow myself to be alone with a man unless I know and trust him.'

Slowly, Mac flushed a deep, dark red.

Grady's eyebrows flew up towards his dark glossy hair.

Both men wore identical expressions of shock and affront.

'Bye,' she said, sweetly, as she opened the front door for them to pass through, then closed it with a soft but final-sounding click. She'd taken a cheap shot but she'd enjoyed it. Whether Mac wanted to apologise for old sins, or even turn sinister and warn her to keep her mouth shut, he could just damned-well stew.

She sailed back into the kitchen, spirits lifting. 'I'm going to begin clearing out Mum's studio so I can bring my stuff in.'

Daisy leaped up. 'Fantastic!'

Her mother tweaked the teenager's curls. 'You weren't as enthusiastic when I suggested we clear it for you to work in.'

Daisy laughed. 'No Wi-Fi out there. I like working in my room where I can watch Netflix at the same time.'

'I'll need a range extender or a separate router for internet access, then,' Laurel said, as they grabbed their coats and took the side door into the garden. The garage was on the other side of the house so they stepped into an open space surrounded by hedges and trees, the lawn wearing its shaggy winter coat. Rounding the corner to the main back garden, Laurel paused to appreciate shapely conifers, wooden seating, graceful arches, and shrubs bearing red or orange berries. 'Your garden's lovely, Rea, even in winter.'

Rea flushed with pleasure, huddling into her coat against the wind that blew in across the fenland that began just the other side of the hedge. 'As Daisy said, I just carried on Mum's work.'

They all turned to look towards the top of the garden. At the end of a stepping-stone path stood the studio, a wooden structure in which Isla had once spent many happy hours on her watercolours of the village. Rea had repainted the outside a pleasing deep grey-blue. In silence, the three took the path, unlocked the door and stepped inside.

Laurel breathed in the faint scent of old paint and gazed at the skylights studding the sloping roof. A stream of dust motes danced in the weak sunlight and for the first time since returning to Middledip she felt a semblance of peace. 'This is going to be perfect.'

A whole community of spiders had taken up residence, judging by the number of old cobwebs amongst the beams above several new crates standing in the centre of the floor. Rea gestured towards them. 'When your paintings were delivered I had them carried straight in here.'

'Brilliant, thanks.' Laurel patted the biggest crate. 'There's work to do before I'm ready to unpack them though.' She opened a nearby cupboard to see Isla's dried-up paints and brushes. 'I feel guilty I never came in to clear Mum's things before, but I suppose I was clinging on to a piece of her.'

Daisy opened another cupboard, exclaiming over water-colour paintings stored in portfolios. She took one out. 'This says it's St Margaret's Church, Middledip. We don't have a church.'

'We used to, which is why we have Church Close.' Rea slipped an arm around her daughter's shoulders. 'Our great-grandfather was the vicar.'

Daisy looked up disbelievingly. 'I'm the great-great-granddaughter to a vicar?'

'The Reverend Glenn,' Laurel confirmed. 'Our family's Middledip roots go deep. Mum used to love recreating scenes from old photos. Look, here's the pub that's now a coffee shop.' She held the painting up for the others to see.

'Wow, yeah, it's The Angel.' Daisy came closer to inspect the slightly buckled watercolour paper from more than twenty years ago. 'Nan wasn't as good as you.'

Laurel gave her a hug. 'Nan didn't do further education, then four years of uni. She had a nice touch, though, and made a useful second income from these nostalgic water-colours. Look at the luminosity of the streetlamp just coming on in the twilight and the way the light falls on the ornamental brickwork at the front of the pub. The artistic gene runs in our family.'

Daisy shrugged. 'I suppose, though Mum's about decor-ating and I'm more of a maker than an artist.'

'It's all artistic,' Laurel assured her. 'Rea, can you remember sitting in here with Mum, working on our own stuff? Trying charcoal, chalk, watercolours, oils or anything we could get our hands on?'

Rea's face softened into a reminiscent smile. 'She split her time between us equally but you were the best. Your clothes were always covered with paint.'

31

'Mum's were, too. I can see her now, her hair piled up, encouraging us.' She blinked away a tear.

'I wish I'd known Nan.' Daisy turned over a painting labelled "Christmas at The Cross in 1920", looking odd without a single car cluttering the road but with plenty of room for a Christmas tree bedecked with silver chains and what looked like candles in jars. 'Can I have this in my room?'

'Of course,' answered Rea. 'We'll frame it.'

Laurel nodded, warmed by Daisy wanting to forge a connection with the grandmother she'd never met. 'We'll buy a frame and I'll mount it. I haven't got a trade framer in this area yet. Finding one's on my to-do list.'

'Grady's got a mate who's got an art shop in Bettsbrough. Lots of people use him,' Daisy volunteered, still flipping through the old paintings.

Laurel moved off to open a cardboard box, discovering inside a stack of old local newspapers. 'Look at this lot! The top ones go back sixty years. I bet Mum rescued them from someone's attic for the photos. You seem to have a lot to do with Grady, Daisy.' She tagged the observation on casually because it was dawning on her that avoiding both Cassidy brothers might not be easy, judging by the comfortable manner Daisy exhibited with Grady and her friendship with Grady's nephew, Niall.

Daisy nodded without looking up from her grandmother's paintings. 'He's cool. Apart from Art December there's going to be an art wall at Middledip Christmas Fair and he's the organiser.' She tilted her head. 'Well, he says "co-ordinator" rather than "organiser". So everyone books through him to exhibit their work on the art wall during the village fair or joins Art December, and sends him photos of their stuff for the Facebook group.'

'Brilliant,' said Laurel, pinning on a smile and resigning herself to the fact that returning to the village meant sharing it with the Cassidys – and perhaps other people she'd rather not encounter again, like Amie Blunt. It was possible that she'd have to tackle the school about Daisy's bunking off in Rea's stead and she hoped Mac Cassidy wouldn't be her point of contact. 'Art December's the village art month, isn't it? What's happening?'

Daisy put the painting down while she explained. 'Loads of people are displaying their work in their house windows for the whole month, with price tags, and I'm making a Google map so everyone can discover what's on offer and then use their phones to guide them to it. The link will be posted on every local Facebook group we can think of.'

'Daisy's going to have my office window for her display,' Rea popped in, emptying a cardboard box of paintings so she could use it as a bin for dried-up paint tubes.

They fell silent, selecting what to keep, such as Isla's paintings and the stash of pristine old newspapers. Daisy checked something on her phone then looked up, beaming. 'They're having the tree lighting outside the village hall tonight. Can I go?'

Seeing Rea assume her worried look, eyes wide and forehead wrinkling, Laurel asked casually, 'Could I come?'

'Yeah, great,' Daisy agreed, tapping rapidly at her phone screen. She drifted away after a while, ostensibly to do homework.

Rea sighed as she wiped dust from the window and watched her daughter jog down the path, huddled into her hoodie. 'I hope she goes to all of her lessons on Monday. I dread the school texting to say she's been skipping again.'

Laurel paused to take in Rea's lines of worry. 'They're onto it that quickly?'

'The electronic registers at every lesson are transmitted to the office and someone checks it there,' Rea explained. 'What doesn't make sense is that it's art lessons Daisy often bunks off. She's all about art! She loves the craft sessions at The Angel and you've heard how excited she is about the art show. Before the summer holidays it was English she skipped but that was always one of her favourites, too.'

'If it's not the subjects she's avoiding then it must be someone in those classes.' Laurel stretched over a box to give Rea a comforting hug.

But Rea was already shaking her head. 'That's the obvious conclusion but I've asked and asked and the school's given her bags of opportunity to explain or to ask for help. She insists it's not anyone or anything. She's been such an easy kid till now but I'm at my wits' end.' Despair rang in Rea's voice. 'After detention and isolation last school year, she eventually returned to her lessons. Then we had the same cycle at the beginning of September term and now again after half-term. I can't get a handle on what's happening.'

Laurel frowned. 'In some ways she seems engaged with school. She told me about dressing as Santa to help with a party for the younger kids.' That made Laurel think of Mac having to wear Daisy's Santa pants and her thoughts flew to the scene of some of her own teenaged problems. 'She travels to school by bus, doesn't she?'

Rea nodded. 'Not much choice. She'd have to walk several miles between Bettsbrough and the village otherwise. That's not acceptable.'

'Of course not.' Laurel returned to work but only half

her mind was now on the studio. 'I'll take Daisy to and from school on Monday. I have stuff to do in Bettsbrough.'

Rea looked up with a frown. 'OK, thanks.' Her expression suggested she wasn't quite sure why Laurel was suggesting it but Laurel had bad memories of the bus to school and one tiny, blonde she-devil called Amie Blunt.

'At least she hasn't refused to go to school completely,' Rea continued. 'I've read about that happening and the parent gets fined.' A tear leaked from the corner of her eye. 'I'm so crap. If I could go out I'm sure I'd be able to support Daisy more.'

Heart hurting for her sister, Laurel pulled her back into her arms. 'It's OK, Rea. I'm here, now. If Daisy needs a visible adult presence at school, it can be me.' They continued their work until darkness fell, when they went indoors to shower away the dust and prepare a meal in the kitchen that had been Rea's alone for so long.

When they'd eaten, Daisy checked the time. 'The tree lighting's at seven-thirty, Auntie Laurel.'

Laurel didn't sigh, but she felt like it. 'We'd better get our coats.'

Rea seemed happy to clear away the dishes so Laurel was soon stepping into a cold clear evening with her niece.

'Wish it was snowing again.' Daisy gazed up hopefully at where the wind chased ragged clouds across a pearly moon. When they'd crossed Main Road she took the route across the playing fields, where it was much darker, though the lights of the village hall and car park could be clearly seen a hundred yards away.

But Laurel couldn't help herself. She hesitated.

Daisy looked around enquiringly. 'What's up?'

After a long, deep breath, Laurel made herself go on. It would be ridiculous to insist they went around by the road when the action was so clearly going to take place on this side of the hall. 'Nothing.'

They had soon crossed the grass, which was just beginning to crunch with frost, and were in a car park full of milling people – what passed for a crowd in little Middledip. Laurel made herself relax, joining Daisy in a noisy queue for hot chocolate and the first mince pies of the season. Daisy seemed to know everyone and Laurel recognised a few faces peeping out from under hats and scarves. She hung back and let Daisy take the lead.

Then a small blonde lady made a welcome speech explaining how they'd decided it would be nice to erect the village hall Christmas tree outside rather than inside this year, so everyone could enjoy it.

After a pause for applause she got everyone counting down, their voices swelling as one. 'Five . . . four . . . three . . . two . . . one . . . hooray!' The lights blazed, illuminating a pine soaring into the night sky, a golden star on top and coloured lights winking from every branch.

Daisy hooted and whistled with everyone else. A singing group burst into a spirited rendition of 'O Christmas Tree' while villagers chatted and the mince pie stand did a brisk trade. Daisy's smile became pensive. 'Shame Mum couldn't come.'

Laurel slipped an arm around her niece. 'Yes, it is. But I'm here until she feels she can cope a bit better.'

Unfortunately, she knew both Daisy and Rea would be missing out on a lot until then.

Chapter Three

In the chill atmosphere of his spray shop, Grady tried to concentrate on masking up the bonnet of a 1996 Bentley Continental. The client wanted a spacescape – was that a word? The moon and stars, anyway. A Bentley wasn't a typical subject for airbrush art and he thought the owner, Les Preedy, eccentric.

When he'd first sought Grady out he'd been dressed in an enormous green woolly cardigan that clashed with his florid face. 'Inherited the car from an uncle and want you to give it a crazy look. Christopher Carlysle said he thought there was a chap here could help me. Going to give rides at car shows.'

Grady hadn't been particularly impressed by the mention of the local bigwig landowner, as Carlysle was known for trying to get something for nothing. Les had had to stump up fifty per cent upfront for the work on his car, like anyone else.

The design, preparation, painstaking airbrush painting and sealing would take Grady about ten days but then the Bentley would look sensational, a crater-filled moon and a burst of stars glowing from the power-bulge bonnet, and comets trailing along the bodywork from the four headlights and grinning grill. The conservative grey bodywork would pop with silver, blue and every shade of fire.

Taking a minute to warm his hands up inside the sleeves of his coat, he gazed at the Bentley absently. Sunday wasn't really a working day but he was too antsy today to veg out with a movie or a book.

He was unsettled by the reappearance of Laurel Hill.

How weird was that?

How weird was she, these days?

Daisy and Rea were great, so what had happened to Laurel? A personality transplant? The sweet, sunny teen he remembered might never have existed. This morning Laurel had shown understanding one minute and been rude the next. Mac had shrugged it off but Grady had been outraged on his behalf over the way she'd embarrassed him. He believed in people taking care of their safety, but he did *not* appreciate the blunt way she'd refused a private conversation. And she'd practically hit them on the arse with the door on the way out. So far as he was concerned, this snooty, snotty Laurel Hill could piss off back to wherever she'd come from.

As if hearing his name in his brother's thoughts, Mac chose that moment to call Grady's phone. 'OK?' Grady answered, economically.

Mac sounded fed-up. 'Yeah. I rang the police and reported what happened. I gave them your details along with Daisy's and Laurel's.' Then, as if Grady had objected, 'I *had* to report it. Jake, my headteacher, was in full agreement. If I don't act, these individuals could go on to give problems to my colleagues. Pranks get embedded in teenage culture and become a thing.'

In his own school years Grady remembered the scribbling of an obscenity on a white board in an empty classroom becoming 'a thing', but not pantsing a teacher and tying him to his car. 'Did you tell the police the kids videoed it?'

Mac's sigh was almost a groan. 'Yeah. Little shits,' he added unprofessionally.

Grady could only imagine how hellish Mac's life would be with such embarrassing footage flying around his school. 'Do you think Daisy will be able to resist talking?'

'Dunno.' Mac sighed.

'She's a good kid.' Grady hesitated, then asked, 'Laurel was odd, wasn't she? She'd been sort of sticking up for you when she called pantsing a sexual assault and then pretty much called you untrustworthy.' When Mac didn't answer he added, 'What did you need to speak to her alone about?'

'Erm . . .' Mac said. 'Aspirations Week at school. We ask successful people to come in and talk to the kids about potential careers. We haven't had an artist.'

'Oh, right.' Grady wondered why Mac would request privacy just for that. 'I wouldn't have minded waiting around while you had that conversation. I was in no rush.'

'Oh . . . I wasn't thinking.' Mac sounded as if he'd lost interest. 'Fancy a pint at The Three Fishes tonight?'

Grady did, and they'd just made arrangements and ended the call when a young, female voice said behind him, 'So, what's next with Art December?'

He jumped to see Daisy standing in the open doorway and hoped she hadn't heard herself and her aunt discussed. Judging from her usual round-faced smile, she hadn't. Her hood was up and her long curls dangled out either side, like a scarf. On the front of her black hoodie it said in red: *Yeah, underestimate me and see what happens.* He grinned. That was so Daisy. He'd become fond of the sassy teen as they'd spent more time together this year, the Middledip arts and crafts scene gaining traction. Last month, Grady had put on a session of airbrush painting, helping people master the art by repeating 'trigger down for air and back for paint' about a thousand times. Everyone from knitters to card makers to artists to photographers had met at The Angel Community Café in the room called The Public, which was a nod to the Victorian building's pub origins. Carola, who ran The Angel, was also head of the village hall committee so she pretty much had the community stuff covered.

He answered Daisy's question. 'Gathering volunteers.'

Daisy beamed, extracting one hand from her big front pocket to raise it. 'Me.'

'Fantastic. So long as Rea's OK with it and it doesn't interfere with your schoolwork,' he said diplomatically. Daisy had told him she'd been skipping lessons and was in trouble for it. It seemed at odds with everything else he knew about her but teens went through phases. So he understood, anyway, from parents such as Mac and Tonya, as he wasn't a dad himself.

'Mum'll be cool with it,' Daisy assured him breezily. 'I'll ask Auntie Laurel, too. Imagine Middledip having a proper artist involved.' Her eyes glowed.

A strange feeling began in Grady's insides. He pretended to need to sort out the zip on his ski jacket while he examined the pins-and-needles sensation in his stomach at the idea of Laurel being involved. Was it alarm? Distaste? Apprehension? 'Will she be here long enough?' he asked, still fiddling with the fastening of his coat.

'She got divorced so she's living with us for a while.' Daisy gave another of her beaming smiles. 'Have you seen

40

her stuff? She gets thousands for a canvas. I was having a nosy this afternoon. Look.' She produced her phone and flicked to her browser. It was open at Etsy and the screen seemed positively ablaze with colour as Daisy thrust it into his hand.

He found himself gazing at an image of a slender, ethereal woman who'd apparently hurled herself into a man's arms, tossing back her head to welcome his lips on her throat. Where her hemline should be, the bold, swooping lines of her scarlet dress burst into an explosion of flowers that flew into the air and somehow entangled with the reds and ambers of her hair. The man's clothes were severe and simple in comparison but every line of his body spoke of the lust he felt for the woman he embraced. Myriad tiny, stencilled designs ebbed and flowed through the kaleidoscope of colours. Grady had never seen anything like it and couldn't remove his gaze. It was delicate, yet bold, and his body tightened as if the passionate woman was pressed against him.

The caption read: *Joyful lovers. Multimedia. Laurel Hill original.* The price was nearly three thousand pounds.

He scrolled down to the next image; another willowy woman in a dress of a hundred blues, smiling dreamily as she paddled in frothing waves – priced at just over four thousand – and then a man, his torso naked, grimacing as if he'd just raced his heart out and was flying through the tape at the finishing line. His hair seemed scribbled with the finest threads of dribbled paint. That one was two thousand five hundred.

'Wow,' he breathed.

Daisy took back her phone. 'Isn't she awesome? She says her work is expressionist, which means the colours reflect mood rather than being real-life, and a little bit impressionist because she doesn't *exactly* paint what we'd see.'

'I'm certainly impressed,' he said, trying a feeble play on words. 'I didn't realise she'd be staying in the village.'

Daisy took the phone back and fiddled with it. 'Mum needs a bit of support, y'know?'

'I know,' he agreed gently. That Rea Grove had become what Melanie at Booze & News declared 'a recluse' was well known in the village. Daisy had told him their GP had diagnosed agoraphobia and Rea now worked from home and had her shopping delivered. Poor Daisy seemed to accept the situation on the surface but he suspected she was bewildered underneath. All he could do to help was be her friend. Friends helped you feel secure.

'I want to make my living from making awesome things like Auntie Laurel,' Daisy said, pulling her hood closer as she turned to leave.

'Did she do art at uni?' Grady picked up his door keys and followed her out. The snow remained now only in shady nooks.

Daisy sent him a suspicious look. ''S'pose.' She so obviously anticipated the *You need to get the grades in your GCSEs and A-levels to go to uni* that he didn't say it. It would only make him the bad guy and she didn't need telling.

Outside, the November afternoon was already turning to dusk. 'Will you be OK to walk home?' he asked.

She cocked an incredulous eyebrow. 'Erm . . . we're in the village.' She added a, 'See you later,' and in a few strides she'd disappeared around the corner into Main Road.

Left alone with his own thoughts, Grady decided he wasn't yet in the mood for the silence of Mistletoe Cottage.

He'd drop in at The Angel Community Café and see if Carola was behind the counter.

Sure enough, he found her amongst espresso machine steam, fading blonde locks neatly twisted behind her head and a smart black polo and trousers beneath her white apron. He supposed she was in her late fifties now but she had the energy of a teenager. She slid a Belgian bun onto a plate and took payment from Alexia Kennedy – Alexia Hardaker now, he reminded himself – ahead of him in the queue, then beamed at Grady. 'We need to sort out a Middledip Christmas Fair meeting,' she said in her quick, efficient manner. Beside the counter were notices for a Christmas raffle and a Christmas pensioners' singalong.

'Thinking the same,' he agreed, ordering a latte.

She turned to the espresso machine. 'We can meet here, in The Public.' Carola gestured towards the doorway that led to the next room. She used to host the meetings and committees she involved herself in at her home on the Bankside Estate. Now she'd come to work at The Angel she found it good for business to hold them here.

'Daisy Grove's volunteered to be involved,' he told her, paying for his drink, then picking up the thick cup and saucer.

Carola beamed. 'Tess Arnott-Rattenbury's happy to help with the Christmas scene for the village hall.'

'Tess? Great to have a professional illustrator on board.' Tess was his landlord Ratty's wife. Middledip was getting quite the community of art professionals. As if to reinforce that thought, as he turned away to pick a table he noticed Laurel Hill seated by herself on a brown leather sofa at the back of the room. A lone coffee mug stood on the low table by her knees and a multi-coloured coat that Joseph would have been proud of was folded on the sofa beside her. The pretty girl he'd known had grown up into a gorgeous, lush woman.

His steps faltered. There were several unoccupied tables . . . but in a few seconds he found himself standing before her, leaving the coffee table as a barrier between them. 'OK if I join you for a minute? If sharing a sofa in a public place isn't against your alone-with-a-man code.'

Her gaze flicked up to focus on him. Apparently, she'd been so lost in thought she hadn't noticed his approach. She blinked, then smiled faintly. 'Help yourself.' She eased along the cushions to make space.

Settling down his brimming cup, he said, 'Welcome back to the village. Daisy tells me you're here for a while.'

She shrugged. Her dark, foxy hair was shorter than when she'd been a teenager, cut in one of those sharp bobs that came to points at the front and a deep fringe above eyes the same startling blue he remembered. 'Thanks. For some months, I expect.'

OK. Guarded, but not unfriendly. It was enough encouragement for him to say, 'I thought I ought to warn you about Daisy.'

Fear flashed in her eyes. 'What? Is she OK? What do you mean?'

He lifted his hands hastily. 'Sorry! She's fine. She's great. I only meant that she's volunteered to help with Art December and the art wall at the Christmas Fair. I think she's going to ask you to contribute work. I don't want you to feel obliged. She showed me your paintings on her phone and she's obviously super-proud but you're a professional and the art wall's a fundraiser for the village hall. Be aware there's an eighty-twenty split of proceeds, in case you want to have your excuses ready. Nobody's under pressure to participate.'

Her expression had relaxed the moment he'd reassured her about Daisy and now she picked up her coffee mug, the forget-me-not blue eyes twinkling over the rim. 'Who gets the twenty?'

'The village hall.' He smiled because she could almost be the Laurel he remembered, the sweet, funny one, always ready to laugh.

She shrugged. 'Not too bad. Galleries take fifty.'

It sounded as if she wasn't discounting exhibiting a piece of work. He could imagine Carola cartwheeling with joy at a potential twenty percent of what a Laurel Hill original brought in. He kept his tone light. 'Art December runs throughout the month but the Middledip Christmas Fair in the village hall is on the 18th and 19th of December.'

She nodded. 'Daisy told me about her brilliant idea of a Google map for the Art December display windows so people can locate what they're looking for. It sounds as if Middledip has a big art community.'

'Growing, anyway,' he agreed. 'Sites like Etsy and ecommerce platforms like Shopify make it possible for makers to find customers without slogging around the country to fairs and shows. Being a maker's become hip as well as fun.' He took up his coffee cup. 'Expecting anyone in the village to offer the kind of price you're used to might be optimistic but having your name attached to the show would be great.'

Laurel opened her mouth, as if to answer, but then her gaze switched to a point over his shoulder. Before he could turn to follow her gaze, arms slid around his neck. 'Hiya,' a familiar female voice crooned. 'Too much caffeine's bad for you, you know.' She giggled. 'We're eating shortbread angels in the corner if you want to join us.'

He'd known it was Pippa from the first word and her

unconcern that her scarf was dangling in his face was typical. She lifted her head to address Laurel, arms still looped around Grady. 'You looking after my man here?' She giggled again, swished her feathery long hair, then, without giving either of them a chance to answer, she cooed, 'Laters!' and tripped off in the other direction. Grady turned and spotted Pippa's sister Zelda waiting at another table. Zelda raised a friendly hand, regarding her sister with bemusement.

He returned the salute and turned back to Laurel, face hot, mystified that Pippa, after moving out of Mistletoe Cottage nine months ago, should act so proprietarily.

'Feel free to join your girlfriend,' Laurel said politely.

'Ex,' he clarified brusquely. 'Pippa and I broke up early in the year. She shared her sister's house in the new village before we got together so she went back there.' At first their paths crossing in the pub or here in The Angel had been awkward, though his feelings for her had vanished over the way she'd ended things. Now, seeing her was just a reminder of his imperfections. 'We're still friendly,' he added drily.

Amusement glinted in her eyes, again bringing the old Laurel sharply into focus. Questions buzzed in his brain like bees trapped at a window. Why had she stopped talking to him all those years ago? Why did she leave Middledip? Why the occasionally snotty attitude? Impulsively, he said, 'I fancy another latte. Can I get you anything?'

She regarded him. Her thick hair shone beneath the bright café lights and a few freckles spangled her nose. He remembered teasing her about them just to see her eyes crinkle up with laughter. He remembered everything. Kissing. Talking about Christmas jobs and coming exams. Kissing under mistletoe. Her school, his school.

Kissing again, even with no mistletoe in sight. Arranging to meet at the under-eighteens Christmas party at the village hall . . .

Then nothing.

Grady had never got to the party because he'd broken his ankle playing football and had been in hospital having it pinned. Reunited with his phone at home the next day he'd texted her an explanation. Nothing. So he texted several more times. Still nothing. Once up on crutches, he'd hopped and swung his way to The Nookery, but his knocks had gone unanswered.

'OK, thanks,' she said suddenly.

He blinked himself back to the present. Oh, yes, he'd offered to buy her coffee. 'Great.' He took her order for a cappuccino and returned to the counter where Carola ruled the hissing espresso machine.

'That's Rea's little sister, isn't it?' she asked as she made angel shapes in the cappuccino froth. 'She's gorgeous.' She took his payment and whisked off to some other task without waiting for an answer.

Ignoring Pippa's fixed gaze, Grady carried the two steaming mugs back to the corner sofa.

'What did Carola say?' Laurel murmured as he set the mugs down carefully and took up his seat again. 'I saw her glancing over here.'

The old urge to tease her returned. 'She said you're gorgeous.'

Blue eyes widened. 'Oh.'

He grinned but decided against saying he thought she was gorgeous, too. He had the feeling it would take only one suspect word to explode this tentative conversation. Instead, he said softly, 'She's the kindest person around, under her slight nosiness.'

Her answering smile was faintly rueful. 'I'm out of practice at living in Middledip. I went for a walk yesterday and people kept stopping to ask what I'm doing here and how Rea is. I'd forgotten how up in your business a village can be.'

He blew the surface of his latte, evaluating this slur on the village he loved. 'I suppose you could look at it like that. Or you could think of it as a close, caring community.'

She snorted.

He put down his drink and looked into her face. 'Is it so terrible if people are curious about you coming back? I am, myself.'

Her gaze dropped. 'I got divorced. Rea and Daisy could use me around. It's not that interesting.'

It was to him. 'Then I suppose people are curious about the way you left. You were part of Middledip . . . and then you weren't. Rea still lived here but it was almost as if you'd died. She hardly said your name.'

She looked taken aback, then flushed and fiddled with a sugar sachet from her saucer. A cartoon reindeer peeped from behind the word 'sugar' on the paper. 'Was Rea . . . upset? I realise now how clumsy I was. When Mum died our aunt wanted to take us in and, also, some of the villagers took "it takes a village to raise a child" literally. Rea fought off all that well-meant but unasked for interference.' She dropped her gaze. Above the chatter of the café the espresso machine hissed and a child cried for a cake. 'A couple of years later I decided to do sixth form at an arts college in Peterborough and my aunt said I could stay with her. It had better facilities than Bettsbrough Community College. Teenagers are selfish.'

Grady debated. Laurel's face was an unhappy pink and

she folded the sugar sachet over and over so that all of the reindeer was hidden but the red nose. Grady could have let the subject drop but what had happened more than half their lifetimes ago still bugged him. 'I don't blame you for taking that opportunity. But I've always wondered why you stopped talking to me months before you went.'

His words hung between them.

'It wasn't you,' she said in a strangled voice, the one she'd used so much after her mum had died. But then her shoulders squared and she tossed back her hair, almost visibly drawing on an adult mask. Her lips drew up at the corners in a polite smile. 'Sorry if teenage me was clumsy with you. I hope we're old enough to put it behind us.'

Grady tried to process what he'd just witnessed. It had been for all the world as if Laurel had suffered a bad moment, then consciously paused to coach herself on how to move past it. He elected to co-operate with her wish to leave the past behind – for now – and returned smoothly to her earlier remark. 'Sorry to hear about the divorce. Pippa and I never got any further than wedding plans. They fell apart.' He didn't say why.

Laurel flicked back her fringe. The geometric hairstyle drew attention to the clean lines of her face. 'Sorry about you and Pippa. In our case, we couldn't give each other what we wanted. The marriage had taken all it could.' She passed the conversational ball like a sociable person at a party. 'You said Daisy showed you some of my work. Can I ask about yours?'

He grinned. 'You know MAR Motors at the Cross? The owner, Ratty, restored a barn behind it and rents it to me as a spray shop.'

She looked interested. 'Ratty is Miles Arnott-Rattenbury,

right? I'm amazed he stayed in the village. After his public school education I thought he was destined for greater things.'

'Some of us think the village is great,' he said stiffly.

Her eyes widened. 'Sorry. I didn't mean to be rude. I just meant that he was bright.' Then her colour rose. 'I mean—'

Evenly, he said, 'You don't have to be stupid to like working on cars. Ratty's built up his garage from scratch. I enjoy working on cars too. I was in hotel management but I like cars better.'

'Of course.' Embarrassment flickered, then it was gone, overlaid by a remote expression. She picked up her coffee mug. 'I didn't meant to give offence. Sorry.' She finished the drink in a few gulps and shoved the mug back on the table. 'Thanks for the coffee.' Flinging on her coat as she gained her feet, she squeezed awkwardly around the end of the table and strode across the café to the door.

Grady watched her go, irritated by her turning up her citified nose at the village he loved but sorry he'd reacted like a touchy kid, ending the conversation on a sour note. He'd been enjoying their tentative encounter. It had felt like sunlight thawing an iron-hard frost. Then he noticed Pippa's attention on him. 'New girlfriend?' she mouthed.

He shook his head so vigorously that it would probably have been Laurel's turn to be offended if she'd been there to witness it. He finished his drink and left the warmth of The Angel, ducking his head against the November wind racing down Port Road in an icy blast.

His fond memories of mistletoe kisses between young Laurel Hill and young Grady Cassidy were worthless. The new Laurel Hill was as chilly as the winter weather.

Chapter Four

It had been a while since Laurel needed to get up promptly on a Monday morning but she'd been lying awake anyway thinking how awkward she'd been with Grady. What had come over her? His questions about her leaving the village must have turned her jittery and at least half her mind had been occupied by absorbing the notion that he was still hurt at the way she'd cut their friendship short. *Still.* It was almost a relief to get up to take Daisy to school.

Breakfast was not relaxed. Rea, who worked for a telesales company from her office at the front of the house, ate quickly, checking the clock. 'I have to log in by eight.' Her brow was furrowed and Laurel wished her sister could have a job she really liked.

Daisy dragged herself into the kitchen, half into her black school sweatshirt. Dumping her backpack in the middle of the floor she helped herself to cereal and a huge glass of milk.

Laurel sipped coffee and gave her a smile. 'What time do we need to leave?'

Daisy shrugged. 'Soon.' She finished her breakfast, said

bye to Rea, then they went outside, where Laurel scraped sparkling frost from the windows of the SUV. When Laurel got in, Daisy gazed at her with a mutinous expression. 'I'm not going to skip school. You don't have to take me.'

Laurel reversed off the drive to turn around in the cul-de-sac of Great End. 'But I'm going to Bettsbrough to the arts supplies shop. Why wouldn't I take you?'

After a moment, Daisy said, 'OK. Cool,' in a voice that suggested the opposite. She hunkered down in her seat and busied herself with her phone while they headed out of the village. After half a mile, she pointed at her phone screen with an air of triumph. 'Art shop's shut on Mondays.'

Laurel didn't let the announcement slow her down. 'Damn,' she said with faux regret because though she'd run supplies down when she knew she was leaving her Chiswick studio, she had a lot to do before starting a new painting. And, anyway, she bought almost everything online. 'I should have checked the opening hours. Still, I have to buy heaters for the studio. I expect that retail park outside town will have some.' She drove on up the lane, over potholes and under frosted trees, their winter-bare branches reaching out as if to hold hands above. Idly, she added, 'The bus to school used to be a zoo when I was your age. Isn't it nicer to have a chauffeur?'

'The school bus is fine,' Daisy answered.

Laurel's hands and feet continued the automatic movements necessary to drive carefully over icy puddles at the edges of the lane. Had there been unconscious emphasis on *bus*, as if to indicate there was something else to do with school that wasn't OK? She gnawed at the problem as they joined the main road and soon they arrived in the residential area where the school stood, its playing fields

52

to one side of classroom blocks that rose several storeys into the air. She slowed the car, peering past the big white sign that said *Sir John Browne Academy*. 'Who painted the school green? And what's the building next to the science block?'

Daisy looked vague. 'I always forget you and Mum came here. It's green so as not to stick out of the landscape so much. Do you mean that building?' She pointed. 'It's a library and a computer suite with a gaming section. Lunchtime geek club. Not my thing.' Daisy settled her fingers on the door handle and gave the first smile Laurel had seen from her this morning. 'Laurel, will you be part of Art December and the art wall at the Christmas Fair? It would be, like, vintage. Not just because you're fam but because you're an amazing artist.'

Thanks to Grady's warning, Laurel didn't feel caught out. Laurel and Rea had talked last night and agreed it was an opportunity for Laurel to share Daisy's interests, deepening their relationship. 'Vintage means "good", right?' she joked, expansively. 'If so, then OK.' It wouldn't be a hardship to contribute a small canvas. She already had something hanging around that would do. Last year she'd had a commission to paint brothers gazing at each other but it hadn't been collected. She accepted commissions on a 'only buy it if you like it basis'. The client had liked it but had lost his job and, with apologies, been unable to buy. She hadn't yet got around to photographing it to list online.

'That's sick,' Daisy breathed, startling Laurel till she remembered 'sick' was akin to 'awesome'. 'We're meeting in The Angel on Wednesday night.' Beaming now, Daisy opened the door and hopped out into the frosty day. 'See you later.' The car door shut with a bang.

Wondering what she'd be required to do at said meeting, Laurel watched Daisy dangle her backpack from one shoulder, clutching her coat across her. When a bus rumbled into the bus bay, stopping with a hiss of brakes, Daisy waited, then waved. A girl and a boy detached themselves from the stream of disembarking students and hurried to join her, the girl's ponytail flying like a flag in the wind. Daisy, presumably responding to their questions, gestured in Laurel's direction, shrugging. Laurel imagined her saying: *my aunt brought me. I said I'd catch the bus but . . . the faaaaaark?* The others laughed, then they all hurried towards the big green building, still in obviously animated conversation.

She gazed after them with an uncomfortably familiar feeling in her belly that was colder than the ice on nearby puddles. This time it wasn't her own unhappiness prompting it, but her niece's. It might not be the school bus or lack of friends but *something* was making Daisy avoid art lessons. Laurel jumped when a polite toot let her know that another car was waiting for her space. Scrambling her thoughts together, she drove off, trying to remember the route to the retail park.

In another hour, now in the possession of heaters, emulsion called White Whisper, draught strip, and some picture frames, she arrived at The Nookery to transform her mum's old studio into her new workspace. Letting herself in through the front door of the house, out of the icy cold, she stacked her purchases on the hall floor, mindful of the proximity of Rea's office. She could hear her, patient and polite as she assumed the role of the voice of someone's company. Her telesales organisation took calls from the happy, angry or disappointed customers of many clients. Remote working was common enough and Laurel supposed it suited Rea's particular issues but it seemed a lonely way of working compared with the traditional call-centre set-up. Then again, Laurel was about to begin a similarly solitary working life. At least there had been artists in the neighbouring studios in Chiswick . . .

She forced the thought away.

That was the past and she needed to forget it. Today was about looking forward.

Keen not to disturb her sister, she grabbed a mug and some instant coffee then carried them and this morning's purchases across the wintry garden. 'Brr,' she exclaimed, when she let herself into the studio, half surprised not to see ice patterning the inside of the windows as well as the outside. Her first job was making coffee and the second rootling through her boxes for her staple gun to fix draught strip around the windows and doors. Once all shut snugly, she turned on the heaters to stop her hands and feet from freezing.

She fetched the vacuum cleaner and sucked up the dust and cobwebs, having to pause to empty the cleaner halfway through. Then she began transforming the boarded walls into a pleasingly gentle white with long even brush strokes that left her mind free to wander to Daisy, who'd already texted: *coming home on bus*. Perhaps taking her to school hadn't been a good idea. Instead of the car providing a cosy, friendly atmosphere, as it had when they'd gone Christmas bauble shopping at the weekend, it had made Daisy suspicious and subdued.

Probably it was as well she'd never had kids of her own if that was the best she could do.

Coasting over the pain that came with that thought, Laurel climbed up on a stool to reach the high bits. She worked all morning and into the afternoon, remembering her mum painting in the same room and realising that now she'd gone through the pain of postponing her other plans, she might enjoy working here. She'd frame a couple of Isla's paintings for the studio as well as for Daisy's room and ask Rea if she'd like some to keep her company in the office.

By the time she'd finished one coat of emulsion she was ready for a break. She didn't need to push herself too hard. It wasn't every week you left your marital home and returned to your childhood village, immediately falling over the reasons you left. An uncomfortable feeling squeezed her stomach.

For nineteen years she'd lived with a horrible experience but, apart from lingering trust issues, she had learned not to be defined by it. She'd set herself free. OK, certain situations gave her a nervy feeling but she'd thought herself way past the awful, frustrated, destructive thirst for revenge she'd once had. Yet in the past two days she'd deliberately made Mac Cassidy uncomfortable. And that *was* revenge. He looked like a pillar of the community these days and was a family man but . . . yeah. She was finding it hard to let him off the hook.

No. She couldn't let herself be dragged back into the past. She was needed in the present.

She stuck the lid back on the emulsion and hurried indoors. Rea was mid-call and it was half past two so had probably eaten lunch already. Laurel ate a sandwich then pulled on her coat against the keen, blustery wind and set out to stride around the village.

First, she joined Main Road. Two men were outside the pub, putting Christmas trees in tubs, a tangle of fairy lights lying on the floor nearby. They all exchanged friendly nods. She marched up on into the Bankside Estate, which

Grady had called 'the new village'. She knew from Rea that it was also known disparagingly as 'Little Dallas' because the bigger houses had porticoes. The really new part, the affordable housing, was called 'Toy Town'. These nicknames were generally applied by those who lived in the older part of the village in the stone cottages, like The Nookery, or red-brick Victorian houses.

When she'd left the village, Bankside Estate had comprised only Great Hill Road and New Street. Now Laurel tramped along a whole host of other streets of modern houses and felt she could have been anywhere – not Middledip at all. A woman busy stringing lights around a tree called, 'Christmas mad, me. Can't wait to get everywhere twinkling. Me and my neighbours are all having a crazy push with outside decorations, this year.' She gestured to where a woman clinging to a ladder hung glittering plastic snowmen on a wall, while a man swathed a porch roof with lights.

As it wasn't possible to be anonymous or unfriendly in Middledip, Laurel called back, 'Can't beat plenty of twinkle.' She walked on, slowing to listen outside a big house where a choir was practising 'White Christmas', their voices rich with the mixture of hope and wistfulness the song demanded. After completing her tour of the estate she exited onto Port Road, back in the original village again, passing the school where cut-out snowflakes adorned the windows. She paused there, too, gazing at a silver tree outside the gates covered with the clear baubles you could buy ready to fill. Children had filled them with coloured paper, drawings or models. The result was charming. When she'd attended the village primary school they used to make a big snowman with a white cotton wool body and a real carrot for his nose.

Further down Port Road she waved to Angel Sissins hurrying along the opposite pavement. Angel was eight or ten years older than Laurel but their mums had been friends and she'd hung out with Rea.

'Hello, stranger,' Angel called across. 'How's your sister?'

'Hanging in there,' Laurel returned, not wanting to go into her sister's anxiety disorder across the street with someone she'd glimpsed only occasionally in the past two decades. 'How's your family?' She knew from Daisy that Toby Sissins was in the year above her at school. He and his little sister would be two of the village kids on the bus with Daisy every day.

'Great, thanks!' Angel tossed back, then hurried on her way.

When she came within sight of The Angel Community Café, Laurel's footsteps faltered. It had been a surprise when Grady had asked to sit with her yesterday but she'd found herself unable to say no, perhaps partly because she'd been feeling conspicuous, attracting curious glances and imagining that the hum of low conversation was villagers either recognising her or speculating as to who she was. He'd offered an olive branch in the form of a cappuccino. In return, she'd been so superior he'd probably felt like sticking the olive branch up her nose.

On impulse, she swung left past Rotten Row and, crossing the road after a couple of cars had sped by, followed the edge of the forecourt of MAR Motors. She rounded the garage building and was immediately faced with a red sign saying 'Grady Auto Art'. Despite the weather, one segment of the bi-fold door was open and she could see Grady himself. His back to her, he was leaning over the bonnet of a car.

She halted. Here was a chance to take her turn brandishing the olive branch and maybe chat about Daisy. It was obvious that they were on good terms. Making a quick about-turn, she hurried back to The Angel and bought a latte for him and a cappuccino for her, as he'd bought yesterday. The steaming cups balanced in a cardboard holder along with sugar sachets, she was soon back at his open doorway and was hit by a sharp smell of paint.

Then she halted.

Pippa – Grady's ex – was standing in the chilly, bright interior, gazing up into his impassive face. 'I'm sorry I hurt you over your infertility,' she murmured.

Laurel must have let out a gasp because both Grady and Pippa swung around. 'I'm s-so sorry,' Laurel stammered. Heart fluttering, horrified at her intrusion into their highly personal conversation and rocked by hearing the word that evoked the grief and pain she and Alex had suffered, she stooped to dump the coffee cups on the floor before spinning around to stumble away.

But she had to pause, hand on the cold wall, because blood was singing in her ears and darkness was advancing on the edges of her vision. Then Pippa barged out of the door and, shoving past with a snarled, 'Thanks a lot,' stormed around the corner and out of sight.

Laurel sucked in several long, slow breaths. The darkness began to retreat. She straightened up just as Grady loomed beside her.

His expression was thunderous. 'What do you want?' he demanded bluntly. Then, after taking a look at her face, he dropped all hostility. 'Come inside a minute. You look as if you've seen a ghost.'

Laurel let herself be steered on jelly legs. Inside his spray shop several old, ripped and pitted car seats were arranged against the back wall and soon she was seated on a dark red one. Grady retrieved the takeaway cups from near the door and held them up with a questioning expression.

Laurel collected her scattered thoughts, angry at herself for her overreaction. It wasn't as if her infertility was a new thing. 'I was snitty yesterday. I brought you an olive-branch latte.'

'And the cappuccino's for you? You look as if you could use it.' He perched himself on the next car seat over, a black one with white paint smears. In silence he added sugar to both cups and stirred, then passed her hers. 'Thanks,' she muttered, taking a sip. As strength began to return, she forced herself to meet his damson-dark eyes. 'Sorry.'

'For?' He raised his eyebrows.

Realising she was curled up like a monkey, she forced herself to relax her posture. 'I sounded up myself about the village and about other people's occupations yesterday. And today I came clodhopping in—'

A single headshake stopped her, but he dropped his gaze. She fiddled with her cup. 'I feel your pain,' she said, bleakly. 'I'm infertile.'

His gaze flicked back to her.

She ploughed on, finding herself hunching over again, as if holding her heart in to prevent it from shattering into pieces. 'I understand it doesn't help to know there are so many of us. One in four, isn't it? Or is that one in four couples? But if you were embarrassed by me overhearing what Pippa said, I just want you to know you shouldn't be and you're not alone.' She took a steadying breath. 'I share that particular grief.' Her words echoed around the cold stone walls, up to the underside of the tiled roof.

It took him several gulps from his cup before he answered hoarsely. 'I'm sorry you're affected too. It's pretty shit.'

She nodded. 'It's what finished Alex and me. We'd been happy.' Her mind flicked through a mental photo album of wedding day, beach holidays, Christmas, snuggling on the sofa, loving one another in bed. The past. 'We're still friends but the constant processes, the repeated disappointment, it took the love away. Or the lust, anyway, which changed the love.'

He was watching her steadily now, eyes thoughtful. 'We didn't get that far.' His voice was gruff, as if the words hurt his throat as they emerged. 'Once she knew I was "defective" – her word,' he added, when Laurel flinched, 'she wanted out. Said it's the woman who has to have all the invasive assistance to conceive and it wasn't fair because she "wasn't to blame".'

'Hell,' Laurel muttered sympathetically. The part about invasive processes was true, though. She'd spent way too much time on the gynaecologist's examination table. She hesitated. 'But Pippa was apologising when I blundered in. Maybe . . .?'

He snorted. 'There aren't enough apologies in the world to change the situation between us.' He cocked his head as he regarded her. 'Do you still . . .' He stopped, then started again, his voice gruff. 'Once I knew I couldn't have kids, I accepted it. It was hard but I don't go round peeping into prams and yearning.'

She paused. He was obviously asking-without-asking something important to him and she didn't want to rush her answer. 'I suppose, I'm the same – now. It took me three years of infertility to accept the truth but eventually I did.' Carefully, she added, 'I don't think there's a right or wrong way to deal with the disappointment. I feel entitled to grieve but I also feel entitled to get on with my life. Just being Laurel and just being Grady is enough, you know. We don't have to ensure the continuance of the human race to be considered valid.' She sighed and loosened her shoulders, giving him a moment in case he wished to continue the conversation. When he showed no sign of doing so, she moved on to what she hoped would be an easier subject. Cradling her take-out cup and enjoying coffee-fragranced steam warming her face, she continued. 'I actually came to ask you something. Rea's worried about Daisy. I am, too.' She managed a painful smile. 'Daisy's like a clam about what's going on at school. Without betraying confidences, do you have any ideas?'

He shook his head. 'I know she's in trouble for skipping lessons. She told me that, not Mac,' he added hastily, obviously protecting his brother though, as an aunt rather than a parent, Laurel had no idea how much discretion Daisy's head of year owed her.

'Rea says she seems OK joining in with the village arty stuff.' Laurel frowned, trying to think herself into Daisy's head. 'Yet it seems to be art she's avoiding at school this year, and last year it was English. The obvious conclusion is that someone in those two classes must be upsetting her. But, if so, why won't she tell anyone? What does she think will happen if she confides?' She sipped her cappuccino while it was still hot. She felt as chilly in Grady's spray shop as she had outdoors.

Grady ran his hand over his clean-shaven jaw. He was lean, not the kind of man who needed a beard to show everyone where his jaw was. He'd grown from gangling boy to beautifully put together man. Hands sexy, capable and strong. Eyes intelligent, with a lurking humour. 'I'm not close friends with Rea. I never had a reason to call round until Daisy started turning up at some of the same art groups as me and I occasionally helped her carry something home. I suppose it took a while to catch on to just how isolated Rea had become and that it's affecting Daisy.'

'Rea has become more anxious.' Laurel sighed. 'Until the last few months, she seemed able to force herself out for certain things. She managed to get to parents' evening at Daisy's school but she was a right state afterwards. She called me about it, in tears.' Laurel remembered her comment yesterday about villagers being up in one another's business and shame washed over her. How could she have been so judgey when she'd stayed away and left Rea to cope? And in the few days she'd been back, when no one had called on Rea apart from the business-like visit from Mac and Grady, Laurel hadn't even questioned where Rea's friends were. The sigh she heaved made her chest hurt. 'I've let Rea down. Let her become isolated. When Mum died, Rea put her arms around me and told everyone, "We'll manage. We'll be fine." I took it for granted but she was still a teenager herself.'

For several seconds he was silent.

'I'd almost forgotten she used to be such a tiger as to refuse help after your mum died,' he said. 'A moment ago, I said "we're not close friends" but I once knew her fairly well, through you. In those days, I was in and out of your house all the time.' Regret flavoured his words.

Tilting back her head, she drank the rest of her coffee and skirted the point about how often he used to visit. 'Before we lost Mum, Rea had talked about uni or travelling but instead she took a sales job to support me.'

He gave a disbelieving snort. 'Are you hinting that you left so Rea could get on with her own life?'

Blood heated her cheeks. 'No, because she didn't try for any of her dreams once I was off her hands, either – though I suppose if we wanted to keep The Nookery then she needed steady income.' She dropped her empty cup and stamped it flat to relieve her frustration and guilt. 'Later, she fell for Daisy's dad Ewan. He was a charmer but, unfortunately, when she got pregnant with Daisy his charm disappeared. He never wanted to be a parent.' She tried not to compare that with her and Alex yearning for their own child but, instead, experiencing assisted pregnancies followed by the bitter disappointment of her body rejecting what it had so reluctantly started. She went on, 'Ewan began cheating. Then he left and Rea took sole responsibility for Daisy, just as she once did for me.' She drew in her knees and propped her elbows on them. 'She was only ever a "tiger" when forced by circumstance to fight for things. What I didn't realise then was that she was also fighting fears and anxieties that, over the years, made her view the house as her only safe place. Instead of wowing the world as the lovely, kind Rea I know she is, she's shut herself away.'

They fell silent. Rain began pattering against the window and hitting the ground outside the open door. Shivering, Laurel looked around, taking in the bulk of an enormous grey car, spray guns on the wall and a small compressor. For a spray shop, it seemed a modest set-up. She wondered whether it was what he could afford and if habitually keeping the door ajar was a cheap method of ventilation.

Grady broke into her thoughts. 'Yesterday, you said "it wasn't you" when I asked why you began ignoring me. So tell me what it was.' His gaze had zeroed in on her.

Her stomach lurched. She cast a glance at the door,

beginning to wish she'd never given in to the impulse to come through it. But here she was and here Grady was and it was probably as well to formulate an explanation that would fly and get it over with. She looked down at her hands, still bearing traces of White Whisper from the studio walls. 'I was a frightened sixteen-year-old but we were friends. I know I treated you badly.' So far, so truthful.

'Frightened?' he all-but barked. Then, more moderately, he added, 'Slightly more than friends, as I remember it.'

'Yeah.' She remembered, too. Wary of the unwanted attention her early physical development had prompted, the only kisses she'd exchanged with boys had been the under-the-mistletoe-but-we're-not-together kind, quick pecks with pursed lips . . . until Grady. With him she'd felt safe to explore the joys of open mouths and caressing tongues and mistletoe had become her favourite festive greenery. They'd been approaching girlfriend/boyfriend status until . . . Laurel swallowed. 'Do you remember Amie Blunt?'

He made a scornful noise. 'Poison Amie? Mac went out with her for a while. I couldn't stand her.'

Here was her opportunity to create a plausible explanation. She lifted her gaze. 'Mac going out with Amie was the problem. Well—' She tried to pick out events to suit what she was prepared to let him know. 'It began with Mac and I having a spat.'

Grady's brow dropped down. 'I don't remember that.'

She shrugged. 'I probably didn't tell you. He's your brother.'

He nodded. 'We've always been close. I've really only got him and his family because our parents have gone now. Dad nine years ago with a heart attack and then

Mum crossed the road without looking about a year later. Hit by a car.'

'I'm sorry,' she said softly, sadness at his lack of family worming its way into her heart. She'd known, through her regular updates from Rea, but it didn't stop her aching at his bleak expression.

He managed a smile. 'Go on with your story.'

She collected her thoughts. 'The village put a float into Bettsbrough's carnival and I was a mermaid. Mac was a merman.'

Grady's eyes crinkled in amusement. 'I'd forgotten that! Mac was pissed to have to wear a tail. Said it was like wearing a skirt.'

She smiled politely. Her own gripe had been the bikini top in the shape of two shells. It had felt as if she'd been picked out for her bustiness – exploited, really – but she'd been too young and unsure to demand a less revealing costume or a different role. 'We didn't really get on. I could hardly believe you were brothers. Mac was a stinging nettle and you a dock leaf.' She moved on with her tale. 'On carnival day, we were supposed to be having a photo together but Mac had moved away from the float with his mates. I was sent to hurry him up and arrived in time to hear him say, "Better go. I've got to have my photo taken with a pair of tits. Nice tits, though." I lost my temper and said, "You should worry. I have to have my pic taken with a dick – and not a nice one." His mates roared with laughter and he swore at me.'

Grady winced. 'Not Mac's finest hour,' he said gruffly.

'Yeah, well. I don't know what version of that his girl-friend Amie heard but she began to bully me on the bus to school. You weren't around, as you went to a different school. She was a year older than me and though she was small she made up for it with nastiness. She followed me off the bus and ripped out one of my earrings.' She fingered the long-healed lobe, remembering the blood and the fiery burn of torn flesh.

Grady stared at her open-mouthed, shock bright in his eyes.

Having entirely omitted what had happened between Mac's coarse remark and the earring attack, Laurel's truth-telling became still more selective. 'Amie said if I told anyone, she, Mac and their friends would say it was a lie, that I'd caught my earring on something and then blamed her. Mac being your brother, you might not have believed me. If you *had* believed me, it would have set you against Mac. It seemed easiest not to tell you or see you. It seems too gauche for words now. I apologise.' She forced a self-conscious laugh, reasonably confident she'd pieced together a believable scenario and would never have to go through the burning humiliation of revealing what had happened on the playing field. 'I was young, terrified by the violence, and everything got distorted.'

Comprehension in his deep brown eyes was accompanied by horrified dismay. 'You *should* have told me! I *would* have believed you and I would have stopped the bullying, regardless of Mac's involvement. Was it the day of that Christmas party we were supposed to be going to together?'

Surprised at the clarity of his memories, she said evasively, 'About then.'

He swore. 'I thought you were mad because I stood you up when I broke my ankle. It was such a crappy time for you. Trust Poison Amie to make it worse.'

Laurel got to her feet, brushing off her jeans, shamed by his warmth and understanding but shying away from talking about that party. 'It was just that you're Mac's brother.' That had been the reason she hadn't told him the truth then and why she wasn't telling him the complete truth now. Mac's little family was all Grady had – similar to Laurel only having Rea, Daisy and Aunt Terri. The thought of risking spoiling his love and respect for the person closest to him . . . No. She didn't care about Mac but she'd always cared about Grady.

Grady rose, too. 'Amie left the village in her early twenties.'

She nodded. 'I think Rea mentioned it.' Then her eyes fell on the car in the middle of the paint shop, its bonnet and side panels partly masked up with blue tape. 'Wow. I just realised that's a Bentley.' Then she caught sight of the artwork across the bonnet, silver luminosity surrounding a cratered moon and an ethereal spangling of stars. She let out a low whistle, approaching slowly. 'That's amazing,' she breathed. 'Is this what you do? You're an air brush artist?' She glanced round to look at him.

He took a couple of paces closer, hands in pockets. 'It's one of my sources of income. I'm largely self-taught. I don't have an art degree.' He looked almost embarrassed. 'I tell people I'm an artist but it seems ridiculous to claim the same title for airbrushing flames on car bonnets as applies to your success in fine art.'

'Sorry. When you said spraying cars I thought you meant for repair. I suppose you realised that and let me carry on sounding up myself. This is gorgeous.' Flushing, she turned back to the lunar landscape. 'I love the delicacy of the moon's halo. I suppose air brushing lends itself to that?'

'Very much.' His hair had fallen forward but he didn't shove it back, as if happy to be half-hidden.

She noticed a sketch book on top of a red metal tool chest on the other side of the car and stretched out for it. Then she paused. 'Do you mind if I look?'

He shook his head, though he didn't look enthusiastic.

She picked it up, enjoying the familiar flexible feel of a sketch pad, and flipped the pages, pausing to study dragons, skulls, eagles and breaking waves. Sometimes he'd taken more than one approach to a subject, working out ideas. Measurements and notes were jotted alongside loose, quick sketches that showed passion and suggested movement while observing lines of perspective.

After a couple of minutes, he stepped around her to the tool chest and opened the wide, shallow top drawer. He pulled out a black A3 presentation folder saying economically, 'I have photos of the finished work here.'

'Great.' She returned the sketch book to the chest and laid the folder on top so she could slowly turn the plastic photo pockets and appreciate his use of colour. The feathers of an eagle's wing were not brown. They were every shade from tawny to gold, the highlights yellow, red and white and the shadows blue and purple. She lingered for a long time over a sea serpent writhing through a boiling sea. It was impossible to categorise the glassy, glossy colours into 'blue' and 'green'.

'It must take layers upon layers,' she observed, dissecting the technique with an informed eye.

'That's pretty much how air brushing works. You create highlights by interleaving white between layers of colour.' He'd moved closer to view the images with her and his breath trickled across her cheek.

Suddenly disturbed by the proximity of grown-up Grady Cassidy, she closed the folder. 'Impressive work.' She side-stepped, making space before turning to face him. 'By the way, you were right about Daisy asking me to be involved in Art December and the art wall at Middledip Christmas Fair. I envisaged just offering a canvas to exhibit but she's assumed I'll come to meetings. I thought it would be wrong to disappoint her. I hope it's OK for me to be around.'

He grinned, sliding the folder back into its drawer. 'Everyone will think it's more than OK. Sorry if you feel dragged in but don't look to me to save you by saying I don't want you involved.' His eyes brimmed with laughter.

Glad to have an opportunity to be light-hearted after navigating tricky subjects earlier, she joked, 'Aw, c'mon, don't make me act like a villager.' Then she halted mid-laugh as she turned and saw Mac framed by the doorway, the shoulders of his jacket glistening with rain. 'Oh.'

He stopped short, glancing uncertainly between Grady and Laurel. 'Sorry if I'm interrupting.'

'I'm just leaving.' Laurel checked the darkening afternoon outside, pulling up her hood ready to brave the weather.

But Mac stood his ground when she made to slip past. 'Laurel, I've already called Rea but I should share the information with you. The police have given a warning to the lad who played that prank and won't need to contact you.' His tone was clipped, as if he was talking to her only because he must. He was probably not enjoying reviving the subject of his embarrassment.

'You OK with that, Laurel?' Grady asked swiftly, giving his brother a quick frown.

She nodded. 'As long as Mac's comfortable with people getting away with humiliating others.' Then she managed to skirt around Mac and leave. Outside she took a deep breath, heart trotting. She half-regretted getting in another jibe but she harboured so much resentment towards Mac the words had popped out. Why the hell couldn't he have left the village like Amie, so she didn't have to deal with him?

Chatting with Grady had felt good. Then in walked Mac and spoiled it, just as he'd spoiled things for her with Grady before.

Grady shifted to watch through the open door as Laurel hurried away, the streetlights forming halos above her in the chilly afternoon. When she'd vanished from view, he turned to his brother. 'She thawed a bit today.' He wasn't going to say anything about them unexpectedly finding common ground in the arena of infertility and ended relationships. Under the guise of brotherly teasing, he added, 'At least, she thawed towards me. She vanished as soon as she laid eyes on you.' He watched Mac's reaction.

Mac hunched his shoulders. He looked tired and his eyes were surrounded by lines of strain. 'She was your friend, not mine.'

'Most people like me best,' answered Grady, still teasing. Then he sobered. 'Did you know Amie Blunt used to bully Laurel?'

Gaze sharpening, Mac looked at him. 'What did Laurel tell you?'

Grady settled his backside against his tool chest and folded his arms. 'That Amie ripped her earring out then said if Laurel told anyone you and your buddies would back Amie up that Laurel was lying. Apparently the bullying began after you and Laurel had a spat.' He then repeated what Laurel had told him.

Mac stiffened, his gaze sliding away from Grady's. 'You

know I went through a troublesome teen patch. I'm not proud of how I was. Amie was up for a lot of sex so I closed my eyes to her antics, even though I knew she hated Laurel and gave her grief. I was trying to apologise to Laurel on Sunday when I asked to speak privately. I guess she realised it and so made that crack about not being alone with men.'

A small shock shimmered through Grady at having to face past unpleasant aspects to his brother's personality. However, he looked so wretched that Grady didn't point out Mac had lied when he'd said he wanted to talk to Laurel about Aspirations Week. Instead, he suggested, 'If you get another chance, just apologise. It's probably better late than never.' He clapped a comforting hand on his brother's arm.

Mac nodded. 'Is she here to stay?'

Grady shrugged. 'For the next few months at least, she said. She's recently divorced and seems concerned about her sister and niece.'

He didn't ask himself why his heart lightened at the idea.

Chapter Five

Tangled in the duvet, trapped in a sweaty dream, Laurel tried to shout to her younger self.

Walking across the playing fields in the dark alone ought *to be safe but go round by the road!*

There are four people drinking on a bench. You have time to turn back to the Christmas lights of the village hall.

Instead, she had to watch helplessly as sixteen-year-old Laurel decided to show Amie bloody Blunt she wasn't scared of her and her horrible cronies – Grady's brother Mac and his buddies Jonny and Ruben.

Young Laurel shoves her chin in the air and doesn't deviate from her route across the grass, ignoring Amie's strident little voice. 'Look at the size of those ugly great hooters. You're a freak, Laurel Hill.'

Heartbeat threatening to choke her, Laurel sneers back. 'You're just jealous 'cos you've got two fried eggs for boobs.' And fury crosses Amie's face.

Laurel tried to drag herself to the surface, to reassure herself that she was thirty-five now and knew how to keep herself safe . . . but the dream refused to let her go.

Amie jumping up and blocking Laurel's path. Mac, Jonny and Ruben, visibly tipsy on cider, laughing and joining in. Amie scurrying behind Laurel like a troll in a computer game to grasp the shoulders of her half-fastened coat and yank them down.

Laurel realising too late her arms are trapped. Struggling. Shouting. Furious. Frightened. Sweating.

Amie crowing, 'You hold her, Mac.'

Mac, wearing the uncertain grin of the drink-befuddled, taking over restraining Laurel, bigger, stronger and harder to fight.

Amie dancing around in front of Laurel, taunting, shoving and . . . 'Let's see those ugly great hooters, then!' Amie yanking up Laurel's top, the glittery blue one she'd worn with a new skirt.

Laurel screaming, 'No! Stop!'

Amie reaching out and pulling up Laurel's bra. The frozen night air and four pairs of eyes on Laurel's breasts. Terrifying. Humiliating.

'Stop it!' Laurel's throat hurting with her screams.

Silence, while stupid drunken young men stare at her breasts. Laurel crying, struggling.

No one coming.

Then she's free and running . . .

Laurel awoke, a hoarse sob dying in her throat as she fought her way free of the duvet.

She jerked upright, her breath easing and the tendrils of the dream slinking away to leave only a pounding heart and an overwhelming sense of shame. 'Bastards,' she muttered. To anchor herself to the present she switched on the lamp. The light made her screw up her eyes but she could see she was in her childhood room in The Nookery, its beams painted black. Rea and Daisy slept nearby. It was Friday – or 4.40 a.m. on Saturday morning, as her clock showed her – and she'd been back in Middledip for a week.

It was a couple of years since she'd last had that dream. This time there was no Alex to cuddle her, whispering that it was in the past, she was fine, those shits were no longer in her life.

One of those shits, unfortunately, was back. Mac Cassidy.

Shaken by the violence of the nightmare she got up, pulling on her fleecy dressing gown and big slippers against the winter night chill, and padded downstairs, switching on lights as she went. In the kitchen, she made a mug of comforting mint tea and drifted into the sitting room where the curtains were drawn shut over the French doors. Embers still glowed in the wood stove and she added screwed up newspaper to reawaken the fire, then huddled on the sofa to pass the rest of the night watching TV.

A few hours later, when it was daylight and she could hear Rea's shower running, she went up to dress before stealing from the house and, not wanting to be interrupted or disturbed, drove a mile from the village. Rain lashed her big car as she pulled over in the gateway to a farm field. She switched off the engine, the wipers halted and the only sound was rain drumming on the car roof.

Laurel unsnapped her seat belt, hoping she'd get Fliss before she left her Ealing home for her Saturday women's self-defence class. She'd considered ringing Alex, because she missed his quiet good sense and strength, but he might be in bed with Vonnie. She didn't begrudge Alex finding someone who might give him what Laurel couldn't. She'd just rather not intrude.

Forward was the way to go. Fliss possessed as much

strength and good sense as Alex, anyway. One day, Fliss, all blonde fluffy hair and confidence, had sauntered into the Chiswick High Road studios where Laurel had rented space and, in her soft Californian drawl, canvassed for artists who'd run community creative workshops. Laurel had volunteered, liking Fliss's easy smile and her opening gambit: 'I'm asking for something for nothing – do you want me to leave right away?' Laurel had been drawn into Fliss's bright orbit, not just because it was the beginning of several years of helping people have creative fun with donated materials but because Fliss, all about empowering people, had run self-defence and personal safety classes where Laurel had learned a lot.

Or, at least, she thought she had, until she returned to Middledip and felt like an angry, intimidated teen again.

The ringing tone sounded in Laurel's ear several times before a sleepy voice answered, 'Hey, you. How're you doin'?' Fliss had lived in the UK for over ten years but south California was still strong in her voice.

Laurel felt a shaft of guilt. 'Did I wake you? I thought you were teaching a class at ten so you'd be up.'

Fliss yawned loudly. 'Class cancelled. Damned hall flooded. Now, why don't we try that again. How are you doing?'

'Bleurgh,' Laurel answered honestly. 'I had that crappy nightmare.' Fliss knew her entire story and so there was no need to launch into a detailed description. 'I've come out in the car so I could talk to you without Rea overhearing and being worried. It's peeing down here.'

'I can hear rain against my window, too. A real "welcome to winter" kinda day. So, you know what triggered the nightmare?' Her intonation suggested that she, at least, thought she knew the answer.

'Being in Middledip. Seeing bloody Mac Cassidy,' Laurel replied gloomily.

Fliss's voice was as gentle as a snowflake landing on Laurel's burning heart. 'Honey, you could tell your sister what happened, if it's got you all churned up having to deal with this Mac character again. You can call me anytime but family support in your village could be good.'

'I know.' Laurel watched the rain trickling down the windscreen. It made the scenery look as if it were crying. 'But I'm not telling Rea. I couldn't bear the questions and it would hurt her to know she didn't prevent what happened. She did so much for me. And she'd probably call Mac,' she added, imagining what a shit show that would be. 'I'm listening to my gut,' she said, utilising a phrase Fliss used when giving tips on street safety. 'I'm here to help her with her agoraphobia and with Daisy, not worry her about things we can't change, especially things that could increase her anxiety. She's easily over-whelmed and it might make her even more protective than she is with Daisy. It's up to me to find a way to move on from the bad old days.' Laurel shifted in her seat so she could crook a knee for comfort. 'Actually, I could use your advice about Mac Cassidy.'

Fliss suddenly sounded completely awake. 'What's he done?'

'Nothing,' Laurel assured her hastily. 'If anyone's done anything, it's me. I just don't seem to be able to stop making him uncomfortable – deliberately.' She told Fliss about refusing to talk to Mac alone and making sly jibes that only he'd catch.

Fliss sighed. 'Nobody could blame you for that. I'm not sure it's the best thing for you, though.' They fell silent while Laurel listened to the rain and watched a tatty red van coming from the direction of Bettsbrough, wipers battling the downpour.

Then Fliss spoke again. 'We frequently talk about not carrying your past into your present but, for you, the two have collided.' She paused, as if collecting her thoughts. 'By refusing to listen to him you're refusing him the means of redeeming himself or apologising. You *could* look on that as you refusing to allow him to make himself feel better. And apologising rakes up the bad stuff for you, so it *might* make you feel worse.' Then she added, 'But clinging on to bad stuff is rarely positive.'

It was Laurel's turn to think. The engine purred comfortingly and she turned on the demisters to clear the windscreen. She tried a weak joke. 'Doesn't getting petty satisfaction out of making him uncomfortable count as a positive?'

Fliss passed over the opportunity to laugh. 'You could maybe stay away from him.'

'Easier said than done.' Laurel sighed. 'He's the dad of one of Daisy's best friends and also her head of year. Rea's asked me to be Daisy's number two contact at school. That means I may need to go in and discuss her skiving. I don't know much about school structure but what if the meeting is with him?'

Fliss groaned. 'That would be a challenge. There must be positive aspects of the village you're living in though.'

The skin at the top of Laurel's cheeks tingled. 'It's a lovely place with fields instead of the endless buildings of West London. I'm with my family. And there's Grady, Mac's brother.' Hastily, she clarified, 'I mean we used to be friends so it's been good to chat with him.'

'This is the guy you spent one Christmas kissing under the mistletoe, right?' Fliss sounded interested.

'That was a long time ago and we didn't get as far as Christmas,' Laurel answered. 'But Middledip's developed its own festive arts and crafts movement. He's the events organiser and Daisy's roped me in.'

Fliss laughed. '*Daisy* roped you in, right? It wasn't that you wanted to be roped in because of Grady?'

Unwillingly, Laurel laughed, too. 'Grady's a good guy. It's just his brother . . .' She didn't take that thought any further. 'How are you getting on without me?'

Fliss accepted the change of subject. 'OK. The artist who stepped into your shoes at the community centre is working out and . . . I'm seeing someone new. A lady who I think is a definite maybe.'

'Whoo!' Laurel teased. 'I need pictures of her. How did you meet?'

'She's over here from the States on a jewellery design course. Her mother's Thai, her dad's from Philadelphia. Her name's Chantana.' Excitement bubbled in Fliss's voice.

Within seconds, Laurel's phone chirped as the photos arrived. 'Wow,' she said, studying the images, one of 'definite maybe' Chantana alone, and one with Fliss. 'She's pretty. Love her silky dark hair. She's so petite she makes you look like a giant.'

Fliss giggled. 'She sure brings out my protective side.'

They talked on until Laurel realised it was past ten o'clock. 'I'd better go,' she said regretfully. 'I promised Daisy I'd help pick up what she describes as "craft stuff" from a smallholding on the edge of the village. I remember the property. A bloke bought it and spent his retirement reversing years of neglect. He used to grow veg and drive a pony and trap. His name's Gabe.'

'Sounds very rural,' commented Fliss. 'I'm thinking now of that TV show, *Midsomer Murders*.'

Laurel laughed. 'Middledip is like Midsomer without the murders . . . so far.' She turned to reach for the seat-belt. The rain had stopped and a weak sun was sprinkling the hedgerow with diamonds. 'It's been great talking to you, Fliss. You've cheered me up.'

'Sure,' said Fliss equably. 'Here's a last thought for you. Only you can decide to let go the past and forgive this Mac guy.'

'You can't decide to forgive someone,' Laurel protested. 'It's a feeling. A reaction. It is what it is.'

'Well, if you're sure,' ended Fliss enigmatically. 'See you, hon.'

After several minutes' thought, Laurel dialled again, this time her aunt Terri's number. Without Terri to run to, teenage Laurel might have crumbled entirely. No-nonsense, plain-speaking Aunt Terri had helped her rediscover her backbone and encouraged her to look to her future. She'd never once asked if she'd left a bad situation in Middledip. Maybe she thought Laurel had just been pining for her mum . . . or maybe she'd just known that her niece had needed peace more than anything else.

'Hello, duck,' came Terri's voice. 'How's life back in Middledip?'

They chatted for a while about clearing the studio and whether they'd see each other at Christmas. 'I could come over to Peterborough one day before that,' Laurel offered. 'Bring Daisy.'

Terri answered guardedly. 'That sounds fun. We'll have to sort out a time.' But then she said she had to rush for an optician's appointment and ended the call without saying when.

Laurel grinned as she started up the car. That was Aunt

Terri, always rushing somewhere, getting involved in something.

The track up to Gabe's place was ankle-deep in mud after days of snow and rain. 'I'm glad you told me to borrow your mum's wellies,' Laurel said to Daisy, squelching along in the olive-green boots. 'This guy, Gabe, I think he's the one who used to drive a pony and trap through the village.'

'Mum says so.' Daisy clutched Laurel's sleeve as her feet almost skidded from beneath her. 'He's still got the little black pony, Snobby. He's so old he just eats or sleeps, except for when Gabe puts him on a leading rein and walks him like a big dog.'

They reached the paddock and, sure enough, there was a portly pony, whiskery and grizzled, long windswept mane across his eyes. They leaned on the gate and Snobby turned his head to inspect them, then turned away.

Daisy gurgled with laughter. 'He won't come over unless you look as if you've got something for him.'

'If that's the same pony, he must be ancient.' Laurel craned further over the gate to see. Then she jumped back as a taller, leaner pony, the pale dappled grey of shadows on snow, materialised from behind the hedge and blew down her nose at them.

'Whoa.' Daisy held her palm out for the ghostly grey to nuzzle. 'Where'd you come from? Has Gabe bought you to keep Snobby company?'

Laurel stroked the velvety nose. 'He doesn't look any more interested in her than he is in us.'

When they turned away, the grey whickered after them. Snobby glanced up with an equine smirk as if to say, 'I could tell from here they weren't packing carrots.'

Over by the red-brick house, Laurel saw that three men had gathered. She recognised Gabe because he still had the silver ponytail she remembered, though it was longer and thinner now. One of the other men wore a cap and had a white fluffy beard, and the last was Grady, his dark hair blowing, a bit like Snobby's mane.

Daisy snorted a quiet laugh. 'That man in the middle looks like Santa Claus.'

Gabe raised his voice to call, 'Hello, there.' His accent sounded clipped and middle-class. Rea had reminded Laurel that he'd been a bank manager until he'd given up the urban grind for a bucolic lifestyle. His marriage hadn't survived his move to Middledip and he was happy alone, wearing mismatching clothing and avoiding haircuts.

As the men ambled over to join them, Daisy said, 'This is my auntie Laurel.'

'Hello, Auntie Laurel,' said Gabe gravely, though with twinkling eyes. 'Meet my uncle Bertie.' He gestured towards the man with the fluffy white beard.

'I'm Bertie Piercy,' the bearded man said. He sounded much like Gabe. 'My bungalow in Aylesbury is being rewired and replumbed so I'm seeking refuge and learning to be eccentric from my nephew.' He looked to be in his eighties, which was maybe ten or twelve years older than Gabe, but judging from the way they grinned at each other, they got along.

Gabe shook Laurel's hand. 'If I'm eccentric then I'm proud of it. You know Grady?'

'We go way back,' said Grady, which led to explanations about Laurel's history with the village.

'Ah, Rea's sister,' Gabe exclaimed. 'How's she doing?'

Daisy soon tired of the catching-up session. 'Have you bought a new pony?' she asked Gabe. 'Is he company for

82

Snobby or are you going to ride him? Or drive him with your old cart?'

Gabe looked pained. 'It's a "pony trap", not a cart. And she's Bertie's pony.'

A beaming smile burst over Bertie's face, as much as could be seen between cap and beard. 'His name's Dave.'

Gabe looked still more pained. '*Her* name's Daybreak.'

Bertie made a scornful noise. 'Cissy name. I didn't mean to buy a girl. What if Snobby gets frisky with her?'

Gabe threw back his head and laughed. 'Even if he had a stepladder and I'd just fed him a tonne of oats, Snobby's too old, grumpy and antisocial. And he's a gelding.'

'He's had the snip?' Bertie enquired with the air of seeking clarity.

'Castrated when he was a colt,' Gabe confirmed.

Laurel assumed Bertie's ignorance was exaggerated for fun but Gabe's next words proved her wrong.

'Bertie bought Daybreak on his way here,' he told them with a resigned air. 'Just stopped at an auction and did it. First I knew about it was some bloke at the door saying he couldn't get the horse box up the track so did I want to walk my new pony up? Lucky she's got her own tack or I wouldn't even have had a halter to put on her.'

Grady, who'd been listening with a smile, asked, 'Are you going to ride her, Bertie?'

'Huh!' snorted Bertie. 'Never been on a horse in my life. Not going to start now. I thought she'd be company for Snobby.'

Gabe rolled his eyes. 'Snobby is a solitary old curmudgeon. Shall we leave these young people to crack on? I'm perished. Bloody wind goes through you instead of round. The barn's open,' he added, in the general direction of Daisy and Grady.

'Thanks,' they replied together and called goodbye as the older men disappeared into the house. Falling into conversation about bags and whips – to Laurel's mystification – Grady and Daisy turned towards an outbuilding and Laurel tagged along behind. Daisy had asked her along and Laurel's aim was to be available to her niece and learn about her out-of-school interests.

She listened as Daisy asked Grady, 'Niall's going this afternoon, isn't he?'

Grady nodded, making for the bowed wooden door of the building. He grabbed a handle and began to wrestle with the latch. 'Think so. What about Zuzanna?'

Daisy huddled into her parka as the wind tugged at her long curly hair. 'Yep.'

Laurel had met Zuzanna because she'd hung out with Daisy at The Nookery and Laurel had recognised her as the girl who'd jumped off the school bus along with Niall. Her parents were originally from Poland.

Laurel asked, 'What happens this afternoon?' as the door to the barn groaned open, releasing an earthy smell.

Daisy switched on a light and glanced at Laurel with a slightly puzzled air. 'Craft Stuff.'

It wasn't exactly a clear explanation. Bemused, Laurel stepped into the dusty building, then paused. Everywhere was vegetation. Bunches of drying lavender and teasel hung upside down and long, thin, glossy brown sticks stood in bundles. Odd objects that looked like absurdly shaped black and brown leather bottles stood on shelves, their peeling outer skin patched with white hairy mould.

'Oh,' she said, as she realised she'd seen something like them before. 'Are these gourds?'

Grady looked up from handing bunches of sticks to Daisy, who took them outside in a shower of dead leaves.

'Yes. Gabe lets me grow them on his land and I dry them in here.'

She stepped closer. 'I worked in an artists' co-op in Cornwall after uni and there was someone there who ran workshops on decorating gourds. She made fantastic stuff.'

Interest sparked in his eyes. 'I wish I'd been there. I've mainly learned from YouTube.' He began picking up various gourds, some as round as apples, others a traditional bottle shape or with a stretched neck that curled around on itself. 'These have been drying since last year. I have a load more out on the vines but I'm waiting for the vines to die so I know they're ready to harvest. I could leave them outside to weather but they don't get so mouldy. The mouldier they are, the more figured the skin.' He picked up a wonky bottle shape and tapped and shook it. 'Not quite dry enough.' He repeated the process until he found one that sounded hollow when knocked and rattled when shaken. 'It's the seeds that rattle. I soak this for twelve hours or so, then scrub it. It'll come out like these.' He pointed to three gourds sitting in the light entering through a dusty windowpane. 'I scrubbed those off a few days ago so they're ready to work with.'

Laurel picked up one of the clean ones and gave it an experimental shake, hearing the rattle of seeds. 'It hardly weighs a thing.'

A smile creased the skin around his eyes. 'They don't. They're the weirdest things, but I can make money out of them. A lot of people only know about pumpkins.'

Daisy reappeared with fewer leaves on her sticks and a lot more on her parka. 'He makes some awesome stuff. I'll take these and do them this afternoon. I was thinking maybe you'd help, Auntie Laurel.'

Laurel scratched her head. 'I'm sorry if I'm being stupid

85

but what are you doing to them this afternoon? And where?'

Daisy looked blankly out from under the fringe that the damp, windy weather had frizzed. 'Craft Stuff.'

Grady must have understood that Laurel needed more precise information. 'The village has a group that meets in The Public at The Angel. The group's called Craft Stuff.' He indicated the grubby interior of the outbuilding in which they stood. 'We're collecting material for the Craft Stuff session. Gabe lets Daisy grow willow whips for weaving like I grow my gourds for carving and painting.'

Daisy giggled, evidently working out Laurel's confusion. 'We've been collecting craft stuff for Craft Stuff. Come see my willow patch.'

Laurel smiled, Grady's explanation having made everything clearer. 'Great.'

They led her past a couple of other outbuildings and three bamboo wigwams that beans probably grew up in summer, then around a greenhouse that held only empty pots. They came out at an untidy patch with Brussels sprouts looking ready to cut and a row of cabbages. On the end was an area of large, dying leaves in manky damp shades of brown and green. 'It's like a pumpkin patch,' Laurel exclaimed.

'Pumpkins, squashes and gourds are all the same family,' Grady said.

Laurel stepped off the path to examine the bottle shapes and fat spheres. 'So many shades of green. This is so pale it's like shallow sea. The next one's dark green like a courgette. I've never seen them like this. The woman in Cornwall used to bring the already dried gourds into the studios and then work on them with mini power tools.'

'I do that part in my workshop at home.' Grady's eyes

glowed with enthusiasm. 'I only bring them to Craft Stuff if I'm at the decorating stage because the little rotary tool you mention is as noisy as a dentist's drill.'

Daisy gave a little hop. 'Grady, is the patterned one ready yet?'

Grady grinned at her. 'It might be.'

'Let's look!' Daisy took off across the patch, zigzagging so as to not step on any gourds.

Grady followed and Laurel brought up the rear, once again with no idea what they were talking about. 'Patterned?'

'It should be awesome,' Daisy called back, which didn't enlighten Laurel. But when she caught up with them, almost slipping over in the sea of mud, she found Grady holding a dirty wooden box tied around several times with sodden string. A stem from the gourd vine ran into the box.

'Come on, Grady.' Daisy gave him a 'get on with it' look.

Laurel edged closer as Grady took out a knife and carefully cut the string. He turned the box then stuck the knife tip in one side and pried. The sides parted with a little coaxing.

'Awesome,' Daisy breathed.

'W-what the hell?' stuttered Laurel. Inside was a living gourd, still attached to its dying vine. It had grown in the shape of a vase, ready decorated by patterns pressed into its skin. It was pallid, almost white, from being grown inside the box.

Grady laughed at Laurel's astonishment. 'You carve out the shape you want in wood and trap a growing gourd inside. It grows to fill the shape you've made. I'll leave the gourd out now to green up. Next year, when I've cut

87

off the top and painted or inked the patterns, it'll be the easiest vase I've made.'

'That's amazing,' she marvelled. 'I once went to a wedding buffet where the cucumbers had been grown in moulds so each slice was heart-shaped but I've never seen anyone grow a vase.' She laughed at the absurdity. When she shifted her gaze to Grady she found he was watching her with a half-smile.

Laurel's cheeks heated. His expression set off the same strange sensation a surprise or a memory might.

'Willow patch next,' ordered Daisy, grabbing Laurel's sleeve and almost pulling her over. She bore her off beyond the gourd vines to where twelve young willow plants grew through black matting. 'No weeding or digging,' Daisy explained. 'When the kit arrives the plants are just sticks. You get a tool to pierce the matting and then you plant the stick in the hole. They grow these long, bendy rods called whips.' She let a handful slide through her fingers. Most of them still had leaves. 'You keep harvesting them and they keep on growing. You weave with them.'

'What do you make?' Laurel wondered once again how this creative, industrious young woman could possibly be bunking off art classes at school.

'Whatever.' Daisy shrugged. 'This afternoon I'm making circlets for Christmas wreaths while the willow's still flexible. I cut what was in Gabe's barn a couple of weeks ago, so the leaves would fall off easily. If I stored it much longer the willow would harden and then I'd have to soak it to work it.'

'What do you do with so many Christmas wreaths?' Laurel asked.

'Sell them,' Daisy answered promptly. 'I've got a load of orders already off the village Facebook page. I don't have to worry about getting them delivered, like I would if I sold them through Etsy, because I can just walk to whoever's house it is and hand it over. They pay me cash so it's mega easy.'

Laurel mulled over this information. She might not be a parent but she felt Daisy was omitting something important. 'I knew you'd bought those baubles for wreaths but I'm surprised Rea and you never mentioned selling them.'

Daisy shifted awkwardly.

Grady's voice came from over Laurel's shoulder. 'Doesn't your mum know yet, Dais?'

She trained all of her attention on the whippy strands of willow, running them through her fingers. 'I'm not doing anything wrong,' she answered defensively.

Hmm.

Daisy was looking mulish. Laurel wanted very much for her niece to feel they were on the same side, but there was definitely a situation to be managed here. Carefully, she said, 'Well, we don't want your mum to think you've been taking orders from just anyone online and intend to go to their houses on your own, do we? Because she's bound to think that's dangerous.' *Because it flaming-well is.* 'What we could do is tell Rea about selling the wreaths when we go home. And we'll make it clear we'll go *together* to deliver them. How's that sound?'

'OK,' Daisy agreed slowly, frowning. 'But I'd only be delivering in the village. Nothing could happen to me.'

Laurel looped an arm around Daisy. 'Things happen in villages, you know.' Her voice caught in her throat. She forced a laugh to clear it.

Daisy turned to Grady. 'Are you going to show Auntie Laurel your workshop at Mistletoe Cottage?'

'Mistletoe Cottage?' queried Laurel, her interest diverted.

'On the corner of Ladies Lane and Port Road? I remember when it was owned by a lady who had two enormous poodles. I can't remember her name. Wasn't she the sister of Gwen at Crowthers?'

'What's Crowthers?' Daisy demanded.

They turned and headed back towards the outbuilding as Laurel replied. 'The village shop. When I lived here Gwen Crowther owned it and the poodle lady was her sister.'

But Grady was shaking his head at Laurel, smiling. 'Gwen's cousin. Those were the biggest poodles I've ever seen.'

'Oh, Booze & News,' Daisy interjected. 'Melanie runs it. She's a right old nosy cow. People call her The Village News.'

'Heart of gold though,' Grady said peaceably. Then, to Laurel, 'Gwen and her husband retired to Hunstanton. Poodle Lady died and someone from London updated Mistletoe Cottage. When they decided they didn't like village life, I bought it. No mistletoe now, though,' he added. 'They cut the trees down where it used to grow so they could make a drive. Times change.'

'Shame,' Laurel said. She'd quite enjoyed the little catch-up but wasn't about to go into memories about mistletoe. Times did change but memories remained.

Daisy collected her willow whips and Grady pulled an enormous bag from under the shelf to carry the gourds. They set off together, pausing at the paddock gate. Daybreak – or Dave – came over again, nodding her head coquettishly.

Laurel stroked her neck. 'Poor you, Daybreak. Your owner calls you Dave, Snobby doesn't want anything to do with you and you're stuck in this paddock.' Daybreak flicked her ears and sighed, her breath clouding in the chilly winter air. Judging by the pale grey sky – and the weather forecast – snow was on the way again. Laurel thought Daybreak would look magical in the snow but hoped she'd be warm enough.

Grady gave Daybreak a pat. 'You used to ride, Laurel. You could take her out.'

She laughed, making Daybreak toss her head. 'I haven't ridden since I was sixteen.'

'She was good,' Grady told Daisy. 'She used to sneak into the paddock at Carlysle House and ride a horse there, bareback, with just a halter. It belonged to the son of the house but he was the kind who only had a horse because his public school mates had one.'

'The horse was a beautiful black gelding called Dark Magic,' Laurel said, realising there were still a few threads to connect 'Laurel Then' to 'Laurel Now'. Poodle Lady. Dark Magic. Grady . . .

'And no one saw you?' Daisy asked disbelievingly.

'I used to "borrow" that boy's pony very early in the morning,' she admitted. 'Your mum did things the proper way. She worked at a riding school near Port-le-Bain to earn riding lessons until she was old enough to earn money to pay for them.'

'You crept off to the Carlysle Estate when there was no one around?' chided Daisy. 'And yet you don't want me delivering wreaths to village people at their houses?'

Grady gave Daisy a pat on the shoulder. 'I used to go with her.'

'Oh.' Daisy lost interest once there was a reasonable explanation.

But Laurel remembered, and she was certain that Grady did, too, that they'd paused and kissed at every stile and the bridleways hadn't felt lonely with Grady's hand in hers.

Although the Craft Stuff session was meant to begin at two o'clock, Laurel discovered that Daisy intended to go straight to The Angel, while Grady peeled off for Mistletoe Cottage.

'Why are we heading to The Angel already?' Laurel asked, pausing at the end of the track to slosh about in a puddle to wash the worst of the mud from her wellies.

'Most people meet for lunch first.' Daisy shifted her bundle of willow, giving her own boots a cursory rinse.

Laurel halted. 'If you're meeting your mates, you don't want me along, do you?' It was one thing to spend time with Daisy to get to know her better, another entirely to get in the way of her day. She imagined herself sitting there like a lemon while Zuzanna, Daisy and other teenagers excluded her by using their own language, like 'peng' – which she understood to denote someone was good-looking – and 'basic', 'vintage' or 'retro'. The latter two would probably be applied her, at the grand old age of thirty-five.

Daisy turned and gazed at her, eyes enormous. 'Everyone will be there. I thought you were coming. They'll all be stoked 'cos you're, like, a proper artist.'

She looked so woebegone that Laurel slung an arm around her shoulders and strode onward towards The Angel. 'If your nan was here she'd say, "She's not *like* an artist, Daisy. She actually *is* one." Mum hated Rea and me littering our sentences with "like".' It made her feel less 'vintage' to have once overused 'like', as Daisy did now. She added, 'No problem about lunch. If you want me there, I'll come.'

'Cool!' Daisy cheered up, clutching her willow as the wind tried to snatch it away.

'Shall I take half?' Relief settled on Laurel's shoulders like a cloak to see Daisy smile again, and not because Laurel had taken some of the willow. It was troubling how the teen had changed in a click of the fingers from relaxed and insouciant to looking ready to cry. Laurel mulled that over as they passed the row of parked cars along Rotten Row, turned the corner and stepped into the bright, bustling warmth of the café.

'Let's dump our stuff before we order.' Daisy lead the way across the main café and into the next room, The Public. There, the same colourful mixture of tiles graced the floor but the tables had been pushed together to form a rectangle, and chairs set around it.

'Hiya,' Daisy called to the three women and two men clustered at one end. 'We'll need five chairs, so is it OK if we grab these?' She indicated five chairs together.

'Yes, you go on, duck,' said one of the men comfortably, one of his hands occupied by a steaming mugful of something and the other with cake.

After securing the chairs with coats and willow whips, Daisy and Laurel returned to the counter of the café, where Carola was simultaneously toasting panini, frothing coffee and instructing two teenage girls on the best way to drape fairy lights on a Christmas tree.

'Yeah, OK, Mum,' expostulated the eldest. 'Sheesh, to think I came home from uni this weekend for this. Emily, can you leave the baubles and help me untwist these lights?'

Emily, who appeared a couple of years younger, continued to rummage in a cardboard box. 'You're doing the lights, Charlotte. I'm checking the baubles.'

'Hey, Emily,' Daisy called to the bauble-sorter.

Emily waved. 'Hey, Daisy!' When Daisy had ordered a panini, Coke and a brownie, she crossed to inspect the contents of Emily's bauble box while Laurel chose her lunch.

Carola, tendrils of blonde hair sticking to her cheeks in the steamy atmosphere, gave Laurel a friendly smile and nodded in the direction of Charlotte and Emily. 'It's not ideal to get the decorations up on a busy Saturday but my daughters only have weekends. We're offering Christmas coffees now it's only five weeks to go. Fancy cinnamon sprinkles or a cranberry shot?'

Laurel said, 'Mm, a cranberry shot, please.' She also ordered a panini and a shortbread angel, unable to resist the liberal chocolate coating on its wings.

The espresso machine hissed self-importantly as Carola clattered mugs and plates. Laurel watched Daisy, who'd crouched next to Emily to inspect the shiny decorations. Even Charlotte, who looked several years older than Daisy, passed a friendly word with her. Whatever was bothering Daisy seemed to originate at school. At least . . . At least, it didn't seem to come from the village. Laurel flipped that point over in her brain.

Her stomach sank. She hoped Daisy's comfort zone wasn't shrinking, as Rea's had. Rea's triggers were situational, like busy places and difficult road conditions. Kids learned from the example of others . . . She smiled wryly to herself. If Daisy stuck to her comfort zone of being in the village and Laurel stuck to her comfort zone of being anywhere but the village, they'd never meet. To help Daisy, Laurel had to get over herself.

Carola popped Laurel's coffee and Daisy's Coke on the counter. 'Here are your drinks. I'll get your cakes and put it all on a tray. Paying by card?'

'Yes, please,' Laurel answered mechanically, her eyes still on her niece who'd moved on to helping Charlotte with fairy lights that had become thoroughly snarled up.

A few minutes earlier, Daisy had had a definite wobble when Laurel tried to pull back from lunch. Was it only that Daisy had wanted to parade 'a proper artist' to the crafters of the village? Or did it go deeper?

Was she beginning to rely on Laurel?

That could be good. It hinted at the deepening bond Laurel hoped for . . . but if a tiny thing like a misunderstanding over lunch could cause those big, tear-filled eyes, Daisy's emotional state must be on a knife edge.

For Rea's sake as well as Daisy's, Laurel needed to discover what was going on.

Chapter Six

Grady was irritated. And the person he felt irritated with was himself, because while he'd been home to get what he needed for Craft Stuff, he'd also changed his clothes at the prospect of removing his coat in the same room as Laurel Hill. He hadn't even intended to attend today's session. He was perfectly happy in his own workshop and only joined Craft Stuff occasionally out of community spirit.

Attending today was stupid.

Yet, still he swapped his bobbly, old woolly jumper for a new, dark red sweatshirt and climbed into clean, better fitting jeans. It was probably pride at looking good at least once to the woman he'd fallen for as a teenager . . . even though the fall had ended in a painful landing.

Teenagers dealt badly with such misunderstandings but now, as adults, they could put it firmly in the past that Laurel had only stopped talking to him because of Poison Amie. It made his fists tighten to think of poor, sixteen-year-old Laurel being bullied like that.

He collected what he needed in a big blue canvas bag then stuffed himself into his coat and set off down Port

Road. In a few minutes he was striding into The Angel. Jodie took his order, her dark hair in bunches, a big smile on her round face. 'Fancy a Christmas coffee, Grady?'

'Too early for me,' he said genially, rather than tell her he hated coffee to taste of anything but coffee . . . except maybe Jameson whiskey once in a while. One of the reasons he liked The Angel was its permanent, heady scent of coffee. 'I see the decs are going up.' He nodded to where Carola and her teenage daughters were heatedly discussing whether a naked Christmas tree was straight in its pot. His vote would be 'no, it's not,' but he wasn't going to enter that fray.

'Yep. We'll be one big twinkle till the end of December.' Jodie beamed. 'We'll be breaking out the Christmas jumpers next. What can I get you?'

He ordered a latte and a sandwich, paid, then carried them into The Public. He didn't generally mind where he sat but when he saw an empty seat beside Laurel he made straight for it. She was alongside Daisy and her mates, including his nephew, Niall. He dumped his bag and coat and deposited his lunch on the table then exchanged a high five and a 'Hey,' with Niall and joked with Daisy and Zuzanna. By habit, he checked Niall looked happy and relaxed. He'd loved Niall since he first held him, a crumpled baby with a wondering gaze, making tiny popping noises with his lips. He'd enjoyed being an uncle, the one who bought the noisiest toys and never minded excursions that involved mud. Now Niall had hit puberty and was interested in girls, music, TV and computer games, they were more like buddies than uncle and nephew but Grady loved him no less.

As Niall was seated snugly between Zuzanna and Daisy and not looking in need of anything from his uncle, Grady turned to Laurel. 'Glad you're here. It means I'm not the only one who's neither a teenager or a pensioner.'

She gave a small smile. 'I've just been introduced to your nephew. Mac's son.'

He flipped the lid off his coffee cup and made sure they got one thing straight. 'Niall's ace,' he said firmly. 'He's great mates with Daisy.'

'Oy!' a woman broke in, pretending to glare ferociously at Grady. She was seated across the corner of the table, her strawberry blonde hair piled on her head, a two-year-old boy industriously eating shortbread by her side. 'Which am I, then? Teenager or pensioner?'

'Teenager, obviously, Tess,' he said smoothly, though he happened to know her next birthday would be her fortieth because her husband had already mentioned a party. 'Laurel, have you met Tess Arnott-Rattenbury? Her husband's Ratty, my landlord at the spray shop. Tess illustrates children's books. Tess, Laurel's an artist.' Then he sat back to enjoy his sandwich and coffee while the two women talked. He noticed Tess's little boy blinking at him and remembered that he'd recently tried to teach the child to wink.

'One eye at a time, Cody,' he suggested, exaggerating his own wink.

Cody giggled and said, 'Ugly.'

'Charming.' Grady laughed. Then he was distracted by the beep that signalled the arrival of a text. It was from Pippa. *Are you free to talk? xx*

He replied: *Busy at the moment.* He omitted kisses. Those days were done.

She came straight back. *Later? I'll call at the cottage. xx*

He stared at the words, shoulders prickling. He didn't appreciate her expecting him to be free at no notice. And 'the cottage'? Yes, she'd once lived there, but her not saying 'your cottage' annoyed him unreasonably, especially as he'd intended to see if Laurel fancied meeting him for a drink later – just as a 'welcome back', of course. *I could call at yours about five* he sent.

Zelda will be here. I'll come at five. Thanks! xxxx

Typical Pippa to only read what she wanted to read – that he'd be available, and to try and pin him down to 'at five' when he'd said 'about five'. He'd never worried about her manoeuvrings when she'd been his girlfriend but now things were different. He returned: *I'll be there as near five as works for me* and slid his phone away, clearing Pippa from his mind so he could listen to Tess asking Laurel how she sold finished pieces.

'Galleries are the traditional route but they take half what the painting fetches,' Laurel was saying. 'Online galleries take less and can get good prices but if I can sell on Etsy my main cost's shipping.' Because she was on his left and Tess was around the corner of the table to his right, they were talking across him and he was able to watch the movements of Laurel's mouth and the subtle shifts of light in her silky, fox-coloured hair.

When Laurel had first left, he'd thought of her constantly, constructing scenarios of her returning to the village and the froideur between them melting away. Time had faded those hopes and if he'd thought about her in recent years it was only because Daisy Grove was buddies with Niall and she mentioned her artist aunt, Laurel Hill, especially at Craft Stuff.

He'd wondered what kind of woman Laurel had grown up to be.

And now he had some idea. She was beautiful, successful, bright and compassionate but occasionally prickly. The open-hearted way she'd reached out to him about his infertility had stunned him. She was in the same unfortunate club, of course, but had looked outward from her own pain to reassure him. *Just being Laurel and just being Grady is enough, you know* . . . She was back in Middledip because she was needed, not because the cute cottages and warm villagers had called to her, but every time Grady looked at her, awareness shimmied up his spine.

The chatter rose around the table. Jodie came to clear lunch things and people around the table began producing their projects, many of which were destined for the fair: Christmas cards and labels; Santas made from felt; plant pots painted with Christmas motifs in red, green and silver; and Christmas ornaments full of tinsel and glitter.

Tess turned to helping Cody make paper chains and Grady took his coloured inks from his bag, aware of Laurel watching. Then Daisy claimed her attention to show her how to weave willow whips into circlets to become the base for her Christmas wreaths, saying, 'If we get them done now they can harden a bit in the next two weeks, then I'll add the decorations. If your first circle's twenty-five centimetres it will be about right when you've woven enough whips in to make it sturdy.'

'OK,' Laurel said obligingly. She pushed her chair back from the table to make room to wield the whips, which were about a metre long. She glanced at his inks and brushes. 'What are you up to?'

'Decorating,' he answered economically. Then he reached into his bag for the bottle gourd he'd been working on, pronouncing, *Blue Peter* style, 'Here's one I made earlier.'

It was satisfying that Laurel's hands paused in weaving her first circle. 'That's a hell of a transformation from the sort of raw material I saw at Gabe's.'

A couple of others looked up from their own projects and murmured, 'Good one, Grady,' or 'That's beautiful.'

Dropping the willow on her lap, Laurel said, 'May I?' and picked the gourd up to inspect it.

It was a vase he was particularly pleased with. He'd cut the neck into an asymmetrical shape and made the top third into a kind of filigree, using his hand-held rotary power tool with its dozens of heads for cutting, drilling, filing and sanding. Then he'd carved a border that resembled a ribbon, ends dangling down the vase. 'I'm going to paint the pierced part cream and the ribbon gold,' he explained. 'But I'm going to start by colouring the body with dark red ink, which will enhance the markings.' He ran a fingertip over the smooth, bulbous shape.

'Will you lacquer it?' Carefully, she passed the gourd back.

'Possibly. The gold paint on the ribbon might need protecting. Depends how it comes out. It's such a free form that I just go with my gut.'

Her eyes smiled. 'That's how I paint. Even if it's a commission, the artist has control.' She turned back to helping Daisy make willow circlets.

He took out the screw-top jar he brought water in, checked his brush for stray hairs and wiped over the vase in case of dust before unscrewing his Indian Red calligraphy ink. He dipped his brush several times, squeezing off the excess on the lip of the bottle to saturate the bristles evenly. Then he began stroking on the colour, brushing out the ink to avoid hard edges. Although he usually became absorbed in his work, he was aware of Laurel's gaze, though her hands remained busy weaving willow.

Daisy and her mates chatted. Niall was working with

wire, frowning over the construction of a red, green and silver 3D star, a wooden form cut at a variety of angles helping him form regular points. Zuzanna was embroidering Christmas cards with silver thread but when she paused to consult her phone she frowned. 'It says here to do the next bit with French knots.' She lifted her voice. 'Anyone know how to do French knots, please?' A woman further up the table smiled and nodded and Zuzanna went to her for a demonstration.

Laurel selected a fresh willow whip from Daisy's pile. 'Can you leave the vase here to dry?' she asked Grady.

'Luckily, yes.' He paused to check his brushwork for streaks. 'But if you leave something to dry you should pick it up by noon on Sunday so the café staff aren't inconvenienced. If you fail to meet the deadline,' he added, reloading his brush, 'I think Carola makes you a member of the village hall committee as penance.'

She tilted back her head and laughed, her hair streaming away from her face to reveal the curve of her throat. He found himself smiling stupidly until she returned her gaze him, then he looked quickly at his vase. A woman called Iris across the table was painting and she asked Laurel about wet-on-wet watercolour techniques. Before long, Laurel was up on her feet to demonstrate washing Iris's piece of card with a pale blue-white, then, in a few strokes and changes of colour, she'd created a robin, beak open, chest out, as if mid-song. The soft, out-of-focus effect of painting on wet paint drew appreciative murmurs from those looking on.

Tess, who'd been watching Laurel's brush technique over Cody's head, entered the conversation about Christmas cards from the perspective of an illustrator, sketching a couple of cutsie animals in demonstration.

Iris, who ran the group by virtue of the fact that she

was the one to collect two pounds from everyone for use of the room, said shyly to Laurel, 'I don't suppose you'd do an official demo some time, would you? How long will you be here for?'

Laurel glanced at Daisy then said, 'My stay's open-ended. And yes, of course I will.' She looked as if she honestly didn't mind, rather than just putting on a sporting face because she'd been put on the spot.

It was great to see her smiling and joining in with a Middledip activity but it meant Grady got no more of her attention. He continued with the red ink over the mottled skin of the gourd, enjoying watching the figuring brought out by the deep ruby translucence. His phone buzzed with another text from Pippa: *Could it be before five? xx*

Jeez! And this from a woman who'd dumped him. Swiftly, he shot back: *Why don't I come to yours when I'm ready so you're not hanging around?*

In return he received a laughing emoji, and: *Because I'm at the cottage already and it's snowing. Haha. xxx*

Shit. She was playing on Grady being too much of a gentleman to leave her standing outdoors freezing. It was just turned four and a chilly grey dusk would be falling. He finished the red inking part of the vase, put it on the drying shelf and began to clean his brushes. He popped a two-pound coin on the table at Iris's elbow.

Any vague ideas of saying to Laurel, 'What are you doing later?' or 'Fancy a drink sometime soon?' washed away like the red ink from his brush.

She called goodbye when she noticed him pulling on his coat. Then her gaze caught on the gourd, glowing red. She sent him a smile. 'That's beautiful.' If it hadn't been before, her smile made it feel that way.

He called his farewells and swung out through the main

103

café, where the Christmas tree was now a spectacular array of glittering, twinkling white lights and glowing blue and gold baubles. He liked Christmas, he thought, stepping out and admiring the gently drifting snow that made the village look like a Christmas card. Christmas, for him, meant arriving at Mac's house with a bag of presents and a half-case of wine, checking out Niall's latest computer games, joking with his colourful, petite sister-in-law while she beat batter and he and Mac peeled veg.

He strode up Port Road with snowflakes kissing his cheeks and the contented feeling of having enjoyed today. Laurel would be in the village this Christmas . . . *Stop being an overeager moron,* he chided himself. *You're reading way too much into her thawing towards you.*

He turned between the hedges of Mistletoe Cottage and loped up the path that was just beginning to cover with snow. Pippa waited beneath the porch, stamping her feet and swinging her arms as if the snow were two feet deep. He fished out his key. 'I don't know why you came so early.'

She answered with a dazzling smile. 'I couldn't wait to see you.'

'Yeah, right.' He unlocked the door with its aperture of stained glass and led the way, switching on the hall light en route to the kitchen.

'Still got the bright red floor tiles,' Pippa teased as she followed.

'And I still like them,' he replied evenly. The people who'd done up the cottage had chosen them and he liked their fire-engine redness, even if they probably hid original quarry tiles beneath.

Pippa unbuttoned her fir green coat and hung it on one of the hooks on the back of the door. He slung his own coat on a kitchen chair.

'I won't have coffee, thanks,' she said, when he took down two mugs.

He checked out alternatives in his cupboard. 'Tea? Hot chocolate?'

She accepted the hot chocolate and he made it then showed her through to the lounge.

Pippa took her old place in the corner of the big, L-shaped blue sofa. He took his favourite black leather chair with the scuffed footstool. 'So, what's up?' he asked, pleasantly. Despite his hurt and disappointment at the way Pippa had reacted to his fertility issues, they lived in the same village and he preferred good terms to bad ones.

Pippa sipped her hot chocolate, her cheeks flushed. 'Do you have to sit all the way over there? Something's happened that I want to talk about. It would be nicer not to shout.'

Grady debated. It seemed petty to stick to where he was comfortable, but considering Pippa's every wish when he'd loved her hadn't earned her support when it mattered. Once, he'd thought he'd spend his life with her. They'd lived together for two years, planned a wedding, joked about their differences – her 'princess tendencies' and his 'liking to get his hands dirty'. They'd spent time with each other's families. But when they'd hit a bump in the road . . . she'd jumped off the relationship bus. Nevertheless, he smiled to remove any sting from his words. 'I can hear you OK. No need to shout.'

She kicked off her shoes and tucked her legs beneath her, then carefully placed her mug on a side table. 'Well,' she began, clasping her hands. 'Something's happened, as I said. And it could be a wonderful thing, if we let it.' Her long blonde hair lay on the shoulders of her black jumper like gold on jeweller's velvet.

He frowned. 'Oh?' She seemed on edge, which put him on edge, too; the kind of edge that felt as if it might hurt.

Pippa tilted her head and gave him a tender smile. 'Well . . . I'm pregnant.'

Grady stared at her, this pretty woman who hadn't been prepared to attempt fertility treatment nor contemplate childlessness. He hadn't blamed her for wanting to be a mother but it had still hurt. His voice seemed to buzz in his ears. 'I presume you're telling me so I don't hear it from someone else so . . . thank you. And congratulations,' he added.

The fine, blonde eyebrows arched. 'The pregnancy wasn't planned,' she said, as if he should have realised. 'We met online. We had a few dates. It wasn't meant to be a "relationship".' She made finger quotes. 'We had a contraception failure. He doesn't feel the need to be involved. Except financially, obviously.'

For several seconds, Grady couldn't speak. Then he managed, 'Sad for the baby.'

'Exactly,' she said, her face lighting up. 'And you and I only split up because we couldn't have a baby.'

'I'm not likely to forget.' The words wrenched themselves from his throat. Surely, she couldn't be suggesting . . .? The air hummed with tension.

Pippa uncurled her legs and sat forward, her voice soft, passionate. 'You wanted to be a dad, didn't you? This is a heaven-sent opportunity.'

He could only gape. His heart seemed to be using his lungs as a punchbag and his skin burned, as if his organs were working too fast.

'Grady, listen,' she coaxed, abandoning the sofa to come and kneel beside him, grabbing his hand with both of hers. 'It's such an opportunity. We always got on well, we're compatible in bed, we still have feelings for each other.' Her hands tightened when he tried to recoil from her. Urgently, she added, 'We'll get back together, then tell people I'm pregnant. *Nobody needs to know the baby isn't actually yours.* You can quietly adopt it, so it legally is, and we'll be a family. It's our happy-ever-after!'

Grady's heart almost exploded with pain and outrage. He erupted from his seat, ripping his hands from her grasp. 'Get out.' His voice was hoarse, his throat constricting around the words.

Pippa stumbled to her feet, eyes wide and bewildered. 'It'll be perfect for us both—'

Deliberately, he turned his back on her. 'Please leave.'

A silence. Then she murmured, 'I think you ought to think about it, Grady.' Her voice was gentle and sympathetic. 'Face it. You're never going to have a baby the biological way. If we'd had fertility treatment the baby would have been someone else's anyway. This is much better because we avoid the actual treatment. You'll be a father and no one will know the truth apart from us.'

He trembled with anger and humiliation and pain. 'It's nice to know that you see me as a fallback position, something you dumped as broken but realise could have a use after all. But no thanks.'

He listened to the rustle of her retrieving her shoes from beside the sofa, felt the disturbance in the air as she left the room. Heard her go into the kitchen for her coat, her shoes tapping up the hall and then the front door opening and closing. He fell back into his chair, stomach churning. How had he ever been in love with a woman who could first wound him, then slice open that wound out of fucking *expediency*?

He did feel sorry for the baby but he couldn't give up his life to be Pippa's easy answer.

Chapter Seven

By evening, the rain had blown away and the temperature had plummeted. Through the kitchen window, Laurel could see frost twinkling in luminous moonlight as her hands performed the automatic movements of slicing veg.

Daisy slouched on a kitchen chair, phone in hand. 'Thanks for sorting Mum out about the Christmas wreaths,' she said suddenly. They'd put the enterprise to Rea when they'd returned home from Craft Stuff, omitting the detail that Daisy had been going to deliver wreaths to people's houses alone until Laurel stepped in.

Carefully, Laurel said to Daisy, 'I know you're protecting your mum by not telling her things that might stress her, but that's not an excuse to do stuff on the quiet that you know she wouldn't approve of.'

Daisy glanced up. Then back at her phone. Then up at Laurel again. Her eyes filled with tears, which she blinked way.

'Daisy?' Laurel said uncertainly, laying her knife down on the chopping board.

Daisy's lip wobbled. 'Is Mum still in the bath?'

'I think so. I told her to take a glass of wine and a magazine in there for a long soak while I made dinner. What's the matter?' Laurel rinsed her hands and crossed the room to crouch beside her niece's chair and stroke the long, tumbled, windswept curls that lay over Daisy's shoulder.

Daisy wiped her eyes on her sleeve. 'How long do you think you're staying?' she asked thickly.

Laurel shrugged. 'Here? I don't know, yet.' *Until I can get away,* she thought. She got up and fetched several tissues from a box on the windowsill and passed them to her niece.

'But for a while? You're not leaving in January, say? Or February?' Daisy blew her nose.

The questions made Laurel uneasy, not just because it was so unlike Daisy to press her but also because it illuminated in a bright, white spotlight the fact that Laurel had no real idea how long she'd be stuck in Middledip. She stroked Daisy's arm. 'I've spent all week getting Nan's studio up to scratch, haven't I? I wouldn't do that if I only planned to stay a few weeks. I'll soon start a new painting.'

'Only . . .' Daisy gulped. 'There's something I can't tell Mum.'

Heart beginning a long, slow dive, Laurel edged her chair closer. 'Because of her agoraphobia?'

'Kinda.' Daisy took a clean tissue and blotted her eyes. Then, 'Not exactly. Just . . . just because I can't.'

'OK.' Laurel rose, got each of them a glass of water and brought over the entire box of tissues from the windowsill. 'Whatever it is, you can tell me.' Her pulse pounded. Behind the calm, in-charge-adult mask she'd just pinned on for Daisy, her thoughts scurried like mice. Was

Daisy in trouble with the police? Or pregnant? She was obviously super-friendly with Niall Cassidy. Then she squared her shoulders. Whatever it was, there would be a way to deal with it. Parents had to so Laurel would find a way, too.

Daisy gazed at her from red-rimmed eyes then flicked a glance at the open kitchen door, as if checking there was no sign of her mother. 'Has Mum told you what happened at parents' evening in the summer term?' she asked, voice quavering.

Laurel shrugged. 'She seemed in a state afterwards, like it was the last straw so far as going out was concerned.'

'I felt so bad for her.' Fresh tears leaked down Daisy's cheeks. 'She made herself go because it was all about moving into Year Ten this year. GCSEs and assignments and everything.'

'Right.' Laurel nodded. She could imagine Rea wanting to support Daisy in an important school meeting.

Daisy hiccupped a sob and grabbed three tissues at once to bury her face in. 'We were late. Mum had been sitting in the car doing deep breathing. She was all sweaty. I said "let's just go home, Mum, it doesn't matter", but she said it did matter and she was going in. Then, in the foyer—' Daisy's face crumpled '—she had a panic attack, clutching her chest and gasping. The only people around were two girls from my year. They were supposed to be helping any parents who couldn't find the meeting. Octavia and Scarlett.' Daisy halted, battling to get the words out.

Heart pattering with alarm by now, Laurel gave her the glass of water. 'It's OK. Take your time.'

Daisy sipped, then cried into her tissue for half a minute, head on Laurel's shoulder. Finally, she croaked imploringly. 'You can't tell Mum.'

'I won't.' A horrified Laurel hoped she'd be able to keep that promise.

'Octavia and Scarlett . . . we don't like each other. They don't like anyone from Middledip. They reckon we all ride round in posh cars and we're up ourselves.' Daisy steadied a bit as the story began to emerge.

'It was the same when I was at that school,' Laurel interjected. 'Middledip's a nice village but not full of millionaires.'

Daisy nodded. 'Yeah, well, that. Octavia and Scarlett are really bitter. They were there when Mum had this attack. And she . . . well, made a bad smell.' In a whisper, she added, as if she had to make sure Laurel got the gravity of the situation, 'She *farted*. Mum couldn't help it. Having a bad stomach during a panic attack isn't funny, but Octavia and Scarlett killed themselves laughing behind her back, holding their noses and pretending to gag. I don't think Mum noticed because she was struggling to get her breath.' Daisy shook her head, more weary and weighed down than any fourteen-year-old should ever have to be. 'We never got into the main hall for the parents' evening. I took Mum back to the car and we sat in there until she could drive home.'

Heart bleeding for her niece, Laurel gripped Daisy's sweating hand. 'That sounds horrible. I'm sorry you had to cope with it. I can go with you to parents' evenings now your mum's made me an official contact at the school.'

'Thanks.' Daisy brushed the offer aside so casually that it obviously wasn't the source of her unhappiness. 'Then Scarlett and Octavia came up to me the next day and said Mum had . . . had—' Daisy had to sip water before she could go on. 'That Mum had pooed herself. They called her crappy knickers and poopy pants. They began writing notes about it and saying stuff in front of people – not exactly what happened but just that there was *something* they knew. Dropping hints. Making the other kids all go, "What? What?".'

'I can imagine,' Laurel said, sympathetically. She saw all-too-clearly why Daisy felt she couldn't confide in her mother. Rea would be mortified beyond bearing. 'Anxiety does affect the gut, which is why exams can give us stomach-ache. Were Scarlett and Octavia in English lessons with you last year and art this year, by any chance?'

Daisy shot her a grateful look. 'Yeah, you've got it. And in those two lessons I'm not with Niall and Zuzanna or other village friends. Octavia and Scarlett get those fake dog poos and put them in my bag. They send me emojis of poo.' She gulped. 'And,' the tears began to ooze again, 'this just arrived.'

She took out her phone and turned it to show Laurel a text. *Hey shitty knickers we've decided you need to pay us not to tell everyone about your mum. A tenner each will do for starters cos we need to start our Christmas shopping.* The message was ornamented by two Mother Christmas emojis and, as Daisy had said, heaps of poo.

Laurel leaned over and enveloped her niece in a huge hug. She wanted to say, 'Who are these fucking monsters? I'll spoil their Christmas shopping!' But she knew that was what Fliss would term 'an unhelpful reaction'. Fliss was big on not meeting violence with violence, or abuse with abuse. She said there was always another resolution. Channelling Fliss, she said, 'The first thing to do is find someone to tell.'

'Yeah.' Daisy leaned her head on Laurel's, as if exhausted. 'But I couldn't tell a teacher because they'd have to tell Mum. If she finds out I've been having hassle because of her—'

'We won't let that happen,' Laurel said gently, easily picturing Rea beside herself with guilt and her stress levels going stratospheric. 'I can come into school. I'm sure that if I explain the sensitivity of the situation we can solve it without them involving your mum – just this once, obviously. Don't worry. We'll fix this. I'll make it stop. It'll be easy to prove if the girls are stupid enough to text you like that.' Laurel held Daisy tightly, hoping she was saying the right things. Maybe she'd call Fliss later and check.

'Thank you.' Daisy hesitated. 'When you talk to someone, can it be Mr Williams, my form teacher? Not Mr Cassidy. He's Niall's dad and it's weird enough going to his house and that.'

'OK.' Laurel had no trouble agreeing with that request. She smoothed back Daisy's hair. 'Didn't you even tell Niall or Zuzanna what was happening?' Daisy's headshake told Laurel how mortified her niece must have been at the prospect of her mum being ridiculed, having seen how tight-knit the three teens were. Aunt and niece sat together until Laurel caught the sound of footsteps on the landing. 'Sounds like your mum's finished in the bath. You run upstairs and bathe your face in cold water so she doesn't know you've been upset. Give yourself a bit of time if you want it. I'll call you when dinner's ready.'

After Daisy had hugged her and scurried upstairs, a shaken Laurel rushed through the final preparations for the casserole before Rea appeared. Poor little Daisy had enabled the bullies by trying to protect Rea.

Laurel had every sympathy.

She'd kept what had happened to her from Rea for exactly the same reason.

Ten minutes later, Rea arrived looking rosy and relaxed from the bath. 'What a treat. I topped the hot water up twice and read all of *Garden News*. I love you being here.'

Laurel accepted Rea's hug and managed a weak joke. 'Only because we can take turns cooking.' With Daisy's agonised confession going round and round in her head she found it hard to concentrate on Rea's chatter. What was the best way to contact Daisy's form tutor, Mr Williams? Better check the school website.

Daisy came down when the casserole was ready, quiet but no longer sporting red eyes.

They all sat down together, Rea exhibiting a feature on greenhouses of various shapes and sizes. 'I'm thinking about having a greenhouse built behind the garage. I could have a nice wooden frame, rather than one of those aluminium ones. This casserole's lovely, Laurel. I can get a power cable put through the wall from the garage for heating.'

'Sounds great.' Laurel would call the school on Monday morning, from the studio. Rea would be safely ensconced in her office. She suppressed a wriggle of regret because she'd intended to start playing with ideas for a new painting on Monday. It had taken her three weeks to pack up in Chiswick, move to Middledip and sort out the studio. Maybe it was having a brush in her hand again at the Craft Stuff session, but her creative mind had begun to show her an image of a woman dancing in falling snow, face upturned, hair writhing around her head and shoulders. She wanted to start thinking about the angle of her neck, the inward arch of her spine and curves of her arms.

But Daisy's problem came first.

Daisy's phone buzzed. She picked it up from beside her plate then put down her fork while her thumbs flew over the screen. 'Laurel, just given your number to Grady, OK?' she said as she returned to her meal.

Surprise shimmered through Laurel. 'It's usual to ask first and send after, but OK.'

'Oh. Soz. But you know Grady,' Daisy answered unrepentantly.

'Do we need to take messages at mealtimes?' Rea asked Daisy reprovingly.

Then Laurel's phone buzzed. Daisy giggled. 'Auntie Laurel, do we need to take messages at mealtimes?'

'Nope,' said Laurel, in sisterly solidarity, and left her phone in her pocket until after the meal was over and the dishwasher was stacked. Then she found a text from a number not in her contacts: *This is Grady. Any chance you could come to Mistletoe Cottage? My head's going to explode if I don't talk to someone and I think you'll understand. Apols for massive imposition.*

Laurel, caught by surprise, returned, *Now?* before realising how brusque and unfriendly that sounded. She sent a follow-up. *Yes. I can come.*

Her phoned pinged immediately. *Thanks! Yes, as soon as convenient. Apols again.*

Laurel looked up as she heard Daisy asking to be allowed to go to Niall's house and Rea saying, 'You know I don't want you walking about on your own in the dark, Daisy. Can't Niall come here?'

Daisy pulled a face. 'What, like boys are automatically safe and girls are automatically not? You have to treat us alike, Mum.'

'Girls are more vulnerable than boys,' Rea began, wiping down the white granite counter tops.

'You wouldn't say that if I was a boy,' Daisy declared, hands on hips. 'Most violence is directed against young

115

men, especially gang fights and knife crime. It's just sexualised crime that's more common against females. Anyway, Niall has Disney+ and we don't.'

Rea argued anxiously. 'We have Netflix and Sky.'

'There's a new Marvel movie on Disney+ tonight,' Daisy retorted, a typically mutinous teen butting heads with her mum rather than the tearful young woman who'd been valiantly trying to protect her for all these months. 'And Mr Cassidy has replaced my Santa suit and I said I'd pick it up.'

Laurel stepped in. 'I'll walk her to Niall's house, if that's OK, Rea. I'm going out.' She gave Daisy's hair a friendly tug. 'It might not be the mean streets of a big city but you can't assume you're safe just because Middledip's warm and cuddly. Stay together, stay safe is a good rule.'

Daisy, happy now she'd achieved her goal, hissed, 'Yessssss,' and punched the air.

'Sure?' Rea asked Laurel, looking half-relieved and half-exasperated.

Laurel replied, 'Sure.' Then she texted Grady again: *Expect me in the next hour.*

'Where are you going out to, Auntie Laurel?' Daisy asked.

Rea pushed the cleaning cloth into Daisy's hand and pointed at the table. 'Laurel doesn't need to report in to us.'

Laurel was glad of it. She didn't madly want to say she was going to see Grady. When they'd been buddies in the past everyone had assumed they were more than friends.

They'd been right.

She didn't need that kind of scrutiny now.

Daisy ran upstairs to fetch something and Rea turned to Laurel with haunted eyes. 'Am I projecting my fears on her, not wanting her to go out?'

Laurel reassured her stoutly. 'No. I think she should have someone with her in the dark.'

Rea's shoulders relaxed. 'Will you tell me if I get unreasonable about her freedom?'

Laurel agreed. Though she'd been easing herself back into life in Middledip, she'd also been reading about helping a loved one with agoraphobia. Showing Rea she was her ally was her priority but her first step would be a behind-the-scenes one: to stop the bullying of Daisy. That should end the truanting and make the flow of school emails to Rea dry up, which would be one anxiety gone. Encouraging Rea through the barrier of fear that locked her into her home was a longer-term goal.

It was nearly eight-thirty when, bundled up against a frosty evening, Laurel and Daisy crossed the village, their breath like clouds and Daisy sliding on frozen puddles. They passed The Three Fishes, which was looking splendidly festive in a network of fairy lights that twinkled from the roof and every wall, with blinking, winking Christmas trees standing sentinel either side of the door. Once they reached Port Road Laurel saw Daisy up the long front path to number 148, and waited for Niall to answer the door before turning away. She retraced her steps as far as Ladies Lane, where Mistletoe Cottage sat diagonally on the corner. It was a part-stone, part-brick cottage, its tiled roof sagging at the ridge. A canopy porch sheltered a front door ornamented by a little window. Laurel gave the brass door knocker two raps.

Grady opened the door. His dark hair looked, as her mum would have said, as if he'd been pulled through a hedge backwards. His expression was set and pale. 'Thanks for coming.' He ushered her in. In the hall, a green lamp with a cream shade cast light on a quarry tiled floor.

'I'm really putting on you,' he said as she hung up her coat and scarf and followed him through a doorway to a sitting room. He plumped down on the edge of a black leather chair. A half-drunk bottle of Malbec stood on a small table, a part-filled glass beside it and a clean glass standing ready. He indicated the wine distractedly. 'Want some?'

His manner was so tense that Laurel thought she'd better say, 'Yes, please.' She took a seat on the sofa, a big corner unit that took up all the space.

He sloshed a measure into the glass and handed it to her. 'I don't know if I'm being a diva. Someone's asked me something and I've taken it so badly, I feel like running round smashing things.' He broke off this opaque explanation to take a quick, nervous swig of wine.

Laurel's brow creased. Never did she remember seeing Grady Cassidy like this. Sometimes he used to growl about his dad or complain about his teachers but she'd never seen him so off-balance, his eyes darting around as if not sure what it was safe to look at. 'And you want to tell me about it?' she asked, curious that it would be her. Why not Mac, when they were so close?

He paused to pinch the bridge of his nose and squeeze his eyes tight shut. 'I'm emotional.'

She settled back on the sofa to sip her wine, giving him time. It seemed to be her evening for people getting emotional.

He began to speak without opening his eyes, as if it were easier that way. 'Pippa's pregnant.'

'Oh.' Compassion and understanding flooded through her. 'Oh, Grady, I'm sorry. I get that being difficult. One of the worst things about infertility is that your condition affects your loved one, and it doesn't get easier when they move on.'

'Loved one,' he almost spat. Angry eyes flew open. 'I don't even want to look at her.'

Laurel said nothing to what seemed an extreme response but her heart went out to him. She would have expected him to be more controlled but could empathise with his misery.

He drained his glass and filled it straight up again, firing out sentences. 'She's not in a relationship. The father's some bloke she met online. He doesn't want the child. She's asked if we can pretend we were seeing each other again on the down-low and she got pregnant. Get back together. Pretend the baby's mine. Says I can adopt it and no one will ever know. Says it's my best chance to be a father. Says it could be "perfect for us". Says we can live happily ever after.'

'Oh,' Laurel breathed, trying to absorb such a shock scenario. 'How do you feel—'

He leaped to his feet. '*Outraged!* She thinks it's OK to dump me as "defective" then take me back on a best-of-a-bad-job basis? She seemed to think I ought to be *grateful*.' He slapped the wall in frustration, his back to Laurel. 'I feel *hurt and furious*. Like the top of my head's going to blow off. No one wants to feel they're not someone's first choice but to use my deepest pain as bait, to present being allowed to father her accidental pregnancy as a reward . . . that's cold.' He slapped the wall twice more. Then his hands dropped to his sides and his head tipped back. 'I needed to tell someone who might understand.'

She rose and went to him, heart wrenching at his obvious anguish. 'Someone who might tell you it's OK to feel like this?'

He let his head fall forward. 'Yes.'

She touched his arm. 'It's OK to feel like this. I'd be bitterly hurt if Alex tried to use me that way.'

It took several moments but eventually he turned to face her. His eyes were dull. 'Thank you.' He returned to his seat and she returned to hers, both picking up their wine glasses like any two people in a normal social situation.

'She always was a princess,' he commented. 'She had childhood leukaemia and her parents were terrified they'd lose her. They, and her sister Zelda, got used to treating her as special.' His smile twisted bitterly. 'When we were together I didn't notice how entitled it made her because, I guess, she saw me as an extension of her. If the rain came, she made sure someone gave her an umbrella big enough for both of us.' He gave a short laugh. 'I'm not explaining very well. But she's pretty and can be sweet. It wasn't until my issues came out and she so readily discarded me that I realised how little empathy she has for others. I've no idea how she'll learn to put a baby first.' He sighed. 'I feel like an expensive pair of shoes.'

Laurel watched him slump in his chair, looking less tightly wound now he was letting everything out. 'How so?'

A smile flickered in the corner of his mouth. 'Pippa's parents bought her some gorgeous designer shoes. She loved them. Lavished care on them. Showed them off. Changed her favourite outfits to go with them. Then they got badly scratched and there was no longer any point to them, in her eyes. She didn't take them to Timpsons to see if the scratch could be repaired. She dumped them and went out to buy replacements.' He took a reflective mouthful of wine. 'Think of me as those shoes. She hasn't yet found the perfect replacement so she's lowering her standards to get me out of the bin and find a way to cover up the scratch.'

'Thing is, shoes don't have feelings,' Laurel commented. She realised with surprise that her glass was empty and, on inspection, so was the bottle.

'She can't think I do, either.' Grady followed the direction of her gaze. 'I'll get another.' He left the room and returned with a second bottle and topped up both glasses.

After a generous slug, Laurel sighed. 'Infertility is shitty, isn't it? You're denied something fundamental, something others take for granted. You feel as if you've let your partner down. When you'd give anything for a planned pregnancy, it stings every time you hear about an accidental one. And when it's your ex . . .'

Grady snorted. ' . . .She thinks you'll leap in to take the role of father because the real one's unsatisfactory.'

Laurel considered that. 'Maybe some people would. We're all different. Alex and I went down the treatment route, which some people don't; but didn't go for adoption, which some people do. Maybe we should have given up sooner because we stopped enjoying trying to make a baby and every process either didn't take or I miscarried. I'm glad he's met a nice woman now, Vonnie. Maybe she, or someone who comes after, might be able to give him babies.' She sipped. 'I hope I'll be big-hearted enough to be glad for him.'

Grady stretched and settled himself more comfortably. 'In those circumstances, I think you will. For you to come out in the cold at a moment's notice to listen to me shows you're big-hearted. Thank you,' he added. 'My outrage filled my head so I couldn't think right. Pippa was so calm when she put her proposition to me, so surprised but soothing when I got upset. I wondered if my feelings might be overreaction or ultra-sensitivity.'

Softly, she said, 'I think you had salt rubbed into your wound and then were expected to be grateful.' Pippa sounded incredibly self-serving. At The Angel Laurel had thought her pretty but if that had once been enough to work magic on Grady, that spell was well and truly broken now.

'Anyway,' Grady put in, with the air of someone in need of a new topic. 'What changes do you see in Middledip?'

Laurel was glad he seemed ready to climb up from his emotional low. 'Rea's always kept me updated with the big news, like the village hall shutting for repairs, the shop changing hands and The Angel opening. The pub's recently changed hands as well, Rea says. I remember going there with Mum for the occasional meal and it was run by a grumpy guy.'

A smile gleamed in his eyes. 'Harrison Tubb, or "Tubb from the pub". Nice guy, under the crusty exterior. He sold out to Ferdy and Elvis. They've got a load of Italian dishes on the menu now and I'm a particular fan of their carbonara. You haven't been into The Three Fishes since you were a kid?' He smiled when she shook her head. 'Too many people to get "up in your business"?'

She laughed. 'Rea wouldn't go with me, would she?'

He was topping up their glasses and opening his mouth to reply when the doorknocker rapped once, then there was the sound of a key in the lock and the front door opened.

'Grady?' called Mac's voice.

Laurel was taking the first sip of her freshened drink. She froze with the wine still in her mouth. Damn.

'You'd better come in as you're half in already,' Grady called, mixed amusement and exasperation in his voice.

The door clunked closed, then Mac appeared, unzipping his coat. He flushed when his eye fell on Laurel. 'Oh. Sorry. Didn't mean to interrupt. I've been texting you, Grady, and there was no reply so I thought I'd check you're OK.'

Grady turned to Laurel. '"Check Grady's OK" is Mac-code for "see if Grady wants to go to The Three Fishes before closing time".'

Laurel scooted to the edge of the sofa and put down her glass. 'If you want to go out with Mac—'

'Of course not. We're talking and we're halfway through a bottle of wine,' Grady said mildly. 'Get a clean glass and have one, Mac.'

Mac hesitated, but then headed for the kitchen.

It would look so pointed for Laurel to dump a full glass of wine on the table and catapult out of the door the moment Mac arrived that she subsided. Mac returned with a glass and took a spot right at the other end of the sofa. Laurel assumed the role of listener as the brothers began to discuss the best pasta on the pub menu.

They tried to draw her into the conversation but her mind was working on her exit strategy. If she waited too long Mac might leave at the same time she did. As she needed to collect Daisy from his house, he'd naturally walk along with her. She shrank from being alone with him, though it was obvious that he'd matured into respectability and she didn't actually think the current Mac would attack her in the dark. If she still didn't want to be alone with him . . . that meant Fliss had been hunting along the right trail. Laurel wasn't willing to afford Mac any opportunity to apologise.

Something for her to think about.

After twenty minutes, by dint of waiting for a moment

when Mac's glass was full and hers was nearly empty, she was able to drain the last mouthful and say, 'Think it was time I was off. Thanks for the wine, Grady.'

Grady looked concerned. 'Shall I walk you back?'

'Not necessary.' She hurried out into the hall to grab her coat and pull it on. 'Daisy's hanging out with Niall and I can almost see the house from here. After that, Daisy and I will be together.' Despite Grady's slight air of bemusement, she called goodnight and was soon hurrying through sparkling frost that coated every car and garden hedge, phoning Daisy as she went.

Daisy sighed. 'But Auntie Laurel, my curfew is eleven. I still have ten minutes.'

Laurel said regretfully, 'Sorry, I misjudged. But I'm just arriving at Niall's house so could you come out?'

'Bet Niall's mum Tonya would like to meet you,' Daisy began.

'Not tonight,' Laurel said pleasantly.

'OK,' Daisy agreed ungraciously.

Laurel had to wait five minutes outside the Cassidy household for Daisy to appear. A small woman with blonde and pink hair came to the open doorway and lifted a friendly hand to Laurel. Laurel returned the salute then hurried Daisy away.

'What's the rush?' demanded Daisy.

'Need the loo,' said Laurel, which wasn't actually a lie, and they strode through the icy village together, huddling into their coats. Every leaf or grain of wood wore a twinkling white jacket and Jack Frost tweaked Laurel's ears until they stung. She tried to jolly Daisy along. 'The streetlights look as if they're wearing Joseph's coat of many colours with so many Christmas lights wound around them.'

'Cool,' responded Daisy, tepidly.

Then they walked in silence apart from the ringing of their boots on the flagstone pavement. They turned into Great End, where the householder on the corner had stuck solar lights into the verge to dissuade pub goers from parking there. In sight of The Nookery now, Laurel slowed, hooking her hand into Daisy's arm. 'You all right? After being upset earlier, I mean. Are you still OK with me phoning the school on Monday to ask to speak to Mr Williams?'

Daisy nodded vigorously. 'I haven't answered the text.'

'That's the right thing to do.' Laurel realised she'd failed to give Daisy advice on that. 'It's best not to even hint that I intend to put a stop to their games. It'll be better to catch them off-guard. I'll need you to forward to me all the messages they've sent you and I expect Mr Williams will want to see them on your phone himself at some point.'

Daisy nodded. She smiled, though probably at the thought of Octavia and Scarlett getting in trouble.

Laurel's mind drifted back to her own experiences, including the counselling she'd taken advantage of herself eight or nine years ago. 'I expect Mr Williams will give you some idea how to act when this is over. I know it's tempting to think of revenge but it's not good. It brings you down to their level and can make you the aggressor. You just need to move on to a happier place.'

''Kay,' Daisy agreed and they carried on the last few yards to The Nookery where Daisy, after shouting hello to her mum, disappeared upstairs to her room.

Slightly more gracious and well-mannered than the teenager, Laurel sought out Rea in the sitting room though, having had two people spill their hearts to her tonight, she wouldn't have minded going upstairs and letting a good book carry her away from reality. 'Hi,' she said, falling into a cutesy rocking chair for which Rea had made black and green cushions.

Rea closed her laptop and tossed it aside. 'Thanks for doing that for Daisy.' She hugged herself, though the room wasn't cold. 'It's affecting her that I'm not leaving the house. I'm hurting my daughter and setting a bad example. My instinct earlier this evening was to keep her home with me for safety's sake instead of looking for a way to get her to Niall's safely. It's made me take a hard look at myself.' She was white apart from the pink slashes high on her cheeks.

Though she was glad Rea was facing facts, Laurel tried to keep her calm. 'Daisy's very mature for fourteen. She understands. It's what I came back for, isn't it? To support you and Daisy?'

Rea crossed and recrossed her legs. 'But I'm so crap, Laurel. I wish I wasn't like this.' She picked up the laptop and slapped it angrily back down on the sofa cushion. 'I've been reading about self-help for those with agoraphobia but they make it sound like it's all down to bad diet and too much caffeine. As if a cuppa and a mince pie could make me feel like this!'

'May I see the site?' Laurel extended her hand and Rea thrust the laptop into it and then refolded her arms as if holding herself together.

Laurel took her time scrolling through the website, trying to absorb what she read and compare it with her own research on living with someone with agoraphobia. 'I agree they suggest lifestyle changes and self-help techniques to help relieve symptoms, but they're also signposting a guided self-help programme and cognitive behavioural therapy.'

'I don't think people believe agoraphobia is real,' Rea said with a sigh, not really addressing what Laurel had said. 'My GP suggested counselling but it sounded as if I'd have to go out of the house to access it. What use is that? "You don't like leaving the house, eh? Well, I know just the thing for you – but it involves leaving the house." That's not helpful.'

'So you dismissed it?' Laurel murmured, imaging Rea forcing herself to the surgery and finding the offered solution so unpalatable she used it as an excuse to run for the safety of this house. The phrase 'this house' echoed abruptly in Laurel's mind. It was as if The Nookery itself played a part in Rea's issues, being both sanctuary and prison. How many forty-year-old people still lived in their childhood home? Her gaze dropped to the stack of home and garden magazines on the coffee table. Rea constantly tended and renewed the fabric of the cottage and felt responsible for it. It was a shame she had no flesh-and-blood relationships outside of it.

An idea flickered tentatively to life. 'I thought I'd pop over and see Aunt Terri,' she said. 'How about—'

But Rea was already shaking her head. 'Not right at the moment, thanks.'

Laurel cursed herself for such an obvious, clumsy attempt to coax Rea out. Her eyes dropped to the laptop screen again, searching for alternatives. 'It says here you can refer yourself to an NHS psychological therapies service. The guided self-help programme can be delivered by phone or online, so probably counselling or CBT could be, too.' She looked up at her sister, taking in the lines of strain around her mouth and eyes.

Gently, she asked, 'How many times have you seen your GP about this?' She hated to think that any GP would leave a patient feeling as unsupported as Rea seemed: agitated because she couldn't go out; unable to go out because she was agitated.

It took Rea several seconds to answer. 'Once,' she finally admitted.

Laurel smothered an exclamation. Getting impatient would only cement Rea's conviction that she was 'so crap'. She kept her voice even. 'Why only once?' She closed the laptop and focused on Rea.

Rea's eyes brimmed. 'Just feeling overwhelmed. Long wait in the waiting room. People. Noise. Smells.'

'And the only thing offered was counselling outside the home?' Laurel pressed.

A hesitation. Then, 'He signposted me to information and offered pills. He did tell me I was welcome to return,' she admitted, making Laurel aware that, in her anxiety, Ria was rearranging events in her mind to justify not looking for the right kind of help.

'But you didn't?' Laurel prompted, gently holding Rea to account.

Rea's chest heaved. 'Loads of companies are happy for you to work at home. I went out if I really needed to and just about controlled my anxiety with deep breathing. Then, a few months ago it just . . . got worse.' She dropped her gaze.

Then, in the foyer, she had a panic attack, clutching her chest and gasping. Laurel could remember Daisy's own trembling anxiety as she recounted the 'bad smell'. Maybe Rea had been aware of the girls behind her laughing, knowing she was embarrassing Daisy. Running for home.

Rea gave a laugh that sounded like a sob. 'I don't think you can understand if you don't experience it. A panic attack is like a band tightening round my chest so that I

128

can't breathe. My stomach knots up. Once it's happened a few times – and it can be triggered by really ordinary things, like being in a crowd or not being able to find a parking space – you get anxious about it happening again.' She sucked in several long, slow breaths. 'Agoraphobia is a really powerful feeling that something is going to go wrong.'

'Except in the house?' Laurel murmured, sympathetic tears pricking her eyes.

Rea nodded. 'Exactly.'

Laurel could see that it wouldn't take too many episodes as Rea described to seriously affect stability and that what happened at Daisy's parents' evening had taken her to breaking point. She shifted over to sit beside her sister on the sofa and take her hand. 'I'm here for you, Rea. I'm not going to pressure you, but I think there's more help available than you're admitting. Maybe you're not ready to hear it. If and when you are, I'll support you any way I can. I'll drive you to appointments, sit with you in waiting rooms, be in the room while you talk on the phone or via video call. Whatever you need.' Vision blurring, she slid her arms around her elder sister and hugged her tight. 'You lean on me – just like I used to lean on you.' This made three people in one evening Laurel had offered a shoulder to but none was more important than her sister. Rea was as fragile as the November ice crusting the puddles outside.

Rea returned the hug. 'You are the best sister in the world.'

'No, you are.' Laurel swallowed a lump in her throat. 'There's no shame in needing help, or speaking to the right person.' It had been Fliss who'd made Laurel see that when trauma touched someone they carried it with them.

Don't let anyone diminish your feelings. It wasn't just horseplay that got out of hand. What happened to you was assault.

Laurel murmured to Rea, 'You're perfectly entitled to understanding and help. Your situation is real.'

Rea laid her head against Laurel's. 'I'm so glad you're here,' she murmured.

'I'll be here as long as you need me.' Laurel's move to the coast receded a few more months in her mind.

Chapter Eight

Sunday. Ten-thirty. Village meeting at The Angel.

Grady. Big, thumping headache. Wished he could stay in bed.

Seated at the big table, he awaited the arrival of the last few attendees, tuning out Carola who was discussing roles with Iris at the other end of the table. The Public was now festooned with flashing white fairy lights. The throbbing in his head kept time. *Ow. Ow. Ow.*

He was halfway down his first large black coffee and had a second lined up on the table before him in a red take-out cup, although he knew he should really be drinking water. His stomach was queasy and his mouth dry. He shouldn't have opened that third bottle of wine. He sighed. When Mac arrived, Laurel hadn't hung around long. Later, he'd suggested Mac think about whether Grady had company before utilising his spare key. Mac had brushed it aside with a fresh comment about Grady not answering his phone. They'd gone on to discuss Pippa's crazy idea and Mac hadn't asked anything about Laurel.

Grady had thought about her, though. The way her loose golden-brown top had set her auburn hair ablaze. The clear blue of her eyes. How soft her lips looked . . .

'Hey, Grady,' said a loud young voice.

Grady jolted back to the present, blinking to encourage his eyes to focus. 'Oh, hi, Daisy. Hi, Niall.' He gave his nephew a gentle arm-punch and said hello to blonde Zuzanna, too. Then he saw Laurel hovering behind the teens. She wore a big black shirt and light blue jeans. 'Hi, Laurel.'

She smiled. 'Hi.' As the teenagers pretend-fought over chairs, Laurel took the seat around the corner of the table from him. 'How are you this morning?' she asked, with the kind of glint that suggested she had some idea of the answer.

He made pitiful eyes at her. 'I think I have a migraine.'

She snorted with laughter just as Carola thumped the table with a book – really? Did she *have* to? – and said, 'Shall we get on?' as if wasn't her who'd been nattering.

Then Tess barrelled in through the door with a breathless, 'Sorry!' and sat down on Grady's other side, exchanging whispered hellos before noisily scraping her chair, rustling her way out of her coat and stirring the drink she'd brought with her.

Carola's smile didn't waver. She knew how to get the best out of people and it was generally by simply asking them to do things so nicely they'd find it hard to refuse her. 'Hello, Tess. What a wonderful calibre of volunteers we have. Not just Tess, a professional illustrator, but now Laurel, a professional artist.'

'And me,' Grady couldn't resist saying. 'An unprofessional artist.' Everyone laughed.

'Oops.' Carola adjusted her glasses. 'And Grady, a

professional auto artist. Is that the correct term? Actually, you're leading the art side, Grady, aren't you?'

Horrified that he'd almost goofed his way into having to do something, he assumed his most winning smile. 'But I was relying on you to chair the meeting, Carola. It's about the Christmas Fair as well and you know so much about committees.'

Carola looked gratified while Grady added under his breath, 'Because you're on all of them.'

Laurel hid a smile.

Business progressed rapidly. Helpers were lined up to erect stalls at the village hall, advertising had already begun on social media and Daisy had created the Art December Google map, dropping pins to indicate where the window displays would be around the village. If exhibitors would send photos of their works to Grady, he'd share them with Daisy for the map and post them on the village Facebook page. Tess would email the promotional flyers to Carola and Grady for printing, and Niall, Daisy and Zuzanna volunteered to deliver them around the village.

Grady began his second cup of coffee.

Laurel acquiesced when Daisy suggested they share a window at The Nookery for the village Art December and exhibit a canvas on the art wall at the Middledip Christmas Fair at the village hall. To aid others with their art wall exhibits, she also agreed to conduct a midweek Craft Stuff session to demonstrate mounting and framing. 'I used to run community sessions with a friend in London. I'm happy to do something here if I'm not treading on anyone's toes.'

'Gosh, no, we're lucky to have you,' breathed Carola, who never actually came to the craft sessions, just let them take place in The Public and listened to her till ring as everyone bought refreshments.

Any enthusiasm Grady might have had for the meeting ran out at the same time as his second coffee. 'Right,' he said, meanly taking advantage of Carola pausing for breath. 'I have the list of exhibitors both for Art December and for the art wall at the Christmas Fair. I'll post a reminder on the village Facebook group in case anyone else wants to get involved. Everyone's got my email, yes? Thanks, Carola. Thanks everyone.'

Carola looked faintly disapproving at this abrupt winding up of his responsibilities, especially when the others began to put on their coats, signalling her part was over too. Grady was just deciding between returning to bed or visiting The Three Fishes to try a hair of the dog for his hangover when he heard Daisy call to Laurel, 'Coming up to Gabe's?'

Laurel tilted her head consideringly. 'It would be nice to see that pony again but is it OK when we were only there yesterday?'

'That was to pick up stuff he lets us store. It's not nice to only visit him when we want something,' Daisy said promptly.

Grady grinned. 'Good point, Daisy. I'd better come too.'

'Also, I want to check out Gabe's holly bushes for my Christmas wreaths,' pronounced Daisy, in blithe contradiction of her first point. 'Our first deliveries are on December 1st Auntie-dear.' She grinned.

'As promised,' said Laurel serenely.

'Can I come and see the pony?' asked Zuzanna, who was quieter than her friends, so that Grady often overlooked her.

'Then I'd better come, too,' said Niall, with the air of one doing them all a favour, rather than simply not wanting to be left out.

It was a small group who called their goodbyes and exited into the frozen morning for the short walk to Gabe's place. The teens led the expedition and Grady, to his satisfaction, found himself beside Laurel on the narrow village pavement. She pulled on a black bobble hat and he wished he had one like it to stop the icy wind bouncing from his thumping forehead. 'You look like a cute elf. Perhaps you could help Santa.'

She snorted. 'Daisy's getting me enough jobs as it is.' She studied him. 'Feeling grim?'

'Yeah. Hangovers suck. Thanks again for last night,' he added.

She shrugged and smiled. They'd walked past the cramped old cottages of Rotten Row and were crossing Main Road. As they passed his spray shop he automatically glanced over to ensure the doors were safely secured. While distracted, he found himself stepping onto a frozen puddle, which promptly cracked. 'Jeez, the state of Gabe's track,' he complained, as ice water oozed towards the top of his Vans.

Laurel, in leather ankle boots, had swerved to one edge of the track to pick her way along tufts of grass. 'The kids, of course, just hurtle into it.' Daisy and Zuzanna, hanging on to Niall's arms, began shrieking as they slithered about.

Their laughter made Grady smile. 'We were the same at their age. I seem to remember a girl who fell off the log over the stream and cried with laughter when she soaked us both.'

Laurel's mouth curved into a smile that told him she remembered, too.

'Teenagers have the ability to bounce back,' Grady went on, opting to follow her example, discovering that the edges of the track were less slippery than the middle but you ran the risk of getting spiky hawthorn twigs in your face.

'Not from everything,' Laurel said quietly.

Grady, thinking of the death of Laurel's mum and the bullying he'd only just found out about, wished he'd thought before he'd spoken. But then they rounded the curve and saw Gabe and Uncle Bertie huddling into their coats at the paddock gate. The two men faced each other, white beard and silver ponytail ruffled by the wind. Daybreak, the pale grey pony who was now sporting a smart navy turnout rug, stood beside Bertie. Snobby pressed his black head to Gabe's arm. It was as if the two animals were taking sides.

But Laurel muttered, 'Uh-oh. Looks as if we're interrupting an argument.' She raised her voice. 'Daisy? Maybe we should—'

Daisy blithely motored on, grinning and waving, while Zuzanna called, 'Hiya! We've come to see the new pony.' Laurel and Grady had little choice but to join the group.

Laurel said to Gabe and Bertie apologetically, 'We've barged into your Sunday morning.'

'Laurel can ride,' Daisy said to Gabe, as if Laurel hadn't spoken. 'She could exercise Dave for you.'

'The pony is called *Daybreak*,' Gabe snapped. Grady felt his eyebrows lift. He didn't think he'd ever heard Gabe snap at anyone. Then Gabe collected himself and smiled – first at Daisy, then at Laurel. 'Do you ride? Daybreak's not a geriatric, like Snobby. She needs exercise several times a week. We were just—' he treated his uncle to a hard stare '—*discussing* it.'

'You put her on that long rein,' Uncle Bertie put in pugnaciously.

Gabe closed his eyes in a 'give me strength' expression before he spoke again. 'She's young. She needs to be ridden. She needs exercise and schooling.'

'You could have her pull your pony trap.' Uncle Bertie's beard jutted.

'She's never been driven,' Gabe explained with overdone patience. 'It's bloody criminal that someone would stuff her in the auction and leave her to be bought by a codger like you who knows bugger-all about horses. She's obviously been stabled because she hasn't even got a good winter coat.'

Bertie smirked. 'You've bought her a coat.'

'I've bought her a *rug* because you're so irresponsible,' Gabe said, emphasising the correct terminology. 'You're clueless about feeding or grooming or mucking out the field shelter – which Snobby doesn't want to share, incidentally, so he bares his teeth at her when she tries to get out of the wind and rain. You don't even have somewhere to keep her when you take her home. You're a bloody silly old sod, Bertie,' he added with exasperated affection.

Defence faltering, Uncle Bertie looked down at his wellies. 'I didn't buy her to take her home. She's company for Snobby.'

Laurel said, uneasily, 'I haven't ridden for years. I have no riding boots or helmet.' She stepped closer to Daybreak, who threw up her head and pranced coquettishly.

'Zuzanna's mum used to ride but gave up because of her bad back. You'd be able to borrow her gear,' Daisy volunteered.

Laurel's eyes widened. 'Oh, I don't think—'

Grady hid a smile because Zuzanna was already holding her phone to her ear. In seconds he heard her say, 'Hi,

Mum. Can Daisy's auntie Laurel borrow your riding hat and boots? OK, I'll come get them, thanks.'

Zuzanna looked pleased with herself as she slid her phone away. 'Mum says you can have them. She won't ride anymore.'

'I don't even know what size she wears,' Laurel protested, not looking particularly grateful.

'About the same as you. It'll be fine,' Daisy said breezily. She turned to Gabe and Bertie, both of whom were wearing hopeful expressions. 'Where's her saddle and stuff?'

Grady murmured into Laurel's ear. 'You'd be doing a good turn but I'll make my voice loud and stop this, if you want.'

She turned to gaze at him with those big blue eyes. 'I can make my voice loud and stop it myself, but it would disappoint them all.'

'Especially the pony.' He watched the teenagers take turns in giving Daybreak their empty palms to snuffle.

Despite her evident misgivings, half an hour later Laurel was mounting Daybreak from the gate, Grady at the pony's head and holding the stirrup. The hard hat had a chin strap and short peak, suiting her as well as the bobble hat had. Once up, she stooped to check the girth, gathered up her reins and stroked Daybreak's neck. 'Let her go.'

As Gabe's hand released the bridle it was as if someone had fired a starter's pistol. Daybreak whirled on the spot, narrowly missing Gabe's knee with a flying hoof, threw up her head and, with a series of snorts, bucked and propped her way across the paddock.

'Eek,' breathed Daisy, eyes enormous. Zuzanna slapped her hand across her mouth.

Laurel's firm voice floated back to them. 'Stop it,

Daybreak.' She sat her bum down into the saddle, kept her hands low and refused to give the pony her head. With a last buck, Daybreak arched her neck and tripped into a neat trot as if that's what she'd always meant to do, mane and tail streaming like ghostly banners.

'Dave looks wonderful,' Bertie marvelled, beaming, elbows on the gate.

Grady thought Laurel looked wonderful, too, as he watched her first few circuits, taken back to those long-ago dawns on the Carlysle Estate when he'd watched while Laurel stole rides on a different under-exercised pony. Then horse and rider broke into a flowing canter down the long side of the paddock, reined back to trot again along the short side, and cantered the long side again, passing the gate in a thunder of flying hooves and clods of mud. Snobby watched, ears pricked, wearing an aghast expression behind his unruly forelock.

Over the next half-hour, Laurel rode figures of eight and put Daybreak through her paces. Then she returned to the gate, the pony's breath clouding on the cold air. 'I'll walk her to cool her down, OK?'

Gabe rested his hand on the gate bolt. 'Hack her round the bridleways. More interesting for you both than the paddock.'

'Yes!' the three teens clamoured instantly. 'We can all go together. It'll be sick.'

'Sick?' demanded Gabe, looking mystified.

'They mean "great",' Grady supplied with a grin.

'Well, OK,' Laurel agreed. 'Daisy, you and your friends need to walk in front though. If you get behind Daybreak she might kick. We'll go down Little Lane to join the footpath, follow the stream to the ford then come back down Main Road.'

Gabe and Bertie waved them off, making for Gabe's house and, if they had any sense, a nice warm drink.

By the time Daybreak's hoofs had clopped past the first couple of houses in Little Lane, Daisy, Niall and Zuzanna were shivering. 'Our feet are frozen. We'll go back to our house,' Daisy said. 'See you there, Laurel.' And they went chattering back to Main Road as if the idea of a hack had had nothing to do with them.

So it was just Laurel on a now sweetly sauntering Daybreak and Grady, hands stuffed in pockets, striding by her stirrup. They turned left off Little Lane with the stream to their right, swollen and muddy, the tree lying across it that had been a bridge for as long as Grady could remember.

Laurel reined in to gaze at the lichened bark of the tree she'd once fallen from. 'I'm amazed it hasn't rotted away.'

'I suppose it will, one day.' The thought made Grady's mood dip. It underlined how fast life could pass. Maybe it was that which made him say, 'I'm sorry you felt you had to leave as soon as my brother walked in, last night.'

She patted Daybreak's neck, saying, 'Good girl,' as if giving herself time to think before answering, 'Not *as soon* as.'

He glanced up at her, though it meant looking into the harsh winter light, which sent pain shooting through his eyeballs. 'OK. You went quiet, then left as soon as you could gulp your drink.'

'Sorry,' she murmured.

He made his voice soft. 'I understand your old antipathies. I've challenged Mac about Poison Amie and I think he feels guilty he did nothing to stop her.'

'Childish of me to still not take to him, huh? It's no reflection on you.' She gazed down into his eyes. 'It was never anything to do with you but I handled things badly.'

140

With a gentle kick she set Daybreak walking along the footpath once more. Tiny, whirling flakes of snow began to fall, making the pony shake her head and snort.

Grady changed the subject, suddenly wanting to enjoy this time with Laurel while the snowflakes shrouded them from the rest of the world. 'Got your studio set up, yet?'

'Ready to go,' she confirmed, a note of enthusiasm creeping into her voice. 'I know what my next subject is and I'll soon start preliminary sketches. I'm feeling antsy after taking the break while I moved here. I made a bargain with myself that I'd give loads of time to Rea and Daisy this weekend, then dive in on Monday.'

He pulled up his collar. 'Can I see your studio sometime?' The snow was beginning to find crevices to settle into, white veins on the packed earth of the bridleway. His feet were so cold he felt as if he were stumbling along on two blocks of ice.

'Sure.' They reached the ford and she clucked encouragingly at Daybreak, who wanted to stop and snort at the water even though they weren't going through it. 'Come whenever. But maybe not Monday. I so need to feel a pencil or a brush in my hand.'

'I'll give you a few days to wallow.' Grady strode beside her and the pretty grey pony, chatting about sketches and projects until they were back on Gabe's track. When she saw the paddock gate, Daybreak tossed her head and whickered happily.

Snow settling on his shoulders, Gabe stood at the gate, talking to Snobby, who eyed Daybreak suspiciously. 'I'll take her from here,' Gabe called. 'Thanks a lot, Laurel. Hope you haven't frozen to death but you've taken a weight off my mind. I don't suppose you'd want to exercise her regularly?'

Laurel dismounted, patting Daybreak's neck to thank her for the ride. 'I'm not sure I can.' She gave Gabe an apologetic look. 'I have to start a new project. If you haven't found anyone else by next weekend though I could probably give her another hour then, depending on what Daisy and my sister are doing.'

Gabe's face fell, but he said, 'I understand.' He loosened Daybreak's girth and removed her saddle, balancing it on top of the gate, gave the pony's back a rub and tossed her rug into place. He took the reins from Laurel's hand and glanced around at the house as if checking they wouldn't be overheard. 'I've no idea why my uncle bought her. He's bonkers.'

Laurel removed her riding hat and rubbed her fingers through her hair, shivering as snow landed on her unprotected head. 'Maybe he thought it was the thing to do, as he was coming to live in the country?'

'But he's not even sure that he's staying,' Gabe protested. 'I offered, because he complains about his bungalow, but he's missing his grandkids and lunching with his mates.' He thanked her again and Grady held the gate so Gabe could lead Daybreak through.

They said their farewells and turned back down the track, Laurel wisely wearing the riding boots she'd just inherited and carrying the ones she'd arrived in. She seemed relaxed and happy. Grady decided to capitalise. 'Fancy a meal at The Three Fishes one evening? Check the place out for yourself?'

She frowned hesitantly, her boots cracking an icy puddle. Then, just when he thought she was going to make an excuse, she said, 'OK. Sounds nice.' But then she added, 'If I'm doing this Craft Stuff session on Wednesday evening we can go after.'

Right. The session would end at nine and people would probably try and keep Laurel talking. By the time they got to The Three Fishes it would be eat-and-run. Then a happy thought struck him. 'It's Tonya's birthday so we're going out for a family meal that night. Another night?' He kept his tone casual, striding from tussock to tussock along the track edge.

The hesitation was longer this time. Then she said. 'Thursday? I'll meet you there.'

Easily, he answered, 'Great.' If she wanted to set the pace, if she didn't want him to call at her house and escort her across Main Road to the pub, fine. Whatever made her comfortable.

She shivered and pulled out her black elf hat again. 'Snow's lovely when you're dressed for it but I'm going home for a hot bath so I'm not stiff tomorrow after such a long time out of the saddle.'

'A hot bath sounds pretty good to me, too. Get rid of the last of the headache. See you later.' He waved goodbye and crossed Main Road, heart considerably lighter than when he'd woken up in hangover hell this morning, assailed by the memory of Pippa's stunt last night. Laurel had agreed to go out with him. He'd kept the invitation casual and it had paid off.

He turned the corner into Ladies Lane and spotted his sister-in-law coming towards him, pink and blonde hair mostly tucked under a hood. 'Hey,' he called. He had a lot of time for Mac's feisty wife.

'Hey,' she replied, beaming. 'I'm going to the shop. Got no wine in the house.' She glanced down at his wet foot-wear. 'You, too? Niall's just turned up soaked and frozen.' Her hood blew back and she yanked it on again. She paused, gazing thoughtfully at the cottages on the other side of the street. Thin veils of snow were beginning to cling to the rooftops. 'I don't suppose there's any point asking you if there was more to that night when Mac was pantsed than I was told?'

Grady laughed ruefully, remembering her astonished confusion. 'Are you still worried about it? It was only a prank . . . though it wasn't hysterically funny at the time.' He remembered the miserable discomfort of huddling into his hoodie at the side of the road in the snow.

'I wouldn't say worried,' she replied. 'But . . . Mac was odd about it. Niall seems to think you and Mac already knew Daisy's aunt but Mac acted as if she were some stranger.'

Grady grew uncomfortable, both at Tonya's question and at his damp, frozen feet. If Mac had chosen to pretend not to recognise Laurel because he didn't want his wife to know his teenage girlfriend bullied her and Mac didn't stop it, he sure as hell wasn't going to enlighten her.

Tonya's gaze swivelled to his face. 'I get the impression Mac once had the big hots for her.'

Gently, Grady explained, 'Erm . . . *I* was seeing Laurel,' certain she'd hear the unspoken, *so Mac wouldn't have felt that way.*

His certainty proved misplaced. Though Tonya grinned, she didn't look entirely convinced. 'Mac would do almost anything for you but that doesn't extend to choosing who he fancied. He'd probably have hidden it from you if he did have feelings for her,' she allowed.

Tonya was family so Grady felt free to take the liberty of slipping his arm around her and giving her a friendly squeeze. 'Tonya Cassidy, even if you're right and I'm wrong and Mac did once fancy Laurel, I am absolutely certain that the only woman he fancies now is you. *Absolutely*,' he repeated for effect. 'He loves you to bits.'

She smiled and blushed. 'I think your Irish ancestry's coming out. You've been kissing the Blarney stone.'

'Mixed Irish and Scots,' he reminded her, letting her go. 'I'm going to learn the bagpipes next.'

It was too cold to hang around chatting in the snow, so Grady was glad to feel as if Tonya's concerns had been put to rest and he could say goodbye and hurry home, keen to warm up. Had Mac ever had the 'big hots' for Laurel? Should Grady ask him? He didn't think so. Better to leave it filed under 'that was then' and just get on with 'now'.

No way would he ask Laurel. That would really scare her off. His feet slowed, though Mistletoe Cottage was now in sight, with its promise of coffee and a hot bath.

Scare her off . . .?

Was Laurel scared of something? He pondered. If so, what? Being stuck in the village? Her sister never improving?

Last night he'd had what amounted to an emotional meltdown when compared to his usual comfortable calm. She'd been collected, compassionate and wise. Yet so much of the time she was wary, like a rescue animal encountering kindness but not entirely sure it would continue.

He could only assume it was that bloody bullying that had made her that way. He wished again that he'd known about it. He'd have stopped it, that was for sure.

Chapter Nine

Laurel, half-dressed, gazed through her bedroom window at the morning mist lying over fields covered in a thin layer of snow, thinking about yesterday, when she'd ridden Daybreak along the bridleway that was just out of sight. Rea had looked so pensive when she'd heard about Laurel's ride, as if counting just one more thing she couldn't do. Laurel had eulogised over the near solitude of rider and horse – OK, and Grady – but after saying, 'I used to enjoy riding lessons,' Rea had changed the subject.

'Are you still going to do it?' came Daisy's voice. Laurel spun around. Daisy's head was protruding into Laurel's room, the rest of her still on the landing. She came all the way in and whispered, 'Are you going to talk to Mr Williams?'

Laurel drew her down to sit on the edge of her unmade bed, noting Daisy's wide, apprehensive eyes. 'That's my plan. Unless you're having second thoughts?' She'd had one herself but didn't want to spook Daisy with it just yet.

Daisy ran her finger along a pleat in Laurel's duvet.

'No, I want you to talk to him. Only, when you came back yesterday you were arsey and said I had to stop finding you jobs.' Her voice was high and strained.

'Oh, Daisy!' Laurel pulled the young girl into her arms. 'I'm not sure it's "arsey" to ask you not to tell Gabe I'd exercise his horse without checking with me first. Of course I'm still going to ring Mr Williams. Sorry if I worried you.'

Daisy pressed her face to Laurel's shoulder, muffling her voice. 'Can I stay away from school today?'

Laurel's first instinct was to say, 'Yes! I'll slaughter the dragon that's been spoiling your life before you go back.' What she actually said was, 'That's up to your mum, and as you'd have to come up with a plausible excuse, and it might worry her, *I* think it might be better to carry on as usual. Let the school deal with it.'

Daisy didn't lift her head. 'I've got art this morning. What am I going to say to them about the money they're asking for? Scarlett sent another text this morning.' Red-faced, she showed Laurel a text. *Don't forget the tenners today.*

Laurel stroked Daisy's soft hair, her heart aching at how easy these kids seemed to find it to make another child unhappy. 'I'll call the school first thing, OK? If you have to talk to Scarlett and Octavia, just say you haven't got any money at the moment.' She paused, feeling she'd been pitched into the deep end when it came to dealing with teenage issues. 'Or . . . I suppose I could drive you and we could go into school together?'

Daisy sat up, wiping her cheek on her sleeve. 'You'd only get as far as reception.' But she sounded half-hopeful.

'I could take you into reception with me and tell them what the problem is.' Laurel began to gain confidence.

'We'll tell your mum that I'm driving you into school again. You can get all sulky about it like you did before,' she added, as if bestowing a treat.

Daisy managed a giggle. ''Kay. Deal.' She threw her arms around Laurel. 'You're cool, Auntie Laurel.'

Laurel gave her a final hug. 'Just don't expect me to keep secrets from your mum in future. This is a once-only deal because of exceptional circumstances, and purely for her benefit.'

They drove to Bettsbrough after a breakfast Daisy had largely pushed around her plate. Once in Laurel's passenger seat, her tapping toes and clenched hands indicated her tension. Yesterday, Laurel had been lulled into unconsciously downgrading Daisy's crisis, though she'd known a conversation with Mr Williams lay ahead. Now, as she left behind the last of the lampposts bedecked with Christmas lights, she knew she was not going to allow her niece to be intimidated for another moment.

They parked a street away from Sir John Browne Academy. The dashboard clock showed eight-fifteen. Laurel said, 'School starts at eight-thirty, right? Let's hang on a few minutes.' She didn't want Daisy's pallor or the presence of an adult to alert Scarlett and Octavia to what was heading their way. Students straggled past on foot, coats above black trousers or skirts, backpacks over shoulders.

When ten minutes had passed Laurel said brightly, 'Right, let's go.' They left the car and walked together to the next street and up to the square-built green school buildings, through the gate in the black metal railings to a door signposted 'Reception'.

'When we came to this school, this was the entrance to the new block.' Laurel hoped her chatter would distract

Daisy. 'But it can't be the new block now because there's a newer block.'

Daisy made no reply.

They followed an arrow along a broad white corridor to where a woman sat at a glass partition, presently open so she could deal with a parent demanding an instant search of the school for his son's training shoes. 'Forty bloody quid, even off the market,' he grumbled. 'Within a week some tea leaf's had them off him.'

The woman, whose name badge read 'Mrs E Jordan', informed the disgruntled man of lost property protocol and dispatched him. Then she smiled at Laurel and Daisy and said, 'Hello. How can I help you?'

Laurel introduced herself and explained her relationship to Daisy. 'As my sister's unable to come to school I'm Daisy's second contact. I have immediate concerns about bullying. Her form teacher is Mr Williams.'

Mrs Jordan smiled again. 'You didn't need to come into school, Miss Hill. You can make an appointment by phone or through Daisy's student planner or parent portal.' She turned her smile on Daisy. 'You won't have registered for first lesson, will you? What is it? I'll let the teacher know where you are.' In the office behind her, a younger woman worked at a keyboard. A person was doing something to one side, a man, judging from the grey jacket sleeve and one black shoe Laurel could see.

'Miss McLaren, art,' Daisy murmured.

The corridor was hot and stuffy and Laurel removed her coat. 'I'm afraid the art class is the problem. My niece won't be joining it until I've spoken to someone about the bullying she's being subjected to.'

'I can make you an appointment—'

Laurel pretended Mrs Jordan hadn't spoken. 'I'll take

149

a seat until Mr Williams can see me.' She indicated four seats against the wall.

Mrs Jordan eyed her unfavourably. 'I'll send Mr Williams a message.'

Then Mac Cassidy stepped into view, showing himself to be the owner of the grey sleeve and black shoe. 'Hello, Daisy. Hi, Laurel.'

Just who Laurel didn't want to see. 'Hello,' she answered colourlessly.

Mrs Jordan turned to him with an air of relief. 'I was just offering to make an appointment.'

Mac nodded. His eyes were wary, despite his smile. 'I should think Daisy could go to her lesson while we see what we can sort out.'

'Afraid not.' Laurel didn't smile. 'Bullying is unacceptable. I'm sorry not to fall in with school processes but Daisy's not attending that class until the situation's resolved.' She felt a surge of power.

After a moment, Mac addressed Mrs Jordan. 'What does Mr Williams' timetable say?' Mrs Jordan tapped her keyboard, then turned her screen so Mac could view it. 'Planning time.' He turned back to Laurel and the mute Daisy. 'Just let me see if I can have a word with Mr Williams.'

'Of course. We'll wait.'

After signing the visitors' book, Laurel headed for the seating area, Daisy by her side. Laurel would have liked to take her hand reassuringly but knew it would destroy Daisy's cred if any student were to witness a four-teen-year-old holding hands with her auntie. Mrs Jordan closed her glass screen and all fell quiet apart from faint voices drifting from elsewhere in the school. Both Laurel and Daisy took out their phones to while away the time.

Ten minutes later, Daisy whispered, 'Here's Mr Williams.'

Laurel looked up from a WhatsApp conversation between the artists at her old studios in Chiswick to see a thin, angular man in his forties loping towards them, clothes conservative, brown hair in no particular style. 'Hello, Daisy,' he said, as he reached them. 'Miss Hill? I'm Mr Williams, Daisy's form tutor. I wasn't teaching and there's a room available, if you'd like a chat.' His smile was boyish.

Laurel felt instinctively that he could be trusted. With real gratitude she said, 'Thank you very much.'

He took them to a small room with scuffed white walls, a big window, a table and chairs. 'Take a seat, take a seat. Now, how can I help you?'

Laurel did take Daisy's hand then, feeling suddenly inadequate and unpractised at standing in as a fourteen-year-old's significant adult. She cleared her throat. 'I know you're aware Daisy's been avoiding art classes. She confided in me at the weekend and I'm here to help her explain and see the situation's resolved. Unfortunately, it concerns her mum – my sister, Rea Grove – and it's important Rea should be protected.'

The next half-hour passed quickly. Mr Williams' smile vanished when he heard Daisy's hesitant, half-tearful account of events. He listened and cast no doubt on her story. He asked questions and expressed empathy. His eyebrows formed an uncompromising line as he read the texts and murmured in wintry tones, 'The sender wants Daisy aware of her identity but doesn't consider possible consequences.' He smiled. 'Don't worry. We'll clear this up.' He continued to gently go over the story with Daisy while Laurel listened, gaining respect for this kind, unassuming man. Scarlett seemed the ringleader, which chimed

151

in with her being the one to send the messages. He talked about Daisy's support network – her village friends – and asked, if it could be managed, whether Daisy would be open to moving to another art class? Yes, Daisy would.

He launched into a little speech about encouraging positive behaviours, commitment to the personal and social development of every young person in the school's care, and providing an environment in which girls could grow in confidence and self-esteem. 'We pride ourselves on our students knowing there's always someone on hand to listen to their concerns, but I do see why you felt unable to talk to us on this occasion, Daisy. You love your mum, right?'

Tears quivered on Daisy's lower lids as she nodded.

After another round of 'don't worries' and 'we can deal with its' he said, 'You've been brave in asking your aunt for help. It was the right thing to do. Do you think you'll be OK to go into second lesson? Yes? You've got a few minutes in hand if you want to visit the loo on the way. Off you go then. I'll see you later.'

Laurel rose to give Daisy a big hug. 'OK?'

Daisy looked a hundred per cent happier. 'Yep. See yers.' A last sniff and she swung her backpack over one shoulder and coat over the other, then left.

Mr Williams checked his watch. 'I'm teaching next lesson but I have a short time if you have any last questions?'

Laurel returned to her seat. 'One concern I haven't shared with Daisy. What's to stop these girls blabbing about my sister's anxiety attack now? It's what they've held over Daisy's head all along.'

He gave another of those wintry smiles. 'We're well equipped for nipping such things in the bud, Miss Hill. After all, if any of us hear the story, it will be obvious where it has come from. I'll be making that plain to the two individuals in question.' He twiddled a pen between his fingers and it caught the winter sunlight streaming through the window. 'We also have PSHE lessons – personal, social, health and economic education,' he added, when she regarded him blankly. 'We're free to address the topics most relevant to our pupils. I shall be talking about relationships with fellow students and acceptable social behaviour. Not for the first or last time.'

Laurel rose to leave. Awkwardly, she said, 'Thank you. I won't be asking you to leave my sister out of the loop ordinarily. It's just . . .'

'I understand the sensitivities in this situation.' Mr Williams walked her back to reception for her to sign out in the visitor's book before he hurried off to teach.

Laurel drove home feeling as light as air, convinced Mr Williams had everything sorted. Maybe she wouldn't have been too awful at the parenting lark. Her happiness dimmed as she acknowledged she'd never have the opportunity.

At least she had a share in Daisy while she was in Middledip, though.

Her car ate up the miles and soon she was swinging into Great End. Through Rea's office window she could see her, headset on, lips moving, looking up to wave at Laurel without faltering.

Laurel went indoors only long enough to grab her paint-daubed overshirt, then, her mind clear of other responsibilities for the moment, she ran up the path to the studio. Inside, she hung up her coat, turned on the heaters and breathed in the smell of paper and new canvas. She grabbed the A3 pad just waiting for her first pencil strokes and switched on her big Mac Pro to search for videos of willowy ballerinas and sinuous Latin dancers.

A pencil jumped into her hand and began to swoop across the paper as she experimented with female figures, upflung arms and trailing legs, thinking of colours and flowers and shapes.

Later, she set up a paint palette to her preference: warm colours, cold colours and finally neutrals. Paper would do for now. It would be a while before she was ready to begin on the kind of large canvas she liked to use for her bold-statement works.

She began playing around with colours for the hair – burnt sienna, ultramarine, yellow oxide for a streaky impression, then flowers of aqua and white. Perhaps the dress could be aqua, too . . . She thought of sea foam and breaking waves on a sunny day in winter.

She worked on, absorbed, humming beneath her breath, until Daisy burst in, face pink, hair flying. She gabbled, 'Scarlett and Octavia have been excluded for the rest of the week and I'm moving into the other art class where Zuzanna and Niall are.'

And Laurel fell back to earth realising, in quick succession, that it was almost four o'clock, she hadn't eaten lunch and she was starving. In Chiswick, she would have worked on into the evening if she'd felt like it with just a few rueful texts from Alex about eating alone to contend with. For an instant she felt like snapping, 'What the hell, Daisy! I'm working.'

But . . . this absence of ceremony, lack of privacy, came with the territory of living and working here. With family.

Daisy was obviously waiting for the big news to be exclaimed over. Laying down her brush, Laurel gave her niece her full attention. 'Wow, that was a prompt result. How do you feel about it?'

Daisy stooped and gave Laurel a huge hug, her ponytail

dangling perilously close to the paint palette. 'So relieved. Thank you, Auntie Laurel. You've made everything right.' Then Daisy's face crumpled and she burst into noisy tears. 'S-sorry, I am relieved, honest. It's just—'

'Relief,' Laurel finished for her. All irritation at being interrupted forgotten, she cuddled Daisy until the tears dried. Then she let the soft, adolescent body pull away, saying, 'You'd better stay for a bit so Rea doesn't see your red eyes.' She texted her sister: *Daisy in studio with me xx*

She looked up to see Daisy examining Laurel's sketchpad. 'You're so cool,' she breathed. 'Figure drawing's well hard.'

'It takes practice,' Laurel agreed. She turned to a fresh sheet on her pad and began going over figure drawing technique, starting with a vertical line divided into eight equal segments.

'I like to begin with the two parts of the torso but it might be easier to think first of the head. We measure all the body in terms of the head. See, shoulders are two head-heights wide.' She dashed in a just-off-horizontal line. 'The crotch comes at the halfway point.' Another line. 'Knees come around the top of the second segment. Decide where the person's looking and find the centre line of the face, centre of the body, so we know where the rib cage arch is.' Swiftly, a stick person appeared on her paper, leaning one elbow on something, head and shoulders slightly cocked towards the dancing girl. 'I like to know which is the supporting leg and get it under the centre.' As Laurel indicated knees, hands and feet with ovals, and sketched in a square jaw and broad chest, she realised she was drawing a man who was watching the dancing woman. His body language was relaxed but focused.

That was what her picture had been missing – someone

155

to admire the dancing woman. She paused. Was he admiring the woman? Or the dance? Something to think about.

Laurel went to her room before dinner for some alone time, emotional from the unaccustomed experience of supporting Daisy, feeling an uneasy mixture of relief at Daisy's smile and guilt at sneaking behind Rea's back.

Discarding her paint-daubed clothes she caught her reflection in the mirror, blue bra clashing merrily with green pants. She paused to consider, dispassionately, how she'd draw her own little frame rather than the more willowy woman of today's sketches. Her top-heaviness was not the classic dancer's proportions of those she'd been watching on YouTube. But ordinary women also danced, women with significant breasts, apple or pear body types and extra chins, didn't they? Why *should* she be studying only professional dancers?

She'd hate to be guilty of making all women think they should possess ballerina bodies.

The subject of her new painting could be a woman whose hips didn't balance out her bust and whose legs could use a couple more inches. Experimentally, she half-turned, throwing up her arms and studying her reflection over one shoulder, noting the crease at her waist, the elliptical shape of her breasts. Then she thrust an arm behind her. Turning up her face, she checked out the mirror again through the corner of her eye. That was an interesting pose. It took a mental effort to hold it because her boobs were thrust out, rather than hidden by loose clothing. Loose clothing had always been her protection against those who thought it was OK to stare. She was fine with men liking big boobs, but not the leering.

She straightened up and studied her body in the mismatching underwear.

Alex definitely used to be a fan of her shape . . . until she stopped attracting him. She missed being desired. Her new painting would be of a woman enjoying being exactly who she was and dancing for the hell of it; the watching man would sexually desire that flawed everyday woman without caring whether her body could make babies. The theme would be: *this woman's not perfect but that's fine.*

'Laurel?' Rea's voice came from just outside the door, startling Laurel into opening it without pulling on her clothes. Rea took a step inside. 'Daisy fancies takeaway. Blimey, you got the boobs for both of us, didn't you?' She gestured at Laurel's overflowing bra.

Yanking open the nearest drawer, Laurel found a clean top to pull on. 'Takeaway's fine by me.' She wished the boob remark, even from her sister, didn't prompt her to instantly hide her body.

Rea checked behind her, then quietly closed the door. Her smile faded, leaving her usual tired, anxious expression. 'I looked into referring myself to an NHS psychological therapies service. I'm waiting to hear from them. And I've registered for some webinars on managing worry and stress.'

Instantly, Laurel forgot her bra size and gave Rea an enthusiastic hug. 'Wow. Good for you! I'm so pleased and proud. Are you going to tell Daisy?'

Rea nodded, but also grimaced. 'It makes it harder for me to back out and I want to do it for her sake. She's too young to shoulder my difficulties or, even worse in a way, have her freedom affected by my fears. I'll talk to her after dinner when she's finished her homework.'

Laurel gave Rea's slight frame a fresh squeeze. 'I think

she'll be delighted you're trying to break out. How about you leave me to clear up after the takeaway dinner while you take her off to the sitting room?'

Though she returned the hug and agreed, Rea sighed. 'I need to get it through to her that there's no instant cure. I've heard people like me called a "shut-in". The longer it goes on, the harder breaking out seems.'

'Remember that if you ever want me to go somewhere with you, I'll come, even if I'm painting at the time,' Laurel promised rashly, though she could feel her artist-self send her a death glare.

'Aw, thanks, kid,' said Rea, using the affectionate term from their teen years.

They all relaxed over takeaway, teasing each other as they sneaked the last spare rib or more than their share of prawn crackers. Daisy had ditched her school uniform and was wearing a purple sweatshirt with *Don't think you can ctrl + alt + del me* on the front. Laurel got Cobra Beers from the fridge for her and Rea, and Daisy was allowed a weak shandy. Laurel enjoyed the lift of mood in the household, even though Rea became progressively quieter as the meal progressed, no doubt because her planned conversation with Daisy drew near.

When the meal was finally over, Rea tugged Daisy's long hair and murmured, 'Can we have a chat? Let's go in the sitting room.' Laurel was happy to undertake the hand washing of foil containers that Rea would use at least once more before recycling, stacking cutlery and glasses in the dishwasher, mind returning pleasurably to her *Everyday Woman* painting.

Just as she'd selected a pod for the coffee machine, her phone rang and she saw it was Alex calling. She grabbed a favourite mug, pale green and iridescent, and answered while slotting the pod into the machine. 'Hiya.'

Alex's softly spoken voice filled her ears. 'Hi. Is now an OK time? I just want to check you're all right. You've been away more than a week.' He gave a short, self-conscious laugh. 'We didn't talk about how we're going to do this. Stay in touch, I mean.'

'It's nice of you to even think of it,' she said, realising, guiltily, that she hadn't had the same thought. She pictured him at home in the blue terraced house they'd shared, the blue Alex used to say matched her eyes, his thick brown hair that seemed to want to grow straight up, his glasses glinting. 'How's everything?'

'OK. How about you?'

'OK, thanks.' She laughed. 'That was a short conversation.' Her coffee was ready so she took it over to the kitchen table.

He laughed, too, then relaxed and told her that the regeneration project he'd been working on for the past couple of years had hit a snag. Alex worked as a project manager on big building sites and snags happened. Water where it shouldn't be or not where it should be. Digging up a plague pit. Archaeologists taking over. Although it was nice to hear his voice, the details flowed over her head.

She blew on her coffee and waited for a chance to turn the conversation. 'And Vonnie?' she asked, when the snag story reached its natural end.

'Yeah, she's good,' he said. After a moment, he added, 'You've not had time to meet someone in the ten days you've been gone.'

Maybe nettled by this being phrased as a statement rather than a question, she answered, 'I'm having a meal with someone, later in the week.'

159

'Oh.' Alex halted.

Laurel tried to analyse that 'oh'. Surprise? Discomfort? Or did he simply not know how to have this conversation?

'An old friend or a new one?' he asked, at length.

'Old, though we went to different schools,' she said, before remembering how aware he was of her history and realising what conclusion he'd leap to. The correct one.

Sure enough, Alex's voice climbed, crisp and shocked. 'Not the brother of the guy who . . .?'

'Grady, yes,' she acknowledged defensively. 'He wasn't responsible for his brother, then or now.'

Alex sounded worried. 'But what's it churning up inside your head, Laurel? What if it brings you back in contact with the brother? Will you cope? I know how fragile you can be.'

'Since when?' she demanded hotly, and almost knocked her coffee over as she jerked upright in the chair. 'I would have thought you'd seen me go through enough to know I'm sodding strong.'

He had the grace to sound sheepish. 'I suppose that's what I meant. You've had a hard time.'

'I admit the treatment and disappointments affected me,' she said, stiff with dismay that Alex, of all people, should write her off as 'fragile'. 'It's also true that being assaulted as a teenager left me with a wariness over personal safety. It made me reluctant to come back here – but I *am* here. Grady and Mac both live in the village and I'm dealing with that, not cracking up. Rea and Daisy need me more than I thought but I'm dealing with that, too.' She thought of the different Daisies she'd seen today: the desolate one going to school; the radiant one bursting into the studio; and the one who'd cried with relief in Laurel's arms.

Alex gave a little groan. 'Oh, Laurel. Don't get too caught up. What about the travelling you'd planned? You owe it to yourself—'

Her temper flared. 'The one person in the world I owe something to is Rea and, by extension, her lovely daughter. It's not up to you to judge my situation. We're not married anymore, Alex.'

Stiffly he replied, 'I see.' So polite. That was Alex's way. He hadn't appreciated her mini outburst, plainly, but didn't snap back.

She sighed. 'Sorry. That was snarky. But you began this conversation by asking how we're going to do this. Well, I vote we don't critique each other's choices.'

'You're right.' Now he sounded remorseful. Laurel knew exactly the small, wide-mouthed grimace he'd make as he called himself to account. 'It's just I know how it messed you up—'

'Alex,' she said, warningly.

It proved quite a short conversation. Short in length and short in temper. Odd, Laurel reflected, as she put away her phone. They'd gone through the deeply emotional trying-to-get-pregnant stuff together without a single cross word.

Chapter Ten

When Laurel stepped inside The Three Fishes she had to pause to absorb the sheer profusion of tiny white lights twinkling along every beam, around the pillars of the bar and in and out of the glasses above. The Christmas tree was smothered with them. They glimmered from behind the optics, turning whisky and brandy to glowing amber and Bombay Sapphire gin to a clear, luminous blue.

Grady's voice distracted Laurel from her admiration of Middledip's answer to Santa's pub. 'Hi, Laurel.'

She turned. 'Oh, hi. I was transfixed by the bling.' She was disconcerted to hear herself sounding breathless. It must be the icy evening air she'd breathed as she crossed the road from Great End. She unwound her scarf and slipped off her coat, glancing around. Nearby occupants of the small circular tables sent her genial smiles and Gabe and Bertie waved from stools set at the furthest point of the bar.

He grinned. 'The Three Fishes has been Christmas-bombed.' His hair, looking soft and freshly washed, curved into the collar of a dark shirt. 'Drink in the bar before we eat?' he suggested. 'You sit down. I grabbed us the window seat.'

'Thanks.' Attracted by the pretty Bombay Sapphire bottle, she asked for a gin and tonic and then crossed to the upholstered window seat and piled her coat on top of Grady's, smoothing her blue denim shirt and black jeans. She'd dried her foxy hair straight and glossy tonight and, for the first time since coming back to the village, she was wearing make-up.

Brenda, a sixty-something lady Laurel suddenly recognised from yesterday's Craft Stuff session called to her from another table. 'Thanks for last night. I've been to Bettsbrough and bought half the frames in the art shop. You made it look so easy to get a professional result. I'm just deciding which pictures to put in the fair and which in my window.'

'Glad you enjoyed the session,' Laurel called back as Grady arrived, her gin in one hand and a pint of something dark in the other.

He slid in beside her and smiled hello to Brenda. He took a long pull from his beer and licked the froth from his lips. 'We went out for Tonya's birthday meal to an Indian restaurant in Cambridge or Niall and I would have been at the session, too.'

'Sounds like a lovely family outing,' she commented, visualising a happy group wolfing down fragrant dishes and relaxing in each other's company. Teasing. Joking. Chatting. She felt a sudden nostalgia for the bars and restaurants in and around Park Royal and sighed. 'I'd love to encourage Rea to do something like it. Maybe just here, in the pub, with me and Daisy.' She studied the chattering, laughing clientele. Might Rea feel better at a table near the door? Or maybe the dining area would be more secluded? Constantly staying in sounded like hell to Laurel.

Grady's brow furrowed doubtfully. 'Do you think there's some prospect of that?'

'Not as yet,' she admitted, seeing the noisy pub suddenly through the eyes of someone who found busy places threatening, even if Rea would know half the people there. She remembered how she'd felt the first time she'd visited The Angel, conspicuous and a subject for gossip. Perhaps Rea felt like that all the time. 'I've been reading about supporting someone with agoraphobia but it's not easy. There's no "cookie-cutter" sufferer so the advice is all about listening and trying to understand. Learning her triggers.' She glanced at Grady, whose dark eyes were fixed on her as he listened. 'I've offered to go with her somewhere but she hasn't taken me up on it so I'm waiting for my moment to invite her somewhere specific, instead of leaving the ball in her court. It doesn't have to be a social situation like this. It could just be a walk.'

She lifted her glass to sip her drink, enjoying the fizz of the tonic and the smooth kiss of the gin. 'She is actually showing a will to change. I want to encourage that.' She didn't give him an account of Rea's distress. That had been a private moment between sisters. Laurel was so proud of Rea for the steps she'd already taken and Daisy had shed tears of hope. The psychological therapies service had acknowledged Rea's self-referral and she'd attended one webinar, which was available online without waiting to be accepted for a counselling programme. She'd chosen to participate in the webinar alone and said it had given her a lot to think about and was 'OK' and 'interesting'.

He nodded. Then, hesitantly, he said, 'Family support's

important. Mac always knew I was on his side, even in his turbulent teen years.'

'I know,' Laurel said stiffly.

He winced. 'Sorry, that sounded as if I wouldn't have supported you over the bullying . . .' He halted, plainly realising his statements to be contradictory.

She put down her glass. 'You see why I never could have told you? You can't be on both sides in a conflict. I'm just surprised that Mac needed support. I never thought of him as leaning on you. He was always hanging around with Jonny and Ruben.'

He shrugged. 'But I'm his brother. Jonny and Ruben went off to uni and never came back to live here.' Grady regarded her meditatively. Then he dropped his voice and leaned closer. Laurel could smell his shampoo. 'Even I didn't fully understand that Mac was ninety per cent bravado. Dad really put pressure on him.'

'How?' Laurel couldn't help asking, intrigued. She'd known Grady's father had been a grim-faced man. The family had lived in one of the older cottages on the edge of the village, marooned in its own plot beyond the ford, and she'd never minded that Grady had come to her house rather than her going to his. She'd presumed Mr Cassidy senior hadn't welcomed his sons' friends.

He shifted restlessly, screwing up his face as if his thoughts were uncomfortable. 'Dad was what's politely termed "traditional" or "patriarchal". Mum was lovely but she let him get away with laying down the law. He made his eldest son his focus.' His smile flashed. 'Dad's name was Cormac. "Mac" actually translates in Gaelic as "son" – did you know that? Mac's full name is Macormac Cassidy, or "son of Cormac Cassidy".'

'I know vaguely about the "mac" prefix on names like

165

MacDougal but I never gave any thought to your brother's full name.'

He laughed shortly then dropped his voice. 'I often wonder how Dad would have coped with my infertility. It's almost a relief that he's not around to know.' His mouth twisted.

Laurel watched the play of emotions across Grady's face, feeling his pain and sense of failure, and saw the exact moment he pushed those unpalatable thoughts away and pulled on his usual expression of friendly calm.

'So, anyway,' he went on. 'Dad exerted control over Number One Son. Mac had to battle not to have his life mapped out for him, from the subjects he took at school to which sports he played. Which sports he *watched* even. We'd be up in our room, playing on Sega, and Dad would drag him downstairs to watch Ireland play rugby on TV.'

Laurel cast her mind back. She hadn't seen much of Mr Cassidy, let alone the way he treated Mac. It was a novel idea that being 'Number One Son' might be a negative experience. 'And your dad was different with you?' she clarified.

Grady blew out his lips. 'Completely. Less was expected of Number Two Son. Sometimes it stung but mainly I was glad I didn't have to resist Dad's grooming, like Mac.'

She sat silently digesting this. 'So you're saying that's what made Mac abrasive?'

He hesitated. 'I'm saying it made him constantly on edge and expecting a fight. He's grown up into a nicer person. Don't you think?'

Laurel didn't want to think that. She ran through her encounters with him since she'd been back. Pantsed on a cold dark evening at the side of the road. Letting Rea, Daisy and Laurel know he'd talked to the police but wasn't out for the blood of the perpetrators. Dealing gravely with her and Daisy at school on Monday. Courteous throughout . . .

But overlaying it all was the memory of Mac pinning her arms behind her back while Amie pawed at her clothes and exposed her naked body to Mac and his laughing, crowing mates.

The fear.

The humiliation.

The shame.

As she couldn't express that without trampling on Grady's enduring love for Mac and opening up floodgates she'd successfully barricaded shut for nearly two decades, it was a relief to spot Bertie Piercy abandoning his stool beside Gabe at the bar and making a beeline for them

'Mind if I join you?' he puffed through his white beard. He pulled up a chair and plonked himself and his foaming glass of beer down. 'Gabe's angry with me so I thought I'd give him a few minutes.'

Laurel was happy to abandon her negative emotions around Mac Cassidy and let sympathy for Bertie creep into her heart. Bertie looked so down in the mouth . . . though she couldn't actually see much of his mouth with that beard.

'What's up?' she asked.

'Gabe can get angry?' Grady marvelled, at the same time. 'What have you done?' He showed no sign of impatience with the old guy for sitting down uninvited.

Bertie swigged his beer and licked the froth from his moustache, which made Laurel feel vaguely ill. 'He's cross with me for buying Dave.'

Grady laughed. 'Maybe if you gave the pony her more dignified name of "Daybreak" . . .?'

A smile stirred in the depths of the white forest that hid the lower half of Bertie's face. 'He doesn't think that's funny,' he conceded. 'I came clean and told him I'd bought Dave – Daybreak – for him, not to keep Snobby company. You see, I'm worried because Snobby won't last much longer. My plan was that if Gabe had Dave, he'd be able to cope with losing Snobby better.'

'Oh dear,' Laurel said gently. 'But Gabe's right that Daybreak probably isn't used to being driven and Gabe doesn't ride. Does Gabe even want to drive a pony again? Isn't he over seventy? The responsibility of a pony in all weathers – and the expense – might not be what he's looking for.'

Bertie winced and stroked the side of his head theatrically. 'That's what the ear-bashing was about. And that he knows Snobby will go and doesn't need me rubbing his nose in that.'

'Maybe there's someone in the village who'd love a free ride in exchange for looking after Daybreak,' Grady offered sympathetically.

'I said that.' Bertie raised his beer as if making an exclamation mark. Then turned to appeal to Laurel. 'Can't you do it, dear? You looked wonderful on her the other day.'

'Gabe's already asked.' She gave the wrinkled hand a pat. 'Maybe on the odd occasion but she needs a proper home with a stable, a full-time rider and lots of love.'

The beard twitched sadly. 'That's what Gabe says. And that now he's got to go through the heartache of finding that new home because I'm clueless.' He shook his head. 'Which is true when it comes to ponies. He won't put her back in the horse sale in case she doesn't get a good home and blew his stack when he discovered I'd actually bought her before she even went into the ring.'

'Outside trading at an auction?' Grady exclaimed, smile vanishing. 'That is pretty frowned upon, Bertie. It's not regulated.'

Bertie's white beard became ever more mobile and his words more clipped. 'So I've been made aware. Apparently I didn't use my brain and now Gabe has to get the vet up to see if she's microchipped so he can check her out online and sell her on in what he calls "a reputable manner".' He cast an injured look in Gabe's direction. Gabe was chatting to two other men and looking grim. 'My name's mud. I think he'd send me home if not for the lack of heat and light at my place.'

A woman behind the bar called over, 'Your table's ready, Grady.'

Grady raised a hand in acknowledgement. 'Thanks.'

Bertie drained his tankard. 'Think I'll go home to the doghouse. Goodnight, all.' He nodded in response to their answering goodnights and went to retrieve his coat from the hooks by the door.

Laurel said, 'Poor Bertie,' as she rose. Realising a need for the ladies' room, she told Grady she'd meet him at the table and headed off, winding her way between tables, exchanging smiles with Brenda and with Iris, who was seated further on.

In the ladies' loo, when she emerged to wash her hands, she found a woman leaning against the wall, arms folded and mouth set. With a spark of surprise, Laurel recognised Pippa, Grady's ex. Had she already been in the pub? Laurel hadn't spotted her.

Pippa gave a tight smile. 'Hello. I'm Pippa, Grady's . . .' She tailed off . . . as if to imply a current bond?

'Hello,' Laurel returned pleasantly. Shaking water from her hands, she took paper towels from the dispenser, eyeing

169

Pippa with interest. She couldn't imagine it was by coincidence that she'd turned up in the ladies while Laurel was there.

Pippa tossed back her blonde locks and smiled. 'Look, this is tricky.'

Laurel waited, drying her hands before tossing the used towels in the bin.

'I know it's not obvious we're together,' Pippa went on, assuming a conspiratorial air, 'but I think you should know I'm pregnant with Grady's baby.' She tossed her head again, as if a swish of her long blonde hair added weight to her assertion.

Surprised, Laurel considered her words then made her voice as gentle as possible. 'Whatever you and Grady are to each other is none of my business. But it would probably make this conversation shorter if I tell you I already know what you suggested to Grady about your baby.'

Pippa's eyebrows flew up. Presumably, Laurel being in possession of such knowledge hadn't been in her plan. Her lip trembled. 'It *is* his,' she insisted, weakly. Then, with a lightning change of tack, she added, 'This has got nothing to do with you.'

'That's right.' With a last smile, Laurel tried sidling past to reach the exit.

Evidently, that wasn't the plan either as, her voice rising several notches, Pippa barked a question. 'Are you seeing a lot of him?'

Hesitating at the door, Laurel considered. She owed Pippa no explanations but she didn't want to be rude or hostile, so she said lightly, 'If Grady's not falling in with your plans, it's not because of me.' She reached for the door handle.

170

'If Grady and I got back together, everything would be OK,' Pippa murmured piteously. 'My parents . . .'

Laurel waited. Surely Pippa was too old to be scared of her parents? She was in her thirties. But then . . . Laurel supposed she was no judge. She hadn't had parents for such a long time, and maybe disappointing parents was hard, whatever age you were. She could see how *I'm back with Grady and we're having a baby* would present an entirely different picture to *I've had a contraception disaster with a man I barely know*. She wished she had something wise and sage to offer, but it wasn't that long since she'd have felt black fury that a woman could treat an unwanted pregnancy like a tragedy. It had once seemed unbearably unfair but, finally, she'd come to realise life wasn't fair. Her IVF treatment not working didn't mean she was entitled to judge Pippa for a broken condom.

'I hope you find a way forward,' she murmured, and slipped out of the close confines of the room with relief. But not before Pippa vented a bitter, 'Don't offer to get out of my way by leaving Grady alone, will you?' The remark was calculated to make Laurel uncomfortable. It succeeded, though she understood that Pippa, rather like Bertie, had got into a situation and now was disappointed others wouldn't resolve it.

Laurel hoped Grady had ordered large drinks because she was going to have to share with him what had just happened. No matter her distress, there was no way Pippa should be lying about paternity. No woman ever should, but it was particularly unfair in his case.

Frowning uneasily, she re-entered the pub and almost tripped over Tess Arnott-Rattenbury talking to Angel Sissins, Rea's old friend. Laurel would have smiled her hellos and moved on but Angel, blonde hair raining around

171

her shoulders, beamed. 'Hello again! Sorry I didn't have time to stop when our paths crossed in the village a little while ago. How do you like being home? How's Rea doing?'

Laurel didn't want to say she didn't think of Middledip as 'home' and thought instead of Rea trembling bravely as she referred herself for help. 'OK, but a bit isolated. I expect you know she's found it tricky to be out and about.'

Angel's brown eyes darkened with concern. 'I don't know much about agoraphobia. Is it OK to visit her? I've wanted to suggest it but hate the idea of going to her house and making her uncomfortable.'

Over Angel's shoulder Laurel could see Grady waiting patiently, idly perusing a menu. 'I think a cuppa and a chinwag could do her the world of good, but it's her opinion that counts, not mine. How about texting her first?'

Angel looked pleased. 'I will, now I know that's OK.'

Before Laurel could take more than a step Tess delayed her by introducing her to someone called Miranda, who was married to someone who worked for Ratty, knew Rea and had ordered a Christmas wreath from Daisy.

Then, finally, Laurel was able to politely excuse herself to join Grady, who was halfway down his drink. He cocked an eyebrow as she dropped into the seat opposite him. 'I thought you'd run out on me.'

She downed half her gin and tonic. 'Sorry. People kept stopping me to talk.'

His eyes crinkled. 'Welcome back to Middledip.'

She laughed, then sobered, as she remembered that one of those conversations had not been of the friendly chat variety. She got the process of ordering out of the way first – carbonara for him and sea bass for her – before clearing her throat. 'Um . . . do you know Pippa's here?'

He cocked an eyebrow. 'In the pub? No, but it's not a massive surprise. She lives in the village.'

Laurel fidgeted, noticing how the fairy lights encrusting the beams above them reflected in Grady's eyes. 'Um . . . I think you ought to know what she said to me.'

Slowly, his smile died. 'Then please tell me.'

Another swig of gin lubricated her throat. 'I'm just going to come out and say it. She told me she's pregnant with your baby.'

Grady's jaw dropped. For several seconds he seemed genuinely speechless. Then, he half-roared, 'She told *you*? Someone she said hello to once but otherwise doesn't know?'

Laurel reached out a hand but didn't quite let it touch his. 'Presumably, her aim was to warn me off. As we're out together, I mean.' Neither of them had mentioned the word 'date'. Laurel was glad. He still exerted a magnetic pull on her but he was also still related to Mac.

Grady gaped. Then thunder entered his eyes. 'What the *fuck*? She dumped me because I can't make kids and now she's telling people I got her pregnant?' He clutched his head, disordering the dark shininess of his hair. 'What is she even thinking? In these days of DNA tests she doesn't stand a chance of making paternity stick. Excuse me.' He jumped up and brushed past her, striding into the body of the pub like a man on a mission.

She twisted in her seat to crane after him but his trajectory took him out of sight, so she grabbed a waitress and ordered two more drinks. Grady looked as if he needed it and she didn't mind keeping him company.

Laurel watched winking fairy lights that hung like icicles down the wall and listened to a woman on another table saying smugly that she'd done all of her Christmas shopping already.

Then, just as their waiter returned with their meals, Grady slipped back into his seat.

He paused while the waiter checked they had everything they needed, then leaned in close to Laurel to murmur. 'Her sister Zelda said Pippa's already gone. Now let's forget her.' He gestured with a firm hand, as if shoving something away. 'Will you help with the Christmas scene for the village hall?'

Laurel was glad he'd put his momentary frustration aside but made him wait while she ate a delicious mouthful of sea bass. 'Aha. You just brought me out to butter me up.'

He grinned as he wound spaghetti around his fork. 'You got me. We've bought this big sheet of MDF board to paint a Christmas scene on and put up as the centre-piece of the art wall during the Middledip Christmas Fair. It'll be for the whole village from the Craft Stuff crowd. I wondered whether you'd rough in the scene and then sort of show people the right technique to paint their bit.'

She gazed at him while he ate his forkful, at the thick black hair and brows, the hopeful expression in those brown eyes. 'Like, maybe a mountain landscape and I'd show people how to paint fir trees and Swiss chalets?'

His eyes brightened. 'Exactly. Tess is involved, too, but can spare only limited time. It would be most of the core Craft Stuff folk.'

'I've done something like it.' She cut up a couple of the melt-in-your-mouth sautéed potatoes. 'It was for a women's group and it wasn't a Christmas scene but the process was much as you describe.' The scene had been a pretty park with lots of women and kids relaxing in the sunshine, eating ice cream or playing ball. Eventually, it had gone up on a wall of one of Fliss's refuges as a positive reinforcement of what family life could and should be. 'Sure. Sounds fun.'

He made a big show of clapping her heartily on the shoulder. 'You're a good woman. We need to have it ready by December 17th, the same day we have to prepare the village hall. The fair is the 18th and 19th, when the school holidays have just started and everyone's in the Christmas spirit.'

'So we've got just over three weeks? Where's the painting going to take place? Surely not at The Angel? It'll get messy with that number of people and paintbrushes.'

His eyes danced. 'Can you imagine Carola's face? No, I have a workshop at the back of the cottage. I can shove aside my gourd stuff and we can work there.' They finished their meal, tossing around ideas for what could go into the Christmas scene.

Tess popped over to their table to say bye, buttoning up a patchwork coat at the same time as diving into the discussion. 'Could I have a corner of the foreground for a Santa and sleigh, sort of whooshing into the picture like this?' She drew an imaginary piece of board in the air and 'whooshed' with her hands.

Laurel never collaborated on her own paintings but loved the occasional chance for a fun community project. 'Absolutely. We'll have the sun over there—' she drew an imaginary circle with an imaginary pen on the top left on Tess's imaginary board '—so everyone knows where the light's coming from. I was thinking maybe mountains coming down to a lake, with ice skaters and chalets. That'll leave you the bottom-right corner.'

'Fantastic.' Tess gave them each a hug before hurrying home.

It was nice to be friendly enough with someone in

Middledip to hug – other than Rea and Daisy, that was – and it gave Laurel a tiny warm feeling. Though she'd been a reluctant returnee, occasionally Middledip felt like home again.

As Tess left, Laurel's phone buzzed with an incoming text. 'Sorry, but I'd better check it's not something important from Rea or Daisy,' she apologised, slipping the phone from her back pocket. But the message was from Alex and short enough to read on the lock screen: *Are you OK? x* She gazed at it, trying to decide how it made her feel. She was the last person to object to friends keeping an eye out for each other – but her *ex*? That felt uncomfortably like being checked up on. If she replied, she'd be reporting in. If she didn't, he might ring.

Grady gave a snort of laughter. 'You're pulling ferocious faces. Has Daisy volunteered you for another job?'

Unwillingly, she laughed, too. 'It's Alex, my ex-husband. I'm just trying to decide whether he's being caring or interfering.' Quickly she typed back, *All OK*, with no thanks and no kiss.

Can't help worrying. Are you still out with the brother? x pinged straight back.

She read the new message, aware of Grady sitting opposite her, his legs inches away, Grady who'd been nothing but a great guy but had copped the fallout from his brother's past behaviour. It felt disloyal to even read the cold and faintly hostile phrase 'the brother'. She tried to think of a message that would end the conversation and make Alex aware he was trespassing too far, without souring their so-far-friendly divorce. Eventually, she typed, *I'm fine. You're not to worry about me anymore*, which seemed to her unequivocal but not snarky.

176

When she put her phone away, she found Grady regarding her with curiosity. 'You're still on good terms?'

'With Alex? So far, yes.' Four people at a nearby table suddenly roared with laughter, making a wall of noise for Laurel to hide her words behind. 'If it wasn't for my infertility, we might have been OK.' Perhaps it was the three gins but she heard herself add, wistfully, 'It was just the trying to make a baby and failing. Then, when even trying became difficult, we knew it was time to call a halt.' She stopped short of actually saying that poor Alex had suffered what he'd termed 'equipment failure'. The memory was too sharply painful, lying side-by-side on the bed, each coming to the bitter realisation that Alex no longer found sex with her exciting. That moment brought it starkly home that they should quit while they were still friends. And Alex should be free.

Grady's eyes were shadowed with understanding. The nearby foursome raised tipsy voices, talking over each other in their eagerness to recount some funny story. He sat up to lean in so he could position his head close to hers. 'I wasn't part of the decision with Pippa, but I see how painful that must have been. I'm really sorry it happened to you.'

Tears prickled at the backs of her eyes. 'Thank you,' she managed, her voice strained by the tightness of her throat. Then the tears reached the front of her eyes and the twinkling lights blurred.

Gently, he passed her a napkin and then laid his hand softly against her arm while she mopped up. 'I'm sorry if the text was upsetting . . . or if I've upset you by talking about it. Will a nice sugary dessert help? Or do you just want to leave? We can have coffee at my place and I can show you the workshop. Or I can just walk you home.'

She wiped her eyes and sniffed, trying to force a laugh, partly because she was aware the racket had dropped at the noisy table and wondered whether it was because they were all gazing at her. 'You always walked me home when we were kids. Daisy gave Rea a lecture about males being as vulnerable as females, but I'm afraid I never thought of that then. Maybe your dad, being the old-fashioned type, taught you that walking girls home was the right thing to do?' She found another napkin on her lap and used that to complete her mopping up operations.

His head came so close she felt the heat of his skin and the brush of his hair. 'No,' he said. 'Walking you home meant goodnight kisses.' Then he pulled away and said, 'Let's get the bill.'

Ten minutes later, muffled up in coat and scarf because the wind seemed to be blowing sleet into Middledip straight from the polar ice cap, Laurel found herself halfway to Mistletoe Cottage before she realised she'd never actually opted for it. On reflection, she didn't mind.

'Any ideas yet on how long you're staying in Middledip?' He hunched his shoulders, sleet spangling his hair before melting. He strode along companionably, arm close but not brushing hers. The comment about the goodnight kiss might never have been spoken.

'Maybe several months, if Rea needs support that long,' she answered. 'Daisy seems happier at school so I'm crossing my fingers that it lasts.' She showed him the crossed fingers then shoved her hands back in her pockets because the night air was glacial and held the metallic taste of the snow that the sleet was fast turning into. The idea of a prolonged stay in Middledip wasn't the anathema it had been a few weeks ago. She could have done without Mac Cassidy still living in the village, his orbit making glancing contact with hers, but, even before Grady had pointed it out this evening, she had realised she didn't feel threatened by Mac now. That fact didn't alter the old yearning for revenge, but it made life in the village more bearable than she'd once feared.

They turned between the hedges of Mistletoe Cottage, passing Grady's red truck. He unlocked the front door and Laurel followed him indoors. Then a thought struck her. 'I meant to split the bill. I can't believe I let you pay for everything.' She'd been on two dates since her divorce, pressed upon her by friends in Park Royal who thought dates a vital rite of passage at the end of a marriage. They'd involved her taking her turn at buying drinks in noisy bars and she hadn't had to face any clash of expectations over a restaurant bill.

He turned to meet her gaze calmly, his hair tumbled by the wind. 'How about you pay next time?'

She'd been about to press cash on him for her share of tonight's expenses. On the other hand . . . the notion of 'next time' awakened a curl of pleasure inside her. 'If you're sure,' she murmured.

Grady showed her down the hall to a red-tiled kitchen where he made her a coffee. Her mug bore the name of a garage in Peterborough; his bore the crest of Peterborough United Football Club. She began to unzip her coat but he stopped her with a shake of his head. 'The workshop's not on the central heating loop because it used to be outbuildings. It's cold until the heaters get going.'

He opened a close-boarded door and they stepped into a long room, carrying their mugs. 'This was the outdoor loo, wash house and coal hole,' he explained, indicating the ribs that marked where he'd taken down walls between three windows. 'But now it's my workshop.'

In the middle of the space a sturdy, battered kitchen table served as a workbench, and it was scattered with tools, including a hand-held power tool. Racks and shelves covered the two narrow walls. A board about three metres long leaned against the house wall. 'That's what we're painting,' Grady said, as he switched on panel heaters.

Ignoring the board, Laurel was drawn down the room to a shelf full of gourds, shining dully under the overhead light, a few in their natural state but others looking as if a rainbow had come down to Middledip and found its home.

One had become a peacock, the gourd's stretched and curved neck painted iridescent blue, ending in a neatly painted beak and knowing eye. The peacock's tail was furled around the lower, bulbous part of the gourd, the geometric 'eye' of every feather painstakingly painted in shimmering shades of blue, green, aqua, jade, black and gold. She moved on to another gourd, painted with apple blossom, perhaps to reflect its squat, apple-like shape. The background colour was matte black and every blossom, leaf and stem stood out.

Another was carved into a fretwork of leaves and twigs. At the top, a painted bird perched on a twig, head back and beak open as if in song. 'I'm going to make that into a lamp,' he said. He turned it to show her the hole in the bottom, ready for a light fitting.

So minutely had she been studying what he'd made that she jumped, not having noticed him moving so close. 'How much will you sell it for?' she asked.

He examined it, one eyebrow raised. The light caught the bird and Laurel saw its eyes were black glass. 'About a hundred quid.' He put it back next to the red-inked vase he'd been working on when she'd sat next to him at

Craft Stuff. It looked complete, now, the pierced section cream, the mottling showing through the transparent red and a broad gold collar between the two.

'Can I buy it for Rea's Christmas present?' she asked impulsively. 'She loves things for the house.'

A dark flush crept up his cheeks. 'You don't have to buy my stuff.'

She hesitated. 'Is there some reason I shouldn't buy it? It's gorgeous.'

His laugh was little more than a breath. 'You're a famous artist. This is more of a paying hobby.'

'I'm not famous; I do OK,' she returned, feeling her own cheeks heat. 'I think you undersell yourself by calling this—' she gestured at the shelves of brightly coloured and carved gourds '—a hobby.'

'OK.' He gestured towards the table where he'd left their coffees, as if to divert her attention. As he'd set the coffee down next to a heater and the long room was taking a while to heat up, Laurel took a stool opposite his. He smiled but he was still flushed and embarrassed. 'I'll fit the light socket at the weekend. But I won't charge you full whack—'

'You will charge me full whack,' she interrupted, scandalised. 'Even at a hundred pounds I think you're underpricing your work. Let's look on Etsy.' As he watched on, she unlocked her phone and searched for 'carved gourds' and 'decorative gourds'.

'Hmm,' she said, after scrolling through a host of images with a critical eye. 'You could easily charge me a hundred and fifty. I presume you have an Etsy shop?'

He nodded. 'I also sell through my Facebook page and Instagram.'

She located Grady Cassidy on Etsy. 'You could increase

181

every price by fifteen to twenty per cent, maybe more.' She looked up. 'Unless you're pricing to sell because you need quick money.' She'd certainly leave cash for her half of the dinner tonight, if so.

His eyes smiled. In the harsh overhead lighting his hair was as dark as the night outside the uncurtained windows, where tiny snow particles were whirling against the glass. 'No, I don't have to rush sales.' He rubbed his jaw. 'But I do sell my stuff pretty quickly so I suppose I *could* charge more.'

She found herself noticing the darkness of his pupils and the golden flecks in his brown irises. 'You sound short of confidence.' She thought about the Middledip Christmas Fair meeting and how, when Carola overlooked him, he'd made a joke about being 'an unprofessional artist', as if used to not being taken seriously. 'Don't give your work away,' she urged him.

Pleasure sparkled in his dark eyes. 'You've given me something to think about because I certainly don't under-price for spray work.'

Then he turned the discussion to the beige expanse of board that was destined to become the Christmas scene. They drank their coffee and gazed at it.

'Needs the dust washing off and a coat of household acrylic primer,' she said. 'I can do the background work in household paint and then we'll get acrylic from one of those budget shops. I think they deliver.'

He shook his head. 'We've had paint donated. The guy from the art supplies shop has given me a load of scratched tubes from old stock.'

She drained her coffee. 'Great. OK with you if I start on Saturday?' She rose and refastened her coat.

He fastened his, too, and turned off the heaters. As they

passed through the kitchen, he picked up a beanie hat and pulled it on over his smooth hair, making the ends stick out at the bottom. 'Old-fashioned or not, I'd like to see you home safely. You going to fight me on that?'

She laughed at his mock-challenging tone. 'No. That would be good, thanks.' It was nearly midnight. She didn't expect masked attackers or bogeymen but, ever since the night that still gave her nightmares, her policy had been: 'be sensible'.

She tugged up her hood and they braved the freezing temperatures together, squinting at the snow flying into their faces. Laurel, wearing medium-heeled ankle boots, slipped on the slippery pavement.

Grady crooked his elbow without taking his hand from his pocket. 'Want to hang on?'

'Thanks,' she gasped, the wind stealing her words as she hooked her gloved hand through his arm. He provided an anchor, steady and sure-footed; a calm, comforting presence in a cold world.

Chapter Eleven

Grady enjoyed the feel of Laurel's gloved hand on his arm, even through the ski jacket he wore against the winter wonderland temperatures. They chatted about the painting of the Christmas scene as the snow veered through the illumination around each streetlight in the night-quiet village, but what he thought about was Laurel. The evening they'd spent together. Her laughter and dancing eyes. Her tears and wobbling lip. The way she'd squared her shoulders before telling him what Pippa had said.

He'd have to deal with Pippa.

The only lights showing at the pub as they passed were in the upstairs living quarters. They turned into Great End and the wind flew to meet them down the close. 'Whoo!' Laurel laughed as sleety snow drove into her eyes, hanging on to her hood with one hand and Grady with the other. In the comparative calm afforded by the dark bulk of The Nookery, only one light shone through the curtains of an upstairs window. She took out her phone and did a bit of tapping and swiping. Lo and behold, a low light began to burn in the hall, outlining the curtain at the window beside the door.

He grinned. 'Smart home technology. Handy.'

'It really is.' The wind flipped her fringe around above her eyes, the fur around her hood framing her face. She went on, explaining the features of the app that controlled the lights. She was smaller than him by several inches. He found himself watching the movement of her mouth in the light from the streetlamps.

She paused uncertainly. 'What?'

He dragged his gaze up to her eyes. Softly, he said, 'I've enjoyed tonight. What do you think about doing it again?' Although they'd had a good evening he wasn't sure of her feelings towards him. She wasn't obvious, like Pippa, who, on their first date, had touched him a hundred times, her hand on his arm or her leg brushing his.

Laurel's lips curved into a smile. 'Sounds good. We could go after painting on Saturday. The pub won't mind our painting gear, will they?'

He tilted his head, smiling at the idea of the village pub having a picky dress code. 'Probably not. But I was thinking about a wine bar in Bettsbrough or a restaurant in Peterborough. And non-painting clothes.'

Her gaze became solemn. 'A date?'

'That would be great.' He smiled again, willing her to smile back.

She didn't. 'Was tonight a date?'

Not knowing the answer, he stroked her arm, the sleeve of her coat cold and damp. 'In the last couple of weeks I've discovered I haven't stopped liking you, Laurel.' Giving her plenty of time to step away, he lowered his head to kiss her. His lips brushed hers, then again. He kissed the corner of her mouth, her cheek, her temple, sliding his other arm around her and shifting closer.

After the slightest hesitation her hands came up to his shoulders and she angled her head so that her lips found his, softly, hesitantly. He let her set the pace and was rewarded when she relaxed against him, though the contact was light through her thick coat. Fireworks burst in his chest as their mouths opened and they sank into a hot, deep, drugging kiss that set him tingling and removed all thoughts from his head apart from *I'm kissing Laurel again*.

It was she who ended the kiss. He would have stood under the porch of The Nookery for hours, uncaring if they disappeared in an icy snowdrift so long as he was kissing her. She gave a soft, breathless laugh. 'So that's why you walked me home, huh? To get your goodnight kiss?'

He knew she was joking to defuse the intensity. He nudged her hood back so he could nuzzle her ear. 'Worked, didn't it?' He kept his hips angled away from her because there was a block of something decidedly not ice-like, hot and burning against his lower stomach.

She disengaged herself. 'I'll see you on Saturday.'

'Yes.' He felt as rocked and giddy as their teenage kisses had ever made him feel. He hoped that, this time, their relationship would sooner or later progress beyond kissing in doorways . . . like into his bed in Mistletoe Cottage, her luscious body naked in his arms. He made sure not to let the thought reflect in his smile, not wanting to send her off with a lust-crazed leer. He watched her open the wooden front door and close it behind her. Heard the lock click. Then he turned for home, becoming aware of ice-block feet and burning-cold hands.

Shoulders hunched, he jogged home, head buzzing, trying to outrun the snow that was trying to infiltrate the neck of his jacket. Despite the niggles about her shuttered expression when he'd talked of Mac, Laurel's kisses had left him hovering six inches above the pavement and he sang under his breath as he burst into the welcome warmth of Mistletoe Cottage. He locked up and loped upstairs, tossing his coat over the banister, shuffling a couple of dance steps across the landing.

Despite texting her ex tonight, Laurel seemed over her divorce and her ring finger had been empty long enough for there to be no white line.

A few minutes after he'd fallen into bed, he noticed a phone notification about a message from someone called Francesca on the Grady Auto Art Facebook page. In case it meant a sale, he clicked it open.

You don't know me, the message began, *but I think you know Ruben?* Grady blinked. Mac's old friend?

Assuming someone was trying to organise a reunion or something he typed back: *My brother had a friend called Ruben but I'm not in touch with him. Have you tried searching for social media profiles?*

He slid further under the duvet, intending to switch his phone to silent but the next message flashed straight up. *I know where he is, thanks. I used to be married to him. I'm still on good terms with my MIL, who lives in Middledip, and we FaceTimed a couple of hours ago. She talks about village doings and she said you're seeing someone called Laurel Hill.*

Grady sat up, stunned. The duvet slumped around his waist but he was too shocked to cover himself up. People in the village liked to talk, he was aware, but surely having a meal with a woman wasn't worthy of this level of interest. He hadn't even known Ruben's mum still lived in Middledip.

Another message popped up: *It's just there's something you should know.*

He watched the screen, heart knocking uncomfortably against his rib cage. Eventually he returned: *What?*

When nothing happened straight away he slid back down beneath the covers. He hadn't drawn his bedroom curtains and turned his head to watch snow settling on leafless branches, making the trees look like elderly ladies with wiry perms. Deep in his gut, something had coiled, as if waiting.

When his phone vibrated, he lifted it up to read the next message.

Ruben got drunk one night and told me about how your brother attacked Laurel Hill when they were teenagers. Grady's heart began beating so hard it made his vision swim. Half of him instantly refused to believe any such thing. The other half whispered in his ear: *that would explain everything.* Laurel treating Mac so warily. Mac being unsettled by her return to the village. And, nineteen Christmases ago, Laurel withdrawing entirely from Grady, then leaving the village the second her GCSEs were over.

Ruben was there. They waited on the playing field for Laurel to walk home. Mac and Amie grabbed Laurel and pulled all her clothes off her top half. Then she got away and ran home crying.

Horrified, for several moments all Grady could hear was the blood pounding in his ears, drowning out the wind that buffeted his window. He felt sick and had to shove the covers back as sweat burst out all over his body.

Eventually, he typed back with fumbling fingers: *Why are you telling me this?*

188

There was a short delay and then: *You ought to know what your family did to her.*

His mouth was dry, stomach heaving. Probably this Francesca had a point but still . . . what kind of person got in touch with a stranger to spout this kind of information about her ex-husband, unprompted? And to someone only indirectly involved? Was she messaging a whole load of people with this? Searching for a foothold in her motivation, he sent back: *What's your relationship like with Ruben now?*

He's a shit, arrived promptly. Grady stared at it. Did that explain Francesca's action? Was she blindly hitting out at Ruben? But how would telling Grady do Ruben any harm? Perhaps she was one of those toxic busybodies who used 'ought to know' as code for 'I enjoy giving people bad news'. Grady was perplexed.

After a few minutes' thought he typed in: *What do you expect me to do with this information?*

The reply flickered up on his screen: *That's between you and your conscience.*

His conscience? Why his? *People lie*, he tapped out, pressing hard, as if he could transmit his anger and fear through the screen to the unknown woman who'd taken advantage of the public nature of his business page to send messages that had begun a deep, black dread growing inside him.

People also tell the truth, he got back.

Then the messages stopped. Grady sent several more questions but it seemed Francesca had left the conversation. He lay back in bed, trembling with frustration and worry. Laurel had spoken of bullying but Francesca had used the word 'attack'. And what she described . . . If it were true . . . A fresh wave of nausea rolled over him. Poor Laurel.

189

He couldn't do anything now but neither could he sleep. He switched on the TV to occupy his mind. So much of the late-night programming was about murderers and rapists that he had to search to find a nature programme about woolly monkeys instead. The screen was filled by tiny primates feasting on berries, hanging from prehensile tails, but what he saw was flashbacks to Laurel's white face when he'd tried to talk to her after he'd had to miss that party at the village hall.

After a couple of sleepless hours, he sent a text for Mac to see in the morning. *Must see you alone ASAP. How about this evening?*

At just after six-thirty a.m. he received his brother's reply: *How about 8? Your place?* Then: *You OK?*

OK, Grady returned, and dragged himself out of bed to face the day.

That morning, Grady had planned to work at home, producing sketches for a client in need of a surfer cresting a wave on the side of his camper van. He did settle himself at the table with his sketchbook, computer and pencils but all he could think about was Laurel. Laurel, emotional over the emptiness of infertility. Compassionate over his problems with his ex. Comfortable enough to kiss him goodnight and make a date for Saturday.

Saturday was only tomorrow but a date with Laurel now felt unlikely as last night's messages ran through his mind like a ticker tape. . . . *your brother attacked Laurel Hill . . . They waited on the playing field for Laurel to walk home. Mac and Amie grabbed Laurel and pulled all her clothes off her top half . . . You ought to know what your family did to her.*

He barely ate, pacing the house, checking his messages

to see if Francesca had answered his later questions, rereading what she'd written, till Mac knocked punctually at eight p.m.

Mac grinned when Grady opened the door, four cans of Brewdog dangling from one large hand. 'I knocked this time,' he pointed out. His hair, as dark as Grady's but cut short and conservative, danced in the wind.

Grady stood back and let him, accepting one of the Brewdogs, taking comfort from the feel of the cold can. Dutch courage might be what he needed as he questioned his big brother, the one he'd looked up to, loved, and pitied for being the one in their dad's spotlight.

Mac followed him into the sitting room. His grin had been replaced with a concerned frown. 'What's up?' he asked, perching on the sofa and snapping open the ring on a can.

Grady took his favourite chair, mouth as dry as ashes. It took a couple of pulls of beer before he could speak, the can trembling in his hand. 'I don't know how to say this. Someone messaged me to say that when you were a teenager you attacked Laurel Hill. Sexually. I have to ask if it's true.'

He'd been harbouring hopes of Francesca's messages being lies. Hoping Mac would be astounded and aghast, bounding to his feet, black brows beetling as he bellowed, 'You can't seriously believe that? Of me? How *could* you?' But, instead, he had to watch Mac recoil as if it had been stones Grady had thrown at him, rather than words. His colour drained, even from his lips, while his eyes grew big and black with horror.

He didn't ask who had sent the messages. He didn't attempt to deny it or defend himself. He just looked beaten.

An icy hand closed around Grady's heart. 'For fuck's sake,' he whispered.

Mac sat back – fell back – on the sofa. 'It wasn't how you make it sound.' His voice was dull and despairing.

Grady became aware of sounds outside. A couple of cars swishing past the house, one pausing at the junction. A dull thud of a closing door . . . or maybe that was the sound of his hero toppling from his pedestal. A sigh began in the pit of Grady's stomach, hurting his chest on the way out. 'Tell me what happened.' His voice was hoarse.

Mac stirred, taking a couple of sips of beer. 'I'll tell you how I saw it. I'm not going to make excuses, but I wasn't the one with the plan that night – that was all Amie,' he added bitterly. 'I liked Laurel but I knew I wasn't her type.' He smiled mirthlessly. 'You were.'

'You liked her?' Grady demanded, thinking how he'd all-but dismissed the idea when it had come from Tonya.

Wearily, Mac propped his elbow on the arm of the sofa and rested his cheek on his fist. 'I never tried to cut you out and, anyway, she was *not* interested in me. That was probably why I trash-talked her. She overheard, prompting that quarrel you mentioned recently.'

Grady felt as if he were being sucked back in time to the teenage world of hidden hopes, in-crowds and loners, alliances, enemies and half-understood politics. Kids bullshitting to make everyone think they knew more than they did. Mac had bullshitted more than most and Grady had never suspected him of feeling anything for Laurel, nor caught on to the consequences. Had he floated around in his own self-absorbed bubble? 'Why did Amie hate her?' he prompted.

Mac grimaced. 'Maybe she knew I'd rather be with Laurel. She used to make out Laurel was disgusting for being—' he paused, as if hunting for an acceptable term '—well-endowed. Used to call her "ugly hooters" and "fat puddings".'

'You didn't just tell Amie to shut her face?' Grady snapped.

Slowly, Mac shook his head. 'I should have. But Amie was my girlfriend and . . .' He blew out a disgusted breath. 'No, no excuses. I knew it was wrong but Laurel didn't want me and Amie did. That kind of put me on Amie's side.' He leaned his head back and shut his eyes. 'That night, four of us were drinking cider on the playing field.'

'You, Amie, Ruben and . . . who? Jonny?' Grady guessed, knowing who Mac had hung out with back then.

Mac nodded without opening his eyes. 'We had an armload of two-litre bottles so I was pretty drunk. Then along came Laurel, walking home from the village hall. Amie started bitching at her and maybe we laughed.' He corrected himself. 'We laughed. When she was nearly past, Amie jumped up and grabbed her coat. It came partway down and trapped her arms. She shouted at Amie and tried to kick her.'

He opened his eyes and sat up, settling a bleak gaze on Grady. 'Amie was like one of those nasty Jack Russells that doesn't seem to realise it's small. It just sets on people. So—' he paused to take a swallow of beer '—Amie yelled to me to hold her.' The look he sent Grady was an agony of apology and regret. 'I was half-drunk. I didn't think, "What? Me, a bigger, older bloke, restrain a girl who hasn't done anything wrong?" I just went, "Durr, OK, Amie. I'll do that for you."' His voice mimicked a dopey cartoon character. Neither of them laughed.

He coughed and gulped from his beer can. 'Laurel was shrieking, scared and angry. Then bloody Amie, she capered round the front of Laurel and got hold of her top and yanked it up. I was stupefied. I couldn't compute what was happening. Laurel screamed louder so Amie grabbed

193

her bra and pulled that up, too. Laurel was exposed.' Another of those dry coughs. 'I didn't *decide* to hold on to her. I didn't *decide* I was part of what Amie had just done. I just turned into a doofus, staring at her naked boobs.' Self-loathing rang in his voice. 'Then suddenly it dawned on me what the hell I was doing and I . . . let go.' He covered his eyes. 'Laurel ran away, crying. Amie was giggling. Jonny and Ruben had stopped laughing. They'd realised before I did what a shitty thing we were doing.'

He drank down all the rest of that can of beer and opened the next. His tone became dull and flat again. 'I finished with Amie that night. She acted all hurt and shocked. I said I didn't want anything to do with someone like her. She scratched my face. I welcomed it, like a punishment. Like a badge saying, "I'm not like you, Amie Blunt" even though, unfortunately, I was. I felt sick.'

Grady felt sick, too. 'What happened when you apologised to Laurel?'

Mac shook his head, lips folded inward into a wretched line, as if he were fighting tears.

Disbelief seared through Grady. 'You didn't ever apologise?' he demanded furiously.

'You think she'd come anywhere near me?' Mac asked, brow furrowing incredulously. 'I called her name once, when I saw her come out of the village shop, and she ran – literally ran. I felt like such a shit.'

'You were a shit.'

'I know.' Mac groaned. 'I've been haunted by it. I wanted to try again to apologise that morning we called at The Nookery. That's why I asked to talk to her alone.' Mac ran his fingers into his hair and tugged at it.

Grady felt as if the foundations of his life were

194

crumbling. 'First you told me that was about Aspirations Week at school, then about Amie's bullying, and now you're finally admitting it was because of what you did. You've lied and lied to me.'

'Yep,' Mac admitted quietly. He clenched his fist against his leg. 'I'm sorry. You must be disappointed in me, Grady. I was drunk and stupid. I never intended any of it to happen and felt shittier and shittier when I saw how upset you were when Laurel blanked you. I hated myself. I straightened out and went to uni like Dad wanted. I never again treated a woman with disrespect. I never let myself get drawn into the mob mentality. I only ever drink moderately.'

That was true. Mac hadn't even got drunk at his own stag weekend. It was small comfort. 'I'm just . . . rocked by this,' Grady muttered. He glugged down the remainder of his beer and reached for another, ignoring the knowledge that it was alcohol that had fuelled that long-ago attack. 'Thanks for finally coming clean but, fuck you, Mac. I could throttle you.'

They sat in silence, Grady rerunning what Mac had told him, struggling to comprehend how quickly drunken ragging had turned into sexual assault, sickened that the brother he'd looked up to could get sucked into it. 'It's no wonder Laurel stopped talking to me,' he rasped. 'If I hadn't bust my ankle, I would have been with her that night, walking her home.'

'I wish you had been,' Mac whispered.

He fidgeted with his can and sent Grady a sidelong glance. 'She could still press charges against me, you know. Time doesn't run out on complaints like that. She could lose me my job and probably my marriage.' His voice was flat, not suggesting he should be pitied or assisted, just reporting the stark facts in a starkly factual way.

195

Images of Niall and Tonya flashed into Grady's brain. He'd always envied Mac his happy little family and couldn't bear to think of his nephew and sister-in-law being hurt. 'You stupid bastard,' he said, bitterly.

One thing was certain, he couldn't face Laurel until he'd had time to process. He took out his phone and texted her. *Sorry, can't make Saturday. Family situation. I won't be home so happy for you to come into my workshop and begin on Christmas scene. There's a key safe by the back door, PIN 161220.* He paused, looking at his own words and wondering, dully, how they'd be received. He added: *I'm very sorry about the date.*

Sending the text felt like the end of something good. His heart felt as heavy as rock, especially when he received in reply: *I understand. Hope everything's OK.*

Mac watched Grady's actions through dull eyes. 'Who sent you the message telling you about me and Laurel?'

'Francesca. Ruben's ex-wife. I can't work out why, really, unless she's one of those people who think divorce is an excuse to hurl shit in all directions.' Grady passed Mac his phone, open at the messages.

As he read, Mac shook his head. 'It's ages since I heard from Ruben and didn't know he'd been married. I don't really know why his ex would do this. What axe does she have to grind? And why approach you, particularly?'

'People are complex.' Grady rubbed tired eyes. 'Maybe her reasons will become clear one day.'

Late Saturday evening, Grady arrived home to a dark, deserted Mistletoe Cottage. He hadn't heard from Laurel since their text exchange on Friday evening and he entered his workshop half expecting to find the board destined to be the Christmas scene as bare and untouched as when

196

he'd left it. Instead, he found it chocked in place with wooden wedges, a collection of paints and cleaned brushes tucked behind.

Over white primer, the ghost of a scene had appeared. A hazy sun glowed from the top left of a winter-blue sky and the light and shade of craggy mountains had been indicated with a broad brush. The right foreground was blank, ready for Tess's Santa and sleigh, and, front left, a hazy rendition of light and shade revealed itself as a lake, as Grady looked at it.

He checked around the workshop and kitchen but found no note or used coffee mug. He checked the key safe and found his key neatly replaced. Laurel had come here, laid the foundation for a winter wonderland, and left.

Unexpectedly, his eyes burned.

He was overtired, he thought. He'd had a long day. Needing to keep clear of the village he'd driven into Norfolk and almost got lost on the salt marshes.

He trudged upstairs, heartsick both that he'd have to ask Laurel about Mac . . . and that she'd never felt she could tell him the truth.

Chapter Twelve

December arrived on Wednesday morning with a frost as hard and beautiful as crushed diamonds.

The studio windows were edged with ferns of ice outside. Even with the heaters on full, Laurel was barely warm enough – although that might have something to do with her being dressed in only thin, stretchy, thermal base layers she'd once worn beneath ski gear.

A video frame was frozen on her computer screen. She, Daisy and Rea had videoed themselves learning street dance from TikTok – bouncing, leaping and laughing themselves breathless as they fought to master the lightning-fast steps – and Laurel had scrubbed through the footage and selected the perfect image as a reference for a sketch for her everyday woman dancing in the snow. She'd been caught mid-bounce, one leg lifted so that the kneecap was at hip level, one arm thrust up and the other down. On canvas, Everyday Woman would wear a flirty short skirt over leggings, Doc Martens and a cold-shoulder jumper, but right now Laurel was working on the anatomy beneath the clothes and had carried the full-length mirror down from her room.

Everyday Woman wasn't a self-portrait but she was using her body as a reference – she was available whenever needed and sure as hell fit the remit of not having the willowy body of a ballerina. Concentrating on her sketches was staunching her tendency to wonder about Grady, about their broken date and the following silence. It was stopping her wondering – more than once an hour, anyway – whether she'd see him this evening when she and Daisy delivered Christmas wreaths to some of the Craft Stuff crowd.

She tousled her hair – loose because Everyday Woman's hair would be – stood on one leg and threw up her arm. Experimentally, she steadied herself with a fingertip on the back of a chair so she could rise up on tiptoe as if ready to leap, trying to replicate how the muscles would look. The weight-bearing leg was fundamental to figure drawing but this leg would have just launched Everyday Woman from the ground so would be slightly different again. Absorbed, gazing between the mirror and the computer screen freeze-frame, she half-registered a flash of movement at the window.

Then a knock fell on the studio door and a low voice called, 'Laurel? It's Grady.'

Surprised at the flash of pleasure that accompanied the sound of his voice, she called, 'Come in,' turning her head to watch the door open. When Grady halted for a long moment before closing it behind him, realisation hit her that she was standing on one leg in long, clinging navy blue leggings and a matching top. Almost overbalancing, cheeks burning, she thudded back onto her two feet and swept up her hoodie from its untidy heap on a chair to yank it over her head. It fell to mid-thigh. Despite the blast of frigid air he'd admitted, heat crackled across her skin.

'You're working,' he observed uncertainly, one eye on the sketch, one hand drifting back towards the door handle.

Her face still scalded. 'It's fine, come on in. I've been wondering about you.' When he didn't respond, she clarified, 'After what you texted about a family situation, I mean. Daisy hasn't passed anything on from Niall, so I thought maybe it was an adults-only thing . . .' She trailed away at the way his pale face pinched in on itself. Oh. It looked serious.

He cleared his throat. 'It's definitely not something to be shared with Niall.' His gaze slid off to the window as if he was suddenly fascinated by Rea's frozen garden, which looked as if it were carved from crystal. Then he dragged his attention back to her. 'Laurel—' He stopped, raising a hand to massage his temples.

Alarmed, she forgot how strange and tingly it had made her feel for him to see her in skin-tight clothing and crossed the few strides separating them. Guiding him to a chair, she pulled up another to face him. With heavy movements, he dragged off his coat and dropped it on the floor. 'Are you ill?' she asked. 'Or is someone in your family?' She only realised she'd seized his hand when she noticed him staring fixedly at their intertwined fingers.

He cleared his throat. And then again. Finally, words wrenched from him, raw and painful. 'Did Mac assault you?'

The words, so out of the blue, rocked her. The studio seemed to tilt, as if they were in the midst of a silent earthquake. A sheen of sweat broke out across her skin. A small sound escaped her throat, something between a gasp and a sob. 'Oh,' she said, weakly. Or it might have been, 'Ow,' because the suddenness of his questions felt brutal.

His unhappy eyes fixed on hers. 'You should have told me.'

Her throat ached with tears. At last, she said, 'I've only ever told Alex, my friend Fliss and a counsellor. There was fear of not being believed. Fear of the story getting around. Fear of people thinking I was a willing participant. Fear of being further exposed and having my privacy invaded. Fear of questions, not necessarily sympathetic. Worry that Rea would crack up if she had one more thing to cope with. And shame. Girls shouldn't feel shame when stuff like that happens but, boy, they do, because people associate them with the offence against them.' She gulped. 'And you . . . To believe me, you would have had to accept the truth about Mac. You love Mac. It would have hurt you. I didn't want that.'

His lips parted, but no words emerged.

She knew from his haunted eyes that he couldn't contradict her. 'I told Daisy she'd done the right thing in telling someone about her bully, all the time knowing I did the opposite.' She slumped in her chair. 'How did you find out?'

He heaved a sigh. 'Ruben's ex, Francesca, messaged me to spill the beans.' His eyes filled with pain. 'She seemed to think I ought to know.' He scrubbed a hand over his face. 'I suppose that, in a way, I agree. It went on under my nose, it affected me, yet I was excluded from the truth.'

A silence descended on them while Laurel mulled this over.

'I've talked to Mac,' he added gruffly.

Laurel saw the desolation written on his face and realised she should end her silence. It wasn't just that Grady *had* been affected but that now the truth was out, a truth so deeply personal to her, it was from her he should hear

201

it. 'I was never worried about anything happening in the village.' She paused, letting her imagination sweep her back to that dark, cold night. 'It wasn't until I was between the swings and the pub car park that I saw people hanging out on a bench, drinking. I heard Amie Blunt's voice and didn't want her to see I was scared.'

'Were you scared?' He pushed back his hair, leaning forward as if braced to meet the facts, however unpalatable.

She shrugged. 'Obviously. Amie was a bitch. But she wasn't alone so I didn't think she'd do more than get verbal. She did get verbal,' she acknowledged. She found herself pulling at the front of her hoodie. 'She said my . . . shape was revolting. She said that a lot, like I'd grown boobs on purpose and had to be reminded how disgusting they were. I ignored her. I thought I'd got past. But suddenly she was on my back like a monkey, pinning my arms. It was horrible, her clinging on to me like that. I fought back.' Her breath was ragged at the remembered fear. The black night. The cruel laugher and the smell of cider. She described Mac joining in, Amie pulling up her clothes, her word tumbling over one another. 'I was terri-fied, humiliated, mortified. Screaming.' Her throat felt raw, as if the screaming had only just happened. 'When Mac let go I ran home. Rea was still up so I sprinted upstairs, shouting about being desperate for the loo. She never saw the state I was in.'

'How long—' He cleared his throat and swallowed. He hadn't shaved for a couple of days and the movement of his Adam's apple was accentuated by dark stubble. 'How long did Mac hold you for? After Amie had . . . done that.'

She shrugged, shaken anew by the storm of revived emotions.

'Minutes?' he pressed. 'Hours? Seconds?'

'Oh. Seconds,' she said. 'It seemed a long time. But he did let go.'

Grady rubbed his forehead as if wiping away sweat. 'You didn't think of going to the police? Without telling Rea, I mean. You were sixteen. They would have listened.'

She laughed without mirth. 'Really? I wonder how many girls that age would report that to strangers. The only witnesses were Mac's horrible mates! Mac and Amie would have denied it and Jonny and Ruben would have backed them up. I could even imagine them flipping the story and accusing me of flashing. And I'd walked across a field on my own in the dark. You've heard the phrase "asking for it", haven't you? It's used against victims all the time.'

She heaved a sigh, her body slackening with fatigue. 'Next day, on the bus, Amie told everyone I was a slut, throwing myself at her boyfriend. That was when she followed me and ripped out my earring.' She rubbed her earlobe. 'She said no one would believe me . . . but if I did tell anyone, she'd rip out the other. I've never worn earrings since.'

His glance flickered to each earlobe as she held back her hair to show him. The rip caused by Amie's viciousness had long since healed without a mark. Or, at least, not one that showed on the outside.

His big body shuddered. 'I'm so sorry, Laurel.'

'You?' She got up and pulled sheets off a roll of blue cleaning paper to wipe her cheeks and blow her nose. 'You didn't do anything wrong. I didn't take care of my personal safety and the others committed the crime.'

'Jeez.' His hands moved restlessly, clenching, unclenching.

'Mac's story. Does it match up with mine?' she asked, wondering if he was about to twist her account to make Mac look better.

He nodded.

She laughed hollowly. 'That's something.'

'Did you ever get the impression that he . . . liked you? Before that, I mean,' he said, tentatively.

She shrugged. 'Define "like". Developing early got me unwanted attention and people compared me to Lara Croft, the computer game character with big boobs. Do you remember that Bowling for Soup song? 'Girl All the Bad Guys Want'? I felt like that was me, attracting the brashest and cockiest of the older boys. It was uncomfortable and threatening. But I was entitled to choose who to like and who not to,' she added fiercely.

'Of course you were. Are.' He clenched his hands even tighter. 'Who would you say was the ringleader?'

She didn't have to think about that. 'Amie. Mac followed instructions. Jonny and Ruben were a willing audience. My role was victim . . . but I'm not one anymore. I know about personal safety and I've taken self-defence classes.' She fell silent, her earlier good mood shattered. She wouldn't be able to work again today. A happy, dancing woman was a long way from her current frame of mind.

Tentatively, he reached for her hand. Surprised, she let him take it, feeling his dry and chilly fingers against hers. His gaze bored into hers and his voice emerged low and full of compassion. 'You know you could still report the incident?'

She nodded. 'I'm aware of my rights. Don't think it hasn't crossed my mind, especially since I've been back here and had to watch your bloody brother living a lovely life. The temptation to take revenge has been immense, starting with leaving him at the side of the road in his boxers that night. Most of the time I tell myself that revenge would make me a worse person, but I've been unable to resist saying a couple of things to make him uncomfortable.' Her shoulders rose and fell on a sigh. 'I was doing a pretty good job of leaving the past behind until I had to come back here.'

His thumb stroked the back of her hand. 'I'm not excusing him, but he seems genuinely horrified. He says he was half-drunk. He hated himself after. He ditched Amie. He never gets the worse for drink now. He wants to apologise.'

'I expect that's why he asked to speak to me alone,' she put in, her words almost running together in sudden fury. 'Apologising might make *Mac* feel better. He'll be able to feel he's made reparation, got rid of guilt. But, me? I'd have to face him. Relive it. Unpack it. Listen to him trying to defend the indefensible. He might even expect forgiveness. Well, tough shit. I don't forgive him.' She made herself breathe more slowly. 'Are you working up to coaxing me to let him apologise? Don't bother. Let him live with the guilt like I've had to live with the trauma.'

He had both her hands now, stroking, soothing. He didn't answer her question but said, 'Now that I know what happened, everything's fallen into place. Why Mac gave in to Dad's nagging and went to uni. Why you stopped speaking to me and didn't hang out in the village anymore. Why you left and hardly ever came back.' He edged his chair a little closer so his arms could encircle her. 'I've no idea if this is an appropriate thing to say but Amie was jealous of you. Don't believe her body shaming. You're lush and gorgeous.' It was a sweet, comforting, non-sexual hug, an invitation to rest her head on his shoulder and share her sorrow.

Until Grady had kissed her when he'd walked her home in the early hours of Friday, it had been ages since she'd been in a man's arms. Alex had treated her as out of bounds the second they made the decision to part not quite two years ago. The two men she'd dated since had stayed at arm's length because she'd kept them there. Fliss and other friends had hugged her, and so did Rea and Daisy, but it wasn't the same as being touched by a man.

She thought of the hot, exciting kiss she and Grady had shared on the porch only a few short days before and her skin turned to goosebumps.

Whatever feelings she had for him felt as dangerous as walking on ice. Fall over or fall through – it was going to hurt.

They broke apart as the sound of running feet came outside and Daisy catapulted through the door, home from school and brimming with enthusiasm. 'Auntie Laurel, are you ready to decorate our Art December window? Oh, hey, Grady.' She gave Grady a friendly nudge.

He rose, managing a reasonably convincing smile. 'Hey, Daisy. I'll leave you to talk to Laurel.'

Daisy looked disappointed. 'Will you be at Craft Stuff tonight? I'm only going for a bit because Auntie Laurel and me are delivering wreaths.' She rubbed her hands together. 'Dosh!'

He scooped his coat from the floor. 'Dosh is always good. I don't think I'll get to this session.'

But Daisy wasn't going to let him get away that easily. 'What about the Christmas scene? Isn't what Auntie Laurel's done awesome? When's Tess going to do her bit? And the others? I want to paint the cable car. We thought red would look amazing against the blue sky.'

Grady paused. 'Those are all good questions. What do you think, Laurel? Are you free to come to my place at the weekend? Daisy's right. There's a lot to do on the scene.' Was it her imagination or was there the tiniest hesitation before he clarified?

Grady's enthusiasm was quite obviously manufactured for Daisy's benefit. Laurel followed suit. 'Of course.' But her heart was heavy as they thrashed out a rough plan for those wanting to work on the Christmas scene. Then Grady finally took his leave, melting away into a fast darkening afternoon.

'Right,' Laurel said brightly, to disguise how sad and unsettled Grady's visit had left her. 'Time to decorate our window, Daisy. Good job your mum doesn't mind us taking over that bit of her office.'

'Yay!'

They spent the rest of the afternoon stringing fairy lights around the office window, Daisy as flushed and excited as a five-year-old. Rea finished work early to join in. They propped up Laurel's portrait of two little boys against old encyclopaedias Rea usually kept in the hall for their aesthetic qualities. Daisy fetched two of her best wreaths, one clustered with blue, silver and pink baubles and ribbon, the other decorated with holly, berries, crab apples and pinecones for those who preferred the compostable option. Daisy ran outside to huddle on the frosty driveway shouting, 'It looks awesome! Really Christmassy! Shall we bring in some holly?'

'Some with berries would look fantastic,' Laurel called back. She tried to fill the hollowness inside her with a dose of Christmas spirit, but it was hard going.

Then, after dinner, it was time for Laurel and Daisy to begin delivering the first Christmas wreaths. While Daisy collected what she'd need, Laurel fended off Rea's worried enquiries. 'You're sure you don't mind?' Rea's eyes were huge with apprehension. 'I know it should be me traipsing round the village with Daisy.'

Laurel shook herself from the thoughts that had plagued her since Grady's departure this afternoon – his shoulders slumped and head down – and gave her sister a reassuring hug. 'That's what I'm here for.' Then, taking this as an opening, she dropped her voice so there was no chance that Daisy, who was bustling about upstairs, would overhear. 'But I do have a favour to ask.'

Rea returned the hug. 'Anything.'

Laurel tried to sound casual. 'I'd love you to come for a quick walk with me soon.'

Rea flinched, though she didn't completely pull away. 'That's not a favour.' Her voice had a hitch in it.

'It is, because you'd be making me happy. I know Angel and Miranda came round the other evening but it would be great if you could at least get out into the village,' Laurel said, feeling her way. Instinctively, she felt it was wrong not to gently encourage Rea because continuing to accept the situation was a form of enablement.

'I know. But staying in is so much easier.' Rea's sigh was hot on Laurel's neck. Then, surprising Laurel, she admitted, 'I had a phone consultation with my behaviour therapist, yesterday.'

'Great!' said Laurel. She was about to bite back with, *Why didn't you tell me?* but tried to understand the vulnerability that might make her sister reluctant to share till she was ready. 'That sounds a significant step.'

Rea went on. 'She'd say you're right to bring it up. She told me about self-exposure therapy. You break going outside into bite-sized bits, just short distances. You do that till it feels more comfortable, then go a bit further. There are a lot of personal stories online where people

208

say they got to grips with agoraphobia by repeating tiny outings until the anxiety dropped. I suppose it's time to give it a go.'

'I'm proud of you,' Laurel croaked, her throat suddenly thick with tears.

Then came a thunder of steps on the stairs and Rea pulled away, whispering, 'Don't tell Daisy till I've actually managed to get out in the street. I don't want to disappoint her if I freak. I haven't been further than the garden since May.'

As it was important for Rea to be in control, Laurel nodded, though she hissed back, 'You can do it. I'll be with you.' She flirted with the idea of asking Rea to come just as far as the gate with them now, to wave them off with their breath freezing on the air as they set off on their Christmas wreath deliveries. But, no, it was wrong to spring things on someone who suffered with panic.

Daisy skipped into the kitchen, bulging black bin liners swinging from each hand. Her sweatshirt said: *Bright as a button – but don't press me.* 'Here are the eight to drop off tonight. I've made raffia loops to hang them by.'

'Great,' said Laurel. 'We need to wrap up warm. It's like Siberia outside.' Soon she was done up like a parcel in coat, hat, mittens, scarf and snow boots, trying to find a comfy way to carry one of the black bin bags and its prickly contents. 'Ouch.' She sucked a fingertip. 'Maybe we should take the car.'

Daisy dropped one of her bags in dismay. 'Aw, Auntie Laurel. We're going to look at everyone's Art December windows on the way. Most people were putting their displays up today. Once we get to The Angel we'll get rid of nearly half of the wreaths in one go,' she wheedled.

Laurel did not feel like trekking round Middledip to

admire village art displays and fairy lights. She felt more like a long, hot bath and a big glass of wine, hoping that tomorrow she'd be able to recapture the joyous dancing of Everyday Woman. But she lived at The Nookery for the purpose of supporting those she loved so she sighed in acceptance, and craned her neck to read Daisy's list on her phone. 'Top Farm Road, Rotten Row, Port Road and two in Great Hill Road. I hope we get rid of the prickliest first.'

They set off in the iron frost. Icicles clung to gutters and the roadside bushes had turned to fantastic displays of lacy ice where cars passing through puddles misted them with spray. A pond in a front garden was cracked like a broken windowpane, the fountain on its last burbles before its jet froze solid. Daisy somehow seemed able to ignore the knife-like wind keening down Main Road and the way it tried to snatch the bin bags from their hands. She happily searched out Art December windows, flushed not just with the temperatures but with the success of her Google map, which led them to displays of paintings, drawings and cheery knitted scarves.

Daisy pointed at a small watercolour and murmured discreetly, 'Is that one meant to be a Christmas tree or a hedgehog?'

Laurel tried to give her niece a reproving look because it wasn't cool for one artist to disrespect another. 'I've never seen a hedgehog strung with coloured lights,' she said diplomatically. Then she snorted a giggle and whispered, 'I've seen better-looking Christmas trees, though.'

Daisy's long hair blew out from beneath her hood like a curly scarf and she finally seemed to notice the arctic temperatures, as they turned right into The Cross. 'Brr-brr-brr,' she shivered. 'Let's deliver the Rotten Row wreath first. Oh, look, Nan Heather's got her Christmas tree up already.'

Laurel didn't remember Nan Heather but she joined Daisy in waving a mitten at the tiny, elderly lady smiling and waving through her window. They knocked on a house two doors up and Daisy took her first twenty-pound note in payment as they delivered a wreath covered in so many baubles it nearly gave Laurel a migraine.

They walked on to The Angel, where they found a jolly gathering in The Public, members of Craft Stuff chattering loudly about sales through their Art December window displays or hurrying to finish ornaments and cards for their stalls at the Middledip Christmas Fair. An elderly guy called Hubert had decided to join the session instead of tending his window at home in Port Road and as he'd ordered a wreath Daisy got rid of four instead of three. Modestly, she accepted her customers' exclamations of delight as they examined their wreaths on woven willow circlets, the artfully arranged leaves, berries and cones cunningly secured with jute twine. As they left The Angel, Laurel paused at the counter to buy two cups of hot chocolate to-go, though, she reflected, Daisy's hands probably needed no warming, what with the way she was rubbing them in glee at pocketing a further eighty pounds.

The east wind poked its icy fingers into their collars as they continued up Port Road, slip-sliding along the icy route past the Art December windows, one with corn dolls, others with scented candles and pretty bird feeders, the word 'art' being applied to all art, craft and making. Laurel finished the last of her drink with regret. She hadn't wanted to rush it but it was almost cold chocolate already.

When they reached Mistletoe Cottage on the corner of Ladies Lane, Daisy turned her mouth down in disappointment. 'Grady hasn't done his window. And he's the organiser.'

She was right. Mistletoe Cottage didn't look one bit festive and its curtains were firmly shut. 'I expect he'll get it done,' Laurel said soothingly, thinking that the cottage looked as gloomy as Grady had when he'd left the studio this afternoon. She linked Daisy's arm to cross Ladies Lane, not wanting her niece to take it into her head to bang on Grady's door and demand he instantly fill a window with Christmas lights and brightly coloured gourds.

A few minutes later, they arrived in Great Hill Road to make their last deliveries and Laurel gave an involuntary 'Ow!' and clutched her hands over her eyes. Every house was festooned with lights – white, red, blue and green, they were twinkling, flashing, flickering around trees or dripping from gutters. Illuminated snowmen posed on lawns and floodlit Santas drove sleighs across roofs.

Daisy gurgled with laughter. 'They've entered the Christmas Street competition. The street that wins gets a Christmas party and chooses a charity to receive a donation. Really, though, they want to get on the telly and in the papers.'

'I wish I'd worn sunglasses,' Laurel grumbled. Then a nearby Art December window caught her eye. 'Oh, look at that lovely hat and gloves. Do I just ring the doorbell if I want to buy them?'

'Or get the phone number from the Google map,' suggested Daisy, not just phone-orientated but keen to demonstrate the functionality of her map. But the house-holder must have heard their voices because she flung open her front door and stood framed in illuminated icicles. Her gaze lit on Laurel. She beamed. 'I knew your mum quite well, duck. You're working in her old studio, aren't you? My, she would have been proud. She was lovely with her painting.'

Laurel felt tears prickle at the unexpectedness of this village connection. 'Thank you,' she whispered, conscious of a warm, floaty sensation to know Isla was still remembered fondly. She didn't bother asking how the woman knew about the studio. News spread on the Middledip breeze. They chatted about Isla buying The Nookery and having the studio built, Laurel bought the hat and gloves and Daisy somehow managed to sell the woman a Christmas wreath to be delivered on Sunday. Eventually, teeth chattering in the Narnia-like freeze, they said their goodbyes.

As they turned towards home, Daisy's phone rang. She answered with, 'Hey,' and a series of, 'Yep. Yep. Yep,' then finished with, 'OK, cool, I'll ask her.' She turned to Laurel. 'Can I hang out at Zuzanna's in Port Road for a bit? Niall's going, too.'

'I don't mind.' Laurel checked the time. 'I'll have to pick you up at ten so you'll only have about an hour, though.' She supposed an hour with your mates was always worth walking across the village for. 'Just call and check with your mum first.'

'Yeah, yeah, school night.' Daisy nodded resignedly. She made the call and secured Rea's permission as they strode towards Zuzanna's house, passing Mistletoe Cottage again, definitely not living up to its Christmassy name. With the Art December windows and early Christmas trees appearing in windows or on lawns, the rest of the village was leaving it behind.

As they approached Zuzanna's house, though, Daisy slowed her footsteps. 'Laurel, a thing happened today,' she said.

As Daisy had spent the day at school, Laurel's thoughts flew to the trouble she'd had with other girls. 'A thing?'

'Yeah. To do with Scarlett.' Daisy frowned.

Damn. Gently, Laurel drew Daisy to a halt. 'Has she been giving you a hard time again, sweetie?' Inside her mittens, her hands clenched.

'No.' Daisy shook her head, her hair snaking out of her hood. They'd stopped close to a bare-branched tree in a garden, through which someone had threaded white lights, and their flickering reflected in Daisy's large eyes. 'She and Octavia have ignored me since they came back from being excluded a week and a half ago. They give me the evil eye, sometimes, that's all.' She shrugged, as if to indicate that she could live with that.

Relief made Laurel's chest go all hot. 'That's good news,' she said lightly. She made to pick up the pace again because even with boots and a hat she was beginning to shiver.

Daisy, however, hung back. 'Scarlett's got a deep scratch across her top lip.'

Unsure where this was going, Laurel waited, conscious of the wind finding a way through the knit of her mittens. Daisy was gazing down Port Road but she didn't look as if she was seeing cottages with Christmassy window displays. Rather, she seemed to be wrestling with her thoughts.

Eventually, she went on. 'Zuzanna sits with this girl in science who lives near Scarlett. She told Zuzanna that the scratch came from Scarlett's mum's fingernail because she, like, hit Scarlett for getting in trouble at school. Over me.'

'Oh *dear*.' Laurel's heart thumped uncomfortably. Feelings of inadequacy loomed as she realised Daisy was looking to her to interpret the situation and probably offer appropriate words of wisdom.

'Well . . .' Daisy drew the sound out as, hands jammed in pockets and shoulders hunched, she switched her gaze to Laurel. 'Do you think Scarlett bullies other people because her mum bullies her?'

Laurel tried to compartmentalise her emotional reaction on the subject of bullies in order to answer objectively. 'That does happen,' she said carefully. 'But it's not an excuse. We can't accept people behaving badly because someone behaves badly to them.' She paused. Then, because she could see another question in Daisy's eyes, she added, 'You're not to blame for any trouble she's having with her mum, OK?'

Daisy, although she echoed, 'OK,' looked far from convinced.

Laurel took Daisy's arm, casting around for a way to make the fourteen-year-old understand that Laurel had the experience to back up her claim. 'I was bullied by two people when I was sixteen. One had a difficult mum.' Everyone had known Amie's mum's reputation for starting vicious arguments in a village known for its friendliness. 'The other had a controlling dad, who also might have set a bad example. *But*,' she emphasised, 'I knew his brother, too, and he was a nice guy. So, to me, that means people don't have to follow the pattern set by their parents.' She decided not to make an allowance for what Grady had told her, that Cormac Cassidy had treated Number One Son quite differently to Number Two.

'But, like . . .' Daisy heaved out a frustrated breath. 'If Scarlett's being bullied then I feel bad for her. It's confusing.'

'It is,' Laurel allowed. 'But just remember that it's not your fault.' They set off again for Zuzanna's house and Daisy chattered about the Christmas wreaths she still had to complete before they could be delivered. She patted her stack of twenty-pound notes in a zipped pocket. 'Loads of the stuff I use is free from Gabe's place, too, so I'm getting, like, rich.'

Laurel laughed and made jokes about Daisy affording expensive Christmas presents, but at the same time she was going back over her own words. *You're not to blame . . . it's not your fault.* She'd never one hundred per cent accepted that about herself. She sighed.

When she'd received counselling a few years ago she'd felt clearer about things than she did now. Right had seemed right and wrong had seemed wrong. Laurel had chosen neither to confront the bullies nor to go to the police because that was what was best for her, not because the bullies deserved a break. It was black and white.

She hadn't thought too much about Mac and Amie's backstories but she realised now that there was a lot of grey in the world and that she was glad she had no idea where Amie Blunt was so she was unlikely to discover if, like Scarlett, she'd had her own bully. She did not want to feel forgiving thoughts towards Amie.

But didn't that mean she was failing to *let the past go*, as Fliss advised? Conflicting feelings and thoughts preoccupied her as she saw Daisy into Zuzanna's family home, a small brick-built place not far from The Angel. Then she turned and retraced her steps up Port Road.

The one thing she did know was that Grady Cassidy was innocent in all of this.

She strode up the silent drive of Mistletoe Cottage, lifted her hand and gave the front door a sharp *rat-tat*.

Chapter Thirteen

It was so long before the door opened that she began to think he'd gone out, despite the illuminated sitting room window and his truck parked in the drive. She pictured him at Mac's house or in The Three Fishes, drinking beer and playing darts under the grotto-like twinkling lights, and began to turn away.

Then, suddenly, he was framed in the open doorway. 'Oh. Laurel,' he said.

She hesitated. 'I'm not sure from that greeting how you feel about it being me.'

He didn't crack a smile. 'There are people I want to see less.' While she was turning that unenthusiastic reply over, he turned towards his sitting room with a polite, 'Want to come in?'

As it was either that or shout, 'No, thanks!' after him and head home, she followed, shutting the front door and hovering at the entrance to his sitting room. He'd already thrown himself into his chair. An empty mug stood on the floor and the TV made car-chase noises from its place on the wall. He turned the racket off and trained his gaze on her, obviously waiting for her to speak first.

'Daisy's worried about you,' she began, which was sort of true, even though Daisy had actually been worried about the lack of window display in Mistletoe Cottage's square window. 'You haven't put up your Art December display.'

His eyebrows clashed at the bridge of his nose. But then they relaxed and he rolled his eyes instead. 'I know it's meant to go up on the frigging 1st of December but I've had other things on my mind.'

She understood but couldn't help an edge creeping into her voice. 'I won't pass exactly that message back to Daisy. Art December means a lot to her. We've been traipsing all over the village, admiring displays. People have really got behind it.'

'Good for them,' he said, uncharacteristically snarky. He stared at her for several seconds. 'Are you going to sit down?'

She stayed where she was. 'I'm not sure I'm any more welcome than the 1st of December.'

His gaze faltered, and then he passed his hands across his eyes. 'Sorry. I'm probably not fit company. When the doorbell rang I thought it was going to be Mac and I don't know how to react to him at the moment.'

Her heart heavy, she took a step back. 'I don't think you know how to react to me, either, do you? Finding out about Mac has changed things, which is exactly what I was afraid of from the start. Bloody Mac,' she added bitterly.

He didn't reply. As Laurel hadn't so much as removed a mitten, she mumbled a goodnight and turned back towards the front door, already anticipating the bite of the polar cold outside as she fumbled to turn the locking mechanism.

'Laurel.'

She swung around, surprised to find him close behind her.

His eyes were dark and dull in his pale face. 'I keep thinking you can take everything from him.'

She let her hand drop from the door. 'Is that why you're barely able to look at me? You're scared I'll finally report him?' Slowly, because she was beginning to overheat, she pulled off her hat, scarf and gloves and opened her coat. 'From counselling, I learned that I didn't experience the biggest trauma ever but that nevertheless it was real. It happened. I acknowledged it in my heart and talked about it.' She stepped closer to him, gazing into his shuttered face. 'Maybe you need to do the same. Acknowledging something bad has happened is a big help.'

He lifted a hand as if to brush her advice away. 'This is not about me.'

'It's affecting you . . .' She trailed off from that thought and circled back. 'As I said this afternoon, I know I'm entitled to report the incident and name names. I was then, and I am now. But what I also know is that *I'm under no pressure to do anything at all*. I'm *entitled* not to. Some people believe there would be fewer victims if every culprit was reported. Others think I'll never get closure if I don't act – and maybe they have a point because coming back here has made keeping the incident in the past well-nigh impossible. Everyone's entitled to their views but *I* choose not to take responsibility for stopping the bad behaviour of others. That choice is for me, not for Mac. I don't wish him well, at all. I don't care if he's panicking that I'm a skeleton ready to rattle out of his closet.'

Grady stood silent and dark in the dimness of the hall. His gaze was on the floor but she could tell he was listening.

She shucked off her coat and dumped it on the stairs. 'You love Mac and I know you looked up to him. He's family and his son and his wife are central to your life. I expect it's horrible to learn he once committed a crime.' Softly, she added, 'That's why I never told you. See?'

'I feel grubby,' he whispered. 'Because of what he did. I'm torn in half. I'm so fucking disappointed. After we kissed I was on Cloud Nine. Now it's spoiled.'

Her throat tightened. She closed her eyes and dug deep for the strength to say the right thing. Something that might make Grady feel better. 'You know, I was always a little scared of the Cassidy brothers. Mac scared me because he was cocky and brash.' She reached out and looped her fingers with his, just the barest touch to help her get out the rest of the words. 'You were just as big and strong and good-looking, but you were also gentle and I could talk to you for hours. You made me feel safe. I was scared because you made me feel a whole lot of other things, things I was barely ready for,' she added reflectively, thinking of long-ago, exciting kisses. And one that wasn't so long ago. She took another breath. 'What scares me about you now is that I still like you. But we're in such different places.'

The silence became charged. Grady's gaze flicked up to meet hers. She felt tingly, half excited and half scared of the risk she'd just taken by sharing her feelings.

Then Grady moved and it was as if they were magnets because the last of the gap between them closed with a little jump. His arms slipped around her and he held her tight against his heart. 'Can you stay for a while?' he asked, voice strained and muffled against her hair.

A giggle straggled out of her, sounding almost like a sob. 'Only till ten. I have to get Daisy from Zuzanna's.'

He actually managed a laugh. 'You still have to be in by ten on a school night?'

She held him tighter, feeling her breasts flatten against the hard wall of his chest as her head found just the right spot against his shoulder. 'I could come back when I've seen her home.' Her whisper surrounded them like a breath of hope.

'Yes,' he groaned, nuzzling her hair, lifting a hand to caress her nape. 'Please come back.' He tipped his head and she lifted her face to meet him, closing her eyes at the heat of his lips on her temples and then her eyelids. Finally, she felt the scalding, silken caress of his tongue as he found her mouth. Laurel made a conscious decision to set aside the bad stuff, which still had to be dealt with because Grady was Mac's brother and always would be, and she sank into the kiss. Every muscle softened, every hair rose, every inch of her skin shivered in hyper-sensitivity that brought her to a state of arousal she rarely remembered experiencing.

Paradise. Bliss. Eden. Serenity.

Security. Trust.

Grady.

The heat between them was incredible. She ran her hands over his back, following each segment of his spine and curving muscle. He began to stroke her, too: the curve of her hip, the dip of her back. He grew hard against her and she pressed against him to let him know, yes, it was OK. But when his hands slid around to her ribs he hovered, hesitating.

She broke the kiss just long enough to say, 'Yes,' then his hand slipped onto her breast and both of them groaned in their throats. His hand slipped under her jumper and the T-shirt beneath, then his touch was blazing across skin and inside her bra.

'You're so stunning, so sexy,' he murmured against her mouth. 'Jeez, Laurel, I've wanted this for half my life.'

Laurel's head tipped back as he caressed the curves of her breasts, the peaks of her nipples, taking his time to learn the feel of her skin. Breathlessly she said, 'I'm not sure I was ready for this at sixteen.'

'I was,' he murmured against her mouth, making her laugh. Then he sighed. 'This freaking ten o'clock curfew's on my mind.' He carried on kissing her but felt for his phone, lifting his head briefly to look at it, and groaning. 'Nine forty-five.' Reluctantly, he withdrew from her clothing, smoothing each layer back into place. 'You're still coming back?'

'If you want me to.' Regretfully, she removed her hands from under his sweatshirt and let it fall back into place.

'If I wanted it any more, I'd burst into flames.' The accompanying grin and wink was pure Grady, a welcome replacement for the bleak misery with which he'd greeted her earlier. Laurel wasn't stupid enough to think that a few kisses and an air of promise would vanquish her problems with his brother but it was a step in the right direction. A declaration that neither of them had caused the problem.

Pulling her winter layers back on took Laurel a lot longer than usual, hampered as she was by deep, distracting kisses.

'I promise you a better time than standing in my hallway later,' he said, when she finally zipped up her coat. Then he pulled his coat off the newel.

'What are you doing?' she murmured, still kissing his jawline as she pulled on her mittens.

'I'll walk you to Zuzanna's,' he said, trying to find his sleeve. 'I need to make certain you come back.'

'OK.' She nibbled his neck as she tried to thread her scarf on without losing contact. 'So why am I kissing you goodbye?'

'We're just kissing,' he said indignantly. 'We like it, don't we?'

She laughed, and he reached around her to open the door, exclaiming, 'Whew!' at the icy blast that greeted them. 'One way to cool my ardour,' he complained, yanking up his collar. Hand in hand until they reached Zuzanna's, they hurried down Port Road to pick Daisy up, calling greetings to Zuzanna, who watched from the door, wrapping her arms around herself in an exaggerated, shivering mime, before shooting indoors.

Daisy gave Grady a sidelong look as they turned the corner by Rotten Row. 'Just been saying, like, the organiser of Art December really ought to get his window sorted.'

'Your aunt's already scolded me. I'll do it soon.' He gave her a friendly shoulder nudge, causing her to scrabble for her footing on the frost-polished pavement.

They joshed each other all the way home, Grady laughing when Daisy pointed out decorated windows and crowed, 'See, everyone got their window display done on time except you.'

Laurel tramped beside them, her smile at their antics disguising the ball of anticipation she carried inside. It was so long since she'd gone home with a man that she'd almost forgotten how it went. Well, yes, she'd been in Grady's house twice before this but she was pretty sure that this time when she went home with him it was going to be . . . well, *going home with a man*.

The ball of anticipation slithered into apprehension. She'd showered earlier and her leg-waxing was recent enough to pass muster but she'd have no armour of flattering clothes, perfume or mascara. She'd have hat-hair instead of glossy hair, her underclothes didn't match and she wore a sports bra because when using herself as a figure model earlier she hadn't wanted anything jiggling free as she'd stretched and jumped.

Was there a way she could discreetly shoot indoors for a ten-minute spruce up?

They turned into Great End and Grady felt for Laurel's hand as he teased Daisy, 'Let's see this window you guys have put together then, so I know what I'm up against.'

Once up the drive, they clustered around Rea's office window where twinkling white lights neatly outlined the rectangle and reflected from the baubles spangling one of Daisy's wreaths. The more elegant, compostable wreath twisted slowly, suspended by black tinsel from the curtain pole above.

Laurel's painting of two little boys caught the illumination from the fairy lights, giving it an ethereal glow in the darkness. The boys regarded each other, one tracing the other's face with his plump, toddler hand. Childhood innocence intensified their bond and wonder tinged their dawning smiles.

'OK,' said Grady gruffly, dropping the teasing. 'You guys have smashed it. Daisy, you're amazing creating those wreaths and selling them. And Laurel, that canvas is damned beautiful.'

Laurel wasn't in the million-pounds-a-canvas bracket but she was accomplished enough that people passed compliments yet, somehow, Grady's simple sincerity brought a lump to her throat. 'Thank you,' she murmured.

'Twelve hundred pounds,' he said, reading the small label she'd popped discreetly on the window board.

She fidgeted. 'It would be more on my Etsy shop but if someone in the village wanted it . . .' She didn't finish the sentence, feeling uncomfortably pretentious that all the windows she'd peeped into this evening sported far more modest price tags.

He turned to her. 'It's a snip. A piece of fine art by an artist of repute should be priced higher.'

She flushed, glad he wouldn't be able to see it in the darkness. 'It's a small canvas.'

Daisy gave Laurel a one-armed hug. 'My clever auntie.'

This prosaic view broke the spell and Grady laughed, tugging Daisy's wildly blowing hair. 'OK, kid, think you've got to go in. Your clever auntie's coming back with me.' Laurel's face burned again.

Daisy's glance flicked from one of them to the other and then fell on their clasped hands. 'Oh, ri-i-i-ght. See you later.' She grinned before she went indoors.

Laurel had missed her chance of making an excuse to nip in for a spruce up because she had no intention of facing Daisy immediately after that *Oh, ri-i-i-ght* and the knowing grin. Anyway, Grady was already pulling her along, huddled into his coat and complaining about turning into a block of ice.

They arrived back at Mistletoe Cottage less than half an hour after they'd left. The hall was warm and welcoming – perhaps some residual heat from their earlier kisses? – and Grady turned to her, softly pulling off her hat and running his fingers through her hair before slipping her mittens off and kissing each of her hands, then unwinding her scarf. He tossed everything on the hall table then unzipped her coat, slid it down her arms and hung it up.

225

He threw off his own coat before she could even reach for his zip.

Then, surprising her, he kissed her temple and asked, 'Glass of wine?'

As she'd kind of thought he might be expecting to simply carry on where they'd had to leave off, she was charmed by his lack of rush. 'Any white in the fridge?' she asked, following him as he clicked a switch and the overhead lights came on in the kitchen.

He poured them each a glass and they went into the sitting room, more gently lit by a lamp. They settled themselves on the sofa, legs entwined. 'You're here to help with my Art December window, right?' He smiled, but it was subdued.

Wondering at the tension that had developed but following his cue, she glanced at his firmly curtained window. 'That's right. Break out the fairy lights.'

He sipped his wine, his gaze skating away from hers and then returning. 'Laurel,' he said at last, voice low as he took her hand in his. 'Are we . . . are you comfortable here? With me?'

And Laurel realised it wasn't so much tension she'd picked up on as anxiety – for her. A warm feeling washed over her. She answered softly. 'I so appreciate your concern but if I wasn't comfortable alone with you, I wouldn't be here.' She stretched forward and pressed a kiss on his lips. 'I was attacked once. We've acknowledged that. Now let's move on. I'm capable of perfectly normal interaction with a man.' Though she did remember that when she'd slept with her 'first', Amie's body shaming still fresh, she'd worried the boy would find her breasts ugly. Thankfully he hadn't – and none of her subsequent lovers ever had, either.

She remembered wishing wistfully that her first had been Grady.

Grady still seemed to need reassurance. 'Even with me?'

Her heart hurt for him, for his vulnerability, for his feeling the unfair and unkind taint of close association. 'You're not your brother. We need to acknowledge that, too.'

With evident relief, he kissed her. Relief turned to sweet, aching longing and then deep, aching heat. Soon, clutching their wineglasses, they drifted up the narrow winding stairs that opened onto a compact landing. His bedroom, however, was huge, with three dormer windows looking into the back garden and a beamed, uneven ceiling. While he switched on lamps and closed curtains, she gazed around. 'I'd never have thought the rooms would be this big.'

'The people who had Mistletoe Cottage before me knocked two bedrooms into one. The second bedroom is a box.' He returned to her and, sliding a hand to her waist, asked conversationally, 'Shall I undress you?'

Heat roared from the soles of her feet. Her voice emerged on a tremor. 'Please do.'

He took her wineglass and stepped her into the pool of lamplight. Unhurriedly, he unthreaded her arms from her sleeves and pulled her sweater and T-shirt over her head in one go. 'Lazy,' she chided him. With a grin, he shucked off his own top, leaving his hair tossed, his eyes gleaming with anticipatory heat.

'You're so warm,' she murmured, stroking his chest, feeling the downy softness of male body hair – always high on the list of things she liked. While his eyes half-shut at her touch, his fingers were busy unfastening her jeans, an activity she didn't help by pressing her hips against the hardness of him and making him groan.

'Jeans weren't designed for sexy, mutual undressing,' he murmured, when he'd recovered his breath.

Taking that as a cue, she wriggled out of hers, seizing the opportunity to shed her socks, too, as thick purple socks didn't lend themselves to sexy, mutual undressing either. His eyes were greedy as they raked over her in her underwear and she suddenly remembered. 'It's a sports bra, I didn't think we'd—'

But he kissed her explanation from her lips, stooped slightly to get his arms around her beneath her bottom and twirled with her in his arms so that he could carry her with him onto the bed. 'You're gorgeous. Beautiful. Sexy,' he murmured. 'And I love sports bras, especially when they have, like this one, a little zip at the front.' To demonstrate his pleasure, he tugged the tag down and the elastic fabric sprang aside, giving him unfettered opportunity to lower his mouth to her breasts. 'Luscious,' he murmured.

Time drifted by as they explored each other's bodies. Dizzily, Laurel thought she'd never before made love with a man who was incredibly sweet and incredibly confident at the same time. He wasn't afraid of asking her what she liked – and trialling it – but seemed to enjoy taking it from there, surprising her, arousing her, until she felt ready to explode.

Then he rolled on a condom and pushed inside her . . . and explode she did.

Chapter Fourteen

Grady was woken by a rustling beside his bed. When he cracked open his eyes he got a glimpse of tumbled auburn hair. Laurel. Memories of the night before sent a shiver of desire through him. He had the pleasantly achy feeling that spoke of energetic sex and he was probably wearing a goofy smile. 'You're running out on me now you've had your wicked way with my body?' he demanded sleepily.

Laurel's head popped up above the level of the rumpled duvet, eyes dancing. 'I don't want to face a stream of Daisy's questions, which I will if she sees me coming in. Rea keeps telling her not to ask me where I've been or where I'm going but . . .'

'. . . She does anyway,' he finished for her. 'It's OK. She's fourteen. I understand.' He stretched and yawned. It was five-thirty on a dark December morning but he rolled out of bed and began to search for his clothes. 'I'll walk you home.'

'You really don't need—'

He waved her protest away. Getting up an hour before

his alarm was due to go off was a small price to pay for a sexy, satisfying, earth-shattering night with Laurel. As she rose to her feet with her top in her hand he swept her into a bear hug, enjoying the feel of those fantastic breasts against him. 'OK?' he murmured against her neck, breathing in the bed-warm smell of her.

She hugged him back and whispered, 'Very.'

'Mmm.' He let her slide down his body. 'We wasted too much time sleeping, last night.'

Ten minutes later, they stepped outside to discover that yesterday's freezing night had become today's freezing morning. He wrapped an arm around her to share body heat and they staggered to The Nookery. He kissed her goodbye on the porch. 'I still like kissing you in doorways,' he whispered.

She gave him a playful nudge out of the way so she could let herself into the house, whispering back, 'I like being in bed with you better.'

He jogged back to Mistletoe Cottage with her kisses still on his lips.

There was no way he'd get more sleep so he made coffee and treated himself to a leisurely shower with Stormzy blaring from his speaker. He felt . . . fantastic. Warm and satisfied and deeply, deeply happy. Dressing in clean work clothes, he glanced at his bed and a glint of gold caught his eye. Shoving aside a pillow, he found a gold chain. Laurel's. She'd looked so amazing wearing nothing but that. He paused to let a wave of lust wash over him. Laurel in his bed, his arms. Him inside Laurel.

He texted her: *Just found your necklace. Xxxxx*

He ate breakfast at the kitchen table while dealing with emails on his laptop, chasing up an order of paint and sealant that should already have been delivered. Laurel's text arrived a few minutes later. *Thank you! Wondered where it was. :-) xxxxx*

When the doorknocker sounded at about eight o'clock, he slipped the necklace from his pocket and hurried up the hall. With a wide grin he threw open the door and held out the sinuous gold chain. 'It was in my bed—' Then he halted. It wasn't Laurel standing on the frosty paving stones, gazing at him.

It was Pippa.

Pale and drawn, she gazed woefully from the necklace to his face.

'Ah,' he said, realising he'd just thrust under his ex's nose – literally – evidence that he was now sleeping with someone else. 'I didn't realise it was you.' He slipped the golden chain back into his pocket.

Pippa burst into tears, burrowing in her coat pocket and finding a tissue to howl into.

Grady stared at her in dismay. What the hell was he meant to do? Invite Pippa in to cry in private? A big red flag flipped up in his brain at that idea, considering that last time he'd let her into the cottage she'd tried to get him to form a family with her and her accidental baby.

He could have groaned aloud. Pippa's situation wasn't his fault or his problem but that didn't stop him feeling shitty to see her in tears. To make things worse, over her shoulder he saw Niall crossing Ladies Lane as he did on school days at this time, en route to the bus stop in Port Road. Niall rarely took advantage of Mac driving to the same school every day as Mac's school day was much longer than his son's. Also, Niall preferred to pile on the bus with everyone else so as to not draw attention to the fact he was the son of Mr Cassidy, Head of Year Ten.

Niall looked surprised. Then he grinned. Oh, no, did

it look as if Pippa was leaving Grady's house, as if it was her who'd spent the night? He imagined Niall telling Daisy and Daisy mentioning it to Laurel which, to her, would feel like all kinds of horrible. 'Hey, Niall,' he called. 'Your mum and dad OK?'

Niall paused. 'Yeah.' Then, as if an afterthought, 'Dad's stressed about work or something. Mum's worried about him and keeps hugging him and stuff. Hello, Pippa,' he added, probably wondering why she didn't turn to greet him. For a couple of years, Pippa had pretty much filled the role of Niall's aunt.

Still sniffling, Pippa didn't even answer. Niall looked hurt and Grady felt a surge of irritation. Pippa was upset but Niall was fourteen and wouldn't understand why he'd been snubbed. Grady gave an expressive eye-roll in the direction of Pippa's bent head before he said goodbye to Niall and wished him a good day at school.

'Why are you here, Pippa?' he asked, keeping his voice neutral.

She blew her nose and took a step. 'Can I come in?'

He stood his ground. 'It's probably not appropriate,' he said gently. 'If you've come to ask what you asked before, the answer's still the same.'

Pippa let out another sob. 'Mum and Dad are coming to ours for Christmas. Zelda's house is tiny and I'm throwing up every morning. They're going to hear. Grady if we were—'

'But we're not,' he said, as evenly as he could considering he was stemming rising anger that she was still trying to put him in this horrible position. Although she might have realised it from him brandishing Laurel's necklace a few minutes ago, he felt the need to add, 'There's someone else in my life now. And I know you've already spun your

232

story to her and she didn't fall for it. Though I wouldn't have made myself a convenience for you, even if she wasn't a factor,' he said, as an afterthought.

Pippa showed him a wretched, tear-soaked face. 'But what about my parents?'

He sighed. Pippa's parents putting her on a pedestal had always been tricky but was no longer his worry. 'Why don't you call them up and tell them that you're pregnant?' he suggested as sympathetically as he could manage. 'Tell them it wasn't planned but you're happy. You're thirty-four, Pippa. Not fourteen.'

With one last reproachful look, Pippa turned away. The desolate droop to her shoulders twanged his conscience and he called after her, 'I'm sure they'll be fine once they get over the shock.'

Relieved that he was free to head to his spray shop, he gathered his things, reflecting that he seemed to have had a close shave with Pippa. In the past, his steadiness had balanced out her irrational side. Devoid of that emotional ballast, she was behaving unreasonably. Suppose they'd succeeded in starting a family when they'd wanted one? Would she ever have been able to put a child first? Cope with sleepless nights and soiled baby clothes? That now seemed a fantastical notion. Grady would have ended up with the lion's share of the parenting . . . although he didn't think he would have minded.

A moment's sorrow arrowed through him. He would never be a parent, and neither would Laurel, from what she'd said. He took a deep breath of the wintry air and came up with a positive.

Look what they'd save on condoms.

*

It was a shock when, only an hour later Pippa's sister Zelda walked into Grady's spray shop. He'd been carefully brushing in a turquoise background for a seascape on the bonnet of a black and white 1949 Oldsmobile Rocket, trying not to dwell too much on his part in devaluing such a classic by the addition of an octopus and several star fish. He'd just muttered to himself, 'The customer gets what the customer wants,' when Zelda's voice rang out, making him commit the cardinal sin of letting go of the paint and air triggers simultaneously.

'I cannot say how shocked I am,' she snapped.

Grady, with a horrible feeling that he knew why she might be shocked, wiped his nozzle to prevent paint spatter when he got started again and pushed aside the booth screens before pulling down his mask. Overspray could hang in the air for hours and he was careful about breathing it in. He usually left the street door open for ventilation but now Pippa's big sister had crept up on him he was questioning the wisdom of that. 'Hi, Zelda,' he said, thinking, not for the first time, how different she was to Pippa. No highlights or big hair for Zelda; no painted nails or constantly changing wardrobe. Zelda and Grady used to get on well, which he'd privately put down to them each being the quieter, more restful sibling in their respective families. 'I'm shocked, too.'

Zelda hesitated, looking wrong-footed. 'I'd have thought you'd be over the moon about the baby. But Pippa says you don't want anything to do with it.' Astonishment rang in her voice. 'You're rejecting your own child?'

His heart flinched at the accusation that he, who would have loved a baby, would ever do such a thing. 'So, now I'll tell you what's shocking me – Pippa's trying to palm a hook-up's baby off as mine.' Then, when Zelda's brows shot up, he added, 'I'm "defective", remember. No swimmers. Firing blanks. Don't let her drag you into her fantasy.'

Zelda turned white. 'She said you got back together one night and a bit of a miracle happened.' But her voice faltered and the expression in her eyes told him she'd realised she'd been had.

He snorted. 'For a miracle to happen you'd at least have to have sex with each other, and that hasn't happened. Pippa told me she's pregnant and offered me the opportunity to take on the baby as my own, saying nobody need ever know I can't father kids.' He spread his hands. 'I declined.' He softened his voice. 'I'm sorry she's having difficulty facing your parents having to face the fact that their princess is fallible.'

Zelda crossed to the stool by the tool chest and sank down on it as if the strength had left her legs. 'Shit,' she murmured. 'Sorry. Why did I fall for that guff? It's not like I don't know Pippa. But when she cries . . .'

He cast a jaundiced eye at the bonnet of the Olds and hoped he wouldn't discover a run when he got back to his work. 'It's like trying to resist a cute puppy, isn't it?' He decided to reinforce what he'd told Pippa by telling her sister, too. 'I've moved on, Zelda. I'm seeing someone. I don't want to embarrass Pippa by refuting her story to the whole village, but I will if I have to. I can't allow her to—' he paused to summon the correct word '—*appropriate* me, as if I'm hers for the taking. I'm not an outfit she shoved to the back of her wardrobe and now realises could be useful. She put me out on the kerb for the bin men. We're done.' A thought occurred to him. 'I'm sorry you're going to be stuck with the situation, as you live together.'

Zelda jumped to her feet. 'That isn't why I came to see you,' she flashed. 'I love Pippa.'

Grady was unmoved. 'Of course you do. Loving a sibling doesn't mean you love everything they do though.'

They exchanged stiff goodbyes and then he worked peacefully all morning, shading in the mouth of a cave the octopus would emerge from. The octopus had been requested as grey but the kind of grey he had in mind would include a lot of blue and pink highlights to make every tentacle writhe. He thought about Laurel and wondered whether she was painting this morning in her studio, half a mile away. And whether she was wearing that slinky, fits-like-a-second-skin outfit she'd been wearing when he'd surprised her yesterday. She must have been using herself as a reference for her work, but he'd hardly noticed because he'd been so upset at the time.

Well, he corrected himself, he had noticed Laurel in figure-revealing clothing. Just not what she was working on.

He was thinking about stopping for lunch when his phone rang and he read *Mac* on the screen. He paused. They hadn't talked since Mac had confessed the major part he'd played in driving Laurel from the village. Not knowing whether he was ready for this call yet, Grady answered cautiously. 'Hey.'

Mac's voice was loud in his ear. 'You're not really seeing Laurel, are you?' There was anxiety, even panic in his words.

'What the fuck?' Grady shot back. 'How do you know?' Then realisation dawned and he rubbed his face, feeling the indentations where his safety mask had been. 'I guess Niall must have loitered on the other side of the hedge to listen to me speaking to Pippa this morning.

236

Yes, I'm seeing her.' Worry wriggled in his gut. He hoped he was 'seeing' Laurel. He was pretty sure one-nighters weren't her usual style but they hadn't exactly laid out a relationship route map. The thought soured his mood. The day, which had begun so delightfully, had swiftly turned to crap. 'We're trying to not let other things interfere, OK? We've talked about what happened with you and Amie and your mates. Neither of *us* did anything wrong.' At his slight emphasis on the 'us' he heard his brother's sharp intake of breath. 'Sorry if that smarts, Mac. It wasn't intended as a dig. It was just so you know.'

'Right.' Mac's voice was low and defeated and Grady wondered where he'd gone to make this call. Did heads of year have offices to retreat to? Was he speaking from his car? An empty classroom? Although he thought of himself and Mac as close, there was a lot he didn't know about him.

Mac sounded defeated. 'I'm sorry. If I could make things easier for you, I would, but if Laurel won't listen to an apology I'm not sure how to fix things.'

Grady answered sombrely. 'You can't rewrite history, brother.'

A few minutes later they ended the call and he stood staring at his silent phone, wondering how things were going to play out with him in the middle between the woman he had feelings for and the brother she had a massive problem with.

Then, as if he'd summoned her, he heard Laurel's laugh, carried to him on the breeze. Striding to the door he caught sight of her back as she strolled up Gabe's track elbow-to-elbow with a slight, hesitant figure. Holy crap, was that Rea with her? Outdoors? He hadn't witnessed that for months and months. How in the hell had Laurel pulled that off?

He unbuttoned his overalls and fought his way free, flinging on his coat and beanie hat, then locked the door beneath the sign for Grady Auto Art and set off in their wake to offer support if Rea got upset.

This morning Laurel had snatched up a two-inch brush and swooped on the canvas she'd primed, ready to be painted, a canvas taller than she was. Excitement had coursed through her as the first lines of her dancing woman seemed to paint themselves – the curve of the spine, the tilt of the head, the spring and stretch of her legs. She felt as if the energy and joy of making love with Grady were exploding on her canvas. Anything could be painted: music, laughter, colour, promise, possibilities and hope. Floods of creative energy had hit her before but never quite so effervescent and consuming.

Despite her frenzy, she hadn't even sighed when her phone alarm told her it was Rea's lunch time. Today, Rea had planned to try to take a walk. Laurel's place was at her sister's side.

Laurel's heart had burst with pride as Rea, pale and betraying agitation with every movement, set her jaw beneath a red hat that looked a lot jauntier than she did and stepped out into another frozen day. The deal had been to get to the corner of Great End and for Rea to peep down Main Road. But once there, though her shoulders hunched anxiously, Rea had whispered, 'Let's go a bit further.' Laurel had felt a deep conviction that questioning the decision would snap Rea's precarious self-control and said lightly, 'We could look at a few of the Art December windows in Main Road. I'll show you them on Daisy's map.' She'd held her breath but Rea had nodded, though rather as if she were saying yes to her own flogging, and put one foot before the other, peeping at watercolours, cards and crochet as the windows came and went.

They got as far as MAR Motors where two cars could be seen inside, one on ramps. Rea paused uncertainly. Then a man near the doorway looked up and called, 'Hiya, Rea. Good to see you.'

Almost as a gasp, Rea said, 'Hello, Ratty.'

Laurel recognised Ratty then, Tess's husband and Grady's landlord. The wind blew his curls around as he ambled over saying gently, 'This your sister?'

Rea's innate good manners kicked in and she made introductions. Ratty displayed oily hands and grinned as he said, 'I won't shake.'

Laurel grinned back. 'Good.'

The tiny encounter seemed to steady Rea, though her gaze flitted from an old Land Rover on the forecourt of MAR Motors to Booze & News across the road. Her breath seemed to be coming faster and more shallowly.

Laurel gave her arm a pat. 'We can go back whenever you want. Or,' she added, as if it didn't matter either way, 'We could see if that pony's still at Gabe's. Daybreak. I feel a bit guilty I haven't been back to ride her again. Maybe I can do something about that this weekend.'

Rea cast a look behind her, as if checking her route home was still clear. Then, voice small and tight, she said, 'All right.'

Laurel didn't want to pop Rea's bubble of determination by peeping into the open door of Grady's spray shop as they passed, but instead told Rea how pretty Daybreak was and recounted what Bertie had told her in the pub.

239

'Gabe's miffed with Bertie, apparently, because he bought her in an under-the-counter deal.'

Rea even managed a tiny joke. 'Must be a big counter to get a pony under it.'

Laurel laughed in delight. Rea was outside, not hyperventilating and engaged enough in the conversation to joke, which was twenty times more than she'd dared hope for.

The ankle-deep mud she remembered from her last trip up Gabe's track had firmed up in the ever-present frost. The sun glinted from frozen grass blades as they passed. 'I should have brought some secateurs to gather holly for Daisy,' Laurel said, when Rea fell ominously silent, her breathing rate noticeably increasing again. 'Don't you think she's done brilliantly fulfilling all the orders for her lovely wreaths?'

Rea was diverted enough to gasp, 'Absolutely.'

Then they turned the corner and there was Daybreak's head over the paddock gate, ears pricked, as if she'd heard them coming. A smile wavered over Rea's face. 'Oh, she is pretty,' she breathed. 'Look at the length of her mane.'

As if understanding, Daybreak nodded and fidgeted from hoof to hoof.

Soon they were stroking Daybreak's velvety nose and scratching her neck. Snobby, in the background, glanced up from grazing but lost interest when he saw that all they were doling out was affection.

Laurel watched, heart full, as Rea murmured to Daybreak and Daybreak nodded that, yes, she *was* a lovely pony. Then came the sound of the house door and soon Gabe was strolling towards them, hands buried deep in his army greatcoat pockets.

Gabe called, 'Morning,' without coming right up to

them. He grinned at Rea. 'Your sister's brought you to see my uncle's stolen pony, has she?'

As he'd probably intended, Rea's attention was instantly captured. 'Stolen?'

'Yes. Silly old sod. No sale agreement and no vetting. Fake pony passport.' He snorted, though with a trace of affection. 'As soon as I got her chip scanned we found her registered as stolen.' He took a casual couple of steps nearer so he could pat Daybreak's neck, too. 'Her original name was Ghostly Girl.'

Rea's smile vanished. 'She's going back to her owners?' She sounded almost regretful, making Laurel dare to hope that Rea was actually garnering some enjoyment from their outing, rather than just clinging on to control by her fingertips.

Then Bertie appeared from the house, his coat almost drowning his slight figure and his beard looking as if he'd been out in the frost too long. 'Hello,' he called. 'You come to admire Dave?'

'*Daybreak*.' Gabe beetled his brows at his uncle and Bertie grinned unrepentantly. 'I don't think you've met Rea, Laurel's sister? Rea, this is my reprobate, pony-rustling uncle Bertie.'

Laurel waited for Rea to shrink from Bertie, who she'd never met. She tried to put herself in Rea's shoes – did two men feel like a rowdy football crowd to her? But Rea surprised her. She greeted Bertie politely but appeared to be awaiting Gabe's answer to her question.

'I'm afraid she can't go back to her owners,' Gabe admitted with a sigh. 'She was stolen seven months ago – we don't know where she's been in the meantime – and she's been replaced in her original home and belongs to the insurance company now.'

'Oh-h-h,' Rea breathed. 'Poor baby.' Once again, Daybreak tossed her head as if nodding.

Then Laurel sensed a presence behind her and turned to see Grady in coat and woollen hat, hanging back at the curve of the track. His slow smile lit his face when he saw she'd noticed him. After checking Rea seemed absorbed by her conversation with Gabe and Bertie, she risked taking a few strides towards him. He stepped forward to meet her and suddenly it wasn't Rea's choppy breathing she was conscious of. Her heart seemed to be jumping all over her lungs.

His gaze was soft on hers but he didn't refer to last night. 'Rea's feeling brave?' he asked, instead.

'She's making an effort for Daisy's sake,' she whispered. 'She's done miles better than I'd dared hope. Our goal was the first corner.'

'Coming here was a good choice,' he said. 'I think Gabe has a gentle magic about him. Everyone enjoys his presence.'

'I wouldn't say it was so much a choice as a panicky inspiration when she looked as if she'd reached her limit,' she admitted.

His gaze shifted to the group by the gate and he lifted his hand to greet them. 'Looks to me that you've judged it perfectly,' he observed. They drifted a little closer as they talked, near enough that Rea wouldn't feel abandoned by Laurel but not too close that another person arriving uninvited might tip her into panic or flight.

She was beginning to look paler now and smile less. Feeling as if she was making her strategy up as she went along, but possessed of a feeling that it would be best to leave now, while progress had been made, rather than waiting for Rea's anxieties to mount, Laurel slid an arm around her sister. 'If you want time for a bite to eat before you're due back at your desk, maybe we should—'

'Yes,' Rea said, instantly. But she smiled and managed brief goodbyes to Gabe, Bertie and Grady.

No one tried to detain her with a last question or comment and Laurel got a lump in her throat as she realised that the good men had realised it was time for Rea to go. Gabe just called, 'You're welcome to come any time. Snobby doesn't talk to Daybreak so she enjoys visitors.'

Rea smiled as she turned away. Laurel tried to keep their pace measured, strolling home rather than running for safety, but Rea was quiet now and less engaged with Laurel's gentle flow of chatter. She half-fell back into the dear familiarity of The Nookery, relief evident, but at least she didn't fling off her coat and declare she was never going out again.

Instead, she acquiesced to Laurel's suggestion of vegetable soup for lunch and they ate together in the cosy kitchen, dunking bread spread with butter without finesse and drinking big mugs of tea. Eventually, it was Rea who alluded to their outing. 'Poor Daybreak, having no home to go back to.' Obviously that had stuck with her.

Laurel took another spoonful of soup. 'She's a well-mannered pony.' She giggled. 'Shame on Snobby for not talking to her. He's like a cantankerous old man who's forgotten how to socialise.' They ate in silence for a minute, Laurel wondering how far she dare try and progress Rea's outings.

'What do you think about having a ride on Daybreak before she goes to her new owner?' she asked at last. 'I'm involved with painting this Christmas scene on Saturday—' her heart gave a little skip at the thought of that taking place at Mistletoe Cottage '—but I was hoping to manage some exercise for Daybreak on Sunday. We could go together and school her in the paddock.'

For a second Rea froze, and opened her lips as if to veto the suggestion. Then she paused, took a breath, and said, 'I'll try. Daisy might like to come along.' A note of pleasure filtered into her voice. 'When she comes home from school I'll be able to tell her where I've been.'

Laurel gave her a big, squeezy hug. 'She'll be stoked.'

A half-hour later, she was able to return to her dancing woman with a sense of optimism. It wasn't the frothing emotion with which she'd worked in the morning but she worked more calmly, blocking in the shadow behind the figure and taking time to return to her sketch, to subsume herself in that light-as-air dance with arms outflung and face turned to the sky.

She wanted every line of her subject's body to shout, 'I'm happy!'

Laurel felt happy today, too.

Chapter Fifteen

Laurel raced downstairs. It was Saturday and she was supposed to be working at Grady's, painting the Christmas scene. He'd just texted: *You OK? xxx*, probably because she'd estimated her arrival as nine-thirty and it was now ten o'clock. They'd made love again for hours last night, hence her unscheduled lie-in after creeping back into her own bed long before dawn, exhausted. She'd already texted back: *Overslept! xxx* and now called the same information in the direction of the kitchen, where she could hear Rea and Daisy chatting.

'I overslept too,' Daisy called back cheerfully. 'Grady's going to go ape. I was supposed to deliver two wreaths to Niall's mum first thing but now she's coming here to collect them 'cos she's visiting Niall's auntie and one's for her. Got to wait in for her.'

A letter lay on the hall doormat and Laurel paused to scoop it up when she spotted her name on the front in handwriting so stylish she first thought it computer-generated script. 'OK,' she called back to Daisy. She slit the envelope to withdraw a sheet of white A4 lined paper covered in black, upright handwriting with flashy capitals and loops. Wondering who still sent hand-written letters, she unfolded the sheet and read.

Dear Laurel,

This apology is long overdue. As you won't let me make it in person, this is the best I can manage.

Her heart stuttered. No. Really? Mac Cassidy had reached out to her? For fuck's sake, hadn't her refusing to speak privately with him been a big enough hint that she didn't want to hear it? Hands trembling, she checked the foot of the sheet and, sure enough, it was signed *Mac*. Swallowing hard, she read on.

I so regret what happened to you and the part I played in it and can only offer you my deepest, most unreserved apology. I was drunk. I had no idea Amie would do what she did. I know I froze in shock before freeing you and you must have thought I was fully participating. I had no idea it would end like that.

But I'm apologising, not making excuses.

When Amie grabbed you, I should have stopped her.

When she told me to hold you, I should have refused.

I should not have stood by while Amie gave you a hard time in the lead up to that night either.

I don't know if you want to hear this but my code changed that night. I've held myself to a higher standard ever since. I just wanted you to know how truly sorry I am and you've been on my conscience.

Mac

Laurel stared at the letter. Was this supposed to make her feel better? She hadn't reported him – couldn't that be enough? Bastard. She'd been happy the past couple of days, moving on with her life, and now he'd made her face it all anew. The familiar feelings of humiliation and shame welled up in her.

The doorbell rang. With her emotions in a spin, Laurel opened the door on auto pilot to see a small woman with pink hair. 'Hi,' the woman said, grinning. 'You're Laurel, aren't you? I'm Niall's mum, Tonya—' She halted, expression freezing.

Laurel gazed at her, struggling to concentrate. Niall's mum. Mac's wife . . .

The instant she made the connection she realised Tonya's gaze was fixed on the letter in Laurel's hand.

Tonya's voice went flat. 'Looks like you have a letter from my husband.' When Laurel continued to stare like a rabbit in the headlamps, she added pointedly, 'His handwriting's quite distinctive. Want to tell me why he's writing to you?'

Laurel really didn't. The idea of telling Mac's *wife* what he was apologising for was repugnant. If ever she'd wished to avoid cross-examination, it was from a woman who could be counted on to be hurt, disbelieving and aghast. In a flash of inspiration, it occurred to her that if Mac and Grady went to the same school their handwriting might be similar. She gabbled, 'I'm seeing Grady. Actually.'

Under her colourful hair, Tonya's face turned white. 'Their handwriting isn't at all the same, *actually*.'

Furious at landing in yet another shitty situation Mac Cassidy had helped create, Laurel felt a sudden urge to give Tonya the bloody letter. Let her see what a shit she'd married. Let Mac explain to his wife—

She took a breath and folded the letter into her pocket instead. No. She refused to be responsible for wreaking catastrophe on Niall and his mum, possibly ending a marriage and breaking up a home. She tried to deflect by saying, 'Mac's nothing to me,' before repeating, 'I'm seeing Grady.'

'Then why lie about the letter being from Mac?' Tonya persisted, reasonably but tensely. Her eyes were troubled rather than angry. 'You might as well tell me. He's been odd ever since you came back to Middledip.'

Then Daisy arrived in the hall with fabulous concoctions of yew and holly in each hand, blurting breathlessly, 'Sorry I didn't get round in time this morning Mrs Cassidy, but here are the wreaths for you and your sister. Are there enough cones and berries? Do you like the seed heads?'

Rea arrived right behind her. 'Hello, Tonya. Do you have time for a cuppa?' As ever, she seemed comfortable with visitors she knew.

Tonya treated Laurel to a last level stare before offering the others a smile that got nowhere near her eyes. 'Daisy, those wreaths are gorgeous. Hi, Rea. I'm a bit short of time for a cuppa, I'm afraid, but your sister was just telling me that she's seeing my brother-in-law, Grady.'

'Are you?' Rea raised her eyebrows at Laurel with a grin. 'Old sparks burst into flames, have they?'

Daisy looked smug. 'Have you only just found that out, Mum? I knew on Wednesday when Auntie Laurel walked me home then went back to Grady's.'

Tonya looked less sure of her ground at hearing these indications that there might be some foundation to Laurel's claim concerning Grady. Abruptly, she said, 'I need to speak to Mac. Thanks for all your hard work on these wreaths, Daisy. I've paid you already, haven't I?' With a last, wooden smile, she turned and strode down the drive, a wreath in each hand.

Rea rounded on Laurel as soon as the door closed on Tonya's small figure. 'You didn't tell me about Grady.'

Having come in on the tail-end of the conversation, neither she nor Daisy remarked on anything odd in Tonya's manner.

Laurel managed a weak smile. 'It's so new. We don't want to be too public yet.' She hoped Rea wouldn't question why, in that case, Laurel had just discussed it with Tonya. Laurel wasn't even sure why she hadn't told Rea before now. Probably, she thought painfully, it was because part of her knew towering obstacles and canyon-like pitfalls lurked for her and Grady. The letter in her pocket was an all-too-stark reminder.

Daisy tugged Laurel's arm. 'Ready to get off to Grady's now? Let's get Christmassy!' Her eyes glowed with excitement.

But the idea of careering straight off to Grady's without time to calm down and gather her wits made Laurel's heart jolt. 'Just give me a few minutes to sort out a few things I want from the studio. I forgot to do it yesterday evening.'

'OK. I'll grab some cereal.' Daisy bounced blithely back towards the kitchen, hair flying, while Laurel grabbed her coat and hurried outdoors. Today, the garden was cloaked in a freezing mist that outlined cobwebs on winter's skeletal shrubs and muffled the sound of her feet on the stepping-stone path. Expecting the Ice Queen to appear at any moment, Laurel fumbled her way through the door and heard it click shut behind her. She sank onto a stool to catch her breath. Sanctuary. Here she was unlikely to be overheard and able to see if anyone approached.

She'd lied to Daisy. The brushes and water pots she intended to take to the painting of the Christmas scene were assembled, but if she didn't grab a chance to collect herself she'd be weird with Grady.

That wouldn't have been too big a problem if they'd been spending the time alone, but Grady had volunteers from Craft Stuff coming and Laurel was to help them contribute ice skaters, skiers, cute chalets and, Daisy's pet project, the jaunty red cable car. Tess would also be along to create her Santa and sleigh.

Laurel's mind flew automatically to Fliss, whose calm good sense and insight had buoyed her so many times in past years. She reached for her phone.

'Hey, you,' came Fliss's warm tones a few seconds later, her Californian accent mellow. 'How're you doin'?'

Laurel felt a rush of affection for the friend she'd had to leave behind in London. 'Mixed,' she said, frankly. 'At least, I hit a good patch but something's just happened to shake me up.'

Fliss didn't miss a beat. 'I'm listening if you want to talk.'

That was exactly what Laurel did want. 'Mac Cassidy wrote me an apology and dropped it through our door. And, believe it or not, I had it in my hand when his bloody wife arrived to pick something up from Daisy. She spotted his handwriting.' She rushed on with the rest of the story, one eye on the window in case Daisy ran across the garden in search of her.

When she'd finished, Fliss gave a little hum as she considered. 'So Mac really, really wants to apologise, huh?'

Laurel was taken aback. 'I suppose so,' she agreed slowly. 'I believe that's just so he can feel better about himself though. I've made it obvious I don't want to hear his apology.'

'And you have every right to feel that way, and to have your wishes respected,' Fliss agreed. Then, after a moment, 'So, what's the situation with Grady?'

Laurel's cheeks heated, despite the frigid atmosphere of the studio. 'We've, um, "rekindled old sparks", to paraphrase Rea.' She knew that sounded self-conscious and stiff but somehow nothing natural and relaxed flowed into her head.

'Oh.' Several long seconds passed. Laurel even took the phone from her ear to check on the screen that the call hadn't been disconnected. Then, carefully, Fliss went on, 'I didn't think you were serious when we talked about the possibility before. Honey . . . would you ever be able to have a normal relationship with him? If you hate his family, I mean? Alex called me with that concern,' she added.

Laurel's stomach lurched as if she'd just stepped into an unseen pothole. 'Why would he do that?' she demanded, astonishment making her voice quaver.

Fliss remained serene. 'Because you went out with Grady. I told him you were no more than friends – because that's what you had told me.'

'We're more now,' Laurel put in. 'Or we were till I got that letter and Mac's wife saw it and suddenly it all feels impossible,' she ended in a rush.

'Maybe it is. Maybe Alex is right to be concerned,' she said gently, as if that somehow was a clincher.

'Alex can butt out,' Laurel snapped. But she knew she wasn't angry with Alex. She was discombobulated because Fliss wasn't saying what Laurel wanted to hear – that what happened all those years ago in the dark playing fields needn't stand between her and the hoppity-skip feeling Grady gave her.

Despite starting late, Grady was enjoying Saturday morning. He'd got his Art December window done so that

251

Daisy couldn't tell him off again and coloured fairy lights now flickered around three of his favourite gourds in the sitting room window that faced the street. Zuzanna and Niall rocked up clutching Monster energy drinks and admired first the window and then the mountain-scape Laurel had begun. Or was it a snow-scape? Last night she'd put in further work with decorator's brushes, a plastic tray her palette, one hand lodged comfortably in her pocket, chatting to Grady. He'd been entranced, not just at how good she looked with her hair pulled back and a paint-stained shirt over her clothes, but also at how with a few swift motions of her brush she'd suggested a forest in the folds of craggy mountains and enlarged the lake. Middledip's Craft Stuff had won the lottery having this amazing artist in their ranks.

Then suddenly, here Laurel was again, following Daisy, laden with brushes, water pots, palette knives and old plates as makeshift palettes. Although she wore a smile on her pretty face, Laurel flicked him a slightly wary look. Was that because she didn't know how they'd treat each other in company? Their two nights together had been full-on but they hadn't yet established ground rules for 'them'. That conversation was high on his to-do list. Maybe tonight they could go out for dinner, away from the village, and officially put 'them' on a 'seeing each other' footing. He wanted that, despite the uncomfortable situation between her and Mac.

'Finally got your Art December window done, then?' Daisy joked, shoving her bag into his arms while she shrugged off her coat.

'Been done for ages,' he fibbed.

Hubert and Iris from Craft Stuff turned up while the rest of them were still sorting out materials, the teens talking over everyone else's conversations. He wondered if they were going to get anything done in this chaos.

But then Laurel moved into action.

She pulled off her coat and gently gave it to Daisy, interrupting giggles over Daisy having worn her Santa suit to help at the Year Seven party. 'Could you hang that up, please? Zuzanna and Niall, could you kindly take Hubert and Iris's coats? Hubert, are you any good at prising lids off paint? Iris, is it possible for you to fill these pots with water? Grady, do you want us to use a slop pail for when water gets too murky or is it OK to pour it down the sink?'

'The sink will be fine.' He was amused that pensioners Hubert and Iris, though more used to leading than following, co-operated with Laurel as readily as the teenagers did.

Next, Laurel set everyone to work. 'Zuzanna and Iris, let's pop in some trees. Take a fan brush and mix some dark sienna and phthalo blue-green, stroking the colour onto both sides of the brush, to and fro. OK?' She turned to the big board. 'Take just the corner of the brush, pop in a trunk.' A small vertical line appeared. 'Then a little pressure this side, that side, this side, that side . . .' Conifer branches began to dance across the trunk. 'As you get lower, press a little harder. The brush spreads and so do the branches, see?' She turned back to her palette. 'Pull in a touch of Indian yellow, just to one side of the colour we've mixed up—' she exhibited what she'd done '—and we just tap in the highlights.' She touched the brush to about half the branches with the lighter colour and everyone murmured, 'Wow,' as the tree seemed to spring into life.

She laughed, making her eyes crinkle, and Grady could

hardly take his gaze off her warm, pink lips. Soon Zuzanna and Iris were painting Christmas trees onto mountain slopes while Laurel showed Niall and Hubert that snow isn't only white, but also blue and grey, and that things grow through snow, not on top. Laurel went back to Zuzanna and got her painting a bigger tree, demonstrating how, with little upward pushes of the fan brush, she could create seedling trees poking through the snow at the foot of its trunk. 'Tap the colour onto your bristles for that,' she suggested. 'And pull up with your brush. Then use a clean, dry brush to mist over the lower part to form the snow line.' Next she showed Daisy how to use the side of a palette knife to create the cable for the cable car, slung between mountain peaks.

Then she turned to Grady. 'Fancy a go at the lake?'

He looked at the expanse of water with misgiving. 'I could do it with an air brush.'

'You'll be fine,' she said bracingly.

He was glad she thought so. 'But I don't get what you've done with the centre.'

'That's because there are skaters. We just can't see them, yet.' She was mixing titanium white with a hint of ultramarine to produce the palest white-blue. 'But we're not quite ready for that, yet. We need the water to turn to ice first.'

With the gentlest of touches of her brush she somehow conjured up a reflection of the tallest mountain and some of the fir trees at the far edge of the lake. Then she took a wide, dry brush, stippled it lightly over her palette and, with slow, confident movements, dragged it horizontally across the lake. As her brush moved, the surface of the water froze before Grady's very eyes.

'That was awesome,' he said sincerely. It was also

awesome to be this close to her, even in a gathering; to feel her warmth and get a whiff of tangy grapefruit from her hair.

She grinned, obviously not seeing a little thing like painting techniques as a cause for congratulations. 'OK, now you. Take a filbert brush and a little water, and brown, black, and green mixed together . . . then mix white into one side of that colour.' She moved even closer to observe his movements with the brush on his own palette. 'Good. Now coat one side of the brush with the dark and one with the light.'

'OK,' he said, mystified, but following along.

She took the brush from him. 'Now we make little curved strokes of the brush . . . and we have rocks.' Rocks began to appear alongside the iced over lake.

'Because something has to contain the water,' he agreed. 'That's like magic.'

'No wand required, only a paintbrush,' she joked. 'Keep the brush the same way because the light's coming from over there—' she pointed to the hazy sunlight on the top left of the board '—and when they're dry we can top them with snow.' She left him painting 'magic' rocks while she turned back to Daisy and got her using the side of her palette knife to sketch out the shape of the cable car. Beneath where Daisy worked, Niall crouched to paint in blue-grey shadows of dips in the snow.

When they broke for lunch, which Carola delivered from The Angel, the kitchen filled with a babble of conversation about how they'd paint Christmas lights on the bigger trees and that when Tess had painted in the sleigh, they'd fill it with gaily wrapped presents. Grady carried in the workshop stools to augment the kitchen chairs and people crowded around the table, munching sandwiches and cakes.

He and Laurel ate sitting on his workbench, looking through the open kitchen door at the others. She texted Rea, but then put her phone away with a sad smile. 'I asked Rea if she'd like me to fetch her for a few minutes but she's declined. My sister doesn't mind being home alone,' she said wryly. 'She's planning the Christmas decorations.'

'At least she went with you to Gabe's,' he said, pressing his arm against hers comfortingly.

Her whole face lightened. 'That was great! But it was once. It would be easy to get carried away but agoraphobia's a complex condition and not simple to get over. She's made herself a notice for her office though.' She lifted her hands as if placing words in the air. 'It says: "The most difficult step is at your own door. Start small. Keep going. It works."'

'That sounds fantastic,' he said. 'And how about you? How are you today?' he murmured, letting his leg rest against hers as a reminder of how it felt when their bodies touched.

She shrugged, and though she returned the pressure of his thigh, she didn't smile.

'What?' he queried, surprised.

She glanced through the doorway to check the others were engrossed in their conversation about how many reindeer would pull the sleigh. 'I received a letter of apology from Mac.'

Ah. That explained her earlier wary expression. He finished a mouthful while he decided on his response, surprised Mac hadn't given him a heads-up on what he meant to do. 'How do you feel about it?' he asked cautiously.

The shoulder nearest to him gave a tiny shrug. 'No

more receptive than when I avoided his apology before.' She turned to look at him, her eyes hunted. 'And then Tonya came to the door when I was reading the letter.' Rapidly, tautly, she recounted Tonya's reaction. 'Why couldn't he just accept I don't want to hear it?' she ended bitterly. 'Tonya recognised his handwriting and knew I was hiding something.'

Regardless of whether the others noticed, he slipped a comforting arm around her, feeling her warmth through his sleeve. 'He must have had his reasons for writing to you.'

Laurel remained within his encircling arm, but she turned the conversation to the Christmas scene and he knew she'd said all she wanted to say on the subject of Mac's letter. With misgivings, he wondered how the conversation had gone between Mac and Tonya.

After lunch he started creating the shadows where ice passed over submerged rocks in the lake. Those shadows indicated there was something going on beneath the surface, he thought, just as Laurel's jerky little sentences had hinted at all that lurked below her surface, too.

Later, Iris laid down her brush and declared, 'This has been lovely, dears, but I'm ready for home.'

Grady was surprised to see it was already three-thirty. He thanked Iris for everything she'd done and admired the way she'd bedecked her trees with snow.

Hubert, too, washed out his brush and went home for a rest, just as Tess called Grady's phone.

'Really sorry,' she said, sounding it. 'Ratty's mum's not well so my childcare's fallen through. Ratty says he'll come home about five. I know I was supposed to be with you by now but will after five do? Maybe we could order pizza for supper and work through?'

'That's fine,' Grady said heartily, trying not to mind losing the chance of dinner with Laurel. He passed on her message to the others and the teens pounced with glee on the word 'pizza'.

'Suits me,' said Niall, who'd been entrusted with the chalet-like mountain-top cable car station and was using a palette knife to create the wooden walls. 'Mum's gone off to my auntie's anyway. She was only supposed to go for one day but then she said she was going for "a few".' He rolled his eyes. 'Mum and Dad were whispering in their room for ages before she went. Then they both acted so fake when they told me about her change in plans. I bet Mum and my auntie are going Christmas shopping together or something. It's lame, as if Mum thinks I still believe my presents come from Santa.'

Grady saw Laurel go white around the lips and his own heart gave a disconcerting squeeze. Had Mac and Tonya quarrelled about Tonya catching Laurel with Mac's letter? Tonya making a snap decision to stay with her sister was weird. He knew she'd have about an hour's drive to and from work.

'Let's break for biccies and hot chocolate,' he suggested, as much to give himself a moment to recover as anything. He managed to give Laurel's hand a squeeze and she returned the ghost of a smile.

Soon after five, Tess arrived in a renewed flurry of apologies, clasping her hands in delight before the snowy scene they'd created. 'That's fantastic. I'll get straight on with the sleigh. Let's Christmas this up!'

Soon a sleigh was dashing across the snow, Father and Mother Christmas holding onto their hats as the reindeers laid back their ears and galloped. The teens either painted heaps of gifts or populated the slopes with skiers and snowboarders wearing Santa hats. Grady added bright red lights and baubles to the snow-laden branches of the fir trees that encircled the lake, only breaking for the pizza delivery and two enormous bottles of cherry cola, which Daisy, Zuzanna and Niall had clamoured for but Grady thought tasted like cough sweets.

Then Laurel began to paint two ice skaters in the centre of the lake and everyone paused to watch the figures emerge from the end of her clever brush, a man and a woman clasping hands and staring into each other's eyes from beneath colourful hats. It's was amazing how Laurel managed to capture them in so few strokes, skates poised mid-stride, the impression of movement complete when she used the end of her brush to scratch in the marks their blades were leaving behind on the ice. Details emerged – a bobble on the woman's blue hat and the distant snow-topped chalets behind the lake. Then, in the same style he'd admired in the paintings Daisy had shown him online, she created a floral explosion of green and white above the skating couple. It took him a moment to realise that the whirling leaves and berries were mistletoe.

He almost expected the newly painted couple to close up to one another and kiss.

'That's *awesome*,' Zuzanna breathed.

Laurel laid down her brush, laughing when everyone burst into applause. Clapping along with the others, Grady wondered if he was the only one to notice that the man's hair peeping from beneath the beanie was black, like his, while the woman's longer hair was a dark auburn. Like Laurel's.

He caught her eye meaningfully and she grinned and blushed. His heart squeezed again, but this time in pleasure.

Before long, the Christmas scene was complete. Snow

topped the cable car's roof and the leading reindeer pranced along with the obligatory shiny red nose. They took photos of each other standing before the scene and agreed not to post them on social media just yet, so their work would have maximum Christmassy impact when it took pride of place at the fair.

To Grady's relief, Tess, who'd come by car, suggested to the teenagers that she dropped them home. They grabbed their coats and followed like ducklings, shouting their farewells and, 'Thanks for the pizza!'

Suddenly, miraculously, the noisy house was empty . . . except for one man and one auburn-haired beauty.

Grady was alone with Laurel.

Fatigue washed over Laurel. 'Maybe I should go, too,' she suggested. 'It's been a long day. My car's outside. People will know I'm here and think you're a strumpet.'

Grady looked tired, too, lines of strain around his eyes, but he slid warm arms around her and kissed the top of her head. 'Being your strumpet sounds amazing. You don't have time to unwind with me awhile? A hot drink and a snuggle on the sofa, away from the smell of the paint, would be excellent.'

She pressed her face against his shoulder, breathing in his heat, feeling his heartbeat. A snuggle did sound excellent. 'OK. Though I think I'm immune to the smell of paint.' His laughter seemed to rumble through them both.

When she was propped against him on the sofa, hot chocolate in hand, one of his arms looped loosely around her, she sighed, letting her head rest on him. 'My stomach's been one big knot all day, especially since Niall said that about his mum going off for a few days. Do you

260

think . . . Your brother and Tonya won't have fallen out over that letter, will they?'

He sighed, his breath gliding over her skin and, to her dismay, he didn't rubbish the idea. 'I've been wondering what's going on at Mac's house today, too. Tonya's lovely but a bit of a firecracker when she's upset.'

'Oh, hell.' She groaned, shutting her eyes. 'I felt so guilty when she confronted me this morning, as if I was having an affair with Mac. Why did he have to write? I was perfectly happy ignoring him as much as possible.'

He put down his mug of chocolate so he could stroke her hair. '*Perfectly* happy?' he queried.

Her eyes remained closed and she enjoyed the slow, languorous caress of his hand, as if he was smoothing the knotty problems out of her head. 'Putting up with things,' she amended. Then, irritated by how passive that sounded, she added, 'No, I was looking forward, rather than back. I was getting over a rocky period and feeling optimistic.' Her throat tightened and so did her voice. 'I was enjoying being with you and pretending your brother doesn't exist.' To prevent herself from dissolving into disappointed tears, she took several gulps of her hot chocolate.

His cradling arm tightened around her. 'But he does exist,' he murmured gently. 'I've talked to him about us.' His hand moved on to kneading her neck. 'I explained that we're trying not to let the past affect us.'

Laurel's stomach cramped. 'So what's going to happen to us? If we keep seeing each other, I mean?' She could hear unhappiness in her own voice, the dull, flat, echo of despondency.

Grady was silent. Though he continued to hold her close, he reached for his hot chocolate again and drank it. When he'd finished, he put down the empty mug and

261

slid his other arm around her too, so she felt surrounded by him, moulded to the shape of his body. 'Mac's always going to be around.'

'I know,' she replied ruefully. 'He's your brother and you love him. It's me who has the problem. I'm making difficulties between you and now I might be making difficulties in his marriage.'

'All unwittingly,' he reminded her. 'You don't think you'll ever forgive him?' he asked tentatively.

'I wish people wouldn't ask that.' She knew she sounded fretful but she also felt a rat because she knew forgiving Mac would make things easier for Grady. 'It's not a *choice*. I could *say* I forgive him but that would never change what I feel inside.'

'I get that,' he whispered, laying his cheek against her hair.

She became aware of the way their bodies touched, and his firm thighs beneath his jeans gave her thoughts a new direction. Should she really let bloody Mac Cassidy sour things between her and Grady? Things that could make her feel as giddy as a lovestruck teenager? She gave an experimental wriggle. 'Are you inviting me to your bed tonight?' She tipped her head back to kiss his jaw.

'You bet,' he said, with a hint of surprise but a host of alacrity.

They made love that night gently and tenderly, as if Grady felt Laurel needed comforting. It *was* comforting, and blissful and exciting. But the spectre of Mac coming between them made it hard for Laurel to slide into sleep afterwards, even warm and sated, nestled into Grady's arms.

She must have slumbered eventually, though, because suddenly she was struggling against arms that pinioned her. Gasping, thrashing, sweating, she pleaded, 'No, no! Stop!'

Then Grady's voice came into the half-light of waking and the hands upon her were no longer clawing but gentle and soothing. 'Laurel. Laurel? *Laurel*, it's OK. You're dreaming. You can wake up. You're safe. It's a nightmare.'

Laurel surfaced with a gasp and a thump from her wildly beating heart. Shit. The nightmare. She wasn't fighting off bullies on an icy December night but safe in Grady's bed in dear little Mistletoe Cottage.

She burst into tears.

Grady gathered her up, stroking her back, kissing her hair. 'Hey, hey. I've got you. That must have been some bad dream.'

When she could control herself, she sank wearily against him. 'Sorry I woke you.'

He stroked her back. 'It's not a prob—' He halted. Tensed. 'Was the nightmare about what happened to you?' Dread tinged his voice.

She nodded. Part of her wanted to turn on the bedside lamp and vanquish the lingering tentacles of the dream along with the darkness, but she didn't want to see Grady and the dismay that laced his voice reflecting in his eyes.

He groaned, letting his head rest upon hers. 'I wish I'd been there with you that night.'

'Me, too. But wishing doesn't change a thing.' She let go of him and began to swing her legs out from under the duvet. 'I think I'd better go home.'

Concern laced his voice. 'It's the early hours. Look, if you think the nightmare will return, we can stay awake.' He reached out of bed to switch on the lamp, causing her to shield her eyes.

Tiredly, she shook her head. 'We both need time to think.'

263

As she found her underwear and struggled into her jeans he came to stand beside her, naked but taking no apparent notice of the chill air. Dubiously, tentatively, he said, 'I suppose there are other places to live than the village, if we had to.'

She fastened her jeans and paused to slide her arms around him, leaning into him for one last dose of comfort. 'I've only just come back to be with my family; you've lived here your entire life and your only family is here. Can you imagine telling Niall you won't be around for him anymore? It's obvious every time you look at each other that you're close.' Grady fell silent, presumably imagining that very thing and unable to dismiss it as unimportant. She released him and reached for her top. 'I won't be responsible for spoiling your family relationships.'

'Have you had the nightmare ever since . . . it happened?'

She wouldn't lie to him. 'No. For several years afterwards, but then it faded.'

'Is the first time since you came back here?' His voice was heavy.

She took in the disappointment in his eyes as he stood before her, goose pimples gathering on his skin. 'The second.'

'Has the nightmare come when you've . . . slept with other men?' He sounded as if mentioning that scenario was an effort.

She ran her fingers through her hair. 'No,' she admitted. 'But I only ever told you and Alex. I've never wanted a man to be thinking about *that* while we made love. I'm not saying you did,' she put in hurriedly.

Wordlessly, he began dressing.

She hooked her bag over one shoulder. 'You can go back to bed. My car's here so I can drive home.'

He nodded to show he'd heard but continued yanking on his sweatshirt and jeans. They walked downstairs together and pulled on their coats.

'I'm sorry I'm leaving you alone but maybe you'll at least get some sleep.' Laurel knew she wouldn't. She'd stay awake and mull over their shitty situation, scared to close her eyes. She opened the front door to be met by a wall of fog swirling like phantoms beneath the streetlights. She fished out her car keys but before she could press the unlock button, Grady slipped his arms around her.

They stood there together in the creeping cold of the freezing fog. Then he cleared his throat. 'When I think of you, in bed or anywhere else, I think of a vibrant, gorgeous woman. I'm pulled towards you as if I'm a magnet and you're the North Pole. My guts twist whenever I think of what happened to you but I consider you much, much more than a victim. You're strong and loyal, talented and intelligent. I'm more than half in love with you and while I acknowledge the difficulty we face, I'm not turning tail.'

Too choked to do more than nod, Laurel gave him a hard hug and hopped up into her SUV to reverse into the silent street. With every turn of the wheels on the two-minute drive home she heard *I'm not turning tail,* and wondered whether he'd silently been asking . . . *are you?*

As sleep felt as far away as the moon, she pulled up outside the silent hulk of The Nookery and took the pathway beside the house and across the ghostly garden to the studio. Letting herself in, she dumped her coat and grabbed a fresh canvas, one she hadn't even gessoed yet, then prepared a palette of red, black and blue. She began almost throwing the paint on the canvas with her thickest brush, working at it in long, angry, frustrated strokes in bitter black, raging red and pissed off purple, forming a tunnel of violent colours that expressed all of her darkness and anguish and disappointment.

It wasn't until she'd painted over every inch of white canvas that she slowed.

Once again she heard Grady's voice. *I'm more than half in love with you . . .* Her heart did a long, slow flip.

She picked up a tube of white paint and squeezed some onto her palette, then mixed in a smidgeon of cadmium red. Picking out a lining brush, she added a small arched tracery of palest dawn pink. It looked a little like hope . . . or light at the end of the tunnel.

Chapter Sixteen

To Laurel's surprise, after her frenzy of anger had spent itself on the – now ruined – canvas, she'd settled down to her work in progress as the dark night eventually gave way to day and the sun burned off the mist. The ebullient joy of Everyday Woman dancing calmed her. The basic figure was now complete and Laurel was pleased at the way she'd captured the instant the woman, mid-dance step, lost contact with the earth.

At about ten a.m., she cleaned her brushes and texted Grady. *Sorry to run out on you last night. Treat you to a pint at The Three Fishes tonight? xx* When there was no immediate answer she went indoors, conscious that it was Sunday and Rea might appreciate some company, having been abandoned all day yesterday. Daisy's music thumped from upstairs as she entered the warmth of the house and she found Rea writing Christmas cards at the kitchen table. A completed stack stood at her elbow. With a pang, Laurel saw the evidence of nurtured threads of friendship, despite her sister hardly seeing a soul, nowa-days. Rea's sweet nature had always drawn people to her and the flood of Christmas cards from old colleagues, past school friends and villagers had already half-filled the tinsel Rea had strung around the hall. However, the sum of her sister's recent social life was a visit from Angel and Miranda, squeezed in between Christmas shopping and kids' school concerts, and the walk to Gabe's paddock.

Rea glanced up and smiled. 'Aunt Terri's been on the phone. She does want to come for Christmas. Isn't that great? She wondered if she could come early and spend longer with us than usual. I asked her if she wouldn't be seeing her friend Opal for at least part of the festive season but she said not this year so I said we'd love to have her. Is that OK? She's a bit down and thinks the simple life of the village might cheer her up.'

Laurel wasn't finding life in the village simple. It was damned complicated. She smothered a yawn and headed for the coffee machine. 'Of course! It'll be great to see her because I never got over to Peterborough for a visit. It's not like her to be down.'

'That's what I thought.' Rea signed a card with a flourish and slipped it into a red envelope. 'Daisy wants to put up the Christmas tree this afternoon.'

'She's held on till the 5th of December?' Laurel clutched her forehead in feigned amazement, making Rea giggle. Laurel put two cups of coffee on the table and flopped down into a chair, watching Rea address the envelope to an erstwhile workmate, stick on a stamp and add it to the pile for posting. 'Rea,' she began thoughtfully. 'How much does Terri know about your agoraphobia?'

Rea paused, gaze downcast. 'She knows I changed jobs and avoid certain situations but she doesn't know . . .' She tailed off unhappily, staring at the box of cards. The top one depicted a cottage with snow on the roof.

Gently, Laurel said, 'I promised I'd try and exercise Daybreak today, remember? Do you feel up to coming with me again?' When Rea's forehead crumpled, she crossed her fingers beneath the table, hoping she wasn't going about things entirely the wrong way, and added, 'As you said, Daisy would love it.' She hoped that was gentle encouragement rather than emotional blackmail. 'You could ride Daybreak, too, if you wanted.'

Rea's jawline firmed. Whether it was the prospect of pleasing Daisy, making more progress before Aunt Terri arrived, or riding a pony for the first time since she was a young woman that convinced her, she blurted a 'Yes.' Then she looked scared and had to wipe a tear from one corner of her eye. Her lips wobbled into a smile as well, though. 'I must, must set myself greater goals. Must think of Daisy. You're so supportive, Laurel. I'm sure I'm not strong enough to do this without you.'

'Of course you are,' said Laurel, bracingly, though she was achingly aware that Rea did need someone.

Fleetingly, she wondered if and when she'd leave the village to find a new studio in Cornwall. She'd helped with Daisy, she was happy to continue to help Rea . . . but she'd plunged into a complete conundrum with Grady. Their relationship felt like a Rubik's Cube that someone had tampered with. Lining up one segment satisfactorily meant another could only be hopelessly spoiled.

Daisy's face, when they went upstairs to break the exciting news to her, was a picture. She looked up from tying hessian bows on a wreath of pine, red-berried holly and black-berried viburnum, and her busy fingers stilled. Her round chin dropped. 'We're going out?' she said, blankly.

Rea, smiling tremulously, slid her arm around Daisy's

soft shoulders. 'I can't promise anything,' she said quickly, when a stunned smile began to form on Daisy's face. 'I might get to the end of the drive and have a panic attack. I might do it today and not be able to manage it next time. But I'm going to try.'

Daisy, almost dumb for once, had to wipe away happy tears. She scrambled to her feet and threw her arms about Rea. 'That's so amazing of you, Mum! I can't believe it. I've tried so hard not to get onto you about going out but I so, so want you to.' Then she halted, looking aghast. 'Have I, like, put you under pressure, now?' Her face began to crumple.

Gently, Rea hugged her closer, her eyes misting. 'No, sweetheart. You've just made me more determined.'

Laurel felt her eyes growing hot, too, realising just how deeply Daisy had been feeling Rea's inability to lead a normal life. Outwardly, she'd coped so well.

Soon they were pulling on their outdoor clothes and boots. Laurel found the hard hat she'd borrowed from Zuzanna's mum and shoved it into a backpack along with a few parsnips because they wanted the carrots for Sunday lunch. 'Ready?' she asked her sister.

'Ready,' Rea confirmed, looking pale and uncertain, and taking Daisy's hand as if Daisy was four, not fourteen.

Laurel led the way through the front door. The fog had left behind a winter-bright, hopeful day, which seemed a long way from the dark emotions that had engulfed Laurel after her middle-of-the-night dash home. To buoy her further, as they stepped cautiously onto the pavement of Great End – as tentatively as three not-so-intrepid explorers stepping onto ice – Grady answered her earlier text. *I understand. Are you OK? Unfort am meeting Mac for a pint tonight. You free now? Or this pm? No Craft Stuff today cos everyone's at home getting stuff ready for the fair. xx* Quickly she replied: *With Rea and Daisy atm. Will get back to you as soon as I know about pm. xx*

As Laurel put away her phone, she saw silent tears streaming down Daisy's cheeks.

Rea noticed at the same time. 'Oh, Daisy!' Half-laughing, half-crying, she wrapped her arms around her daughter, right there on the pavement outside their garden gate.

When Daisy choked, 'Mum, you're so awesome!' Laurel dissolved into tears too and joined the hug.

When they'd mopped their eyes, they went on. In Main Road, the pub was getting ready for its lunchtime opening, and Elvis was setting out a chalkboard bearing holly leaves and *Don't miss our Christmas Menu!!* followed by a flamboyant drawing of a Christmas pudding. If he thought it odd that the three of them were holding hands, his friendly greeting didn't betray it.

As she had during Rea's last outing, Laurel chatted gently, hoping to provide distraction. Halfway down Main Road Rea paused and slung one arm around a lamppost as if seeking an anchor. Daisy's eyes widened, clearly worried that Rea was about to bolt for home.

Laurel wasn't going to put direct pressure on her sister but she didn't see why she shouldn't introduce a subject that might distract them both. 'Have you ever done any horse riding, Daisy? Daybreak has a lovely, smooth gait. I'm looking forward to being up on her again.'

Rea shot her a look that appeared half 'thanks for finding something to motivate me further' and half 'I know you're using Daybreak as bait', but she released the lamp-post from her rigid embrace and took a few more steps.

Daisy's expression relaxed. 'Daybreak's very sweet but

I'm not getting up on her. It looks a long way down. I like to keep the gate between horses and me in case they kick me with their wooden feet.'

Even Rea laughed. 'Hoofs aren't wood. They're made of the same stuff as toenails, aren't they?'

They were passing MAR Motors by now and the cars on the forecourt reflected the glare of the sun. Daisy giggled. 'Then why would I go near an animal with mega-toenails? That's gross.' At the corner, they turned into Gabe's track.

Laurel glanced across at the door to Grady Auto Art but it was firmly closed. She continued the jokey conversation, wondering aloud whether Daybreak would like her 'toenails' painted and, if so, what colour, letting the gentle silliness carry them around the curve of the track and up to the paddock. There she produced the parsnips.

Snobby, seeing they had food in their hands, actually broke into a shambling trot to the paddock gate, tossing his head in greeting and barging in front of Daybreak, despite being half her size. 'You're a hooligan,' Daisy scolded the little old pony. Snobby suffered pats as they broke each parsnip into pieces and scrupulously divided them between him and the pale grey beauty of Daybreak. The moment he'd blown over their hands to check the last scrap had gone, he turned tail and shambled off to the far side of the paddock.

By then, Gabe and Bertie had come out. 'Have you come to ride Daybreak?' Gabe called hopefully.

Laurel found herself laying a friendly hand on Rea's shoulder. 'Yes, please, and could Rea, too? She was always better than me because she went to lessons for longer.'

'The more the merrier. Daybreak desperately needs exercise.' Gabe went to fetch Daybreak's tack, leaving them

272

to chat with Bertie. Daybreak remained with her head over the gate as though eager to be part of the conversation. Then her ears pricked and she swung her head to watch Gabe approach with her tack, almost knocking Uncle Bertie off his feet.

'Aw, look at her,' breathed Rea. 'She's excited.'

Laurel climbed over the gate to remove Daybreak's rug, gave her back a quick once-over with a dandy brush to get rid of anything that might irritate her, took the numnah from Gabe and settled it on Daybreak's back. Then she lifted the saddle with a grunt. 'I'm sure saddles didn't use to be so heavy.' She slid it into position so the pony's hair wasn't all brushed the wrong way underneath, then buckled the girth.

Next thing she knew, Rea had come through the gate, bridle in hand. 'Can I see if I remember how?' She did, and in moments Daybreak was shifting the bit in her mouth while Rea deftly buckled the cheek strap.

Laurel took the first ride. While she didn't want Rea to become disengaged by waiting, she wanted to ride the freshness off the pony so Rea's courage wouldn't be rewarded with a bumpy ride on a bucking pony or even a fall. She trotted and cantered Daybreak for ten minutes, then pulled up at the gate where Rea, happily, was still watching.

'Ready, sis?' she asked.

Rea nodded, looking more enthusiastic than she had about leaving the house, so Laurel dismounted and gave her the riding hat, hoping it wasn't too sweaty. Rea fastened it on happily enough and went to Daybreak's head. 'I'm going to ride you now, sweetie. OK?' Daybreak nodded.

Rea very properly checked the girth, mounted from the

gate and pulled the stirrups up a hole as she was shorter than Laurel. Then she whispered, 'Come on,' and gave Daybreak a little squeeze with her calves.

Laurel, in her new role as a spectator, slid an arm around Daisy, who was welling up again at the sight of her mum doing something in the great outdoors. Watching her sister walking Daybreak around the perimeter of the paddock, then shortening her reins ready to trot, Laurel thought it was worth returning to the village just to have this moment.

At first, they all leaned their arms on the top of the gate and watched in silence. Then they began to relax and chat. Rea rode figures of eight, getting Daybreak to change legs, which she did beautifully. Gabe went indoors and brought out hot drinks, then carried over a bench from outside the back door. He and Bertie perched on that while Laurel and Daisy perched on the top rail of the gate.

'Daybreak's certainly getting her exercise today,' Gabe observed, nodding towards where Rea was now riding with crossed stirrups, extending Daybreak's stride. Finally, when the drinks had gone and Daisy had spent a few minutes foraging amongst Gabe's hedgerow for more materials for wreaths – she'd earned nearly three hundred pounds already and orders were still coming in, she told them proudly – Rea finally lengthened Daybreak's reins and walked her up and down to cool her.

She returned to the gate to untack before putting the rug on Daybreak. 'Thank you for the loveliest ride ever,' she said solemnly to the pony. With one last stroke of Daybreak's velvet muzzle, she turned her out to graze.

Laurel's eyes stung again but Rea's eyes were shining. She was smiling. In fact, she was beaming.

'Gabe,' Rea said in a rush. 'Can I talk to the insurance company about buying Daybreak?'

After a stunned second while they gaped at Rea as if an alien had come down and possessed her body, everyone answered at once. Was Rea sure what having her own pony meant? Exercising several times a week. Vet and farrier bills . . .

Rea stuck out her chin. 'Could I pay you rent and leave her here, Gabe?'

'Well . . .' Gabe rubbed his jaw. 'You could, but that pony really needs a stable, Rea. And a stable means mucking out.' But to this unpromising beginning he added, 'I wouldn't mind you having a stable put up in the paddock, if it was one with a stable mat rather than a concrete base. I'd be happy to share costs with you for feed and farrier and instead of paddock rent you could take over arranging that for both ponies.'

Rea whipped out her phone and began searching online for preowned stables, head close to Gabe's. Over their bent backs, Daisy widened her eyes at Laurel. *Is this OK?* her look plainly said.

Laurel gave a tiny shrug. *Beats me.*

Equal parts excited and worried, Laurel watched Rea show Gabe a double stable. 'Look, it's under a grand. You could put Snobby in the other stable. There's also a tiny tack room at the end. We'd have to find someone to fetch it and put it together, though.'

Gabe rasped his grey-stubbled chin. 'Maybe the old boy would like something better than the field shelter,' he acknowledged. 'My nephew Ben might help us. He's got a truck and all the tools.' He raised his gaze to Rea. Softly, he said, 'You're happy to look after her, are you? Because I couldn't take over for you.' With a roguish twinkle he added, 'I'm getting too old for shovelling shit.'

Rea, who'd looked downcast for an instant, giggled. She did stop and bite her lip, though.

Then Laurel heard herself say, 'I'll help, if you have a few bad days, Rea.' She thought it was right to acknowledge that Rea might not always be able to look after Daybreak. It was a giant stride to go from months of not going further than the garden to coming down here each day to muck out and ride a pony and it wasn't fair to rely on Daisy, who distrusted Daybreak's 'wooden feet'. At the same time, she felt that crushing Rea's ambition would also crush whatever confidence she had been able to muster.

A smile that rivalled the winter sunlight blazed across Rea's face. 'Are you really sure, Laurel?'

Laurel gave her a hug. 'Let's just hope the insurance company hasn't already got someone interested.'

Gabe snorted. 'You don't think they've got a private ad out, do you? Her name will be down to go back to the sale. Though that way she'd at least be bought from the ring and not as part of some shady side hustle.' He beetled his brows at Bertie, who looked abashed behind his beard.

Rea fairly threw herself into Laurel's arms, nearly beaning her with the peak of the riding hat she still wore. 'You are the best sister in the world.'

Gabe, perhaps understanding that to invite Rea indoors would be too much, too soon, disappeared into the house for a few minutes before returning with the insurance company's contact information and Daybreak's details. Rea took the sheets of paper and nodded as she listened to Gabe's suggestions as to how to proceed.

Then, all at once, she seemed to run out of steam and the glance she sent down the track held a trace of longing. 'It must be well past lunchtime,' she said, tentatively.

Laurel shrugged easily. 'Daybreak's grazing happily, so she's started without us. Shall we go home?'

Daisy's eyes gleamed wickedly. 'I could eat a horse.'

A laughing light returned to Rea's eyes. 'Don't say such things in present company or I won't teach you to ride my pony.'

Daisy snorted inelegantly. 'No, thanks.'

They left Gabe and Bertie and strolled down the track. Rea looked tired with the effort of being out for so long, but a small smile was never far from her mouth.

At Grady's spray shop the door was still closed but Laurel's heart lifted when she spotted a light through the window. She decided not to see whether Rea would be OK the rest of the way home with Daisy though. It wasn't very fair when she'd said she'd be there and Daisy would likely want to see Grady, too, and this was one occasion when Laurel didn't want to share him. Accordingly, she scurried up Main Road with her sister and niece, saw them into The Nookery and then called a cheeky, 'See you later!' and turned to scurry back the way she'd come.

'Oy! What about the Christmas tree?' Daisy bellowed after her.

'Later,' Laurel tossed over her shoulder. 'You get it all out of the cupboard and I'll be back to help, soon.'

She reached the spray shop flushed and breathless, opened the door and stepped inside. 'Hiya.'

Grady was checking paint stocks, pencil in hand. He straightened with a blazing grin and outstretched arms. Laurel met him halfway across the cold concrete floor and slid against him for an enormous, fierce, wordless hug. His stubble tickled as it brushed her hairline.

He pressed soft kisses on her chilly skin. 'Sorry I already had plans with Mac tonight. I want to know what's going on with Tonya . . .' He broke off uncertainly.

She hugged him harder, though her stomach took a tumble at this reminder of the trouble caused by Tonya catching Laurel with Mac's letter. 'He's your brother and you want to support him.' With an effort, she added, 'And mend bridges. I want what's best for you.' She wondered whether that would ever be her. Or was that crying for the moon? Instead of voicing such misgivings, she murmured, 'Sorry I freaked on you last night. I won't be like that next time.'

He sighed hotly down her neck and she felt him relax. 'That there's going to be a next time is all I need to know.' Then he kissed her properly, deeply, pulling her up on her tiptoes so that they both almost overbalanced.

When he let her up for air, she laughed. 'I've just realised I must smell of horse.'

He settled his hands comfortably on her bottom. 'Doesn't matter. Though . . .' He winked. 'I'm quite partial to sharing a shower, if you feel the need to clean up.'

'Mm,' she said, pulling his head down for another kiss. 'I do have a Christmas tree to decorate but it's a way to save hot water.'

He broke the embrace to reach out for his keys. 'Not the way I do it.'

At The Three Fishes, the Christmas grotto look was in full shimmer and the staff members were wearing Santa hats. The pillars around the bar were studded with notices about the Christmas raffle, carol singing and the Christmas lunch. A couple of noisy groups in the dining area cheered as their crackers snapped and the reflections in their wine glasses only increased the mass bling effect.

Mac was waiting at a small table in the corner near the darts board, two pints of beer before him. Grady had manoeuvred around the cluster of darts players to reach him, and Mac shoved one beer in his direction as Grady took the vacant seat. This particular table was usually considered part of the darts area and utilised by those not currently in a match but at least a darts match in full swing created a wall of sound between the brothers and the rest of the pub.

Mac's jaw looked tight and one of his knees jiggled. 'How's everything with you?' he enquired woodenly.

Grady took a few mouthfuls of beer. It was rich and cold, the taste lingering on his tongue. 'Mixed,' he said, eventually.

Dark eyes, so like his own, settled on Grady. 'I'm causing you bother, eh? Sorry, mate. I know you're disappointed in me.' Mac looked away, jaw working.

'It's not like you murdered someone, but I think we have to face the fact that there are repercussions,' Grady said carefully.

Mac nodded and sank half his beer in one draught.

'So . . . Niall tells me Tonya's gone to her sister's,' Grady said cautiously. 'Trouble?'

Shoulders rising and falling on a big sigh, Mac nodded. 'Do you know I wrote an apology to Laurel?'

Grady nodded. Over the other side of the room he could see Carola from The Angel marshalling a double row of people dressed in red tops and recognised the village singing group, the Middletones. They looked about to burst into song and there would probably be a collection after for the village hall or a Middledip kid who needed treatment. He suspected Carola may have been the inventor of crowdfunding.

'Do you know how Laurel took it?' Mac looked unsure if he actually wanted the answer. 'Don't suppose she said, "Wow, maybe he's not so bad. I won't glare daggers at him in future"?'

Grady shook his head. 'She'd already refused to listen to your apology. You writing it down to force-feed it to her . . . If you'd asked me first, I would have advised against it.' Nausea rolled over him. This was horrible, walking a tightrope between Mac and Laurel.

Mac frowned. 'At school, apologising is seen as a good thing. It makes the individual face what they've done.'

'It can also be perceived as allowing the perpetrator to feel better about themselves and their actions,' Grady said carefully.

Mac looked green. 'Like, cleaning my conscience so it's nice and shiny? I didn't mean it like that.'

Grady's beer began to lose its appeal. 'Do you have any kids that think they can do what they like so long as they say sorry nicely afterwards?'

'Suppose so,' Mac admitted reluctantly. Both knees were jiggling, now. He rubbed his hand over his mouth.

Across the pub, the Middletones burst into 'Let it Snow'. A few people joined in the chorus and one of the darts players grumbled, 'That lot put me off,' when his dart missed the board. The excuse was greeted with a chorus of catcalls from the other players.

'Tonya saw Laurel with the letter,' Mac said shortly. 'Came home near to tears, wanting to know what the hell was going on. I had to tell her something so I said I was apologising for standing by while Amie bullied Laurel.

Tonya seems to have swallowed it but was really disappointed in me.' He paused to finish his beer. 'She accepts everyone does something shitty when they're a teenager but writing to Laurel without confiding in her about it first, that seems to have really upset her. She accepts I've apologised and it's up to Laurel now, but she says it's caused a trust issue between us. She needs time off from me; hence the sudden visit to her family.'

Grady couldn't hold back a snort. 'With respect, Tonya's not the victim here.'

Mac forehead crinkled miserably. 'I know, but, fuck, Grady, she doesn't know the whole truth. I couldn't look into my wife's eyes and admit what I did. She might never feel the same about me. And I'm not sure you ever will either, now you know,' he added.

Grady let the silence between them hang. 'Let it Snow' ended and the Middletones received a round of applause – neither Grady nor Mac joined in – before they began 'Mistletoe and Wine'. Finally, he said, 'Mac, I'm . . . involved with Laurel.' He wanted to tell his brother about Laurel still suffering nightmares but knew she'd hate him exposing her vulnerability to Mac, of all people. 'I had the hots for her when we were kids and I do now.' He hoped Laurel would forgive his directness but this was his brother. 'I'm unwillingly in the middle of this, pulled two ways.'

Mac gazed at him and Grady thought he caught the glint of tears in his brother's eyes. 'I couldn't be sorrier,' Mac said. He sucked in a breath that audibly wavered. 'But there's something else. Ruben doesn't have an ex-wife called Francesca.'

It took Grady several seconds to close his gaping mouth and order his thoughts enough to speak. 'That makes no sense.'

281

Mac frowned. 'I know. I tracked Ruben down through LinkedIn because I thought maybe he'd want to know what his ex was saying.'

And warn him that the truth's out, Grady supplemented silently.

'Apparently, he lives and works in Lancashire and has never had a relationship with anyone called Francesca. He's with a woman called Elena,' Mac continued. 'They have two kids. And as for his mother being in The Three Fishes to see you with Laurel, she hasn't lived in the village for years. She moved to a retirement flat in Norfolk when his dad died.'

Grady let the information sink in. Then he pulled the messages up on his phone again. *I used to be married to him. I'm still on good terms with my MIL who lives in Middledip . . . she said you're seeing someone called Laurel Hill . . . there's something you should know . . . your brother attacked Laurel Hill . . .* 'So this is all bollocks. Someone wanted me to know the story, so they found a way to do it. But why?'

Mac tugged nervously on his bottom lip. 'Sometimes people do just feel a story ought to be told. Or maybe someone wants to come between you and me?'

'Why?' Grady demanded, not buying it. 'And who?'

'Revenge,' Mac said heavily. 'Maybe Laurel's trying to blow us apart. It would make things easier for her.'

'No!' Grady slapped the table, making several darts players look around in surprise at the whip-crack sound. 'Laurel's not like that and if she was going to do it, why wait until now? Why not tell me the day after it happened?'

Several seconds ticked by. Then Mac nodded. 'OK. You're right. So, someone's trying to make mischief for you.'

You ought to know what your family did to her . . .

Grady read from the messages again. 'They wanted me to see things might never work out with Laurel.' He felt his face set in grim lines. 'I can only think of Pippa.'

Mac began to nod, but then frowned. 'But how would Pippa know what happened?'

Chapter Seventeen

Middledip Christmas Fair
December 18th and 19th
10 a.m. to 4 p.m.

The enormous red banner hung over the entrance to the village hall. Inside, the foyer had been transformed into a coffee shop by volunteers, their coffee pod machines in a row on a counter and their patio sets pressed into use as café seating. Gold and red tinsel twirled and balloons hung from the beams, swaying every time the door opened. Laurel had already drunk two cups of coffee and eaten a scone and was beginning to think about buying another.

In the past couple of weeks the village had roughly doubled the number of lights and Christmas trees on every cottage, and the hall itself was a clamour of cheery voices and jolly Christmas music. Bauble-bedecked stalls trying to out-Christmas one another ran down the middle and around three sides, while the art wall was situated against the fourth. The Craft Stuff Christmas scene was the centre-piece of the art wall and would remain after the fair was dismantled, ready for the Christmas parties that would take place in the space in the coming week – tots, teens, over 65s, and the yoga and Pilates groups. Laurel smiled to see the ice-skating couple again, eyes only for each other. It reminded her of Grady's eyes twinkling as he silently got the joke that the couple looked like them.

Carola, never one to miss an opportunity, had installed her daughter Emily to persuade people to pay a pound to guess where in the scene Santa was supposed to have hidden the reindeer food. The nearest guess would win a bottle of champagne and funds raised would go to the upkeep of the village hall. Laurel had paid her pound and guessed it was hidden amongst the rocks, because Grady had painted them.

Her other contributions to the art wall were already on display: three of her mother's watercolours of the village alongside her own canvas of the two boys, which she'd taken from the Art December window at The Nookery, to Daisy's disgust. Isla's pictures were not for sale but Laurel's bore a 'POA' sticker, along with her phone number. She had no expectation of selling but Grady and Daisy had wanted her to exhibit.

Not having her own stall, Laurel had helped others set up, stood in for them during loo breaks and fetched drinks and snacks. She'd based herself at Grady's stall of sensuously shaped, beautifully shaded gourds but then Mac and Tonya had hoved into view and she'd wandered off in the other direction. She didn't mind. It was a relief to see them smiling and back together, as Grady had already told her they were, and they were Grady's family. They were there to support him and Niall. That was good.

Alone and at a loose end, she thought, wistfully, it was a shame that Rea would probably rather scale the village hall roof without climbing gear or a safety net than come inside with this babble of chatter and laughter. It would have been nice to exclaim over the stalls together, buying gifts or ornaments.

Instead, Rea was happy being left behind. She was in talks with the insurance company about buying Daybreak. Her first offer had been refused but she'd raised it five hundred pounds and that had been respectable enough to be considered. The representative had also confided that it would be a lot less trouble to the company for Rea to buy Daybreak than to arrange for her to be collected and transported to a sale. Rea was so excited she'd asked Laurel or Daisy to go with her to visit Daybreak every day this week. Laurel hadn't thought *that* would happen when she'd introduced her to the pony, and silently congratulated herself – and her sister – every time Rea suggested it.

She wove her way through villagers exclaiming over everything the fair had to offer, to where Daisy, Niall and Zuzanna shared a stall, relaxed and happy as the school term had ended yesterday. Red tinsel threaded Daisy's dark curls and green tied up Zuzanna's blonde ponytail, while Niall sported reindeer antlers. Laurel bought two silver wire stars from Niall, getting in before his parents progressed this far, and a Christmas decoration from Zuzanna, made from gold tinsel wound round a wire circlet and hung with tinkly silver bells. Then Laurel turned to Daisy, eyeing the prettily crafted wreaths of holly, cones, berries, baubles and, her especial favourite, a wreath featuring a handful of nuts, which she bought as a present for Grady and Mistletoe Cottage. Last night, Daisy had presented Laurel with a wreath of laurel leaves and red berries, which now hung in pride of place on the studio door.

'Daisy's selling more than Niall and I put together,' Zuzanna said enviously.

'It's true – look!' Beaming, Daisy discreetly opened her cash belt to exhibit a wodge of notes.

'Wow!' Having paid, Laurel left her purchases behind the stall while she wandered on.

She checked back to see what Grady was doing and found that Mac and Tonya had moved on but Grady was talking to two men about a bird house, painted to look like a pear-shaped cottage with roses around the door. He'd shaved his prices for the village show and he, too, had gaps in his display. Laurel didn't approve of him underselling himself but when she'd said so he'd kissed her, winked, and said, 'It's the village show.' He loved Middledip. It was part of him just as he was part of it. All morning Laurel had watched people calling to him, shaking his hand, clapping him on the shoulder. His ready smile had flashed in return, dark eyes gleaming beneath thick brows and hair sweeping his collar.

Carola – head of the village hall committee, organiser of the fair, friend to half the village – whizzed by then, blonde hair swishing busily as she said, 'Hi, Laurel!' But she didn't stop to chat.

Then Laurel heard several familiar voices all calling, 'Laurel!' at once.

Hardly able to believe her ears, she swung around to see a group of people hurrying towards her through the Christmas Fair visitors – Alex, Fliss . . . and Aunt Terri? Terri beamed from beneath her cap of short, straight hair, coat open over her usual untidy ensemble. Fliss's fluffy blonde hair was a halo almost as bright as her pink corduroy jump suit. Alex's warm eyes smiled through his trendy specs.

They caught up with her, all of them beaming and talking breathlessly. 'Alex and I arrived at The Nookery at the same time as your delightful aunt,' Fliss said, giving Laurel a hard, exuberant hug.

'Rea said you were here so we came to surprise you,' added Aunt Terri, taking her turn with the hugs.

Alex took Laurel by the shoulders and studied her face. 'You,' he said, 'look great.'

Laurel gazed at him, at them all, taking in their faces, flushed from the cold air outside. 'I'm stunned. I wasn't expecting you.'

Something flickered behind Fliss's eyes, though she still smiled. 'Just checking you're OK.'

'Right.' Laurel nodded. 'The best way to do that was to surprise me? And you and Alex thought it would be great to come together?' They were making her feel hemmed in, too hot in her Christmas sweater with goggle-eyed reindeer on the front, and she wondered how they were all bearing the closeness of the hall while still muffled up in their coats.

Fliss shrugged, her smile still stretching her lips but not quite lighting her eyes. 'Sure. Why all the questions? We just wondered about you.' Then, wilting under Laurel's stare, she conceded, 'Alex got in touch – I told you that – and I guess it was me who suggested we come and see for ourselves . . .'

'See for yourselves,' Laurel echoed, slowly and thoughtfully.

Fliss seemed unbalanced by being questioned and relieved when Alex jumped in. 'Aren't we allowed to want to know how you're getting on?' he demanded, giving Laurel's arm a reassuring rub.

She switched her gaze back to him. 'I'm fine,' she

answered. She knew she sounded brittle and suspicious, but springing themselves on her like this . . . she didn't appreciate being checked up on as if she might not be able to manage her own life. Sure, Fliss was a great friend and Alex had been a wonderful husband . . . but it felt like they were overstepping her boundaries.

The smile she turned on her aunt was several degrees warmer. 'Aunt Terri, this is great! I didn't expect to see you for a week or so.'

Terri beamed. 'Your lovely sister said I could come when I wanted. I fancied a break from everything at home.' A shadow passed over her face but then she smiled again. 'Christmas in the village was always wonderful.'

Before Laurel could answer, Fliss, wearing an apologetic expression, put in, 'Terri, would you mind terribly showing me to the ladies' room? I guess you know the village hall?'

'Of course,' answered Terri, too well-mannered to point out she'd barely talked to her niece yet. 'It's off the foyer.'

They wandered off and Laurel was left alone with Alex . . . well, 'alone' apart from the hundred or more villagers thronging around them, making the air ever more stifling. She looked at him and lifted one eyebrow.

He smiled disarmingly. 'I wanted to come and see you. Vonnie and I have broken up and, now I'm single, I'm inundated with women looking for Christmas party dates. I came to ask you back for protection.' He laughed, but there was a wistful note to it.

Laurel barely noticed the surprising news about Vonnie. She was too busy being nettled by both his words and manner. 'I'm not sure why I'm supposed to find it funny that you'd make use of me like that.'

He sobered. 'Wow, that joke missed its mark.' Then, when Laurel continued to regard him steadily, ignoring a family bustling past, arms full of finds from the pre-loved toy stall, he said, simply, 'I'm missing you. I ended things with Vonnie because your absence is so hard.' He edged closer when a woman caught his sleeve with the holly on one of Daisy's wreaths. 'I got to thinking . . .' He drew a long, slow breath. 'Plenty of people are perfectly happy without children. I don't like being divorced.'

Laurel's heart gave an uncomfortable thump. 'Why decide that now? We were divorced for almost a year before I actually moved out.' Realising she sounded prickly, she softened her voice. 'Sorry. You took me by surprise. I meant that we agreed our marriage had run out of steam. Both of us.' The slightest emphasis on the word *both*. 'You no longer found me desirable.'

Alex flushed, glancing round uncomfortably. 'Every guy has a failure now and then.'

Some children pushed past, laughing. 'I'm not . . .' What? Criticising? Complaining? Laurel wasn't sure what word to use and felt her cheeks fire up. 'It was confirmation that the joy had gone out of . . . it. That's all I meant. We both knew it already but that's what made us accept it.'

He rubbed the back of his neck. 'I think we jumped too soon. Took two decisions at once – not to persist with fertility treatment *and* to give up on the marriage. We should have made the first decision then waited until we were less raw to consider the second.'

'Well . . . OK,' she conceded, pushing back her hair. 'With hindsight, maybe you've got something there. But those decisions *were* taken. You seemed relieved. You began seeing Vonnie and I—'

'Hiya,' said Grady's voice in her ear. His hand slipped around her waist. 'I've got Mac to take over my stall while I grab lunch.'

Laurel turned, relieved and glad to see him but also knowing his presence could only escalate the tension.

Before she could introduce him, Grady said to Alex, 'Hello. I'm Grady Cassidy.'

Alex stared at him as if he'd just said, 'Hello, I'm a piece of dirt that came in on your shoe.' It even took him a second to accept Grady's proffered hand. 'Hello,' he said, hollowly. The look he turned on Laurel was full of reproach and alarm. He switched back to Grady. 'I'm Alex Lazienko, Laurel's husband.'

Grady smiled coldly. '*Ex*-husband, I think? Pleased to meet you.' He didn't sound it. 'Sorry to be rude but I only have half an hour.' He took Laurel's hand and his smile was as warm and sexy as ever, despite the way he'd bristled at Alex a second earlier. 'But I can eat on my own, Laurel, if you want to carry on your conversation.' He presented her with the sandwich box she'd left beneath his stall.

Laurel's head whirled. She felt bad for Alex, but he had turned up unannounced. 'No, I'll come with you now. Sorry, Alex, but I already have plans.'

But just as Laurel made to move off, Fliss popped up like magic, eyes sparkling as if she'd just nabbed cheap tickets for Glastonbury. 'Quick, I've left Terri holding a table for us all in the coffee shop.' She glanced at Grady and, after an instant, stuck out her hand. 'Why, hello. I'm Fliss Smith. Won't you join us?' She treated him to her best California-girl smile.

It would have been beyond pointed to take their lunch boxes elsewhere so Laurel let herself and Grady be swept along to where they found Terri guarding a table with four chairs. When Grady was introduced to her she nabbed a vacant chair from a nearby table, somehow managing to tell him at the same time that she remembered his mum from when the village had a Women's Institute. 'I wasn't a member but I used to join them in the pub afterwards. Nice crowd.'

Someone came to take their order. 'Hardly got any food left,' she said, pencil poised. 'Rocky Road, flapjacks, cheese straws – which are a bit crumbly but taste good – and white chocolate cookies.'

Laurel and Grady ordered coffee, the rest ordered cake as well as hot drinks.

Grady and Alex were quiet and Fliss kept looking between them and Laurel. Luckily, Terri chattered happily about recognising this person from school and that person from her long-ago paper round. Laurel nodded as she listened, making certain to maintain a smiling mask for Aunt Terri but feeling increasingly angry and awkward. Did Alex and Fliss feel entitled to judge her and make Grady feel uncomfortable? Every so often, he and Alex locked unsmiling gazes.

After a while, Fliss addressed Laurel. 'When are you coming down to meet my new girlfriend, Chantana? She's sweet and beautiful. You'll love her.'

'I'm not sure.' Laurel tried to smile but it felt stiff and unnatural. Fliss had always been *her* friend. Fliss and Alex had only known each other through her so why had they kept in touch? Just to judge Laurel and find her decisions wanting? Fliss had helped Alex ambush her and Laurel felt hurt and angry.

Terri paused, a piece of flapjack in her hand. 'You've got a girlfriend, have you?' she asked Fliss.

Fliss smiled. 'Sure. We got together a few weeks ago.' The edge of resignation to her tone said, *Are we going to have a problem because I'm gay?*

292

Laurel certainly hoped not because there was enough tension being generated by the two silent men at the table.

But Terri just smiled back. 'I like to hear of people being happy.'

'I sure am. Thank you.' Fliss's smile relaxed.

Then out of the bustle and noise around them emerged yet another source of tension – Tonya. Her hair was turquoise now, a change since she'd called at The Nookery and put Laurel on the spot. Grady had already warned Laurel that Mac had smoothed things over with Tonya by telling her a half-truth about why he'd written to apologise and Laurel's stomach twisted at the thought that Tonya might be here to check out Laurel's version. Happily, although she gave a half-smile to the table at large, her gaze lingering for an instant on Laurel, she then focused on her brother-in-law. 'There's a woman at your stall who might want to stock your stuff at her shop in Peterborough.'

'Thanks, I'll come.' Grady rose, picking up his barely touched sandwiches and coffee, but he hesitated, glancing first at Laurel and then at Tonya.

Laurel flushed, realising his quandary. He didn't want to suggest she bring her lunch back to the stall with Mac there. Poor Grady was stuck in the middle. So was Tonya, really, though she had the added disadvantage of not knowing exactly what she was in the middle of. As none of this mess was the fault of either one of them, Laurel dredged up a smile. 'No problem. I'll catch up with you later.'

Grady headed off with Tonya.

When Laurel turned back from watching them go, she was met by twin, round-eyed stares from Fliss and Alex. Fresh annoyance prickled down her spine.

293

Clearly unaware of what was causing tension but realising her niece was upset, Terri put her hand over Laurel's. 'Are you OK, duck?'

But before Laurel could reply a rotund, rosy woman arrived crowing, 'Terri! What are you doing here? How lovely to see you! Lizzie's here, look. Come over for a minute.'

After Laurel had given a smile and nod to show she was fine, Terri, explaining that Lizzie was an old friend, allowed herself to be dragged away.

Laurel waited till her aunt was out of earshot then rounded on Alex. 'You acted like an arse with Grady.'

Alex spluttered. 'Me?'

'You,' Laurel snapped.

Unfortunately, Fliss chose to chip in. 'I have to say, Laurel, I'm a little concerned. Grady obviously thinks you're an item.'

Laurel leaned forward so she could speak without the whole village hall hearing. 'I'm sorry if this makes me appear ungrateful for your past support, Fliss, or not sensitive to everything we've been to each other, Alex, but I don't need you turning up like uninvited guard dogs, sniffing suspiciously at everyone. Yes, Grady and I are trying to be "an item" but it's tough and knotty. Whether I try to unknot things is up to me.'

Silence.

Then Alex glanced at Fliss. 'Would you mind . . .?'

'Not at all.' Fliss got up to join Terri, entering the ongoing conversation in her easy way.

Alex turned back to Laurel, his gaze serious. 'Laurel, I haven't stopped loving you. This isn't about me being protective. It's about me trying to get you back.'

Laurel jolted with shock and her first thought was, *but*

I've got Grady. Her eyes filled with tears at the impossibility of saying that to the man she'd once loved. 'I'm sorry, Alex. I think I'll always love you . . . in a way. But it's no longer the right way.'

Alex's face turned a dull, unhappy red and his lips curled. 'Surely *he's* not the reason?'

'Why not?' she demanded fiercely.

Hotly, Alex snapped, 'Grady's brother—'

'His brother. Not him,' she interrupted.

Alex sat back and folded his arms, clearly fighting frustration. 'Seriously, Laurel, how would that ever work? I can't bear to think of you ending up sitting next to his brother at family occasions, feeling disgust, having that dream.'

Tears spilled unexpectedly from her eyes at this voicing of her own fears and she whisked them away. Before she could force out a reply, Grady's furious voice came from behind her and, clearly, he'd arrived in time to hear some of the conversation.

'You ever go by the name of Francesca, mate?' he demanded.

Alex's mouth fell open and a new tide of colour swept up to his hairline.

Laurel twisted in her seat to gaze at Grady. 'What?'

His eyes were dark and stormy. 'The messages telling me what happened said they were from Ruben's ex, Francesca. Well, Ruben doesn't have an ex by that name.'

Truth dawning, Laurel turned back to stare, horrified, at Alex.

He flexed his jaw. 'I'm not going to apologise. You two need to see that it's never going to work. It was for your own good—'

'No it wasn't,' Laurel denied through stiff lips, biting

back a couple of swear words in deference to the number of children running around, laughing and chasing the balloons that drifted down from the beams. 'All you knew by the time those messages arrived was that I had been out for a meal with Grady . . . so you were just jealous.'

The guilt in Alex's eyes was enough to tell her she was right. Without another word, he shoved back his chair and stormed across the café to mutter in Fliss's ear. Fliss looked surprised but nodded and excused herself from Terri and her friends. Alex strode towards the door and then out through it.

Eyebrows curled in worry, Fliss returned to where Laurel still sat, stunned, stooped and gave her a big hug accompanied by a tolerant, forgiving smile. 'I guess we're on our way. I expect you'll call me when you need me, right?'

Laurel returned the hug. 'Thank you. I don't expect you meant that to sound condescending.'

Fliss straightened, shock bright in her eyes. 'No. I really didn't.' She hesitated. 'Wow, we really have upset you. I'm genuinely sorry.'

Laurel smiled, reminding herself that, until today, Fliss had only ever been a damned good friend. 'And I'm sorry if you think I'm being prickly. I've always valued your good sense and you're right, I've felt free to call you whenever I needed counselling. Maybe I've done that too much and maybe I've been oversensitive today, feeling as if you were staging an intervention. Let's arrange something for after Christmas. I'll visit you,' she added.

Fliss cocked her head, looking from Laurel to where Grady still stood at her shoulder. 'Oh-kay. Both necessity to arrange and venue noted.' She looked hurt.

Laurel gave her another hug, trying to convey that they were still friends but even Fliss wasn't always right.

Fliss collected her and Alex's coats from their chairs and left. Laurel got up and slipped her arms around Grady, so sad her legs would hardly hold her. 'I'm sorry you heard what Alex said. Obviously, he must have known you were standing there, and I didn't.'

'I realised I shouldn't have run out on you like that. I asked the lady with the shop to come back in ten minutes.' He hugged her tight against him, gaze steady and honest, as it always was. 'Don't apologise for Alex. I hate him trying to put doubts in your head but it was great to hear you stand your ground.' He dropped a kiss on her lips.

He sat back down to talk while Laurel finished her coffee and settled her emotions, then Grady returned to his stall to keep his appointment.

Aunt Terri was no longer in the coffee shop so Laurel wandered back into the main hall where shoppers crowded around the stalls. Niall and Zuzanna were still selling their wares, though Daisy's section was empty. Her cash belt must be bulging.

Then Laurel spotted her niece, arm linked with Aunt Terri's, gazing at the watercolours painted by Isla. Laurel halted, watching them through the shoppers, imagining Terri reminiscing about Isla – her sister, and Daisy's grandmother. She was about to join them when her gaze caught on a family with three boys and a woman pushing another woman's wheelchair. Laurel stared, a chill slithering through her.

Amie Blunt.

Her heart gave such a kick she was surprised people didn't hear it. Anger boiled through her, making sweat pop on her cheeks. But the urge to flee whirled inside her, too.

What the hell?

She sucked in a big lungful of air. Run? No! She was a grown woman, not an unsure, vulnerable teen. Squaring her shoulders, she marched nearer to the cavalcade until she could hear Amie call the woman in the wheelchair 'mum'. *Mum?* The older woman bore little resemblance to the greyhound-thin, grumpy Delia Blunt who Laurel remembered, ever ready to deal out indiscriminate tongue-lashings. Wow. Laurel had only known Amie's mother by sight but she was more comfortably built now and seemed to have found her smile.

With horrible fascination she stalked the group, hovering when they stopped at the stall manned by Iris and her husband. Mrs Blunt spoke thickly, as if she might have suffered a stroke. 'We live in Northamptonshire now – me, Amie and the grandkids. Amie's brought me back to Middledip to visit friends. They're sitting down having a cuppa but I wanted to see the stalls,' she said. She chatted with Iris and Laurel, unashamedly eavesdropping, learned Delia actually lived with Amie and the boys, Harry, Sebby and Josh. The family seemed on great terms, happy and relaxed with each other and joining in the conversation. Had Amie forgiven her mother for her hard ways? In the old days, Delia Blunt would never have won parenting awards.

The kids smiled and laughed with Amie, too. Was *Amie* a nice mum? That was hard to grasp.

Laurel, absorbed in conjecture, didn't realise the party had turned until they were face-to-face. Deliberately, though her heart gave another thump, Laurel stood her ground.

Amie looked up with a smile. Then she froze. Her gaze skated away and she made to steer the wheelchair past.

Emboldened by the nervous gesture and feeling the need

to face the diminutive person who had once made her life a misery, Laurel said, 'Hello, Amie.'

Amie hesitated. Then she pinned on a smile. 'Hello, Laurel.'

'Hello,' chimed in Delia in a friendly way. She glanced round expectantly at Amie and Amie had little alternative but to introduce Laurel to her mum and her sons. Red patches had bloomed on Amie's cheeks while the rest of her face remained pale.

Delia beamed. 'It's lovely to be back in the village for the weekend. My Amie's very good to me.'

'Really?' said Laurel, politely. She raised her eyebrows in Amie's direction. It could have been the correct expression to accompany that neutral, 'Really?' Or it could have been, *Really? You?*

Amie cleared her throat. 'I've thought of you over the years, Laurel, and wondered how you got on after you left the village.' Her voice was strained.

Laurel replied evenly. 'It was the best thing for me in difficult circumstances. Easier on my sister, too, Mum having died a couple of years earlier and Rea struggling to cope. She didn't need me hanging around being miserable.' It was an oblique conversation but she was pretty sure it was finding its mark because Amie looked stricken.

Delia chipped in, 'Oh, my duck, that must have been early for your mum to be taken. Did I know her?'

'Isla Hill,' Laurel replied. 'I was fourteen when she died and sixteen when I went to live with an aunt.'

'Isla. I knew her slightly. Everyone was very sorry when she died,' Delia said sympathetically.

'Thank you,' Laurel answered gravely. Fishing for information, she asked, 'And do you have other family here, Delia?'

Delia snorted. 'Used to have a husband. That useless so-and-so. He wasn't a good man. We were a lot happier when we left the village so he couldn't find us.' The bleakness in Delia's expression caught Laurel off-guard. There was a world of pain in the eyes that looked back over the years.

'I'm sorry.' Laurel found herself meaning it.

Then the oldest of the boys, Harry, broke in. 'Can we go off now and buy our presents?'

'Yes, OK,' said Amie. 'You'll keep Sebby and Josh with you, won't you?'

Impatiently, Harry nodded, though the middle boy, Sebby, protested that he didn't need Harry to babysit him. Delia murmured hoarsely, 'You got what I gave you?'

Harry nodded with a secretive smile and Laurel guessed it was Amie they were present-buying for. The old hatred gripped her and she said, with a sideways look at Amie, 'There's a nice jewellery stall. Lovely earrings – though I never wear them myself.'

Harry nodded politely, but looked surprised she'd discuss what he might buy someone when they were standing right there.

Amie went a deep, dark red at Laurel's pointed reference. She caught Harry's sleeve as he turned to go. 'Can you take Nan to her friends in the coffee shop first? I've got a bit of private shopping to do, too.' She sounded mysterious, probably so Delia would go without argument.

'Sure thing,' said Harry. He took Amie's place at the handles of the wheelchair and began to forge a path through the crowd, calling, ''Scuse, please. 'Scuse.'

Then Laurel and Amie were alone – apart from half the village milling around them – in the village hall where they'd attended parties and fairs throughout their childhoods. Across the playing fields outside was the spot where Amie had humiliated her. Further on was the spot where she'd snatched Laurel's earring, tearing the lobe in two.

'I am so, so sorry,' Amie said, her silvery little voice higher than ever with strain. Tears and fear filled her eyes in equal portions. 'I'm ashamed. I always was. I was an angry kid and you seemed to have everything I didn't – looks, friends and catching the eye of my boyfriend.'

'I didn't do anything wrong,' Laurel shot back, her voice vibrating with anger.

Amie gave a watery smile. 'That just made it worse. I was horrible for a couple of years. Mum gave me a hard time at home and Dad was twice as bad to both of us, but that's no excuse. I don't know if you'll believe me but I'm glad you're such a success. I heard about it through school friends on Facebook and thought it served me right, you doing great and me scraping by. Thank you for not upsetting my family by telling them how I used to be. Me and Mum, we tried to reinvent ourselves and be better people, do better by my kids. My kids are the world to us both.'

Laurel was stuck for a reply. Amie, freed of the presence of her children, hadn't snarled and snapped. Instead, she looked ashamed.

Then Laurel's eye was caught by Mac strolling towards them, Niall and Tonya at his side. He paused, looking horrified at the sight of her talking to Amie. She couldn't help a tug of satisfaction.

Then Amie's son Sebby panted up, whispering something about money for Nan's present. In silence, Laurel watched Amie take a ten pound note from her purse and make sure Sebby tucked it in a pocket that fastened. It must be happening in families everywhere, adults giving kids money to buy gifts for the other adults in the family, kids choosing carefully, preparing surprises, showing their love. The little ritual silenced Laurel and touched her heart. She'd never do that with her own child but she'd always helped Daisy buy Rea's present before Daisy became a Christmas wreath entrepreneur.

Now Amie was answering Sebby's next earnest enquiry. 'Yes, I'll go and sit with Nan while you shop. Don't waste money on cards because you can make those. See you in a few minutes.' She pressed a kiss to Sebby's forehead, hesitated, gave Laurel a last look and melted away.

Laurel was left staring after her, her emotions fizzing. Another apology, but it hadn't made her feel better.

Still, the knowledge that Amie appeared to have forgiven her mum for whatever had happened in their home niggled at her. But then, neither of them seemed to have forgiven Amie's dad for whatever *he'd* done. Laurel hadn't forgiven anyone and Alex and Fliss had come all this way to try and get between her and Grady, who hadn't done anything *to* forgive. Her head began to ache as she tried to make sense of it all.

To confuse her still more, when she looked for Daisy and spotted her back at the stall with Zuzanna, she found another girl with them, dark hair in a series of plaits, and when Laurel went and introduced herself the girl nodded and said, ''Lo. I'm Scarlett.'

Laurel felt her eyebrows flip up. Scarlett? She glanced at Daisy, who was looking at Laurel with apprehensive eyes. Laurel said, 'Um . . . I'm going home for an hour, Daisy. Can I have a word before I go?'

Daisy nodded.

'Is everything OK?' Laurel asked, when they'd found a

quietish corner near the artwork. 'I take it that's *the* Scarlett? From art class?'

Daisy turned pink but she met Laurel's concerned gaze squarely. 'She came over to see the art wall. I told her about it at school.'

Fatigue and headache were making it hard for Laurel to think straight. 'I'm confused. She and that other girl made you miserable.'

Daisy nodded. 'Yeah, but she's, like, unhappy. We started talking again before the end of term.'

Not for the first time, Laurel wished Daisy had come with a training manual. 'I'm sorry she's unhappy. You didn't think it served her right for how she was with you?' The music coming over the PA, which had been gently reverent carols all morning, switched suddenly to a rousing rendition of 'Jingle Bell Rock'.

'Not really.' Daisy managed to look both earnest and determined. 'Or only at first.'

Laurel tried to make sense of this. 'Is it that you think she'd make a better friend than an enemy?'

Daisy look struck. 'That's true but I didn't think it. I just thought . . . she seems to have a shit life. I feel sorry for her. And now Octavia and Scarlett have fallen out about some boy.'

Laurel's mind fleeted back to Fliss and she wondered whether they'd 'fallen out about some boy' today too. 'So you befriended her?'

Daisy shrugged. 'Isn't that OK? People make up, right?'

'I suppose so.' Laurel pressed a hand to her aching forehead. 'Do you want me to hang around?'

Daisy was already turning back towards the stall. She laughed. 'No, thanks, Auntie Laurel, I'm not a child. Laters.'

'Laters,' Laurel echoed. Daisy accepting Scarlett had come out of the blue and Laurel admired Daisy for being so certain in her views. Despite Scarlett having made Daisy miserable, Daisy had reached out to her and Scarlett had responded.

Laurel headed for Grady's stall and found him talking to a woman about decorating gourds. He glanced up when he saw Laurel and though he smiled, concern shone in his eyes. 'You OK?'

'Headache,' she responded briefly. 'Think I'll head home. My aunt's here so I'm guessing Rea will be whipping up something delicious in her honour. I ought to help. It's tonight you're meeting buddies in Bettsbrough for a Christmas meal, isn't it?'

He nodded. 'Shall I see you tomorrow?'

She agreed and, after giving her the sort of smile that was for her and her alone, he turned back to the waiting woman. Laurel headed for the exit, eager for fresh air and quiet. She'd almost made it when a small figure with turquoise hair stepped in front of her. Laurel had to hide a sigh.

Tonya smiled politely. 'Just to clear the air,' she said. 'Mac told me why he wrote to you.'

Laurel nodded warily, knowing Tonya had been told only half the tale.

'I know it's horrible to be bullied,' Tonya said gently. 'But Mac's apologised and you're seeing Grady. Can we assume you're ready to let it go?'

Her question rubbed Laurel the wrong way. It was as if Tonya thought Laurel had been making demands for appeasement, whereas all Laurel had wanted was to be left alone. 'I didn't ask him to write to me,' she responded fairly pleasantly.

As she made to move past, Tonya remarked, 'Your brother's always your brother. Girlfriends come and go.'

Laurel's head whipped around and she stared at Tonya.

Tonya had the grace to look sheepish. 'Sorry. That was unnecessary.'

Unexpected tears rushed up to choke Laurel and she hurried off to reclaim her coat from the rack inside the foyer, wrapping it around her before stepping outside. She paused when she realised that snowflakes were twirling down from the winter sky, already filling corners and dotting car windscreens. The icy air tightened the band of pain around her forehead but still she breathed the freshness with relief.

Slowly, she began to walk towards The Nookery, Tonya's words echoing in time to her feet. *Your brother's always your brother. Girlfriends come and go.*

Unease swept over her. Tonya's comment hadn't been madly friendly but it made a good point. An inarguable point. Mac was Grady's brother. Always had been. Always would be. The sting of snow mixed with hot tears on her cheeks all the way home. She wiped her eyes and slipped indoors hoping to get up to her room unseen, but she hadn't bargained on brushing up against the glittering, gaudy Christmas tree that was taking up half the hall, which bore not just the usual generous helping of baubles but also the surplus from a batch of silver bells Daisy had bought for her wreaths.

The tree rustled, the bells tinkled and Rea came barrelling out of the kitchen, face pink. 'Laurel! Isn't it lovely that Aunt Terri's here? I'm doing a roast because you know how she loves them. You did see her at the show, didn't you?'

Laurel pulled herself together. 'Yes, isn't it great? Sorry, got a headache. Not thinking.' She didn't say she'd

305

forgotten her aunt was in the village hall at all and had simply rushed home.

Rea's face creased in concern. 'Poor you. I hope you're not getting a migraine.'

Laurel seized on the excuse. 'There were lots of twinkling lights and shiny things so maybe that is what's lurking. I'll take a couple of pills and nap for an hour, then I can help you with dinner.'

'It's OK,' Rea said, beaming again. 'You take your time.'

Laurel escaped to the peace and quiet of her childhood bedroom. She took paracetamol, then lay on her bed watching the snowflakes blowing against her window, first sticking like little white stars and then sliding down to gather in the corners. After a while, she turned to her phone and searched the internet for personal stories about being bullied. Such a wide-spread problem unsurprisingly led to many shared experiences but every story seemed rounded-out by clear conclusions and opinions. Was Laurel weird to feel so conflicted, unable to 'let it go' and forgive but equally resistant to seeking closure via revenge? Everyone else seemed able to pick a route.

Once she would have thought she'd ticked the box marked 'I have moved on', but then she returned to Middledip and became an emotional time-traveller, pitched back into teenage anger and pain.

The big difference was that *then* she'd ruthlessly cut off her feelings for Grady. *Now*, those feelings were filling her up.

Grady had grown up into a great guy. She enjoyed his company and appreciated his humour and intelligence. He was a generous lover. Every time she knew she was about to see him she felt lit up like the houses that had entered the Christmas Street competition.

306

Her thoughts chased each other in circles and up dead ends until she was glad to hear Daisy and Aunt Terri arriving home, chattering about the snow, which had settled on her windowsill and now inched up the glass. She put on her game face and ran downstairs to listen to Daisy crow about her sell-out day as she brandished handfuls of cash. Terri gave Laurel a big, hard hug. The way she held her a beat too long made Laurel wonder whether her aunt had somehow clocked that Laurel's day as the Christmas Fair hadn't been the relaxing, trouble-free fun it ought to have been.

Over steaming plates of roast beef and Yorkshire pudding, Rea, eyes shining, announced, 'I've joined the British Horse Society. I spent half the afternoon on their website, reading about pony care and management. I'm going to ride Daybreak again, soon. I feel all floaty and safe when I'm up on her back.' She chatted happily on and Laurel found herself gazing at her sister as if she were talking about the secret to world peace rather than horse owners' public liability insurance.

Rea was excited by something out of the home and planning for a future that would take her regularly outside The Nookery.

Laurel wanted to cry.

She'd wanted to cry several times today – tears of frustration, anger, hopelessness and hurt – but now she wanted to cry tears of joy. She wasn't daft enough to think Rea was 'cured', but it was such a relief to see her gaining courage. Laurel could draw comfort from some of what had happened since she'd returned to Middledip: Daisy was attending every lesson at school without Rea ever having had to know that her panic attack had catapulted her daughter into a horrible situation, and Rea was receiving regular telephone counselling sessions. Rea kept the contents quiet but for the occasional, thoughtful remark, but said they were definitely helping.

Terri, who'd never been told how bad a patch Rea had been going through, took the conversation at face value. 'Are you going all horsey again, Rea? I remember you working at the stables when you were young.'

Rea relating the story of meeting Daybreak, illustrated by photos of her and the advert for a pre-owned wooden stable, carried them through the meal. It wasn't until Daisy had gone up to her room to watch YouTube that Terri poured herself a fresh glass of wine and regarded Laurel and Rea over the rim.

'I want to tell you both something.' Her voice held the trace of a tremor. She took several gulps from her glass. 'I don't know if you ever realised, but I'm gay.'

Laurel paused, examining this idea. 'I didn't know, but it had crossed my mind as I've never known you to be in a relationship with a man.'

'Same here,' agreed Rea.

Terri gave a gusty sigh. 'Mum – your granny – wasn't as relaxed about it as you. It was why I left the village and got in the habit of keeping my private life private. It wasn't till I heard Laurel's friend Fliss talking about her girlfriend so casually that I wondered why I'd kept it from you all these years. You're not shocked, are you?'

Laurel gave Terri's arm a small squeeze. 'Of course not. I think the majority of people wouldn't be, these days. Thanks for telling us.'

Terri took another slug of wine. 'Well, as for that.' She cleared her throat, her gaze flicking between her nieces. 'I've told you for a reason.' Her fingers began to pleat the kitchen roll they'd used as napkins. 'My friend Opal is . . .'

Laurel felt that mental 'clunk' that came when a piece of a picture fell into place. 'You're in a relationship with Opal? The woman you've been friends with for years and go on holiday with?'

Eyes glazing with sudden tears, Terri nodded. 'She's married, as you know, so more fool me to have waited. Waited for her kids to grow up. Waited for the youngest to finish uni. Waited for the eldest to do her masters.'

'Oh, bless.' Rea passed tissues to her aunt and took one herself. 'That's so sad, Aunt Terri.'

'Yeah.' Terri blew out a gusty sigh. 'When Opal said she couldn't go on holiday with me this year, I said I understood because the economy's tough. Then her husband explained the reason she wasn't going – they're saving to go and live in Jamaica where both sets of parents came from. Opal couldn't meet my eye.' Terri's mouth twisted in a grimace. 'She hadn't been able to face telling me. I suddenly realised that I hadn't been waiting for the love of my life, but having an affair with a married woman. I don't know if they'll get to Jamaica but hanging around to find out would be hell. And if she goes, staying at home, alone, wouldn't be much easier.'

She managed a ghost of a smile. 'I decided to look into retiring to Middledip, where I grew up.' She looked from one to the other as if half-afraid they'd react with dismay. 'That's why I asked to take an extended break here over Christmas. It'll give me time to look at houses.'

Rea reached across the table where their dirty plates were still stacked and took her aunt's hand. 'It would be fantastic to have you in the village. You stay as long as you want.'

'I agree.' Laurel topped up their glasses, hoping they'd think her eyes were brimming over Terri's story rather than the rush of realisation it had unleashed.

If Terri had come to this decision a few months ago, Laurel might not have dashed back to Middledip. Perhaps she'd have waited to see whether Rea and Daisy would need her at all, or whether Terri being nearby would have been enough.

She wouldn't have met Grady again, falling for him and putting him in his current no-win position. She'd have missed out on a lot of joy . . . but also this intolerable sensation of looming loss.

Chapter Eighteen

As if the first day of Middledip Christmas Fair had been too successful, the second day fell flat. Grady could see why. Daisy wasn't the only one who'd sold all of her stock on Saturday. With only the picked-over remains of knitted bobble hats and wooden toys to buy, visitors were spending more time in the coffee shop than around the stalls, and stallholders began to pack up early. The inches of sparkling white snow visible through the windows down one side of the village hall made everyone want to be outside.

He didn't mind. His gourds weren't cheap but he'd sold more than half what he'd brought, including five items to the woman with the shop who'd approached him yesterday. Remembering Laurel's remonstrations about underselling himself, he'd refused to cut his prices any further than he had for the show and had expected the woman to fade away. Instead, she'd grinned and arranged to visit his workshop on a buying trip in the New Year. She'd invited him out to dinner, too, but he'd smiled and said he was involved with someone.

That 'someone' had been on his mind yesterday evening, even as he'd eaten an enormous Indian meal, sunk a few beers and caught up with old mates from his days as assistant manager at Port Manor Hotel, before he turned Grady Auto Art into a full-time job. He'd called her this morning but the arrival of a customer had made him cut the call short. Now, his heart skipped and his hands began to pack his remaining gourds into boxes. As the art show wouldn't need to be dismantled until Monday evening, he was free to dump his boxes in his truck in the car park. Soon his boots were leaving prints in the snow that drifted down like white feathers as he strode away from the village hall, which looked as if it wore a woolly bonnet, and towards The Nookery.

The shortest route between the village hall and Great End was across the playing field. Suddenly, he felt the ghost of teenaged Laurel walking beside him, leaving behind the party lights and starting for home on a frozen evening. Faltering when she noticed the group around a bench but then refusing to be cowed. Spending the rest of her life wishing she'd turned back . . .

He shook away the knowledge of what happened next and who'd been involved and, slithering occasionally on the snow, hurried across Main Road where every house had a Christmas tree or advent candles in a window.

Hoping to find Laurel in the studio, he took the side path and was glad to find the ghosts of earlier footprints heading only one way across the garden. Plants poking through the blanket of snow reminded him of painting the Christmas scene and Laurel saying, 'things grow through snow, not on it'. The studio lights were on and he caught a glimpse of Laurel standing close to a big canvas, lips half-parted in concentration. Her hair was pulled back and a big shirt spattered with paint covered the lush body he loved to hold.

He hesitated, wondering whether to disturb her. But then she must have seen him from the corner of her eye because her smile blazed, a smile so welcoming it made his heart bounce about. He stamped snow from his boots before letting himself in through the door.

She welcomed him warmly. 'Finished at the fair already?'

He closed the distance between them and, avoiding the loaded paintbrush in her hand, dropped several kisses on her face, grinning at the pink paint flecks on her forehead. 'It's dead today. I packed up early.' He rested his cheek against hers to study her canvas. Last time he'd seen it, it had been little more than a sketch of light and shade.

Now, much of the main body of the painting was done. A happy, dancing woman turned her face up to whirling funnels of snow while a man watched, entranced, from the shadows. The woman's dress and hair fragmented into an explosion of flowers that seemed to eddy in her wake. The reflection gleaming in an icy puddle at the woman's feet was so realistic he wanted to touch it. The top right corner of the canvas, which was just taller than Laurel, was in deepest black and red shadow overlaid with tiny stencilled patterns. 'Awesome,' he breathed.

She nestled against him. 'I've been building up texture and now I'm using the wrong end of the brush to scratch in movement in her hair. Sgraffito.'

'It's so obvious you're trained and I'm self-taught,' he observed, absorbed by the vibrant, joyful picture. 'Look at the blues and purples in her hair.' She felt so right in his arms that he pulled her closer.

'I saw the same use of colour in your portfolio. Expressionism isn't just using the colours you see, but the colours you feel. It's the tonal value that counts. If you took a monochrome photo it would look correct. And art students are left to find out a lot themselves, too, by the way.' After a few more moments contemplating the canvas she discarded her brush and changed the subject. 'Did you see who was at the fair, yesterday?'

He only half-registered a sudden tension in her. He was finding new details in the amazing painting and marvelling at the woman who was Laurel: compassionate in helping her family; hot in his bed and his dreams; talented enough to produce this stunning work of art. 'I saw all kinds of people.'

Her body shifted within his arms as she sighed. 'I saw Amie.'

Shock rippled thought him. He jerked back to stare into her face, which now wore a tight, troubled expression. 'Amie Blunt?' he demanded.

'We spoke.' Her tone gave little away.

'Were you OK? How did it go?' he demanded, alarm sharpening his voice.

She smiled but her eyes were unhappy. 'She's caring for her mum and she has three sons.' Her skin had paled, as if picking up the reflection of snow through the window. 'She said she'd thought of me over the years. I made a mean remark to her kids about buying earrings.' She reached up a hand to finger her lobe, absently. 'When the kids went off shopping, she apologised. For some reason, apologies bring out the worst in me and I made no attempt to let her feel better about herself. Amie and Mac both did the same – private apology after public bullying. It feels like letting themselves off the hook.'

Grady's heart sank. 'You know Mac can't make a public apology because he'd be in trouble with his job if it got to the wrong ears. Would you feel *better* if he said sorry in the middle of the pub?'

Her stomach heaved at the idea. 'No!' She groaned, leaning her forehead against his collarbone. 'Am I letting myself off the hook about forgiving them by setting parameters that are impossible to meet?'

'I didn't say that,' he answered gently, aware she was no longer sinking her body against his. 'But I do wonder how you're going to move forward.'

'So do I. *So* do *I*.' She pulled away.

To maintain contact, he took her hands. He'd known this conversation was coming because his position between Laurel and Mac was untenable and unsustainable, but he hadn't yet worked out how to navigate or negotiate any kind of peace. His shock and dismay at learning what a negative role Mac had played in Laurel's past was too new. His feelings for her were too recently renewed. In the back of his mind lurked the idea of finding a way for Mac to redeem himself in Laurel's eyes . . . but how?

Suddenly, Laurel spoke again, her voice small. 'Tonya suggested that if I can't let the past go, I should remember that Mac will always be your brother but girlfriends come and go.'

'Damn.' Irritation boiled up in Grady. 'I love my colourful sister-in-law but she doesn't know the whole story.'

Laurel's lip trembled. 'She's got a point though. It would solve the whole problem if I left you alone.'

'That's ridiculous,' he snapped, fear and shock blazing through him.

'How can you argue with her logic?' she demanded. 'He'll be your brother all your life. How many girlfriends have you had?'

He stared at her, searching for the right words. 'We don't have to take Tonya literally. Don't let Mac-of-the-past spoil everything for Laurel-and-Grady-now.'

Laurel dropped her gaze. A tear splashed on her oversized shirt, landing among the paint spatters. 'I keep explaining to people that I can't choose how I feel. I just feel.'

She was silent for so long that Grady murmured, 'Shall I leave you to paint?'

She nodded without making eye contact. 'Thanks. It might make me feel better.' The blazing smile she'd greeted him with might as well not have happened. It had been, he supposed, a reaction surprised out of her on first seeing him but then the issues between them had surged up and made her sad and uncertain instead.

Despondently, Grady trudged back across those damned playing fields through snow that seem determined to make the village beautiful despite the ugly situation he had to deal with, the landscape softened as the flying flakes wrapped it in cosy white arms. The village hall car park was almost empty but the lights still blazed from inside. Guilty that he didn't feel like lending a hand with dismantling the stalls, he cleared his windscreen of its snowy coat and started his truck, his headlights reflecting off the whirl of snowflakes in the frigid air.

He'd only brought the truck to transport the gourds and was parking on his drive barely a minute later. Turning up his collar against the flakes that seemed set on sneaking icily down his neck, he unloaded his remaining stock and broke down the empty boxes for recycling, stamping on the cardboard to relieve his battling emotions.

He was in love with Laurel.

He loved Mac but was currently feeling resentful towards him.

He felt powerless to prevent these two different loves colliding with catastrophic results.

Indoors, he hung up his coat and kicked off his boots. His doorbell rang. His heart lightened. Perhaps Laurel had discovered the muse had deserted her and she'd followed him home.

He flung open the door . . . and on the doorstep stood Pippa. Her hair was damp and speckled with snow. Her nose was pink. He tried not to sigh but Pippa had become about as much fun as a mozzie in your bedroom when you're trying to sleep.

'I tried to tell them but I couldn't,' she said, drearily.

'Who?' He was too engrossed in his own problems to interpret this opening gambit.

She shoved back her uncharacteristically bedraggled hair. 'My parents. About the baby.' She fished for a tissue from her coat pocket and blew her pink nose, her eyes already a matching shade. She laughed mirthlessly. 'You've no idea what an uncomfortable place a pedestal is.'

Grady groaned aloud. 'For fuck's sake, Pippa, you have to call a halt to this. I'm sorry, but I'm still not going to stand in for the father, much as your baby deserves one.' Seeing her face crumple, he repeated, 'Sorry.'

Then, for the second time in an hour, he had a crying woman in his arms. Automatically, he patted Pippa's back, wondering, with blank astonishment, whether her family truly had all become fantasists; if Pippa really thought her parents incapable of believing she was a human being with human needs and a life that didn't follow plans.

After Grady left her studio, Laurel tried to work on scratching in whorls with the wrong end of her brush to create an impression of movement.

Grady's face hung between her and her canvas: dark eyes that reflected every emotion and finely-shaped lips that made her want to kiss. The man who'd filled up her heart when she hadn't realised it was so empty, and was now filling her with conflict.

Realising that, far from losing her worries in her work, she was regretting letting Grady go as she had, she cleaned her brushes and then yanked on her coat. Outside, the snow was already filling in Grady's arriving and departing footprints. She debated whether to stop at the house to exchange her comfy, paint-spattered Vans for boots but she was too impatient to see Grady.

She pulled up her hood and hurried around the side of the house and along Great End, enjoying the eye-popping bling of The Three Fishes Christmas illuminations as she stepped into Main Road. Passing feet had churned the snow on the pavements but the gentle white blanket on roofs and gardens was muffling the noise of cars gliding cautiously in each other's wheel tracks.

For some reason, the winter wonderland made her feel hopeful, like a girl in a romantic movie racing through a village turned to white frosting to meet her lover with no clear idea of how they were going to resolve things but an urgent feeling that they should. The movie soundtrack would swell along with the love in the heroine's heart as her feet carried her faster, faster towards the happy-ever-after ending to the story of two people who belonged together, shared a history and the more recent misery of infertility. She'd wear a lovestruck smile and stars in her eyes as she rounded the hedge of the quaint, snow-bedecked cottage home of the hero and . . .

. . . Discover him hugging his ex-girlfriend on the door-step.

She – literally – skidded to a halt, the slush slopping icily over the top of her Vans, slithering in icy rivulets beneath the arch of her foot.

She could hear Grady's voice, though not what he was saying. The tone was firm, reasonable. Pippa was nodding and snivelling. He was patting Pippa's shoulder. It looked brotherly and he wore a frown of mixed impatience and concern, but still Laurel felt shocked and excluded, stupid for ploughing here through the snow. Her plans, like her footwear, had been inadequate for the situation and her heart felt as miserably frozen as her feet.

Grady had other problems in his life apart from Laurel's emotional undulations. It would do him no favours for her to barge into what looked like a difficult conversation with Pippa.

If this *was* a movie, Laurel and Grady, as heroine and hero, would probably adopt Pippa's baby, like rehoming a puppy when the owner couldn't cope. Or they'd somehow beat medical fact and make a miracle baby of their own – probably born on Christmas Day. Real life wasn't like that though. Even in the movies, a wish that things were different wasn't always enough.

Relationships needed hope for the future. Until she could offer him that, nothing had changed.

She turned back towards the warmth of The Nookery, her family and dry feet.

Chapter Nineteen

Laurel had always considered Monday morning blues the fate of other people. Rea, for example, rolled her eyes as she took her travel mug of tea into her home office, ready for another day of remote call-centre working. She wore a smart, office-wear blouse on top and her leggings and fluffy slippers below, suggesting video meetings were part of her Monday schedule.

Daisy, embracing the school Christmas holidays, had not yet made an appearance.

Laurel, though normally considering herself blessed to earn her living creating, today felt no pull towards the studio. Grady hadn't contacted her yesterday evening and neither had she contacted him. Her time had been spent writing her Christmas cards, rather tardily, and trudging through the snow to post them in the red box outside Booze & News or through the letterboxes of Iris and Hubert from Craft Stuff and Tess and her husband Ratty.

There was nothing to stop her contacting Grady but she felt as if she had nothing new to offer . . . and now she was plagued by the thought that, if she wasn't around, Grady's relationship with Mac could resume its former stability and depth and Grady could accept the alternative Pippa had clearly been offering when Laurel arrived at Mistletoe Cottage yesterday. Being an adoptive dad could be as fulfilling as being a birth dad and Grady would make a *great* one.

If only Laurel's heart didn't stop whenever she thought of being without him.

Wistfully, she remembered Fliss's hurt little comment that no doubt Laurel would call when she needed her and realised she would indeed like to make that call, even if Fliss held the conviction that Grady wasn't good for her. Laurel felt the reverse was true and that she wasn't good for Grady, but could see why Fliss had come along to see for herself. Laurel had been snippy because Fliss had chosen to share that mission with Alex and so seeking her counsel now felt an imposition.

By way of testing the water, she sent Fliss a photo of her Everyday Woman canvas.

In return, she received a GIF of a plump, red, satiny heart, revolving on a string of tinsel. It made her smile but was not an invitation to progress to a conversation. Her own heart as a GIF would be much more battered and tarnished, but its fate was down to her alone.

Unable to paint, she busied herself with emails and renewing her car tax. When her phone rang, displaying an unknown number, she answered absently, anticipating a cold call or automated message.

'I'm trying to reach Laurel Hill,' said a business-like female voice.

Tuning in, Laurel replied, 'Hello. This is Laurel.'

'My name's Selina Sullivan,' the voice went on. 'I'm an

art dealer based in Peterborough. I have a client who's seen one of your pieces and has asked me to make a deal.'

'Great,' said Laurel cautiously, opening a web browser on her laptop and tapping 'Selina Sullivan' into the search bar, which led her to a professional-looking gallery website. 'I'm interested in knowing which piece and why a client's acquiring through you. My work's on Etsy or with a gallery, physical or online.'

'I understand this particular piece has only been offered privately and in a limited way,' Selina replied. 'My client saw it on show in—' a pause while she presumably consulted a note '—Middledip village hall. The photo I've been sent is of a modest canvas, a multimedia, expressionist representation of two small boys, one touching the other's face. Apparently, the ticket said POA and gave your phone number.'

'Oh!' So much for her assumption that she'd never sell a canvas through the Middledip Christmas Fair. 'I wonder why the prospective buyer didn't just ring me her or himself.'

Selina didn't comment on that. 'Is the piece still for sale?'

'It is.' Laurel put on her business hat, reciting the canvas's exact dimensions and the relevant paints and techniques. 'The price is twelve hundred pounds, unframed but packed and delivered in the UK. But that's without commission. What's your commission rate, usually? Because I haven't even tried this in my Etsy shop so I don't feel much appetite for sharing proceeds.'

'Right.' Selina sounded noncommittal.

Laurel anticipated that Selina would now return to her client, or pretend to, and come back to say she could get her client to pay more but yes, there was a commission, still reducing Laurel's bottom line. Laurel would counter that she'd try it online for a couple of months and come back to Selina if it didn't sell. Selina would hint that the client would have found another picture to buy by then. Laurel, secure in the knowledge of her bank balance and her worth as an artist, would still decline. Selina might offer to reduce her commission, as her client had apparently sourced the painting. Laurel would refuse again, unless that gave her the sum she wanted. The buyer could always call Laurel direct and make the deal.

'Shall I leave that with you?' Laurel asked politely.

'Get back to you as soon as,' Selina agreed breezily.

The call reminded Laurel that she'd left the canvas in the village hall, along with her mum's watercolours, and she'd need to go between seven and nine this evening to reclaim them. As organiser of the art wall, Grady would be there.

Her heart warmed, despite the grim knowledge that what they had might come to nothing. 'Probably', in fact, rather than 'might'. If only Mac Cassidy would just vanish . . . Maybe when Santa delivered Christmas presents to the village on Saturday he'd take Mac with him to the North Pole.

She was grinning at this thought when Selina Sullivan called back. 'OK,' she said, in the same brisk no-nonsense manner. 'But can I pick it up and have a look at what else you've got while I'm at it?'

Laurel wondered whether she'd misunderstood something vital and a big 'but' was in the offing, so tried to pre-empt any misunderstanding. 'So, I'll receive twelve hundred pounds?' She didn't want to discover Selina would net off a hefty commission and claim that was the deal.

As it was, she'd have to cough up twenty per cent to the village hall fund.

Selina didn't cavil. 'Agreed. I'll text you the details you need to invoice me, then I'll transfer the funds. Can I pick it up tomorrow?'

'All right,' Laurel said, wrong-footed by a sale of such dreamlike ease and speed. The text containing the dealership email and street address came through within minutes of the call ending, so Laurel created an invoice and sent it over. Within an hour she saw a bank notification of a twelve-hundred-pound credit from Sullivan Fine Art. Oh-kay. She called Selina back. 'Thanks for prompt payment. When would you like to come for the painting?'

'I have an appointment in your area about 1 p.m. tomorrow. Noon would suit me,' Selina suggested.

'Great.' Laurel gave her instructions about coming around the house to the studio rather than ringing the bell and interrupting Rea on a call, said goodbye and checked her bank account again. The money was still there. At least something was going right.

Grady's nephew Niall had been at The Nookery all afternoon and into the early evening. He and Daisy had cooked themselves pizza. Laurel hadn't been hungry but Rea and Terri had dined on steamed fish and vegetables, trying to keep the calorie count down ready for the Christmas overeating still to come. Christmas Day was only five days away and they were absorbed in planning the baking and adding things to the supermarket order.

Daisy had taken to wearing Christmas pudding earrings and sparkly tops, quite a change from her usual dark hoodies. Niall wasn't one for sparkly tops but Daisy had pinned a flashing-nose Rudolf badge to his hoodie.

'Can we all go to the village hall together?' Daisy asked Laurel, through a mouthful of pizza. ''Cos you'll be taking your car, right? I thought we could give Niall a lift with his drawing and display easel.'

'Sure,' Laurel agreed easily.

'Cheers.' Niall beamed. 'Mum and Dad are at Dad's staff Christmas party.'

Laurel resisted the urge to say, 'Even better,' and offered, 'We can help you carry your stuff inside,' instead.

Presently, they drove the couple of minutes to the village hall, Daisy claiming the passenger seat by joking with Niall, 'It's my auntie's car so you get the loser's seat in the back.'

Niall pretended to weep, cracking Daisy up, and Laurel grinned at their happy, teenaged joking around. When she drew up in the car park near the big Christmas tree, now authentically laden with snow, and saw Grady's red truck, though, her smile faded and her stomach flipped. How much easier life would have been if, when she'd met the adult Grady, she'd experienced nothing stronger than faint recognition. It was hard to dismiss her stomach, pulse and heart acting as if they were in the mosh pit at a rock festival, without caring about Pippa or Mac. She wished her brain would follow suit.

The teenagers raced off, each trying to make it into the village hall entrance first. Laurel gathered up the cardboard, bubble wrap and tape needed to transport the artwork safely, before following. Inside, the hall looked very different now. In place of decorated stalls and crowds of shoppers was echoing space. Only the part-dismantled art show remained and the standard village hall Christmas decorations of balloons and tinsel. A shiver went through her. It was eerily reminiscent of that long-ago night of the

325

under-eighteens party when the same floor on which her feet now echoed had been for dancing. She'd avoided the mistletoe because Grady hadn't been there.

But this time Grady was.

He was laughing with someone, shaking back his hair before lifting down a framed drawing of a black cat with white socks and placing it carefully on a table. Several people milled around with cardboard and carrier bags and now the art wall bore more empty spaces than exhibits.

Grady looked up with a grin as Daisy and Niall skidded up to him, then his smile softened as his gaze slid past them to her.

By the time Laurel joined them, Daisy was already asking, 'Can you get my nan's paintings down, please, Grady? And Laurel's?'

'You're certainly too short to get them yourselves,' he joked, carefully lifting down each painting in turn.

Laurel had wondered how he'd be when they met again, after being so pensive and frustrated when they'd talked yesterday afternoon. But the moment his hands were free he gave her a hug and a kiss on her nose, and relief flooded through her.

'Hey, that's my auntie you're messing with,' Daisy warned, mock ferociously.

Grady released Laurel. 'That's not messing,' he retorted. '*This* is messing.' He ruffled Daisy's hair, pulling it over her face and making her squeal.

Then he went to his list on the table and ticked off their items as collected. While Daisy rearranged her curls and Niall wrapped his picture for the short journey home, Grady caught Laurel's hand and pulled her close enough to murmur in her ear, 'How about you come back to mine? The last people collecting work have just arrived. I'll be locking up soon.'

'Great,' she whispered, disregarding – but not forgetting – their obstacles the moment she got the opportunity to be with him.

She dropped Niall home first, helping him carry the easel to the door of his comfortable family home, happy she needn't venture into Mac's house. For once, Daisy and Niall didn't ask to be allowed to hang out because Daisy had picked up two last-minute orders for wreaths and needed to go home to make them. Laurel stowed her canvas in the studio and Daisy took Isla's watercolours indoors, destined for Rea's office. Then Laurel skipped back to Mistletoe Cottage, just as the snow began again, whispering down as if Mother Nature had spotted that people and cars had churned up the last fall and wanted to tidy it up.

Grady's truck was already in his drive, and its cooling engine ticked a greeting as Laurel passed. She didn't have a chance to knock as the door opened and she found herself tugged inside and kissed deeply, urgently, robbing her of breath and sending her heart and stomach crazy as the door closed behind her. Wordlessly, he unzipped her coat and threw it to the floor, pulled off her hat and tossed it over his shoulder.

She gurgled a laugh. 'Grady . . .!'

'Upstairs?' he whispered, sliding his hands up inside her top, skimming over her skin, cupping her breasts.

His intensity was contagious. 'Upstairs,' she agreed. Stairs could be difficult when you were trying to kiss and undress each other but they made it to the top somehow, crashing across the landing, and bouncing through the door and onto Grady's bed. Before long he was cradling her naked body against his, kissing, nibbling, loving her.

She thought of nothing else – literally *nothing* – for the next couple of hours.

But afterwards, after Grady had been downstairs to grab a late-night snack of biscuits and hot chocolate, her anxiety began to surface. 'I saw Pippa crying in your arms last night.'

He stilled, a dunked biscuit halfway to his mouth. 'She was upset. I repeated that there's no future for us. I think she instigated the hug.' He sounded defensive.

Laurel stared at the island of froth on the top of her hot chocolate. 'It crossed my mind that maybe if I wasn't around you'd find a way to make a life with Pippa. Have the chance to be a dad.'

Grady swore. 'It's not Pippa I'm in love with.'

Laurel wasn't sure if she should apologise but still asked, 'But just say I wasn't in the picture—'

'I would not be setting up a family home with Pippa,' he finished firmly. His expression softened. 'I want to be with you, Laurel. Full stop.'

Although he smiled, she realised she'd caused offence and changed the subject. 'I have a dealer visiting the studio tomorrow at noon.' She told him about Selina Sullivan buying the picture of the two little boys.

'It's a good picture. I like it a lot. Congratulations on the sale,' he said, the smile becoming more natural. Then he kissed her neck. 'Stay the night?'

Relieved that the uncomfortable moment had passed. Laurel was unable to resist.

Mounting her stock on the wall would usually be fun, but Laurel found herself not to be in the mood on Tuesday. Though a dealer would understand it was her workplace, it would look better to have a display area rather than canvasses stacked against the wall, so she soldiered on. Then she fetched milk in case Selina wanted coffee, leaving it in the snow outside to keep fresh. She didn't think the weather would put Selina off. She'd sounded far too purposeful to let several inches of snow disrupt her day.

Bang on noon, she spied a tall woman with short nut-brown hair striding up the garden path towards the studio and opened the door to welcome her.

'Selina Sullivan,' the woman said, shaking hands before unbuttoning her tailored wool coat and hanging it up next to Laurel's parka. Underneath she wore an olive-green trouser suit with black boots. She glanced around. 'Great set-up.'

Laurel had placed the picture of the boys on an easel where it would catch the light coming in the window. Blues, greys and greens were the dominating colours but hints of purples and oranges lit the work up.

'Nice.' Selina moved closer, stepping this way and that so that the light caught the canvas at different angles. 'How did you build up texture?'

Laurel indicated the boys' denim dungarees. 'Threads of cotton and some tissue in the acrylic. The tiny stencilled wheels that swirl around them were chosen because both boys love cars. It was a commission that was never picked up.'

'Their loss.' Selina gave a decisive nod. 'Can I look around?'

'Help yourself.' Laurel made coffee while Selina took her time, gazing at paintings of running men and twirling women, children on a beach fascinated by the contents of their bucket. Laurel sat quietly watching, sipping coffee. To her, staring at a picture was exactly the right way to absorb it, not asking for constant commentary or the story behind every brushstroke and mark of the knife.

The work in progress, Everyday Woman, Selina left till last. Then she pulled up the other chair and sat beside Laurel, just gazing at the woman dancing in the snow. Finally, she said, 'Self-portrait? Or not? Can't make up my mind.'

Laurel laughed into her coffee cup, making the steam puff against her face. 'Me, neither.' She tilted her head to regard the canvas, which was nearing completion, now. 'A lot of my female subjects seem to come out willowy, like ballerinas. Sub-consciously, I must have thought that's how beautiful women look. One day I decided there was nothing wrong with short, curvy women. I did use myself as a model to get the form and the movement right. And the mood? Well . . . I was trying to reflect the me I wanted to be rather than the me I feel I am. Freer.'

Selina didn't look away from the painting. 'As a bean-pole myself, I used to hate women with "curves", like you.' She was using 'hate' in an exaggerated, jokey sense but the word lanced through Laurel, right into the spot in her heart where she nursed the hurt and pain of Amie Blunt's old torment.

'I used to have bullies like you,' she heard herself say, unforgivably shortly. 'Shall I wrap the boys' picture up for you?'

Selina rose, looking wary. 'Gosh, I'm sorry. I was rude, wasn't I? I should have said I envied women with curves.'

Laurel found herself fighting tears at the stupid, over-sensitive way she'd let the past overshadow the present. 'No, I was touchy,' she said, summoning a smile she didn't mean. 'You know us temperamental artists.'

Laurel wrapped the painting, first in paper, then bubble

330

wrap, then card. She held the parcel out to Selina. Though she smiled, she was suddenly sorry to see the little boys go. For so long they'd hung around in her studio in Chiswick, and lately here, waiting to be claimed.

As if sensing her dip in mood, Selina took the parcel with a smile. 'My client will give these boys a good home, I promise.'

Chapter Twenty

The last few days before Christmas whizzed by. Coloured lights shone magically through a crust of snow. The Middletones sang around the village to raise money for various charities, the raffle at The Three Fishes was drawn and Grady won a massive box of Ferrero Rocher, which he brought to The Nookery to present to Laurel. As it was Daisy who opened the door, she assumed he'd come to share with the entire household and ushered him in to watch *How the Grinch Stole Christmas*. Daisy, Rea and Terri squashed together on the sofa, Niall sprawled in one chair and Laurel and Grady shared the other. As they screwed up Ferrero Rocher papers and hurled them at the Grinch, Laurel giggled, enjoying leaning on Grady's chest and feeling his laughter shake through them both.

Both of them pretended to forget the debate about Christmas Day they'd had that very morning because Grady always went to Mac's for most of it and Laurel couldn't see herself within the walls of Mac's home.

'Ever?' Grady had asked, sounding resigned but dismayed.

Laurel had examined her imagination and confirmed, dolefully, 'Ever.' She'd sighed. 'You're welcome at The Nookery any time but I know you can't just dump Mac and family.'

He'd replied indirectly. 'Let's spend Christmas Eve together so we'll have that and Christmas morning.'

And she'd pasted on a smile to say, 'Lovely! Though I'll need to leave early to help with the meal at The Nookery.' The conversation had only emphasised that she caused Grady problems.

Scarlett, her rift with Octavia continuing, arrived most days on the bus from Bettsbrough to hang out with Daisy, Niall and Zuzanna, who seemed to have opened their ranks to her. Laurel once listened unrepentantly at Daisy's door, more than half expecting Scarlett to be snarky or intimidating away from the adults. She wasn't. Her laughter rang out often and no one passed a cross word.

Terri was well ensconced in the spare bedroom, and Laurel was beginning to feel one person too many at The Nookery, now the main bathroom had to be shared three ways instead of two. Although they hadn't actually seen each other since last Christmas, Terri and Rea spent loads of time together. They'd always got on well, sharing interests in the home and garden and even liking the same things on TV. Rea had finished work for her Christmas break and now Terri walked to Gabe's paddock every day with her to see Daybreak. It only needed the sale agreement to be signed and money transferred and Daybreak would officially be Rea's. Rea hadn't hacked yet, but she rode in the safe familiarity of the paddock. Her love for Daisy had provided a trigger to her venturing out of the house but it seemed to be pretty, grey Daybreak who helped soothe her anxieties the most. Gabe's nephew Ben

– who was on the other side of the family to Bertie – was soon to build the stable. It was lying in pieces outside the paddock, ready. Meanwhile, Daybreak was wearing two rugs and sharing Snobby's field shelter whether the curmudgeonly old pony liked it or not.

Rea and Terri also spent hours poring over the brochures Terri had downloaded for suitable properties on sale in Middledip old village, where she was interested in living. Her hot favourite was a sweet cottage just around the corner in Main Road, only a few minutes' walk away. It had two bedrooms and a bathroom upstairs and most of the downstairs had been knocked into one open-plan space, which Terri said 'saved on doors'.

Ten times a day it crossed Laurel's mind that she could leave Middledip if Terri was so close. She felt guilty, because she'd made promises to Daisy that she'd stay a while, but surely Terri was a good enough substitute?

She was certainly sufficiently free to leave the village to go Christmas shopping in Cambridge amongst the stores decorated to their ceilings in glittering Santas, holly, snowflakes and lights, her steps automatically taking up the rhythm of the brass band playing Christmas songs at the arts and crafts market. She expected to enjoy getting a taste of a city again and then feel reluctant to return to Middledip. But she didn't. Middledip felt like home again. She'd come to relish having country walks on her doorstep and the peace and clean air of the streets compared to gridlocked traffic of West London. Trees, hedges, gardens and cottages were relaxing compared to end-to-end shops and offices. So now, added to 'should she leave?' was '*could* she leave?'

From the work perspective, it would be easy. Find a place, pack up and go, just as she'd exchanged Chiswick for Middledip.

Her Everyday Woman painting was almost complete. She'd thought it represented her finding herself and dancing for joy. Now she wasn't so sure. Maybe it was just a short, curvy woman making a fool of herself because there was nothing to dance about when the admiring man in the shadows might be beyond her reach.

On Christmas Eve, Grady waited for Laurel to arrive at Mistletoe Cottage, which he'd ensured lived up to its name by hanging mistletoe in every room. He'd just about bought the entire contents of a stall in Bettsbrough and tied the bunches with glossy red ribbon. The Christmas tree was threaded with extra twinkle lights and the fridge was full to bursting with festive fare. He was trying not to mind that they'd be separating after exchanging gifts on Christmas morning. He'd spend Christmas Day with Mac while Laurel's Christmas lay at The Nookery. He knew he could have joined her but couldn't be that rude to Mac, Niall and Tonya, when they'd never failed to include him in every family event and celebration.

Christmas brought logistical issues for lots of couples. *Whose turn is it to go here? How much time should we spend there?* The last couple of years, everything had been fine. Pippa had got on OK with Mac and Tonya, and Grady with her mum and dad. It had been easy for Grady and Pippa to divide their time and everyone had seemed happy. He hadn't had the problem that Pippa couldn't stand the sight of his brother.

Grady and Laurel not spending Christmas Day together wasn't symptomatic of their short time back together but of a bigger, thornier issue that occupied his mind. He thought he had a solution, if he could get Laurel to agree . . . but it meant a sacrifice on his part.

Laurel was due around eleven and Grady had dressed in black jeans and a soft cream-coloured jumper. He'd planned a light lunch to leave room for scoffing Christmas chocolates while they watched TV, snuggled up on the sofa. For the evening meal he'd gone totally traditional with turkey, cranberry sauce, roast potatoes, a colourful host of veg, Yorkshire puddings, pigs-in-blankets, bread sauce and every other trimming he could throw in his supermarket trolley, including two bottles of champagne.

He had something to ask her.

She arrived promptly, wearing a soft blue-grey dress that skimmed her body and made her eyes bluer than the brightest winter sky. He slid his arms around her, positioned her carefully beneath the mistletoe in the hall and kissed her. 'Merry Christmas, gorgeous.'

She smiled, vanquishing the tiny lines of strain around her eyes that told him she was as aware as he that the festivities were highlighting the problem in their relationship: Mac. 'Merry Christmas, handsome.'

He took her overnight bag. 'Blimey, this is heavy.'

She grinned. 'Don't be a wimp.'

Wanting nothing more than to get as close to her as possible, he suggested they stow the bag upstairs.

Once in his room, she took in the bunch of mistletoe hanging over the bed and laughed. 'Now that I like.'

'One of my better ideas,' he breathed. Their pleasure in each other's bodies took over and he undressed her slowly, making jokes about her being his Christmas present, making her gasp with his hands and mouth and watching her eyes roll back with pleasure. Afterwards, they lay in each other's arms and watched as fresh snow began to fall, whispering against the window.

'Fancy a walk?' she suggested. 'I love tromping about in snow and it's a genuine white Christmas.'

'Sure,' he said, happy to agree to just about anything.

They ate soup and rolls first then set off hand in hand, crossing to Church Close where Laurel pointed out the red-brick house where her grandparents had brought up her mum and aunt Terri, then they took the path to the bridleways that encircled Middledip, crossing the Carlysle Estate and its home farm. Laurel looked amazing in boots, a long black coat and blue hat and gloves. He ached with longing for their relationship to work out.

The fields looked as if they were made of cotton wool, while trees held out their leafless arms to embrace the snow. They met no one. The world around was hushed but for the squeak of snow crystals beneath their boots and their discussion of weighty matters such as whether you could hear snow land and whether 'burn' was the right word for the way your ears stung in the cold.

Then Laurel told him that Daisy had performed the feat of befriending her erstwhile bully.

Without engaging his brain before he spoke, Grady said, 'Good for her,' then wished he'd opted for something more noncommittal as Laurel became pensive. They trudged in silence for a while after that, trailing footprints through the winter landscape, their coats sprinkled white as if from a giant sugar shaker. When they'd walked for an hour, they took a path back onto Little Lane and slipped and slithered their way up through a village full of brightly lit Christmas trees, back to Mistletoe Cottage.

Grady understood Laurel's quiet mood. He'd praised Daisy for forgiving her bully, which must have seemed a criticism of Laurel for not being able to do the same. In actuality, he agreed with her that feelings couldn't be controlled. Daisy felt one way about Scarlett. Laurel felt differently about Mac. He understood why she couldn't forgive Mac. It made his heart heavy but he understood. What he'd planned to ask her jumped to the front of his mind.

It seemed like the kind of conversation that would go well with alcohol, so after they'd shed their coats and boots and left them to dry he took the first bottle of champagne from the fridge.

She raised her eyebrows and managed a smile as she watched the festive froth and sparkle he poured into glasses. 'Champagne in the afternoon?'

He kissed her mouth. 'Why not?' He grabbed a box of chocolates for good measure, leading her into the sitting room, where it was warm and the mistletoe dangling over the sofa gave him a reason – no, an *obligation* – to kiss her. Ensconced on the soft cushions, they toasted each other with the bubbling champagne.

Then he looked into her eyes. 'You've thought about leaving the village now that your family no longer needs you so much.'

All light left her face but she didn't contradict him. 'Leaving might be best.'

He traced the line of her silky cheek with one fingertip. 'Let's leave together.'

Her eyes widened, lips parting in shock.

His heart ached at the idea of leaving so much he loved but he pressed on. 'If you can't be truly happy in Middledip, if you would always worry about crossing paths with Mac, we could start somewhere new, together. I love you. I don't want you to be sad.' He smiled. 'I know things would still be tricky regarding Christmases but we'll find a way around that.'

Rather than lighting up with pleasure, as Grady had thought she might, she paled. 'But—' she began.

Then the front door opened and Mac shouted, 'Grady, our bloody rice cooker's up the spout. Tonya says can we borrow yours because all of her cousins are coming tonight for a curry—' He halted in the sitting room doorway. 'Oh. Shit. I'm supposed to knock. Sorry.' He looked guilty and sheepish, eyes flitting to Laurel, who instantly looked away.

Irritation welled up in Grady, not just at the interruption or Mac forgetting he was supposed to knock, but that his actions made leaving the village necessary in the first place. With an effort, he stifled the urge to tell his brother to piss off. 'It's OK,' he said shortly. 'But it's upstairs somewhere because it takes up too much room in my kitchen. Just hang on.'

It wasn't until he was yanking things out of the narrow storage cupboard under the eaves of his bedroom that a chill stole over him as he realised he'd left Laurel alone in a room with Mac. She'd hate it. *Hell.* But he could hardly dash back downstairs and bring Mac up with him now.

Laurel stared at Mac. Mac stared back. He shifted uncomfortably. 'I honestly didn't contrive this,' he said. 'But as we've ended up here together . . . and Christmas is a time—'

She just knew he was going to say *for forgiveness*. He was going to try again to apologise! Fury reared up in her at the way he kept ignoring her wishes and the desire for revenge smashed over everything else, sweeping away her knowledge that she was better than that. She saw the perfect opportunity to hurt Mac Cassidy in a way that would change his life as he'd changed hers.

And she took it.

'You can be the first to congratulate us,' she said, waving her champagne. 'Grady's just asked me to move away from the village and live with him. And I've said yes.'

Mac physically reared back. His face turned perfectly white. 'Grady's going to leave?' he repeated stupidly.

Laurel's throat dried. Mac looked so stricken, so shocked, she might as well have punched him.

And she couldn't have felt worse, even if he had punched her back.

Grady's feet thundered on the stairs and he arrived back in the room, the stainless steel rice cooker in his arms, power lead trailing.

Before Mac could speak, a female voice called, 'Grady! Your door's open so I've come in. I hope that's all . . . right.'

Then Pippa was in the doorway, a fluffy hat framing her face, looking from Grady and Laurel to Mac. Then she burst into tears. 'I just can't tell them, Grady! I just can't. I came to beg but you're . . .' She waved a hand at Laurel and the champagne.

Grady gazed at her, speechless and looking haunted.

Laurel was still watching Mac's face. It was pale and shaken but he was the first to gather his thoughts. He laid a friendly hand along Pippa's arm to prevent her hurling herself on Grady. 'I don't think this is the place for either of us right now, Pippa.' He twinkled at her, as if she were one of his students come to him with a tricky problem. He hefted the rice cooker under an arm and gently turned her around.

'I know what you're upset about,' he said understandingly. 'How about I come back with you to see your mum and dad? These announcements are often easier with someone else present. I can defuse things by congratulating everyone about how wonderful the news is.' His tone brightened as they moved together to the front door. 'I'm sure they'll be fine about the baby once they know. You can tell them that single parenthood's a choice you've made – they knew you longed for a baby after all. They'll love being grandparents.'

He turned and gave Grady a last painful smile, before closing the door.

Laurel stood motionless. She felt about two inches tall. To help his little brother, Mac had just risen above the blow she'd deliberately dealt him.

Grady, his voice sounding unnatural, said, 'That rather intruded on the moment.'

Laurel looked into his dark, troubled eyes and knew he could read her answer in hers. 'I'm so sorry you're in the middle, Grady,' she whispered, fumbling to put down her half-drunk champagne. 'I love you, too, but I can't take you away from your only family. Or make you choose them or me at Christmas or any other time. You deserve more.' Tears welled over her lower lashes, probably beginning rivers of mascara down her cheeks. 'Leaving here won't make you happy.'

Her tears fell faster, dripping off her chin and making dark splotches on her dress. 'Aunt Terri wants to come back to the village and Rea's suggested she lives with us while her house is sold. She's keen to help Rea with Daybreak and Daisy isn't being bullied anymore. Rea's begun to go out. It's time for me to go.' She sucked in a breath that shuddered on a sob. 'Alone.'

Grady stood as still as an ice statue as Laurel shoved her feet into her still-damp boots and dragged on her coat, fishing her car keys from her pocket. 'I know it's me who's the problem here,' she cried helplessly, as she battled with the front door.

'Yeah,' he agreed dully, as he opened it for her. 'I'm beginning to see that.'

And then she felt as if she *had* been punched. Hard. Right in the heart.

Chapter Twenty-One

Laurel put on a smile along with a blue sparkly dress and embarked on Christmas Day at The Nookery. No way would she risk spoiling her family's Christmas by telling them she'd soon be moving away. She'd spent half a sleepless night browsing properties she could rent, solo, no longer feeling like being part of an artists' community. A cottage by the sea would be good. Or maybe a light-house. At the top. Alone. Without Grady. Without Grady forever, now. He'd offered his heart on a plate but it was too difficult, too complicated, too compromising for her to take it.

She was leaving Middledip and him behind. For the second time.

But first there was Christmas to get through, and it hurt to realise she'd messed up having the planned Christmas Eve and Christmas morning with Grady, the only chance she'd ever have to celebrate the festive season with him.

Nobody at The Nookery commented on Laurel's presence at breakfast when they'd expected her to be at

Mistletoe Cottage. Rea just gave her a cranberry croissant and coffee to accompany the gift opening. Daisy, who'd earned almost five hundred pounds making Christmas wreaths, had splashed her cash. There was a new helmet and breeches for Rea and a green numnah for Daybreak because she thought it would look better than the blue one. For Aunt Terri there was a silver bookmark, and for Laurel a sumptuous book depicting the works of Édouard Manet and a print of Manet's grave at Passy, in the snow.

'You shouldn't have spent so much!' Laurel gasped, turning the glossy pages. 'But, oh, this is so beautiful, Daisy. Thank you.' She fell into contemplation of *Chez le Père Lathuille* and the way the man gazed into the face of the woman. It took a polite cough from Daisy for her to realise she hadn't handed out her own presents.

For Rea she'd bought the beautiful gourd lamp from Grady. Rea looked dazed. 'That's just gorgeous,' she breathed. For Terri there was a 3D puzzle of a cottage – to celebrate her choosing a cottage in Middledip – and a bottle of craft gin. Daisy received fleece pyjamas bearing the legend 'You got this', chocolate and marshmallow bombs and a Nike top. 'I didn't think of Daybreak,' she apologised to Rea. 'I'll give her an extra parsnip later.'

From Rea she received a pair of green suede ankle boots and from Terri a multi-faceted crystal hanging in an ornate silver ring. 'It's a home star,' Terri explained. 'You hang it in your window. When you're lost, it'll bring you home.'

Laurel gave her a wordless hug at the idea of Middledip being 'home' because her heart felt so ice-like it wanted to slide from her chest and shatter on the ground.

She thought of past Christmases with Alex and knew he and Fliss had been right to worry about Grady – and Mac. They'd been right, too, that Laurel would be unable to get over the past. She slipped away to her room to make Christmas calls to them both and was relieved to discover that Alex was back with Vonnie. Sheepishly, he made an admission. 'I think my dramatic declaration of love at the Christmas Fair did come from jealousy. It was you getting back with your first love.' Laurel felt as if her heart had broken in two. *First love*. Had Alex always known – even before Laurel herself?

Fliss was much easier. She just said, 'Happy holidays! Don't think I've forgotten your promise to come see me in the New Year.' Then she put the call on speaker so she could introduce Laurel to her girlfriend Chantana and they could all chat.

Comforted by mending fences with two people who'd been important in her life, Laurel pinned on a smile and went downstairs to join the kitchen chaos as they all prepared the kind of Christmas dinner where they'd be expected to eat at least three times as much as needed, wear a silly hat and pull crackers.

Laurel laughed at the cracker jokes and drank wine, not betraying for a moment the regrets revolving in her head alongside Grady's last words. It was her. It *was* her. Her whose heart was too small for forgiveness, who'd assumed the stance of a heroine sacrificing her man for his sake . . . because any alternative was too hard for her.

It was her who couldn't be happy and she'd hurt Grady horribly along the way.

Groaning that they'd eaten too much, after dinner everyone cleared up then set off to walk through the village – even Rea, with Daisy holding her hand. They saw a few villagers, wearing new scarves and hats, kicking through the crispy snow that a hard frost had preserved, walking dogs or carrying gifts.

'Hello, Rea!' called several, sounding delighted to see her. 'Merry Christmas!'

Belatedly, Laurel recognised the kind hearts of people living in Middledip. Enquiries as to Rea's well-being had not been ill-willed sticky beaking, but genuine wishes to know.

They took Daybreak her Christmas parsnips and drank cups of glühwein with Gabe and Bertie.

Then Daisy wanted to take Rea to see the entry into Christmas Street. 'They didn't win but no one really cared,' she said. 'Honestly, Mum, it's just totally bling.'

Rea's eyes widened anxiously, but then she smiled and said, 'OK.'

Everyone went quiet and Laurel was sure Daisy and Terri, like her, were trying not to cry at valiant Rea's bravery while Rea, duly impressed by Christmas Street, took loads of pictures on her phone.

When they finally arrived home, Daisy stepped over something lying on the doormat and said, 'Whoops, Santa's been again.' She picked up a small parcel and passed it to Laurel.

As they'd all clustered around, Laurel didn't feel she could race upstairs to tear off the wrapping in private. She parted the gold paper to find a jeweller's box and, inside, a silver pendant in the shape of a forget-me-not, its petals of bright blue topaz and the centre of gold.

'Is it from Grady?' Daisy asked, apparently unaware of Laurel being unable to speak around the cricket-ball-sized lump in her throat. 'I'm surprised he didn't give it to you yesterday.'

Rea, obviously more sensitive to Laurel's pain, hooked her arm into Daisy's and steered her away. 'Want to open the choccies?'

Daisy, who seemed to have received a bottomless stomach for Christmas, cried, 'Yeah, awesome,' while Rea and Terri left Laurel to take her necklace up to her room and put it on with shaking fingers, gazing into the mirror at what might have been.

She knew it didn't take a topaz forget-me-not to ensure she remembered Grady.

Christmas dinner was over.

Grady's face and throat ached from forced smiles and fake laughter. Slipping out to take Laurel her present had fallen pancake-flat when he'd discovered The Nookery empty. He could have hung on to his gift and tried again later but it had been small and he'd been pissed off at the unsatisfactory way he and Laurel had left things so he dumped it through the letterbox and trudged back to the festivities at Mac's house.

He'd taken his phone out a hundred times to text Laurel and then put it back. *Merry Christmas* seemed a ridiculous thing to say, in these miserable, hopeless circumstances. Merry? Not much.

He stared out of Mac's window at lights flickering along the rooftop of the house opposite. Usually, anywhere in the village was familiar and comforting, but today, for the first time, it wasn't where he wanted to be. Mac came up to shove a Jamesons in his hand, glittering in a crystal glass.

'OK?' Mac asked. He knew Grady wasn't OK, because Grady had told him Laurel's decision, so Grady understood it was bro-code for, 'Just how horribly gutted are you?'

'Will be,' he replied, taking a sip of the peaty amber whiskey. Bro-code translation: 'I don't know how I'll get through this but she's left me nowhere to go. I want to cry like a child.'

Mac slung his arm around him and hugged him so hard Grady's shoulder cracked. Bro-code translation: 'I'm so fucking sorry.'

Wordlessly, Grady hugged him back. Bro-code translation: 'We'll always have each other.'

Laurel sat through Christmas Day TV: an old Morecambe and Wise show and some gig by one of Daisy's favourite bands, which she was apparently able to watch at the same time as gaming on her new red Nintendo Switch. Rea and Terri chattered about the cottage in Main Road and Terri excitedly emailed the estate agent asking to view it when the world reopened after Christmas. She and Opal had agreed not to exchange Christmas wishes and Terri had said bravely, 'A clean break's best.' She did check her phone, though.

So did Laurel. She wanted to thank Grady for the beautiful forget-me-not, which lay as light as a feather against her throat, but didn't know when or how.

Hopelessness lay on her like an iron weight.

Grady's brother would always be his brother. Look at the way he'd turned on the big brother tap yesterday and ushered Pippa out as if she was just a minor matter to be dealt with, not a woman who'd never let up in her demands that Grady do something totally unreasonable. Mac had executed his intervention perfectly, almost as if saying to Laurel, 'Look how brotherly I am.' Like she didn't know. Like that wasn't the crux of the whole damned mess.

Her sleepless night caught up with her and she found herself drowsing in the chair before the TV, not really part of the conversation until Daisy's clear voice said, 'Won't you, Laurel?'

She blinked her way back wakefulness. 'Won't I what?'

Daisy was holding both their coats. 'Niall's invited me round to play his new Xbox game. Mum's been out once today. Can you walk me round there? Or,' she added, brightening, 'I could go on my own. It's not like it's late.'

Laurel looked owlishly at the big old-fashion mantel clock. The hands stood at just after seven.

'You're not walking on your own,' Rea said quietly. 'Maybe you could just leave it for tonight?'

Daisy set her jaw. 'But I want to go. Laurel will do it.'

Rea looked reluctant. 'You shouldn't expect, Daisy. Maybe Terri could—'

She looked so uncomfortable that Laurel interposed quickly, 'I'll do it, Rea. I need to thank Grady, anyway.' She hoped she didn't sound as nervous as she felt about that.

She'd have to see him again sometime. Her overnight bag was still at his place and in it was her gift to him. It seemed farcical to give it to him now but also weird and churlish not to. It was a small stone sculpture from a gallery in Cambridge, a couple twined about one another, not quite touching but shaped so that if only you could just push them together they'd fit perfectly. You couldn't push them together, though, because the stone wasn't sculpted that way. Now, that seemed an analogy of the way things were between them.

She reached to take her coat from Daisy, heart shrinking from what she had to do, when her pain was still so raw that she'd failed to live up to their hopes. For a moment she wavered, considering asking Terri to take Daisy after all.

Then she thought of the notice in Rea's office. *The most difficult step is at your own door.* She pushed her arms into her sleeves.

349

All the way to Mac's house, Daisy chattered about her Christmas gifts. For Laurel it was a journey that passed too fast. The village was in the grip of an iron frost that kept snow on rooftops and made everything glitter as brightly as every fairy light and Christmas tree the village could conjure up. But Mistletoe Cottage. That was in darkness.

Laurel's nerve shattered.

It was ludicrous to thank Grady now, when he was with Mac. What had made her think that was a good idea? She'd see him tomorrow. Or write him a note. Yes! He'd put the necklace through her letterbox so she could post a 'Thank you' through his.

When they'd reached Mac's house Laurel hugged Daisy and said, 'See you later.' She hung back down the path, ready to wave and depart as soon as the door opened to let Daisy in. But the person who opened the door wasn't anyone Laurel had seen before. He was an older man wearing a new-looking cardigan and an orange paper Christmas hat.

'Merry Christmas,' he bellowed boozily, clutching a glass of something amber. He was unsteady on his feet. 'Helloo, dear, you're one of Niall's friends, aren't you?'

Laurel stilled, unprepared to abandon Daisy to some unknown drunken man.

Daisy just grinned. 'I'm Daisy.' She turned round to Laurel. 'This is Niall's granddad, Tonya's dad.' She made to go in through a front door decorated with one of her own wreaths.

'And who is this?' Niall's granddad demanded of Daisy, waving his glass in Laurel's direction.

'Laurel,' Daisy said obligingly, slipping past.

The man carried on at the top of his considerable voice.

'Laurel! Lovely Laurel! Laurel's here, everyone. Come in, dear, have a drink.'

It was mortification rather than the frost that froze Laurel to the spot. Then Daisy turned back. 'Grady's here and Mum and Terri will be asleep in front of soppy TV by now so you might as well come in.' Daisy's expression said that perhaps she hadn't been as unaware of the situation between Laurel and Grady as Laurel had thought.

Then there was Grady, easing Niall's granddad out of the way. 'Coming in?' he asked softly. 'You'd be very welcome.' His eyes grew wary as he added, 'It's up to you.'

She knew why he'd added the rider. He was telling her that everyone else in the situation had done everything they could. Only she could do more. She took one step closer. 'Thank you for the beautiful necklace. Your present's in the bag I left at your house.'

'You're welcome. The stones are the bright blue of your eyes.' He didn't suggest they go to Mistletoe Cottage. She knew, and he knew, it would be just another way of not facing up to the big problem between them.

She sighed and her breath hung between them on the freezing air. The next part of Rea's motivational notice returned to her. *Start small*. 'Maybe just a Christmas drink?'

He blinked, then smiled and stepped aside. 'If Tonya's dad's left any.'

In the hall, he took her coat and hung it near the front door where she could get it if she needed to run. She managed a wavering smile. 'You're treating me like I treat Rea, not pushing her, letting her make her own decisions.'

Grady leaned one shoulder on the wall, hands in

pockets. He didn't try to touch her or kiss her – he obviously hadn't brought any of the abundance of mistletoe that had festooned Mistletoe Cottage – but his eyes caught on the forget-me-not necklace before returning to her face. 'Is that wrong?'

She thought about it. 'I suppose not.'

Noise poured from a nearby room, audience laughter from a TV show, women's and men's voices and Niall snorting, 'Daisy, you can get lost if you're just going to pig all my chocolates!' Grady offered his hand. She took it. Together, they walked into the big living area full of Mac's family that was, of course, Grady's family, too.

Tonya said, 'Oh! Hello, Laurel.' Then she added, curiously, 'This is an unexpected pleasure.' But she smiled, as if prepared to be friendly or was even pleased Laurel was there. Her turquoise hair had been swept to one side, suiting her elfin face. She shared a seat with an older woman who looked so much like her – though with naturally silver hair – that she had to be her mum. Tonya's dad had fallen to ribbing Niall and Daisy about sharing the chocolates.

And Mac Cassidy sat in a leather armchair, wearing a frozen expression.

Laurel began to skate her gaze past him, as usual. Then she forced herself to look, to see the tall man with short hair, like Grady but not like him. She made herself absorb this image of him with his family around him – wife, kid and in-laws sharing Christmas drinks and snacks. He looked so . . . normal.

Slowly, he rose. 'Laurel,' he said.

Laurel realised that he was waiting for her to say something. She had, after all, just stepped into his home. It was good manners to speak to the host. 'Mac. Hello.'

352

Grady stepped in and introduced Laurel to Tonya's mum, Mim, and Tonya's dad, Ted. Ted raised his glass to her and Mim said, 'Hello, dear.' She looked at Laurel curiously, probably wondering why Grady had introduced this statue into the room.

Laurel managed, 'Nice to meet you, Mim, Ted.'

Tonya suggested, 'Get her a drink, Mac,' so Mac asked her what she'd like. She took a glass of wine, wondering whether Tonya had made the suggestion with automatic hospitality or whether she wanted to encourage Laurel and Mac to interact.

Daisy called, 'Auntie Laurel, can you move? We can't see the telly.'

Uncertainly, Laurel looked around, wondering where to move to. Grady, whose fingers were still linked with hers, guided her to a chaise longue, which they had to sit on sideways to share. 'I hope you haven't eaten too much Christmas pud,' he said. 'Tonya's about to remind us it's an antique.'

'Certainly more valuable than you,' Tonya said good-naturedly. Then, to Laurel, 'My chaise is a bit of a family joke. None of the Cassidys but me appreciates the finer things.'

Niall sniggered. 'It's just an overgrown chair, Mum. Get over it.'

'It's very nice,' Laurel said to Tonya. 'I'll sit gently.'

Everyone laughed and she realised her heartbeat had been thundering only when it began to calm. Her fingers were gripping Grady's like a vice and she relaxed them. He grinned at her, as if in tune with her thoughts. When she was halfway down her wine and everyone had returned to watching TV, or talking, he leaned closer and murmured, 'Can we go somewhere quieter?'

She nodded and they rose and slipped from the room, Laurel conscious of Mac watching them go. Grady led her into a small room off the hall. When he switched on the light Laurel saw a desk and chair, bookcases and a computer.

Then she gasped. On the wall opposite the desk was her painting, the one of the two little boys gazing in wonder into each other's faces.

'That's yours!' Grady exclaimed.

'But I've just sold it to Selina Sullivan, an art dealer from Peterborough,' she answered, dazedly. 'She said the client had seen it at the village hall. I couldn't understand why they didn't just call me to acquire it.'

A voice joined in from the doorway. 'I wasn't sure you'd sell it to me,' Mac said. He took another step so that he could shut the door behind him. 'I wanted it because—'

'Oh, that photo,' Grady chimed in, in the voice of one for whom light had only just dawned. He cast around until his gaze fell on a framed photo on the windowsill. He picked it up and showed it to Laurel. It showed two little boys, darker than the two in her painting, but the smaller one was touching the older one's face with exactly the same trusting innocence. 'Mum had this picture of us framed. I'd forgotten about it.'

She stared, fascinated that Mac Cassidy would pay so much for a painting just because of its similarity to an old photo.

Mac spoke again. 'I wanted the painting because it reminds me of something very precious. My brother. Selina Sullivan is a friend of a colleague and acquired it from you as a favour. She was full of praise for your work. Told me I'd made a shrewd buy. She thinks it'll gain value.'

Laurel was completely at sea. The entire conversation was surreal. The situation, too – standing in Mac Cassidy's study, talking about a painting he'd wanted so much he'd involved a third party to get it.

He sighed and moved past them to the desk, flopping down in his big chair as if it was somewhere he spent a lot of time. He directed his gaze to Laurel. 'You don't want my apology, so I won't try again but I am going to say one thing. At school, we tell kids that humans have the ability to change. I know I've changed, and I've made certain never to get involved in anything like that again.'

She stared at him, the man who'd been anathema to her for so long.

At her lack of response he said, 'Don't leave the village without Grady. I'll go, instead.'

'What?' whispered Grady. His fingers tightened painfully on Laurel's.

Mac avoided his gaze. 'Teachers move around the country when good jobs come up. I'll find some to apply for. That way I won't be on your doorstep.' He leaned back and linked his fingers behind his head in a boyish gesture. 'I can't think of any other way to make reparation. I can't make a public apology and sacrifice the happiness of my wife and child. I sent you the letter because I was trying to make things right for Grady. He said he was seeing you and you were refusing to let me apologise in person. As a teenager, he was mad about you, but I didn't realise that properly till I'd mucked everything up. He was so upset when you stopped talking to him that I felt even worse than I already did. So I tried to clear the way so he could see you now.'

Laurel had to lean against Grady as the room began to spin. 'I thought it was to make yourself feel better.'

355

His eyebrows lifted. 'Well, it wasn't and it didn't. You're my very own Ghost of Christmas Past, Laurel, the personification of my greatest regret. I was horrified when you came back.'

She licked her lips. 'It will be tough on Tonya and Niall if you relocate.' And Daisy would be devastated to lose Niall.

His gaze dropped. 'Families have to relocate because of careers. Tonya and I have talked about the possibility in the past. We never discounted it.' He unclasped his hands and rubbed his palms on the legs of his jeans. 'There's no perfect answer to this mess but it's the least damaging solution I can come up with.'

Laurel remembered how adrift she'd felt at leaving the village when she was just a couple of years older than Niall. She thought of Grady, beside her, quivering in shock and Mac interceding with Pippa, acting like a proper big brother to take the pressure off his sibling. She groaned. 'You're making me responsible for your family's happiness.'

'No,' Grady contradicted her, voice shaking. 'He's making *himself* responsible. He can't rewrite history. This is the best he can do.'

Hopelessly, she cried, 'I don't want to leave you behind, I don't want Mac to take Niall and Tonya from all they know. But I can't take you away, either.'

Silence. Then Grady said, 'You could still choose to stay. I want you to.'

Laurel turned and slid her arms around him, hiding her face against his shoulder while her thoughts whirled. Mac loved Grady and Laurel loved Grady and the person who held the key to keeping everyone in Middledip was her. But could she use it?

Mac looked tired. 'Grady, I don't think I can carry on living here, not knowing if she's going to bring my life crashing down. When Laurel came in tonight I thought she'd come to tell my family the truth. I nearly had a heart attack.'

Hearing those words, Laurel pressed still harder against Grady, aware of his heartbeat galloping while the rest of him stood perfectly still. Mac was offering to do something really difficult for Grady.

Could she do something really difficult for Grady, too?

Could she force herself to believe that the present Mac was no longer the Mac who'd done her harm?

Five seconds passed. Ten. Then she lifted her head and turned to gaze at Mac. 'We have to find a way of turning the page.'

Grady made a small movement.

Mac's eyes were like black marbles, fixed on her.

Laurel sniffed back a sob. 'I know we traditionally do this at New Year's, but I'm making a Christmas Day resolution. The past is the past. You're Grady's brother and if you're OK with him then you are with me. No one but us needs to know what a stupid drunk boy did one night.' She looked at Grady through a haze of tears. Suddenly, her heart felt like a helium balloon that someone had just set free – lighter than air, no longer weighed down by bitterness and blame. 'Which means the village can be our future.'

Then Grady was squeezing the breath out of her and Mac was on his feet, saying in a choked, emotional voice, 'You're a good woman, Laurel. Good enough even for Grady.'

Chapter Twenty-Two

'Where have you three been? Playing sardines?' Tonya's dad Ted roared as Grady and Laurel finally followed Mac into the sitting room. 'Why didn't you invite me?'

'Because you're slaughtered,' Mim explained serenely.

'I'm not,' Ted roared, red-faced and laughing. 'Give me some more of that Jammy-something, Mac.'

Mim wagged a finger at him. 'You've had enough Jamesons. I'll make you a cup of coffee.'

'OK,' he said grudgingly. 'If I can have a mince pie, too.'

Laurel, who felt as if a tonne weight had been lifted from her heart, laughed. 'May I have coffee and a mince pie, too?' Then she and Grady undertook making coffee for everyone but Daisy and Niall, who wanted Monster energy drink.

As they moved into the kitchen area, Laurel caught Tonya glancing from Mac to Laurel. Mac gave his wife a blazing grin and a hearty kiss. Tonya asked no questions but sent Laurel a smile that looked like relief. Laurel guessed Mac would never tell Tonya exactly what had happened at Christmas nineteen years ago . . . and neither would Laurel. She wanted Christmas Now, not Christmas Then, and to look forward to Christmas Future.

Soon Laurel and Grady were back on the chaise, no longer sitting politely side-by-side but squashed together with their feet up, careful with their mince pie crumbs for fear of Tonya's wrath.

After half an hour of joining in the chatter, Grady murmured, 'Maybe we could get off to my place?'

'When I've seen Daisy home.' Laurel hoped Daisy wouldn't demand a later curfew as it was Christmas.

'Aw,' said Daisy, who was hanging over an iPad with Niall.

Mac began to say, 'I could—' But when Laurel looked at him he stopped, an expression of horror flashing across his face, as if realising Laurel might not trust him alone with her niece.

Laurel got round that awkward moment by saying, 'Everyone who fancies a walk can go. Maybe in an hour?'

So, when the hour had passed, Laurel and Grady, Daisy, Niall, Tonya, Mac and Mim – Ted was snoring peacefully in a corner of the sofa – set off for a crisp, late Christmas walk, crunching the snow, gazing at lights and slipping on pavements. Cute cottages looked as if they'd come from the front of a Christmas card and the lights strung over The Cross twinkled red, blue and green.

Laurel walked with her mittened hand tucked into the crook of Grady's arm. Daisy and Niall rushed ahead, trying to scrape up snow from garden walls, which proved too crispy for snowballs. The sound of voices singing 'Hark! The Herald Angels Sing' drifted from someone's house and out onto the night air as the stars twinkled above.

When they'd just about completed a circuit of the village they arrived at Great End and Laurel popped into The Nookery along with Daisy to check Rea and Terri didn't mind being abandoned.

Rea tilted her head mischievously. 'I'm presuming things are OK again with Grady?'

Laurel blushed while Daisy said, 'They've been cuddling *all evening*,' as if she thought such behaviour needed curbing.

When Laurel stepped back outside, settling her hat more firmly around her ears, she found only Grady waiting for her. 'The others have gone home,' he said, dropping kisses on her face.

'Oh,' she said, breathlessly. 'Did they get too cold?'

'No, I told them I wanted you to myself,' he said comfortably. 'I think you said something about my Christmas present being at Mistletoe Cottage?'

They hurried past the pub, silent for once, though still sporting so many Christmas lights it could probably be seen from Mars, then fell into step along Ladies Lane. Soon they were inside lovely, welcoming, warm Mistletoe Cottage and Grady turned on the lights on the tree, beaming out through the window to light the village, like everyone else's. Bunches of mistletoe still hung everywhere, though a few of the berries now lay on the carpet like pearls. 'Your present's upstairs.' She kissed his mouth. He tasted of chocolate, coffee and Jamesons.

His eyes glowed. 'Sounds like my favourite kind.' He ducked into the kitchen and emerged with champagne and glasses. 'Christmas Eve was so disastrous that we never got around to this.'

Her heart squeezed at the sudden desolation on his face. Then his smile swept it away and he hustled her upstairs to his bedroom, where her bag waited. Such a lot seemed to have happened since she'd left it there.

Grady poured the champagne, though Laurel thought she was fizzing enough already, and they toasted each other. Then they cuddled on the bed while Grady opened his present, wrapped in silver and tied with red ribbon. 'So this is what made your bag heavy,' he marvelled when he finally revealed the sculpture of the couple, turning it in his hands, running his fingers over the smooth lines of the two naked bodies. 'I like this. It's horny.'

Laurel choked on her champagne. 'It's not supposed to be horny, you Philistine. It's a celebration of the beauty of the human body.'

'The sculptor picked two particularly sexy bodies to celebrate,' he observed, undaunted. Tugging her to her feet, he took her over to the full-length mirror and tried to copy the pose of the sculpted couple. 'It would work better without clothes. Then these two sexy people would be us.'

She giggled, rubbing happily against him. 'Nakedness could be arranged.'

But he leaned out of her embrace to pick up the sculpture again and examine it. 'Would you mind if I changed it?'

She stopped short in surprise. 'Don't you like it? I'm not sure about returning an original sculpture to a gallery but I can keep it and you can choose something else.'

He quirked his eyebrows at her as if she'd gone mad. 'Of course I like it! I love it. I just want to change it a bit.' He turned it so she could see the base. 'I want to cut through the base so the man and woman touch. Then I'm going to glue them together with something fierce like epoxy resin, so they're together forever. Like us.'

Laurel melted against him and kissed his neck. 'That sounds perfect. But . . . do it later, OK?'

He put down the sculpture and let her lead him to the bed. 'Later works for me. Let's not waste this mistletoe.'

Loved

Under the Mistletoe?

**Then why not try one of Sue's
other cosy Christmas stories
or sizzling summer reads?**

**The perfect way to escape
the every day.**

Hannah and Nico are meant to be together. But fate is keeping them apart . . .

A heartwarming story of love, friendship and Christmas magic from the *Sunday Times* bestseller.

This Christmas, the villagers of Middledip are off on a very Swiss adventure...

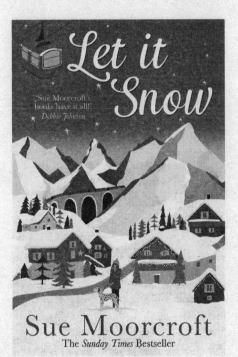

Escape to a winter wonderland
in this heartwarming romance
from the *Sunday Times* bestseller.

One Christmas can
change everything . . .

Curl up with this feel-good
festive romance, perfect for fans of
Carole Matthews and Trisha Ashley.

It's time to
deck the halls . . .

'I love all of Sue Moorcroft's books!' *Katie Fforde*

The
Little Village
Christmas

Sue Moorcroft

Return to the little village of
Middledip with this *Sunday Times*
bestselling Christmas read . . .

*For Ava Blissham,
it's going to be a Christmas to
remember...*

Count down to Christmas as you
step into the wonderful world
of Sue Moorcroft.

Home is where the heart is
...but what if your heart
is broken?

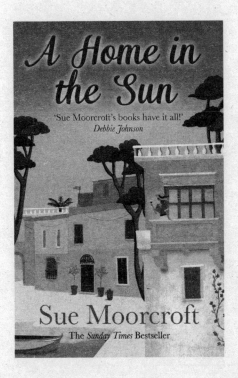

A gorgeous summer read about
new beginnings from the
Sunday Times bestseller.

*A sun-baked terrace.
The rustle of vines. And the
clink of wine glasses as the first
cork of the evening is popped . . .*

Welcome to Italy!
Dive into the summer holiday
that you'll never want to end . . .

Sparks are flying on the island of Malta . . .

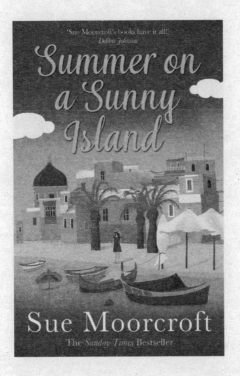

An uplifting summer read
that will raise your spirits
and warm your heart.

Come and spend summer by the sea!

Make this a summer to remember
with blue skies, beachside walks
and the man of your dreams . . .

In a sleepy village in Italy,
Sophia is about to discover
a host of family secrets . . .

Lose yourself in this
uplifting summer romance from
the *Sunday Times* bestseller.

What could be better than
a summer spent basking
in the French sunshine?

Grab your sun hat, a cool glass of wine,
and escape to France with this
gloriously escapist summer read!